# THIS

# WITHOUT

# A NAME

# THINGS WITHOUT A NAME

## Joanne Fedler

ALLEN&UNWIN

This edition published in 2011
First published in 2008

Allen & Unwin
Sydney, Melbourne, Auckland, London

83 Alexander Street
Crows Nest NSW 2065
Australia
Phone:  (61 2) 8425 0100
Fax:    (61 2) 9906 2218
Email:  info@allenandunwin.com
Web:    www.allenandunwin.com

Cataloguing-in-Publication details are available
from the National Library of Australia
www.trove.nla.gov.au

ISBN 978 1 74237 587 8

Author photo by Richard Weinstein

Set in 12/15 pt Adobe Garamond by Midland Typesetters, Australia
Printed in Australia by McPherson's Printing Group

10 9 8 7 6 5 4 3 2 1

**Derbyshire County Council**

| OW | |
| --- | --- |
| 3652914 | |
| Askews & Holts | 01-Oct-2012 |
| AF | £21.99 |
| | |

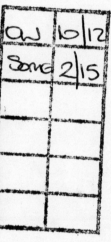

*This book is dedicated to all those who suffer in
silence behind closed doors.
There is a name for your suffering.
And a door to a better place.*

*If a man knows more than others, he becomes lonely.*
Carl Jung


*Look at your wounds. That's where the light enters.*
Rumi

*Nonna taught me how to read.*

*My first book was made of cardboard and had pictures with words next to them.*

*Nonna pointed at the letters next to a picture of a house. H-O-U-Z.*

*She pointed at the letters alongside a bird. B-I-R-T.*

*Because she has a thick Italian accent, I learned to read English with an Italian accent.*

*'NONNA—is me. FAITH—is you. Everywhere you look, up, down, here, there, things have a name.'*

*'Why must things have names?' I asked.*

*'Otherwise how must we know what it is? Things need names for onderstanding. So if you ask for* fiore, *a flower, I don't bring you* ragno, *a spider.' And she wiggled her nine fingers like a spider's legs.*

*'But I like spiders,' I told Nonna.*

*'Yes, but a spider is not a flower.'*

*'What about things that don't have names?' I asked. 'Like the colour of yesterday and the things we forget.'*

*Nonna lifted her four-fingered hand to her mouth like she was holding a truth from slipping out. She smiled briefly before she answered me:*

*'They don't exist. And if they do, they are* dimenticato. *Lost.'*

# 1. scissors

I should have stayed in bed this morning instead of dragging my skinny arse into work to face the music.

Not that it is my fault that Priscilla's sister was stabbed to death with a pair of scissors. But, at the very least, I should have thought of something useful to say.

This, right here, with Priscilla in the chair across my desk, weeping into her sleeve first thing on a Friday morning, is the challenge of my work. I have to come up with something useful. The bereaved refuse to be comforted. Grief is like a crime scene and trespassers are not welcome. People in shock are not looking for meaning, so best to leave the philosophy out of it. I always go for *useful*. A name for what has happened. Something with a 'what-to-do-next' element. Facts stay where you bury them; you can find them long after the tsunami of disbelief has passed. That's when people are trawling for nuggets, broken shells, shards of glass. Anything they can cling to.

Unfortunately I am one of those things people tend to cling to: Faith Ava Roberts (no relation to Julia), legal counsellor at SISTAA, which stands for Sisters in the Struggle Together to Alleviate Abuse, a hell of a mouthful for someone with a split lip or a broken jaw.

My desk in this small room on the south side of SISTAA's premises does not inspire or console. It is second-hand, covered with large coffee stains, ballpoint pen scribblings and a few incomprehensible carvings (apart from the *YOU CAN'T MAKE ME* I recently discovered gouged on the underside when I was on all fours trying to coax a praying mantis into an empty tissue box). It could tell a few stories, this desk of mine. Funding for this work is rare, and astonishing, like a desert flower or a luminous beetle. When you come across it, it sort of takes your breath away because of all the things it makes you think are possible. New desks aren't top of the list while mattresses, sanitary pads and formula for babies in shelters are vying for priority. But I'm not complaining (Nonna says there's nothing more '*ondignified*')— it's a functional desk with a box of tissues and one of those squishy stress balls on the right-hand corner, and three drawers down on the left-hand side where I keep my spare asthma pump, my pens, a stapler and a pair of scissors I am trying to coax back into the 'stationery' and not 'lethal weapon' cubbyhole of my mind.

Scissors. Beats paper, beaten by rock. Libby and I used to play to decide who'd get the last piece of Turkish Delight. Best of three. I always let her win. That's what big sisters do.

My pair of nail scissors lies somewhere at the bottom of my bag for when I visit Nonna, to cut her toe- and fingernails because, being blind, she claims it's difficult to judge where nail ends and flesh begins. But two things: old people need to be touched, even if it's to have their nails cut, and there is seriously *no* point in arguing with Nonna.

You can go your whole life with your little quirky systems in place, like how you arrange your CDs alphabetically but your DVDs in

4

genre, or how you smell everything before you eat it without any idea of what it is you're sniffing for but you'll know it when you smell it. Or how you scrutinise ingredients on every packaged product so you don't end up carelessly eating parts of animals that really belong on the animal itself. Or always opt for 'scissors' in word association after 'paper'. And then someone fucks it all up. This is how things in your brain get scrambled. Instantly and unexpectedly, like a burst appendix and the 'I'm-sorry-to-have-to-inform-you's. And you are left, in the penitentiary of your thoughts, thieved of your ability to ever look at a pair of scissors in the same way again.

On the counsellor side of my desk is my swivel chair, which can do three full rotations if you give it a real push-off and sit cross-legged. On the client side are two plastic stackable chairs. Against the wall is an old sofa with a dark blue throw that covers its blemishes and worn-down armrests. There's a filing cabinet here next to my chair where we store all documents and statements in alphabetical order. I warned you it was nothing to get excited about.

I think that maybe my desk—my office, for that matter—is depressing (and given my friend Carol's condition, I don't use that word lightly). Not that the women who walk in here aren't already up to their fractured eye sockets in misery. If you walk through our doors, depression is probably the least of your problems. You only have to look out the window to see the stretch of the sky, the ancient patience of tree trunks, the sizzle of ecosystems, nothing too small or insignificant. And then there's the sea . . . punk waves slapping you silly, laughing all the way back out. Outside you're in something bigger. The inside, with its walls, closed doors and waiting rooms has a way of stunting happiness. Thankfully we have Barbara, who sits at reception, a radiant human frangipani, who disrupts the straightforward correlatives we're dealing with: shattered tibias. Shattered dreams. Broken ribs. Broken hearts. Joy doesn't creep in here by mistake. Unlike children's wards in hospitals which have illustrated storylines along the walls. Humpty Dumpty. The cow jumping over the moon. Little Red Riding Hood. To make you forget that you're hooked up to a dialysis machine or awaiting a heart transplant. Or dying of cystic fibrosis like Joshua, who made it to three months short of seventeen. Not that Josh noticed the walls. He was too fixated on my nonexistent bust. Carol says that giving away my virginity to him as a sixteenth birthday present was 'the height of pathetic martyrdom, not to mention a cop-out on romance'. But I'm not sorry. Romance isn't everything. It's just an optical illusion. Ambience, at best.

I tell Priscilla that in the violence against women movement, we call what happened to her younger sister, Sanna, who had two kids (nine months, still breastfeeding, and four years, with all her milk teeth), *femicide*. Priscilla nods. I can tell this piece of information is not very useful to her. Right now. But maybe later. When Sanna fades in memory, as all people we lose do, and becomes a story Priscilla tells about her life, with a stray thread which, if she follows, will lead her to other similar stories, and she realises her sister was one of thousands. The victim statistic, a cog in the machinery of gender violence. But you can't tell someone her sister is a cog. What you know to be true is sometimes the thing you need to keep most to yourself.

'Why?' she asks me. 'Why?'

I don't answer her. It's not like the question was directed to me specifically. In any event, the answer is so impersonal, it's brutal.

When you're seventeen and desperate for a date to take to the formal, your mother says something like, 'Where there's a will, there's a way,' dialling Ron Hadley's number. And Ron, who idiotically signed the Valentine's Day card he sent you three years ago *Your secret admirer, Ron Hadley*, for which you have punished him with your indifference ever since, says, 'I'd love to,' with a breathless keenness you know is not asthmatically related. And while you hope he won't try to kiss you with his froggy lips (not that you have anything against amphibians, quite the contrary), at least you've found *a way*. Why should it be any different when you want to stop someone from walking out the door and scissors happens to be at hand?

People like me have filing systems for the fallout: deceased. Multiple Abuse. Trial pending.

'Why?' Priscilla asks again. That's grief for you. Highly repetitive. I could tell her that domestic violence is like smoking and drinking. I could, but I'm not going to because her sister has only been dead for thirty-seven hours. Bad habits. If the switch ever happens, it'll be gradual. Like global warming. Violence against women isn't going out of fashion any time soon. Unlike my boots, which 'don't do anything' for me, as my sister Liberty would say. They are noticeably scuffed and worn down at the heels which I have glued back several times already. Perhaps they are a little disgusting. Libby has emphasised that I won't get a date until I realise that first impressions actually *do* matter and that moccasins went out with Bucks Fizz. I think now about Sanna's shoes. They will stand there in her cupboard, worn into the exact indentations of her feet, collapsed arches and all, until they are given away to charity in a black garbage bag or scavenged by next of kin who have no aversion to the foot odour of deceased relatives.

Priscilla is wearing three-inch heels on dark brown Hush Puppies that have not come from a Big W or Kmart winter special. The kind Josh's mum, Mrs Miller, wore. I look up at Priscilla. I wonder whether she and Sanna are the same shoe size so she can wear her sister's shoes. I notice I am hoping this is the case. But it's really not my place to hope.

I give Priscilla a small sad smile. The kind you reserve for the likes of Mr Williams who sits outside Desai's Corner Café with his crutches to go with the $2 coin you toss him, to distinguish yourself as the one dishing out the benevolence. It is a smile that I perfected sitting in a children's hospital ward. Lifting his oxygen mask to speak, Josh would say, 'Don't smile at me like that, Faith . . .' and I'd blush, a bright splash leaching up my neck to sabotage my freckled cheeks, because he'd caught me—mourning before he'd even died. But I need this smile because in my work there are no quick fixes, short cuts or magic tricks. Most of what I do is damage control. Sifting through the shards of what's already broken. A kind of archeology of intimacy gone wrong.

Here at SISTAA we're only supposed to offer support and advice. Theoretically our clients have to do the fixing and healing themselves.

Most of them, though, are looking to be saved. If you take the time to read the sign on my door, it says *Legal counsellor* not *Saviour*. 'Saving' is not in my bio as a special skill. Neither is 'psychic', by the way. It's not something you advertise. Besides, when people find out, they always ask retarded questions like *Should I leave my husband? Will I die young? Do you do lottery numbers?*

I'm Thirty-Four And Unmarried (which, despite the way my mother introduces me, is actually not my middle name). With a dead-end job. I can't help the thirty-four—everyone ages. I am unmarried *by choice*, but apparently by all civilized standards this makes me somewhat of a weirdo, probably a lesbian. Thankfully, the only person's opinion that counts is Nonna's and all she cares about is that I'm having '*sesso sfrenato*' (great sex) even if it is *sesso pre-matrimoniale*. Which I'm not. As for the dead-end job, it didn't seem so dead-end eight years ago when I started here. The other option was to renew my contract at Bergeron-Turcotte Attorneys. 'You could be a partner, Ms Roberts,' Edward Turcotte drawled at me from behind his desk, a blowfish in a pinstriped suit, with a faint moustache of sweat on his upper lip, 'If you play your cards right . . .' And I swear, he winked.

Nonna calls them God's whispers. These moments typically involve doctors, phone calls in the middle of the night, the occasional coffin. But a wink will do it. As I stood in my ironed pants-suit facing Edward Turcotte, the fancy address, expensive décor, the memos about dress code and the quips about 'hysterical female clients' snapped into focus like those 3D images you look at forever, and just when you feel like either this is a hoax or you've got cancer of the eyeballs, the hologram pops up at you along with the entitlement you suddenly feel to call people stupid who can't make it out. I knew then that delivering horse manure has more dignity and worth than a career in a law firm, where 'I'm-going-to-bone-your-ass-for-every-cent-you've-got' smiles are all about generating long lunches and BMW convertibles.

Dad was 'a little alarmed' when I left BT Attorneys. After forty-two years at Golden Life Insurance, 'things go wrong' is the well-worn armchair of his psyche. I can't say what he was like before death sidled into our living room and settled down like a Persian cat indifferent to anyone's allergies, depositing its hairs on everything and everyone. 'I hate what I do,' I ventured. 'Besides your mother, who doesn't?' Dad reasoned. 'Work isn't supposed to be fun. Otherwise it would be called Fun, not Work.' *Job satisfaction isn't the Be All and End All in the BST.* The *Big Scheme of Things.*

A drop from a five-figure to a four-figure salary is 'irresponsible and foolhardy,' Dad said softly, which was just another way of him giving me his blessing.

I had this rogue thought that helping people might work for me. That was my first mistake. At SISTAA, I don't 'help' as much as 'facilitate people's unhappiness'. This place is a hospice for the human heart, and palliative care is about how you're going to die, rather than what's left of living. But it was an honest mistake. Besides, there's only so much money a single person who doesn't have a drug or gambling habit needs. So here I am.

I guess, given the alternatives, my job at SISTAA isn't that bad. I have my own office. My boss doesn't wink at me. And my stapler doesn't jam or do that half-hearted gig of only going through some but not all of your pages. Don't laugh—death and tragedy we can all handle. It's the small things that break us apart.

The hardest part of my job is getting women to understand: they've got to do it for themselves. Which is why I've got a stress ball on my desk and nails bitten down to the nail bed. My clients are a bloody helpless lot. They couldn't organise a love story with a happy ending if their lives depended on it.

I make a mental note to myself to get all Priscilla's contact details before she leaves today. I am hoping at the very least to score a personal history for our Survivor Speak-Outs. A sister telling her murdered sister's story is a coup no matter which way you look at it.

I repeat the word *femicide.* I offer it to Priscilla, like a small thing that needs to take her hand. She doesn't even acknowledge it, like a mother numb with postnatal depression. Her anguish thrashes around, a neglected, rejected infant itself. Maybe if I knew the word in her native language it would help. But I can't even say, 'I'm sorry for your loss,' in Somalian or whatever it is they speak in Somalia. Learning Somali has, surprisingly, never made it onto my to-do list.

My face feels tight. I can't remember if I toned this morning. The past twelve hours have been rather a blur. I touch my cheek and feel a flap of dry skin. I try to pick it off but I have no nails to speak of. So I just sort of rub it.

It is autumn outside and why I am telling you this is because the website said try to 'focus on something that makes you happy' when I feel the urge to bite my fingernails again, and autumn, shedding its leaves like butterflies released from captivity, makes me happy the way it makes some people sad. Josh liked autumn. He said it communicated something real about life. The letting go. The beauty before winter. Josh lived in a kind of autumn his whole life.

I am looking out the window at the autumn branches when Priscilla lays her head on my desk.

I want to reach out and move the file she is crying on.

But experience has taught me a few things. And I don't.

# 2. bird

It was a Wednesday.

Grief has a memory all of its own.

'*Faith has an uncanny memory for trivial detail*,' she'd say. I think maybe we grow into the descriptions our mothers make of us the way we do with the clothes they put away for when we're bigger.

I had just lost my first tooth. I hadn't expected it to be such a shock, but losing any part of your body is like the beginning of disappearing. I was sliding my tongue in that strange new space between my teeth and thinking about Nonna's lost pinky and how she must miss it, when I found something. It had fallen from a nest in the tree above. A black-and-blue-crested baby wren with a deformed wing, maybe broken in its fall. I cupped it trembling in my hands.

It flickered, a soft tickle of life in my palm. I brought it into the house to where my mother was breastfeeding Libby. I asked her if we could take it to the vet.

'I'm busy with the baby,' she said. I begged her. She shook her head.

'It'll die if we don't do something,' I pleaded.

She pulled me to her, her hand a tight fist on my hand-knitted purple jumper Nonna had made sure had both blue and yellow butterflies because I couldn't decide which I liked better, so close I could practically taste the tangerine and honeysuckle of *Emerald Dream* by *S T Lorder* which Dad always bought her for birthdays. It burned my tastebuds. She made me look her in the eye and she said, in a voice that pricked my skin and tumbled my insides like clothes in a washing machine, that even if we did, the bird would never survive. Once a human hand had touched it, the mother would reject it and kill it.

I knew she was lying. I told her a mother would never kill its own baby. Not a real mother. A stepmother like the wicked queen in *Snow White*, maybe. She squeezed my wrist and told me I was too little to contradict her and when I had been to university and raised a family she would be happy to revisit this discussion. She told me I had better leave the bird outside if I knew what was good for me. So I did only because her sobbing scared me, especially that shuddery thing that came out from the back of her throat. The next morning it was dead just where I had left it. Lying on its back, its little legs curled in like baby fronds. She helped me bury it. A compensation of turned earth. But she never said 'I told you so'.

That's when I understood how lethal love can be.

Sometimes, the best we can do for the things we love is not to come too close.

# 3. tissues

I am not going to refer Priscilla to page 67 of our manual where it says:

> *The most dangerous time in an abusive relationship is when the battered woman decides to leave. If her abuser believes she is serious, the injuries he inflicts on her are very often fatal. This is what is known as separation assault.*

For one thing, the training manual is for staff only. And for another, this is not the time to start taking out texts and explaining the dynamics of abuse. You have to know how to read a situation and offer appropriate input.

It's not that I didn't see this coming. I've inherited Nonna's '*donna della natura*', which manifests as gastric spasms and a silence so perfect it squeals in my ears. The books in the New Age section call it *prescience*. But without superhero powers to swoop through the sky and snatch someone from the claws of evil or dash through the time barrier to turn back the clock, knowing how things are going to end is lame and quirky, like being able to make flower shapes out of your tongue or wrap your feet around your head Chinese acrobat-style. Not to mention useless. Given the choice, I'd have opted for size C cups over premonitions, considering how much easier it is to get a date when you actually have breasts.

SISTAA's 'Client–counsellor boundaries code' makes it clear that staff may not cross certain lines. We do not send in our troops, like the government's doing in Iraq. All those young, eligible, sexually available men putting their lives on the line, and for what? I guess that's Genevieve's point when she says the only advantage of patriarchy is how perfectly it models what *doesn't* work. We are not permitted to give out our personal mobile numbers or home addresses to clients. All contact with clients must be done via the SISTAA pager, which passes from hand to hand each weekend like an electric eel. You can rely on that thing going off any time between 2 am and 4 am, when men stumble in drunk. It's the opposite of what you would call a perk of this job.

We are not allowed to let the professional get personal. It's not good for us. And it's not good for our clients, it *fosters co-dependency* and is *disempowering in the long term*. But how I'm feeling in this moment isn't good for me either. I am hot and even irritable. Right now my own skin feels like a wetsuit I can't jiggle out of because of a stuck zip. I reach into my drawer and take out my asthma pump.

'Excuse me,' I say to Priscilla, and I inhale deeply. And again.

Priscilla doesn't notice. She is haggard with grief, which I might mention right now is singularly narcissistic. Her eyes, since I saw her last—seven days ago, when she brought Sanna here to get an AVO—have swallowed her face, leaving it emaciated and spare.

14

'She knew,' she says, 'she knew he would kill her. She told me, even the day we were here, she said, "This piece of paper won't stop him, it will anger him . . . and he will finish me off . . ."'

I nod sagely.

I have a clear mental picture of Sanna (whose full name was Sanna Najma Leta, a three-word poem that rolled off her tongue) speaking from the couch against the wall, 'He'll kill me . . .' and weeping softly. Priscilla put an arm around her shoulder, in an embrace of shielding intimacy, oblivious to the fact that the next time she would be wrapping her arms around her sister's body it would be frozen in rigor mortis, her face mutilated beyond a sister's recognition. Foreboding should be flagged with luminous post-its. Not vague intestinal cramping which can just as easily be confused with genuine bona fide PMS.

Our stats show that only one in about two hundred clients threatened with death is in any real danger. Abusers are bullies and most don't have the balls to kill. On the whole, 'He'll kill me' is meant in the way you or I might say, 'I didn't return my sister's call—she's gonna kill me.' Exaggerations, much as they appeal to one's sense of the dramatic, aren't reliable as a rule. I need things to be just what they are so I can separate the bullies from the psychopaths. I'm always hoping for bullies. The psychopaths give me sleepless nights.

Sanna's history was just like any other abused woman's:

— J raped S several times (at least five she can recall) over past year (no charges of rape ever laid)
— S admitted to hospital with fractured ribs (June last year)
— S laid charge of assault, withdrawn two days later due to threats by J
— J accused S of 'sleeping around', threw S against glass window, broke her nose and scarred her face (December last year)
— no charges laid
— S admitted to hospital with internal bleeding, lost a pregnancy (May this year)
— no charges laid.

It's all mapped out there—the cycles of violence, fractals of conflict in perfect escalating proportions. It has a kind of elegance, this syndrome, like a twister, or a tidal wave. Our only chance was to eliminate the one factor over which we had any control—opportunity.

I warned Sanna—a couple of times—that once she got the AVO she had to leave the house and stay with her sister. She moved in with Priscilla. But then (and it's no use crying over spilled milk, referring to the manual or saying I told you so) she returned to collect some of her belongings. When she thought he was at work. And without a police escort.

Still. Losing a client is never easy.

Not that we lose them often. If it gets to more than a handful a year, it's not a good year.

My dad did a big insurance payout for a mine some time ago. 'Like spaghetti,' the union official said. Those words stuck in my head like some ghastly word association you make up for an exam and can never, no matter how you tilt your brain, siphon away. The lift cable broke and that lift plummeted a couple of kilometres underground so that when it finally hit the earth, the bodies of the twelve miners were squeezed through the wire mesh of the cage 'like spaghetti'. My dad shrugged. 'It Happens,' he said.

Given that *It Happens*, you need to make sure that you did your job. Which I did. I personally phoned Mr Mahmod at the local court; we secured the most tightly laced AVO forbidding the boyfriend from coming within a hundred metres of the deceased. I know it was served, I have a copy of the sheriff's notice of service in the file. We talked through an exit plan from the relationship and I got her a place in an emergency shelter for . . . yeah, for tomorrow, which is kind of ironic. *Ironic* in my work generally involves a corpse or some other atrocious outcome. The shelters were all full last week. See, she may have been Priscilla's only sister, but she was just a name on a waiting list to everyone else. I marked on her file in big red letters, *Urgent follow-up needed*. That file now sits on my desk looking at me. If paper could scorn, it would be sneering. If you're into symbolism, the words I penned in red bleed at me. *Urgent*. I'm in touch with how feebly that word conveys the imminence of death. I swear next time I'm going to write, *He's going to kill her*, though Genevieve would have a fit at me if she saw it. She's big on professionalism, which sometimes means suppressing the urge to state the fucking obvious.

The thing about statistics is that every so often someone ends up being the one in the one in two hundred.

I swallow. A headache murmurs at me from behind my eyes. But you can't rush bereavement. Not for caffeine withdrawal. You just have to wait.

Priscilla tells me that her sister's corpse had to be uncurled from a foetal position. 'Her hands were covering her head . . .'

I listen. Part of my job is to receive the horror, as though it were a changeling with an unspeakable deformity. And hold it just because it is human and I've been asked to. *Someone's Got To*. Points of clarification are fine, even necessary. Credibility checks are imperative. Not that women lie. But prying is out. Some things you *need* to know, others just feed the monsters in the shadows. Morbid curiosity is a shark that jumps out and tears at you. You can kid yourself that it's worked its way from the wild into the protected harbour of your psyche. But sooner or later you have to grasp that it's *your* shark. It hasn't just risen up from nowhere. Or gnawed through a barrier. It's come *from* you, not some beastly underworld you've inadvertently been swallowed into.

I glance around my office looking for some inspiration, but my lone poster REAL MEN DON'T ABUSE WOMEN seems supercilious in the circumstances. Bare would be better, but there was that memo from Genevieve.

It was circulated the day after an interiors consultant who called herself Anna Kay Li left her lingering perfume in these grungy corridors. We seldom reject services offered free of charge even when the direct benefit to our clients is dubious. And some people have more goodwill than brains when it comes to acts of altruism. She had Oriental eyes framed by Mortitia Addams black hair. I couldn't help following her around as she staccatoed her way down our corridors in stiletto heels which gave me that pain you get behind your eyes when you eat ice cream too quickly. She smelled of honey melon, ripe as summer.

'Oh my God! You simply! have to! get rid of the locks on the fridge and cupboards. It feels like a prison in here!' Even her pauses were punctuated with exclamations.

'Desperate people steal and our clients are a desperate lot.' Genevieve has a knack for verbal economy when it comes to exchanges of niceties.

'Hmmmmm!' She scratched her chin with her nails which looked—I could be wrong—like they had some kind of diamantes embedded in them. 'How about some colourful ribbons?!'

'Forget it. Easy to cut.' Genevieve glanced at her watch.

'I know where you can get some gorgeous! brightly coloured! bicycle chains, they come in lavender, periwinkle blue and hot pink . . . Don't you just adore hot pink?!'

My sister Libby would have loved her.

Genevieve shrugged. 'Sure . . . whatever . . .'

And then, 'We have to do something about the bare walls! They make one feel so bleak . . . even more abused!'

Next day, Genevieve issued a memo, telling us to put *something bright and inspiring* on every wall. Carol put up her favourite poster of Annie Sprinkle's *101 Uses for Sex* which includes:

- *sex to make you laugh*
- *sex as an antidepressant*
- *sex to cure an asthma attack, and*
- *sex as a good deed. Give the needy an occasional mercy fuck.*

It wasn't up for twenty-four hours before Genevieve insisted she take it down and issued her with a written warning about *provocative behaviour*, which is her third warning in the past year. In protest, Carol's kept her walls bare. I had a really great *National Geographic* poster of a funnel-web spider to which Genevieve responded, 'And this is going to inspire abused women in what way?' and so it's rolled up with an elastic band in the cupboard. I replaced it with the standard SISTAA poster in primary colours. But you don't need a degree in psychiatry or feng shui to know it's not winning any prizes in the Non-Chemical Pick-Me-Up Awards this year. Not on days like this when post-mortems are on your mind.

I remove my pad from my desk and start to take notes. It's a coping mechanism, but also, maybe . . . I don't know . . . maybe these facts will be important for the inquest. I write Priscilla's name in the top left-hand corner of the paper. I don't know what else to write. Instead I doodle a jewel spider, which is one of the most beautiful creatures you'll ever see with its little ring of black spines and yellow, white and black markings like nature was boasting or something.

I feel a sudden collapse of the scaffold of my composure. My work is over. The game's been called: Sanna's boyfriend with the scissors in the bedroom. There's finality in that. I can't press rewind. I can't unmutilate Sanna or bring her back. I can't even flout SISTAA's code of conduct and offer her the pull-out couch in my lounge, fresh linen and all.

'You did all you could.'

I replayed the message a couple of times. Genevieve's voice on my answering machine last night was trim. Superbly professional.

What she was really saying was *forget what you know about the legal system and the value that is placed on the life of a single woman (a dark-skinned one at that). Move on before you get stuck here. Move on so you can be at work tomorrow morning.*

But how can you forget what you already know?

'Beyond individual tragedies and setbacks,' Genevieve always says, 'is the war we are fighting.' But I think only people who don't have anyone to lose really believe that.

Down at Shoalgrove Beach on a sunny day you can catch a guy with hair tied back in a ponytail who builds sand sculptures—mermaids, dolphins, castles with moats and turrets. I once heard a kid asking him how long they lasted. 'Till the tide comes in, mate,' he said, sculpting an eyelash out of sand. Like the sand artist, in this

19

work we have to start afresh every day. Memory is either a fragile web or a fickle whore, I don't know which. I would share this thought with Priscilla, by way of comfort, time heals all wounds and so on, but I didn't ask to be the keeper of memories and these are early days.

I look at my ragged hands and my fingers which all look as though they have been individually abused. I cough. I am doing something Important and Useful: I am bearing witness to this injustice. That's the name I give to writing notes when a client has been butchered to death.

I look over at Priscilla. Her eyes look at me with a sorrow I cannot meet.

'There will be justice, won't there?' she asks.

I avoid her gaze.

I swallow again.

'For my sister . . . there will?'

'We'll do whatever we can,' I offer.

And then she starts to wail. A high-pitched animal-like wail that fills my depressing little office and circles me, roping me in tighter and tighter, suffocating me and rattling my nerves.

I pass the box of tissues to her.

As I do so, I notice it is empty.

# 4. dragonfly

'Romeo and Juliet' was his favourite song, so I let him play it while
we had sex. Josh thought it would make it more 'romantic', but
it made no difference to me. I don't like Dire Straits with all that
squealing electric guitar. I prefer 10 000 Maniacs. Especially
that song, 'Trouble Me', with that line about trust, you know, which
is all we can offer, but I wasn't choosing the music.

Josh and I were in kindergarten together and because I had
asthma and he was always needing oxygen, we made friends over our
struggle to breathe. I know what it feels like when your chest closes
and you feel like you're asphyxiating even though there is air, air all
around, but you can't take it in. Like in the Coleridge poem, except
that was about the sea and thirst.

After kindergarten Josh and I always ended up in the same class, which he said was Destiny with a capital D. I called it coincidence with a very small c. He said those were just two different names for the same thing. To me, the one is meant to be, and the other is random and I can't think of two things less like each other than that. I lent him my books to catch up whenever he came back from hospital. He said my handwriting was 'perfect'.

Josh was always coughing and sweating—he explained it was the disease that did it to him, and also affected his growth. Though his birthday was a few months before mine, he looked younger by a couple of years. When we got to about twelve, I just shot up and left him behind.

I once looked up cystic fibrosis in the Encyclopedia Britannica. There I read a line that made me need six consecutive inhalations to breathe normally again:

*There is no cure for cystic fibrosis and most individuals with this disease die young—many in their twenties and thirties from lung failure.*

I guess Josh knew all along, but that was the first time I realised.

I once asked him if he was scared of dying.

'Yeah,' he shrugged. 'I guess.'

'What are you afraid of?' I asked him.

'That I'll die before I have sex,' he smiled.

I think that's when I decided. It wasn't a 'mercy fuck' like Carol's poster says. I did it because he was my friend.

He got really sick around his sixteenth birthday. But I told him in hospital that I was going to give him my virginity as his sixteenth birthday present. 'That's the coolest present anyone's ever given me,' he said.

If you care about someone, you don't mind so much that things hurt, or aren't the way you imagined. It wasn't very 'romantic' but that wasn't the point.

He used a condom we stole from his father's drawer in his parents' walk-in wardrobe. While Josh was rummaging through the drawer, I noticed his mother had three pairs of shoes that were all the same. Olive-green Hush Puppies. Mrs Miller was a headmistress at a girls' school, and always looked officious and neat. Mr Miller had the bearing of a man of about seventy, even though Joshua said he was in his fifties, with a paunch and just about enough hair that you wouldn't call someone a liar for calling him 'bald'. It was just the thought that Mr Miller might need a condom that got me thinking in that way you always wished afterwards you hadn't. I tried very hard not to think about Mrs Miller's meticulous headmistressy fingers applying that condom had I not slipped it on Josh's penis instead.

We had to use some olive oil from the kitchen cupboard. It was the only lubricant we could find at such short notice, and Josh was a little embarrassed, but I told him I really liked the smell of olive oil. It made me think of soil and things that grow. He touched my face and I guess that's how I came to understand what 'tender' means, not just in a dictionary kind of way but in the way it makes a little part of your heart flutter wildly like a dragonfly on a waterlily. Then he kissed me, which was probably the weirdest of all because I had seen so much phlegm come out of his mouth over the years, when he'd spit up the heavy mucus that clogged his lungs. When he wasn't doing that, he'd be telling really crap jokes or repeating something from Monty Python or the Goons. Then there was his laugh which rattled from the bottom of his rib cage and ricocheted onto you, so that you found yourself tugged into laughing too.

He kissed my breasts and held them like they were scoops of gold. It helped that he had such tiny hands.

'Where's your G-spot?' he asked me.

I shrugged. 'I have no idea.'

'Do you think this is it?' he asked, touching my clitoris.

'Could be . . .' I said.

Though it was my first time as well as his, the part I remember best is watching him, because I knew, as much as he did, that this was his one and only chance. That framed it with poignancy. When things are enclosed like that, it has a bearing on the experience itself, because you're not only in it, but sort of out of it too, looking in. And it's the knowing in the watching that hurts. I wanted to stretch it out for him like the longest piece of bubblegum. But his biology outmuscled my intentions. I didn't measure it in real time, but I'm sure there are TV advertisements for dishwashing liquid that last longer than Josh did.

He pushed his penis inside me. It felt like a regular Tampax going in without the cardboard. It hardly hurt. He held onto me like I was saving his life. I shut my eyes tight. Only a few seconds later, it was all over. I opened my eyes.

'I'm sorry I'm not Tyler,' he said.

'I wouldn't want you to be Tyler,' I lied.

I lied because this was his moment and I didn't want to spoil it.

I don't know whether he knew or whether it didn't matter, probably both, because the next thing he said was:

'I love you,' he said. 'I love you, Faith Roberts, I love you.'

I don't care that Carol thinks it was ridiculous or even pathetic.

He was my friend.

It was no big deal.

Except of course, to Josh.

Maybe it was the nicest thing I've ever done. It could be.

# 5. spider

Sometimes I feel like I'm being followed, watched.

Nonna says it's God. I hope she's right and it's not one of my client's husbands, like that time Sheldon Stanmore stalked me in his blue Toyota hatchback for a week, blowing smoke rings from the rolled-down window behind dark glasses. Abusers have control issues and are hyper-sensitive to feedback on this very point. The police couldn't do anything because he hadn't actually threatened me physically. I came home every night and bolted my door before I threw up in the toilet bowl.

I like to think that maybe it's Josh. Keeping an eye out for me.

Today I am hoping it is not Josh because I cannot find my butterfly pendant. I have retraced my steps. I've tried shepherding my intuition, but prescience doesn't respond to requests.

A butterfly once landed on Josh's open palm to die. It alighted, and didn't move again. Josh encased it in resin and made it into a pendant for my fifteenth birthday. 'A fossil of handcrafted amber,' he called it. That's the sort of thing he was good at. He always glimpsed treasure where you'd swear blind there was nothing to see.

I knew today was going to be a bad day.

When I walked in last night from Desai's café with my bread and milk for the week, and saw the luminous red *1* flashing on my answering machine, my stomach curled in like a sea anemone.

'Look Faith, it's Genevieve here . . . I thought I should just let you know . . .' she began.

Sometimes just a few words are enough. Throwaway comments on first dates are personality microchips revealing everything you'll find out in time, including the way someone will break your heart. The first thing Josh ever said to me while we were standing in line outside kindergarten was, 'Can I stand in front of you? I like to go first.' From Genevieve's opening words, I knew she wasn't calling about a pay rise or a marine biologist who lives in her building she wants to introduce me to.

I spent most of the night on the floor next to the telephone where my knees gave in, the Desai's Corner Café packet lying sprawled next to me, the milk on its side, the bread squashed. I must have dozed at some point.

Because I dreamed of Josh.

'I love you Faith Roberts,' he said in my dream. 'You're perfect, you know.'

I am trying to usher Priscilla out of my office.

Seeing me has not made any of this better for her. I'm not sure what she was hoping for. I didn't have any tricks up my sleeve last week. This week is no different, except that her sister's body is in the mortuary with one of those tags attached to her big toe. I'm not sure if that's really where they tag you or just how they portray it on *CSI*.

I'm not saying feet aren't important, toes in particular. But I have wondered what's wrong with the thumb. It's just a thought.

Priscilla doesn't want to leave me.

'I'm going to get on the phone and speak to the police officer in charge, to make sure that they move on arresting him,' I say to her. This only brings on a renewed shudder of sobs from Priscilla. 'He must die,' she says to me. Another thing about grief—it is alarmingly vengeful.

I nod. 'He . . . he . . . must definitely be brought to account for this . . .' I open the door. She makes no move to go.

'I will kill him with my own two hands,' she whispers.

'Please don't,' I offer. 'Then you will be arrested and go to jail, and who will be there for your children? For Sanna's?'

'He must suffer . . .' she says.

'Please . . . don't do anything . . . rash . . .'

'Rash?' she asks, clearly a word in English she understands only in relation to red welts on skin.

'Foolhardy,' I offer.

She shrugs.

'Risky . . .' I say. 'Don't put yourself or your family in danger. Your family needs you. We need you here at SISTAA, to help us, to make sure this doesn't happen to anyone else . . .'

She gives me an odd look. 'Anyone else?'

I smile. Small, sad. It has absolutely none of its desired effect.

'I don't care about anyone else, I care about *my* sister . . . you were supposed to protect her . . . that's why we came here . . .'

'I'm so sorry . . .' I stammer.

'Sorry is too late,' she says, turning from me. I hear the *click clack* of the three-inch heels of her smart brown shoes down the passage.

If I didn't know any better, I'd say my day couldn't get any worse. But today is also my mother's birthday and we're all getting together tonight at Papuzzi's, her favourite Italian restaurant at the wharf. As of this moment, I am still empty-handed in the gift-department and judging from the reception area when I walked in—which was packed with women and kids as if AVOs were on some kind of special—I don't know when I'm going to get a gap to make it to the mall. I also want to check how my eBay bids on that green beetle bracelet and hematite spider key ring are doing. But it's difficult to relax when the waiting room is wall-to-wall with broken people waiting for you to save them from the desperate habit they call their lives. It's like a doctor's waiting room out there, people flicking through celebrity gossip magazines, being made to wait on verdicts that could change their lives. I sat with Josh in enough waiting rooms to know that doctors always run a casual hour and a half behind schedule. You wouldn't mind so much if they were performing emergency brain surgery. But, and I only know this because I once went on a date with a doctor, doctors spend five minutes examining and twenty-five 'catching-up', with patients they play golf with. Waiting is underrated as a form of torture. But it is.

Doctors either don't know it or they don't care.

Poverty hangs around here like a teenager with nothing better to do. Slouching in the doorways, quietly disgruntled, infecting everyone who sits here waiting to see me. Not that wealth gives anyone immunity. Christina Bryant was in here again last week with a funny little piece of cardboard over her nose. Maybe it was a special nasal bandage. I watched from my window as she reversed, and inched forward in that brand-new four-wheel drive until it was perfectly parallel-parked. I filed the photos she brought in of her facial welts. 'The new NOKIA,' she clarified. 'No one should consider buying anything else, it's taken digital technology to a new level.'

We've been over it. I even drew the cycle of violence for her. You are here, I said, circling *honeymoon phase*. She nodded. I then took out my yellow highlighter. I highlighted *tension-building* and *acute battery*. 'This is what follows,' I said. 'It always does.' She nodded again. What you commonly find is that knowing a name for something is probably not as enlightening as you'd expect it to be.

It can't be easy for her. When you're accustomed to uniformed home-help and catered dinner parties, you have Edward-Turcotte-in-a-pinstriped-suit expectations when it comes to legal representation. It takes a certain downscaling of pride to actually walk through our grubby doors and take your place in line with other miserable women who, despite their tatty clothes and bus tickets, are just like you.

'Do you know who I am?' Doctor Bryant said quietly into the phone to me. 'You better get her to drop the charges. Or she'll be sorry, and you'll be even sorrier,' he advised me. I could hear the nurse calling him in the background. Doctor Bryant is one of the finest cardio-thoracic surgeons. There are people who owe their lives to him. I discussed it with Genevieve, and we decided bully, not psychopath. 'Lock your doors when you drive, and when you get home,' Genevieve said reassuringly. So I've added a notch to my usual state of hypervigilance. I think I know I do not want to die because Doctor Bryant has taken a contract out on me, or something equally wasteful. That would be a truly pathetic way to die. Not that I think I will. I've got insurance—my parents have had their share of 'losing a child', which puts me in that mythologically unlikely statistic where lightning strikes twice. Still, you can never be too complacent. Rich people have more money than they know what to do with sensibly. And a cornered rich man can throw money at a problem with a kind of ingenious flamboyance I wouldn't even know how to apply to my own wardrobe.

Now that Priscilla has left, despite the looks on these women's faces, and the guilt it induces in me, I am going to have a cup of coffee and check on my eBay bids. Genevieve's always going on about 'taking care of our own needs', and this morning these are mine. These women have been abused for so long, another half an hour waiting won't make any difference in their lives. And at some point I'm going to have to slip out to buy my mother a present. I've been putting it off, but my deadline is seven o'clock tonight. I've still got no idea what I'm going to give her. She is one of those spiritual and unmaterial-istic individuals—a fabulous personality trait on all occasions save a birthday, because none of us, not Dad, nor Libby nor I, ever knows what to buy her. No matter what we end up giving her, she always says, 'You shouldn't have spent all this money on me . . . I wish you'd given it to AIDS orphans or the RSPCA.' Which makes you, the giver of the expensive gift, feel like a piece of shallow shit.

Barbara winks at me. 'You okay?' she asks, nodding in the direction of Priscilla's dramatic exit. I wince and nod.

She smiles, revealing the whitest teeth—one day a talent scout is going to steal her for Colgate's marketing campaign and then we'll be stuffed and even the reception area will become depressing with nothing to compensate for the side table of fake flowers and stack of *National Geographic*s from St Vincent's. Barbara folds her arms across the colossal reef of her bosom which looks like it could nurse an army. Her three strapping sons, each over six foot, grin, mischief in Levi's, from the family photo on her desk. Jai. Tyler. Bailey. A tribute to testosterone.

'I just made fresh coffee in the kitchen,' Barbara says.

'Thanks,' I say. I didn't get much sleep last night.

'And have one of Dave's cranberry and pear muffins on the kitchen counter,' she nods.

'If you just clone that husband of yours, you could retire in luxury.'

Barbara chuckles. 'There's lotsa them out there . . . you just aren't looking right.'

'Obviously. And Barbara, I need a new box of tissues.'

'Check your bottom drawer,' she says.

I feel drained with gratitude for people like Barbara. There is pride and dignity in replacing empty tissue boxes if you come to the task with her territorial conviction. She carries the key to the cupboard of provisions like a protective amulet. Not a stray pencil gets past her beady eye. If Barbara doesn't authorise it and hand it to you, you've got no chance of getting it. Being on her good side comes easy to me, but if you don't manage it—like Carol hasn't ('*that girl's gotta get her act together, she brings you down,*' Barbara says)—you're stuffed.

I return to my office and open the window to let some air in. And there he is. In the left-hand corner, between the filing cabinet and the ceiling. A spider. An ordinary little harmless house spider. Speckled brown and tiny.

I sigh.

I open my office door, smile apologetically at the row of waiting faces, and make my way into the kitchen to look for a bucket. I find one under the sink but it has something wet and detergent-like in a viscous swirl at the bottom. Rahima, our cleaner, does not come to her job with quite the same dedication as Barbara. So I drain the fluid in the sink, and wash the bucket out. There is no paper towel anywhere, so I shake it out over the sink. Coaxing the spider down from the ceiling only to have him drown in the bucket or be poisoned by household cleaning agents would be one of those cruel twists of fate I come across way too often in my work. I find a broom with a few measly bristles in the closet in the laundry. I walk through the waiting room with the decrepit broom and bucket. The women look at me with interest. Some with perplexed anxiety.

I spend the next fifteen minutes trying to entice the spider into the bucket. He scurries out of sight behind the filing cabinet. Little things commonly confuse a helping hand with danger. It's very understandable, really.

If I were Carol, I would have crushed it. But it is no small relief for me to state that I am not Carol. It is terrifically enterprising of her to augment her income on weekends, even if it involves an oversized tutu of lavender taffeta. I admire it. But I can say with a special kind of certainty that I was never meant to be the Candy Floss Fairy. The last time she was admitted on 'suicide watch', I begged her to let me call the mother and just cancel. 'You can't do that to a child! You can't fucking promise to be there and then let her down at the last minute,' she sobbed and I was afraid she'd rip the drip out. A very large nurse with a mole on her cheek who smelled of garlic asked me to leave because I was 'upsetting the patient', but that just made Carol more hysterical. They tranquillised her after that. It was one of her better episodes.

In hospitals, you probably don't realise how much you want the olfactory safety of Dettol. Bleach. The smell of sanitised precision. Not the curry from the night before. Metabolised garlic, odorous and faintly faecal, makes me nervous now. Smells attach to situations, it's one of those things over which you have no control.

31

'Just this once,' I told Carol. Nonna says that Carol makes me a '*stupida*'. After three hours in her itchy tutu with that leotard scrunched up my bum like a thong, I could see Nonna's point. I ended up doing my entire repertoire of magic tricks Nonno Antonio had taught me. The swarm of sticky four-year-olds dangled their shimmery wands in my face and pelted me with preschool insults like 'That's easy,' and 'You're just hiding it in your hand.' Children are merciless in a way that their stature misrepresents. I hadn't done those tricks in years—not since I did them for Josh before he died. Funny, some things you can't forget, much as you try.

Like the way Libby tried to snatch and tear my copy of *Charlotte's Web* Nonna bought me when I was eight. 'For me?' she yelled. Nonna tried fobbing her off with a jelly baby from her bag, but Libby managed to tear the front cover in which Nonna had written: *For Faith, because death is in life and life is in death. You are SOME KID. xxx Nonna.* I fixed it with sticky tape. Over the years, it's lost its stickiness and become brittle. I know it was just a silly childhood story and spiders can't weave *SOME PIG* in their webs. But there it is. The extent of my sentimentality. It's not an 'overcompensation', as Carol puts it. I just don't kill spiders. But that's social workers for you—overanalysis as a substitute for self-insight.

But now I've wasted too much time trying to get this spider outside where he belongs and I haven't switched on my computer, checked eBay or got myself a coffee. I don't want to start my day running late like every doctor on the planet who truly believes that ten years in medical school makes his time more precious than yours. As if you don't have lives to save.

I leave the bucket and broom in the corner of the room. I'll get him later.

For the fourth time today, I walk past the phalanx of women. I watch my feet so as to avoid eye contact. I head for the kitchen again and this time I pour myself a cup of black coffee to which I add two-and-a-half sugars and concentrate on stirring as I file past the waiting women yet again.

I walk over to the front desk where Barbara is sitting.

'What can I get my mother for her birthday?' I ask her.

'If you'd given me enough notice I'd have asked Dave to bake her his if-I-die-now-I-can-die-happy cheesecake—why you left it so late?'

'A suggestion would be my first choice over a lecture, Barbara. My mother has everything.'

'Let's see, what does one give a woman who has it all? Fame, fortune, a loyal husband and two beautiful daughters, even if one of them hates men.' She lets out a hearty chuckle.

'I do not hate men . . .' I say. 'I just don't see the point of most of them . . .'

She shakes her head at me.

'You got to love men, Faith . . . you got to love them . . .'

'Spoken like someone married to the guy who bakes muffins with cranberries. Please think about what I can get for my mother . . . I don't have much time left . . . and you can send the first one in . . .'

Back in my office, I switch on my computer and wait, sipping from my hot mug. I rummage at the back of my top drawer, again, but it's not there. I can't understand it. I don't lose things. I have just enough time to delete an email inviting me to *enlarge my penis fast* and check my eBay bids—I've been beaten to the hematite spider key ring by *discodude*, but I'm still in the running for the green beetle bracelet which has another ten hours and twenty-four minutes to go.

I mentally note that at the time I would like to be outbidding *silverfarenheight* and *polyesterpimp* for the bracelet, I will be in the clutches of a waiter and my family will be ordering food that has been prepared without a thought for the number of dolphins that died, chickens that were tortured or cows that were pumped with hormones for it to end up on their plate. Nonna always says, '*Nascondere ditale speranza in cuore*, hide a thimble of hope in your heart. *In caso di emergenza.* For emergencies.' But hope aside, I know she's going to bale tonight.

I impulsively put in a ridiculous bid—$25 for that bracelet which is probably worth $10, max.

Outbid that, *silverfarenheit* and *polyesterpimp*.

# 6. magic

Nonno Antonio always made magic for me.

He could take his thumb on and off.

He could make coins appear from behind my ear.

He taught me that 81 is a magic number. 'Nine is magic, because of Nonna's fingers, and also nine times nine is eighty-one. *Molto magico!*'

He could even find the one card you had picked from a whole deck, even though you put it in the middle and he shuffled them.

Then for my eighth birthday Nonno Antonio gave me a magic set.

'*Tenere d'occhio*,' he said, 'watch carefully', as he moved his hands slowly. One by one, he showed me how to do all the tricks. You hide the ring in your glove. You warm the one coin by holding it. You always know which card you're showing.

He showed me how to do all the tricks.

Then he said, 'You try.'

'But they're not magic,' I told him. 'It's cheating. What about real magic?'

Nonno Antonio laughed. 'There is no *magia reale*,' he said. 'What you think? I'm an old man, not a superman. Magic takes the eye to the place where you want it to look—*mago* makes people believe,' he told me. '*Illusione ottica, un gioco di prestigio*, sleight of hand. *Mago* is *dominare*. In control.'

Nonna got cross with him.

'*Robetta!* Rubbish!' she said. 'Only *buffone di corte* cannot make *magia*, must make *illusione ottica*, hoptical hillusion,' she snorted. And she doused Nonno Antonio with a glug of Italian admonishments. *Stupido* was somewhere in there.

'*Marziano!*' she huffed, which I think means, 'Man from Mars'. Nonno Antonio shrugged.

I never did play with that magic set.

Not until Josh was so sick.

'How'd you do that?' he gasped when I made my mother's black queen appear from behind his ear.

'Magic,' I choked back.

# 7. polaroid

> *When a woman has been subject to abuse over a long period of time, she may suffer from low self-image, dependence on others and an inability to do anything for herself, rendering her incapable of making decisions or acting on them in order to change her circumstances. This is what is known as learned helplessness.*

Training Manual, page 34

'Have you seen, you know, that butterfly pendant I wear sometimes . . . ?' I ask Barbara hopefully. 'I had it on last week . . .'

'Sorry, no,' she shrugs.

I sigh.

'I'll keep an eye out for it, but if you've dropped it here, chances are, it's gone walkabout.'


'I'm sorry, he's not in right now, can I take a message?' the female officer says.

'I'm calling from SISTAA—the women's crisis centre in the inner west. I've left three messages for Constable Simpson already, I think we may just proceed with a formal complaint against him,' I say. 'If he doesn't return this call.'

There is a silence for a moment.

'Can I ask what this is in connection with?' the female officer asks.

'I'm just trying to verify whether or not he was the officer who took the complaint of one of our clients—Dianne Gibson, she was gang-raped by three men about six weeks ago outside a church in Williamstown?'

'And if he was?' she asks.

'He didn't give our client a copy of her statement,' I say, 'and . . . I just want to go over some of the questions he asked her.'

'I can check on the statement for you, but what sort of questions are we talking about?'

I clear my throat.

'Just two in particular. We recommend that police officers taking statements in rape cases avoid questions like "Did you enjoy it?" and "Did you climax?" Generally speaking.'

There is a short pause.

'I'd just proceed directly with the formal complaint,' she says.


'I can't talk now, Libby,' I say into the phone.

'You can never talk,' she says huffily. 'I just want to find out what you're giving Mum for her birthday—so we don't overlap or anything . . .'

'I'm sure we won't.'

'We're going the beauty therapy route,' she says. 'Me and Chris.' Like she ever was anything separate.

'We definitely won't overlap,' I assure her.

'So what are you getting her?'

'It's a big surprise,' I say flatly.

Rania Demas is enormous. She has weary eyes and acne-ravaged skin. She is dragging a scrawny little boy in one hand and carrying a green recyclable grocery bag containing what appears to be a pair of man's boots in the other.

I offer her the sofa, which she takes gratefully, sinking into it with a billow, clutching the bag tightly to her. The little boy sits down beside her and scuttles into her curves like a crab in a rock crevice. She scolds him to keep still and be quiet. He nods.

She's chasing maintenance. I know this not because of prescience. When you've worked here long enough, you start to see patterns. People are more predictable than their individuality would suggest. Women always drag the kids in with them when it's maintenance. Showing is the pop-up version of telling.

She's been married for eleven years. Four kids. Messiah, her husband, hasn't come home in over eight months.

'Do you think something's happened to him?' I ask.

'Don't think so,' she says. 'He phones . . . sometimes . . . when he's . . .' and she makes a gesture with her hand like a bottle.

She hands me a maintenance order. I peruse it briefly. It's dated six months ago.

She looks at me with vacated eyes. There is too much room there where love has been unattended. I smile at her.

A looseness flops about in my belly like a broken dial on a compass. It feels a bit like hopelessness, but it could just be viral. I concentrate very hard on the handwriting on the maintenance order. With Rania at arm's length from me, saying 'My husband, Messiah' like that, solemnly, I try not to think about Josh's best line from the *Life of Brian*. 'He's not the Messiah, he's a very naughty boy.' I clear my throat.

Chris told us that he and some friends once stole an old man's crutches while he was swimming in a pool. 'You should have seen the look on his face.' I wasn't being passive aggressive, the way Libby said. I didn't laugh because I didn't think it was funny. Rania is balancing. Hope is a zimmer frame. If I kick it out from under her, she'll fall. Here, in my office. Her husband has gone for good. That's what I know. What I see before everyone else, is usually the shape in the darkness. I've got a lot to get through today. I can't afford to get stuck on a dead-end case.

Instead, I tell Rania about the private investigator who volunteers his services. I tell her his name is Ray Osborne, no relation to Ozzy. None at all. She nods. I tell her he sometimes traces maintenance shirkers. I emphasise the *sometimes*. I jot down a few details in a new file. Later, I will be able to say *I did all I could.*

'What's in the bag?' I ask.

She smiles dazzlingly, her sweetness readily surfacing. People need so little encouragement, really.

'His Blundys.'

I nod. 'Why are you carrying them around with you?'

'He loves these boots. He'll be back for them. And when he comes, I'll have them. For him.'

When your sister's first fiancé offers to help you with the drinks and then grabs your bottom while you're getting ice from the fridge, it is incredibly bad luck that your pretty little sister has not followed you so she can see for herself. I didn't tell Libby. You just have to trust that an asshole will give himself away. Sooner or later. But this, like Rania and those boots, is really what is meant by love is blind.

Rania sighs. She shakes her head. 'I need money for groceries now . . . this boy has not eaten since yesterday,' she says, and for good measure she smacks him on the arm, the kind of brutal motherly affection that bewilders children. He winces, but does not cry out.

'How much do you need for groceries?' I ask her.

'Maybe fifty . . . maybe seventy . . .' she says. 'Just for some bread and milk, maybe porridge . . . No meat, it's too expensive . . .'

I have two hundred dollars in my wallet I was going to spend on my mother's birthday present. I open my bag and I take out my wallet.

'Rania, you cannot tell anyone what I am doing now. And you cannot come back and ask me for more in the future, do you understand me?'

She nods earnestly, but there is an impatient smile at her lips.

'I will say I did not give this money to you, do you hear me? I will tell them you are lying. I will say you stole it from me. I could get fired from my job, do you understand?'

She nods.

I hand over two hundred dollars to her in fifty-dollar notes.

'Hide it away,' I say to her.

She folds the notes into a small bunch and sticks it into her gargantuan bust.

'Come back in a week's time and we will see if we can find your husband.'

'Yes,' she says.

'And Rania . . .'

'Yes?'

'Do you want to be chasing Messiah your whole life?'

She looks uncertain, but she says 'No,' anyway.

'You must make your own money,' I say.

She nods.

'We may find him this time, but he will just run away again.'

She nods again.

'So you must forget about this man. He is no good.'

'No good,' she repeats.

'You should burn his boots.'

She looks taken aback.

'Make a big bonfire, and throw them in.'

She puts her hand over her mouth and shakes her head.

'Okay,' I say. 'You don't have to burn his boots. Do you want help to find a job?'

'Yes,' she says.

'Then let's speak to Barbara who will make a time for you to see Maryse. She's the counsellor who helps people to find jobs. If you have no skills, we can teach you some skills—we have some programmes to teach women how to cook, how to sew, how to clean.'

'I'll learn,' she says.

'That's the only way . . .' I say to her.

She smiles.

'Can you just hold that for a moment,' I ask, taking the Polaroid camera out of my filing cabinet. It's not the latest NOKIA, but it captures fresh wounds well enough. Sometimes clients complain I've taken photos without their permission, to prevent us using them in evidence. So now all clients must sign 'A permission to take photographs' form in case they turn hostile witnesses to their own assaults. But just the other day, someone claimed we forced her to sign the permission form. It doesn't matter what you know. You always feel like shit when that happens.

'And the boy too,' I say.

She puts her precious packet on the floor and lifts the boy up by his armpits and holds him like a domestic animal on show. He is not happy about it at all. He wriggles like a cat being hugged.

'Smile I say.'

The boy starts to cry.

She scolds him in her native tongue. He tries to smile between his tears.

I take a photo.

'Thank you,' I say.

She drops the boy. I open the bottom drawer of the filing cabinet where I keep a stash of lollipops. We are down to the last few but I take out a pink one and a green one and hand them to the boy, one in each hand. He takes them from me without smiling. In my second drawer is a box of *HIV KILLS* condoms. I grab a handful and stuff them into Rania's hand. She nods and slips them into the packet with her husband's Blundys.

On the way out the door, Rania turns to me with startling intensity, and says, 'God sent you to me . . . to save me . . . God bless you . . . I will never forget you.'

I nod a little.

'I'll come, I'll come to learn to make my *own* money,' she says.

I lead her to Barbara, and say, 'Can you help Rania to sign up for our Sistaas-Are-Doing-It-For-Themselves programme?'

41

I leave Rania in Barbara's capable hands, which I'd trust to pull a baby out of my womb, if my womb had any intentions of having babies.

I know that Rania won't pitch up for any of our programmes. Learned helplessness is harder to give up than a lifetime's smoking habit. What I also know is that I will see her here again, with all her children at her flank, and I'd better have an empty wallet or else I'll be suckered into this treacherous charity all over again.

But at least I have my mother's birthday present developing in my office.

I've got it right. For the first time in thirty-four years.

# 8. corner

As far as nicknames go, it wasn't crippling. Fussy Faith. I just couldn't bring myself to eat things with faces after I discovered that chops came from lambs, which have the kindest eyes. That research project on dolphins in Year 8 ended my love affair with fish fingers and anything that lives in the sea that had the misfortune to end up on a plate. It exasperated my mother, as if I was somehow 'doing it on purpose', the 'it' being making her life harder than it already was, hadn't she suffered enough? From the hurried irritation in her delivery of my baked beans or lentil burger, I always knew that, in my mother's eyes, there were hundreds of things in the world I could have chosen to be other than Fussy. Like Normal, for example.

'She just refuses to go out into the playground,' Sheila, my kindergarten teacher told my mother.

My mother agreed, *it just wasn't normal.*

I wished I had a name for what I could see.

Bernard Baker, at the age of four, was a sadist in training. If I Googled him today, he'd be serving time for grievous bodily harm or murder involving dismembering of body parts. Actually, he's probably a surgeon with a long waiting list. He kicked things, not out of rage but out of some scary kind of joy—balls, if you were lucky, but anything else he could get his foot against, including snails, lizards and even the school tortoise. I once saw Tammy Lemay flick a grasshopper that had landed in her skirt into the water table and proceed to pour soapy water over it with a little plastic Hello Kitty teapot until it just gave up, enduring what must be recognised as about as undignified a death an innocent creature could suffer. I watched as kids crushed ladybugs to 'hear their wings crunch' and squished earthworms in boredom: 'Watch this pop!' 'Did you hear that?' 'Yeuch, look at its green blood!' As far as Sheila was concerned, this was, 'age-appropriate play'. To this day, playgrounds scare the crap out of me.

Back at home, my mother extracted a promise from me that I would not stay in one corner all my life for fear of hurting things.

So I ventured out.

Tentatively.

Once, when I was about ten, I was wearing my red trainers when a homeless guy who slept under the bridge called out, 'Hey Dorothy, where's Toto?' I bought him a cheese and mushroom pie with my pocket money because if I'd had a dog, which I had wanted forever, I would have called him Toto. The pies weren't fresh, but he didn't mind. Someone must have called the police. Vagrants hanging around kids. It didn't look *normal.* Three police officers in full uniform were on the scene before that pie was finished. As he was led away, he turned back to me and said, 'I guess we're not in Kansas anymore.' I was nauseous with shame.

My mother was furious. 'Do you have any idea how dangerous it is to talk to strangers?' she asked me.

He smelled a bit. But he was just a harmless homeless guy. That day I figured something out. It's *normal* to treat old folks, amputees and cripples—just people struggling for love like the rest of us—as sinister and as if human misery were contagious.

It helps explain why people miss the real dangers. Fathers who steal into their daughter's rooms at night. Invitations by uncles to sit on their knees. Cigarettes. And the occasional pair of scissors.

What you see is not what you get.

You have to get things, to see them.

I sometimes fold into myself, in self-pity that is more about a devastating loneliness, when I imagine, with a startled jolt, that since Josh left, I am truly the only one who knows this.

# 9. pit bull

I'm standing at the fax machine, faxing a copy of Rania's maintenance order to Ray Osborne, when Carol sidles up to me.

'Come belly dancing with me.'

There are times when silence is the only way you can spare someone's feelings.

'You know what your problem is?' she says, leaning into me.

I shrug.

'You are sexually uptight.'

'And I was worried it was something serious.'

'Belly dancing is in, Faith, I'm telling you . . . my therapist said it would release some of my deep-rooted pain.'

'She's making fun of you,' I suggest.

'You know, you are no fun anymore.'

'I can't imagine what makes you say that.'

'In fact, I don't think you've ever been much fun.' Carol rakes her fingers through her short-cropped blonde hair. 'I think I'm the fun one and you're just tagging along for the ride.'

Ray Osborne's fax line is busy.

'Remember that time I told that guy I'd bite his flaccid dick off and feed it to the ducks?'

'Yes, that was a lot of fun,' I say. 'Fending off drunks in car parks . . .'

'We were like Thelma and Louise.'

'They drove off a cliff, Carol.'

'What a way to go . . .' she sighs.

'That is your pathology speaking,' I say.

'You're a selfish cow if you won't come with me to belly dancing. When do I ever ask you to do anything?'

I sort of snigger. Carol's 'ask' clearly doesn't include 'manipulate', 'guilt into doing' or 'emotionally blackmail'.

'We need to do *something*,' Carol whines. 'I'm sick of sitting around and waiting.'

'I'm not waiting for anything.'

Carol, unfortunately, has been waiting for Corey to leave his wife. It's been, what, seven years this summer?

'I'm working on my online dating profile, do you want to hear it?'

I grimace.

She stands back and narrows her eyes at me. 'You are not a participant, Faith,' she announces.

I nod vaguely again.

*Fun-loving, outgoing, thirty-something, writer of poetry for the soul and sprinkler of fairy dust. I'm an invitation to the best party of your life . . .'*

I am, it appears, lost for words. I blink several times.

'What?' she says. 'This is me, isn't it?'

I avoid eye contact. I wobble my head a bit.

She feigns a yawn. 'Faith, I need you to get some new staples for me from Barbara.' I nod. 'And some sticky tape.' I nod again.

'And I can't find my red pen.'

'Don't abuse this friendship,' I say.

Carol leans against the water cooler.

'I heard about the scissors,' she says.

I nod.

'Kids?'

'U-huh. Two tiny ones . . .'

'D'you reckon you could use a pair of scissors again once you knew your mother had been . . .'

'Who knows, Carol?' I snap. 'Maybe there is life after scissors . . . maybe you go on to Swiss Army knives, maybe you just go through life tearing things.'

'Whoa!' Carol says, gesturing with both hands. 'It's been a horrible week for everyone—I've had sixteen rapes alone—so don't start pulling rank on me.'

'I can't find my butterfly pendant.'

'How'd you lose that?'

I shrug. Miserably. 'I wore it last week to work . . . I never lose things.'

'It'll turn up. Do you want to go out for drinks later?'

'We're doing the happy-family-goes-out-to-a-really-expensive-restaurant-thing tonight, my mother's birthday. Maybe afterwards?'

'I need to get laid later,' she whispers conspiratorially. 'I seriously need a good fuck.'

'Thanks for the update,' I say.

'Anyone with a dick will do, at this point. Do you think Barbara would lend me Jai or Bailey or Tyler?'

'I try to think three times before verbalising things.'

As I say this, Shaun Hamilton walks into reception.

'Mmm . . .' Carol says to me.

'I'd rather fuck a pit bull with syphilis and a cactus for a cock,' I say to her.

'Aw g'won, he's kinda sexy.'

'Give me a pit bull any day.'

* * *

Some things do not excite me. Fashion week. Foxhunts. Paris Hilton. The Ribs 'n' Steak Shack Eat-All-You-Like-for-$20. Gallagher and Cullinan Solicitors.

I didn't apply to G & C after law school because, despite my top results, I don't play cricket or rugby. That automatically excluded me from participating in their compulsory *outdoor team-building culture*. Sometimes just one story holds everything you feel about a certain thing. In this case, Gillian Brown. Brilliant up-and-coming attorney. She'd been overlooked for partner. Again. She sued them for sexual discrimination. The media fed off her for months, while her entire life was paraded, ridiculed and finally destroyed in court, in a blaze of castigations about her instability and incompetence. Given her outstanding performance in her eight years there, it hurt to watch. Not because I cared about Gillian Brown per se. A Year 7 report surfaced in which it was recommended she repeat a year (the same year her mother died of breast cancer) and an ex-boyfriend they raked up testified that she was a nymphomaniac and had been on medication for chronic depression for years. You couldn't help feeling sympathetically exposed. Like that embarrassment you get when you see someone lose control of their bowels.

All that weight on such a small surface area. She was an idealist, just trying to make an anti-discrimination point. I believe she now works in cosmetics. It's a big joke at G & C—if you can't handle the heat, put on some lipstick.

'There's a Shaun Hamilton from Gallagher and Cullinan Solicitors on line four for you,' Barbara said, putting the call through. That was just five months ago. I managed three inhalations from my asthma pump before the call bleeped. I guessed we'd probably just served him with an AVO or he'd been taken on as defence counsel by Doctor Bryant.

My mother says it's only people who lack confidence who need to publicly announce their personality treasure as if it were a scientific fact, when it only really counts if discovered by third parties. Like the way butterflies always came to Josh. He never had to say it. You just needed to watch him. Shaun Hamilton's second sentence to me was:

'I'm all about integrity.' At that point, I stopped biting my nails. *Insecure—small penis?* I scribbled on my notepad.

'Humility *is* overrated,' I returned.

But—and I didn't see this coming—that was followed with: 'I'd like to volunteer my services at your organisation.'

I spat out a nail shard from my mouth.

'And what exactly is it you think you can do?' I asked. My thumb was bleeding a bit from where I had gnawed too deep.

There was silence.

'What's your name?' he asked. See, if I were a recalcitrant bureaucrat refusing to release information because of a technicality, one could forgive his tone. But I'm not. I paused long and hard before answering him. 'Faith Roberts, if that's an answer to my question.'

'Listen, Faith,' he said, 'you need me.'

'The only thing I need is my asthma pump,' I said.

'Not you. Your clients. Your organisation. You need me.'

'How do you figure that?'

'How many convictions do you get, on average? How many rape convictions?'

I swallowed. 'Very few cases ever go to trial.'

'Exactly,' he said. 'What, about one in ten, one in twenty?'

'About.'

'And of those, how many convictions do you get?'

'We have about a one-and-a-half per cent conviction rate,' I said. 'Which is a vast improvement since last year, when it was one per cent.'

'And what, in your professional opinion, is the reason for such a low conviction rate?'

I laughed. 'That is a long conversation, Mr Hamilton. There are hundreds of factors.'

'Would you say that victim credibility is largely a problem?'

'I would say that a male judge's perception of a woman's credibility is generally an obstacle for us.'

'Exactly. And who better to prepare your clients for a male judge's cross-examination than another male who understands the way men think?'

50

I sat there quietly for a while.

'I will prepare your clients for cross-examination. I'll get them to cry when they need to cry, to be convincing when they need to be convincing. You and I both know that victim credibility fucks your chances of getting a conviction. I'll help you get more convictions.'

I don't like it when people use the word 'fuck' when I don't even know what they look like. It assumes something, I don't know what. Like maybe that I swear. Or fuck. It's overfamiliar.

'We can't pay you,' I said.

He laughed. 'Sweetheart, on the salary I get here, I don't need your pennies. I'm just a really nice guy.'

If I thought 'I'm all about integrity' and 'fuck' coming from him would jar my sensibilities, I clearly hadn't contemplated 'sweetheart'.

I had a professional obligation to inform Genevieve, though my guts ached and the silence in my ears was deafening. Genevieve's instructions to me were, 'Don't stare a gift horse in the mouth. Get him checked out for a criminal record first.'

When Ray Osborne gave him the all-clear, I was tasked with calling him back to gratefully accept his offer.

'You won't regret it,' he smirked into the phone. 'By the way, are you related to Julia Roberts, you know, from *Pretty Woman*?'

I think I snorted.

Since then I call him whenever we've got a trial coming up. He drops everything. He's never let us down.

Shaun saunters back past us.

'Hello groovy chick,' he says to Carol.

My friend smiles back and says, 'Hi' like she's a teenage bimbo who thinks it's irresistible to be referred to in the diminutive with an adjective as diminishing as 'groovy'. And she calls me pathetic. At least Josh was my friend.

I check my watch. It's nearly my tea break. I look over at the waiting room. It's like housework, this work I do. Just as you sweep up the mess, more arrives through the door.

* * *

When I return to my office, I consider that perhaps I need a plant.

Maybe if I have something that lives and breathes and maybe even flowers, it will cheer up this room.

I check the Polaroid. It's done. On the back I write in childish print, *Thank you Miss Helene for your kindness, Rania and* . . . I didn't get the kid's name. *Jacob*, I write, making something up. It's Biblical, it'll do.

I then put the Polaroid in an envelope and seal it. On the back I write, *Happy birthday, Mum. You've just fed a family for a month. I hope I have finally understood the generosity of your heart. Love, Faith.*

Yes, a plant. A plant is what this dreary office needs.

# 10. smile

Tyler Holden once scored twenty-seven goals all by himself against St Michael's which held the basketball championship trophy and had done so for the past fifteen years. He wore a blazer with National Basketball Championships on the lapel after our school wrested the trophy away from them. He was really tall, as in six foot four, and that was surely a sign that he was meant for me. As in Destiny with a capital D. All the other boys, my age and older, were afflicted. With stupidity, acne or a hideous combination of both. Tower isn't a romantic word when it's a verb and it's used to describe what you do to every boy on the planet. Though I never did get to stand exactly next to Tyler except once in line at the canteen, he made me feel the way girls like to feel next to boys—smaller. In a crisis, if say, we were attacked at gunpoint, or I was being dragged by a current, I figured, what with stature on his side, *he* would be the one to rescue *me*. That thought almost made me giddy.

He never really saw me, as in looked at me and said, 'Oh, that's Faith Roberts, she's so tall with freckles, and with eyes like leaves of a Chinese chestnut tree . . . I wonder what books she reads.' I was just background, like sky, except not blue and I didn't want to be.

There really was one fatal mistake that I made when it came to Tyler. And that was telling Lisa that I was in love with him.

'He's kind of geeky,' she giggled.

He did have long legs and bounded like a puppy dog on the basketball field. But he was fast. And he wore glasses. Which made him look smart. Like he read books from the nonfiction section and would know things like the Latin names of spiders and the life cycles of monarch butterflies.

I didn't care what Lisa thought. 'I think he's cute,' I said.

Lisa's brother Todd was in Tyler's class and Tyler sometimes hung out at Lisa's house after school. She offered to 'put a good word in for me' when Tyler was around. Maybe I should have asked her what exactly that word was. As soon as she said this, I got a sick feeling in my belly. I thought it was nerves. But it was a premonition.

Four weeks later, Lisa and Tyler were 'fixed up', as in going out. They held hands. He played with her hair. He even kissed her as in French-kissed. Right in front of me.

Lisa acted like I'd never said a word to her. As if she never thought he was a geek but thought he was cute all by herself.

Only Josh could tell I was drowning from the inside. Every time I took out my asthma pump he'd grab my arm and say, 'That bitch.' And I would scowl at him for exhuming my pain which I'd buried deep in the earth, not displayed in a glass cabinet. I hated how Josh didn't need me to translate for him. 'Stop reading me,' I would say. 'Sorry,' he'd shrug.

I would sit with Tyler and Lisa at lunchtimes while she lay with her head in his lap and he stroked his long beautiful fingers over her eyebrows and I ate my wholewheat cucumber and cottage cheese sandwiches which felt like sawdust in my mouth and pretended to be gazing at the horizon, where the wide blue sky pressed itself against the earth's body. I wanted some of that tenderness. I wanted it so much, I found it hard to speak.

The only time Tyler ever said anything to me was the day after Josh died.

'I'm sorry about your friend,' he said in between mouthfuls of his hotdog, tomato sauce gathering at the side of his mouth.

Though my stomach squelched at the smell of the sausage, I smiled at him. It was too big a smile for someone who had just lost her best friend.

He backed away, nervous.

# 11. african violet

I finally have Constable Young, who has been assigned to Sanna's case, on the line.

He assures me that 'everything is under control' and a 'warrant has been issued for the arrest of the "suspect".' He believes the autopsy will be done today and we'll have a report for trial. 'We've also seized the weapon for evidence,' he says. 'Disgusting way to die, not your average domestic violence dispute . . . She must have *really* pissed him off.'

I am pressing on my thigh so hard that I am hurting myself.

I thank Constable Young for all his assistance.

I did underline *URGENT* on the file. I did. I take Sanna's file out. I did. There it is. I underline it again now.

I instinctively reach for my throat. It is bare, just the smoothness of skin. My pulse quickens. I don't lose things. I also don't wear jewellery as a sort of personal rule, but Josh's necklace was different. It sat in the hollow of my throat as if it were made to fit, which I guess it was. Nonna can't wear tight necklaces or scarves. She says it's because she was hanged in a previous life. 'What for?' I asked. '*Infedeltà*,' she replied.

I survey the pile of files on my desk. They are stacked up in a tumbling tower of statements, formal letters and notices. A stationery of despair.

In the next hour and a half I see three more clients: two are straightforward AVO applications, and I inform my third that if she refuses to lay charges against her boyfriend for assault this time, there's really nothing more to say.

'But I love him,' she tells me.

Love. It's a word I'm beginning to despise.

By the end of the morning, I have a sore head.

'You've got blood on your pants,' Carol says. 'Did one of your clients bleed on you?'

'Shit,' I say.

'No, blood,' she says.

I excuse myself to go and wash it out in the bathroom.

Carol and I walk down to the main road in our jackets, the loose ends of which flap restlessly in the gasps of wind. We pick up a falafel and a shwarma on the corner. On our way back, as we pass the alleyway alive with scuttling McDonald's wrappers and Dunkin' Donut boxes, my eyes are sucked to *This City Scares Me More And More* graffitied on the wall. I've seen it a thousand times before, but every time, something deep in my belly groans. It could just be the smell of Carol's lamb shwarma. She is a hardened carnivore despite my best attempts to explain to her in the most uncensored detail the cruelty every small lamb suffers to end up in marinated chunks between the

57

folds of a pita bread. I have a very sensitive nose and can smell fear a mile off. Her shwarma reeks of an abattoir and lambs aren't dumb.

I tell her I need to find a place that sells plants. I am overdue to give blood, but today has only so many hours in it. Carol suggests Gardens R Us on Wentworth Road. We can probably make it there and back in our lunch break as long as she drives. When I drive, I get honked at all the time. Like forty-five kilometres an hour is a heinous transgression. I swear child molesters get more respect than slow drivers. Sixty kilometres is only a *suggestion* as far as I can tell. You're allowed to do less. It's not that people don't care—road rage is proof that people care. They just expend their consternation on the wrong things, bearing down like stiletto heels on small transgressions. I usually just turn up the volume on my radio. If she's in the passenger seat, Carol slinks down and pretends she's my grocery shopping.

In the nursery, we wander amongst the agapanthus and the impatiens. Among the bright flowers, Carol looks like a garden fairy with a peroxide habit. I clearly don't appreciate what is so scary about 'going natural'. She belongs in a kinder world, but you can't give people their childhoods back. It's a flaw, I guess. But I didn't make the world.

'I want something practical and hardy,' I tell her.

'Get something bright and joyful,' she suggests.

'What about something hardy and ridiculously cheerful?'

'Beauty doesn't have that kind of stamina,' she says wistfully, breaking off a petal from a yellow rose. She flings her comment carelessly, unaware of how she litters spoken things that stop a day in its tracks. This is her poetry. Not the tortured rhyming lines she intermittently pens for my inspection.

'I want to get married in a rainforest, with a carpet of rose petals,' she murmurs.

'Just don't ask me to be your bridesmaid.'

'You, my darling Faith, will be the maid of honour.'

I shudder.

We take advice from Edmond, benevolence in overalls, with for-bearance in his eyes and an unhurried gait which makes you feel like you're moving in slow motion, as if he's got all the time in the world. It is either very relaxing or very irritating, I can't decide which. I explain my office gets no sunlight but that I want something that will flower. He shakes his head sadly. 'Flowers need sun,' he says. 'Plants need sun.'

'Okay, I'll take it outside for some sun.'

'A plant is not like a dog that needs a walk,' Edmond says. 'It must be happy where it sits. It must be loved.' He looks at me. 'Do you know what I mean?' His old eyes twinkle.

'Okay, okay . . . just give me something that can survive with the minimum sun and the minimum love.'

Eventually he picks out a lilac African violet in a little pot. I feel like a mother as I clutch and pay for it at the counter.

As he turns to leave us, he looks at me and I think he says, 'Such a beautiful girl. Such sad eyes.'

I look at Carol. She giggles silently.

He can't possibly be talking about me.

But like the sting of a prophecy, his words attach to me. Beautiful. Sad.

Back in the car, Carol says, 'And the award for Giving a Geriatric a Long-Awaited Erection goes to my good friend Faith Roberts.'

'Could you just *not*, for once,' I say to her. 'Not everything is about sex, Carol. Besides, he wasn't even talking about me.'

'You're right,' she says. 'He must have been talking to your pot plant.'

On the way back to SISTAA, Carol tells me that she overheard Genevieve talking on the phone and it looks like she's going to intro-duce compulsory debriefing counselling for all the staff. I feel a slight constriction in my chest.

'What exactly does that involve?' I ask.

'Just talking through your cases, and whatever else is on your mind.'

'I write reports about my cases, I don't need to talk about them.'

'Yes, but you don't write reports about whatever else is on your mind.'

'I don't need to, that's what you're for . . . and slow down will you, it's a sixty zone . . .'

She chuckles. 'I've been paying psychologists and psychiatrists for twenty years. I'm only too happy to get some counselling for free . . . and I'm doing exactly sixty . . . um . . . sixty-four.'

'I don't need free counselling. And besides, look where all your therapy's got you—hung up on some married man for almost a decade . . . and you want to fuck Shaun Hamilton, for godsakes— take that into therapy.'

'Hehehe,' she giggles. 'Why don't you just admit you're a lesbian, and be done with it?'

'I would, if I was,' I say to her, 'but I'm not.'

'Fuck me . . .' she says, '. . . and I'll tell you if you are.'

'I am NOT fucking you,' I say to her. 'I *want* to sleep with men . . . in theory . . . There's just no one that appeals to me.'

She grows quiet.

'You once nearly fucked me,' she says painfully.

'I was drunk,' I say. 'And you climbed on top of me . . .'

'You kissed me back.'

'Are you still on those pills?' I ask her. 'Because I'd up the dosage if I were you.'

'Is the lunatic inside my head getting to you?' It's a joke, but she's not smiling. And neither am I.

I don't answer her. It's all mangled and contorted. Our work, our relationship, our history. I get confused. It feels as if there never really was a time before we met. She's not my sister. I'm not responsible for her. I don't know what she is. She's there. It could be comforting. But it isn't. Carol doesn't speak to any of her family and often tells me, in a way that makes my throat close, that I am her family. It's not that I have anything against families per se. I just don't want to be needed in that way.

\* \* \*

60

I was standing right behind her in line at university on registration day. The motorbike helmet she had looped her arm through was getting in the way. She was ruffling through a wad of documents looking for something in particular while the registrar in her pink seersucker jacket tapped her pencil and rolled her impatient eyes at the rest of us in the queue. People make assumptions. Truly, I didn't mind. I was too busy taking in her scuffed thigh-high black boots, fishnet stockings and unnatural blonde hair colour to notice that she was crying.

Suddenly the registrar realised something was wrong. She softened immediately, maternal and sturdy: 'Don't worry, dear, take your time. I've got nowhere to go.'

But Carol's shuffling became more urgent, panicky. She dropped a whole lot of papers to the floor, which scattered like mice, and as she bent to pick them up, the helmet fell off her arm. I bent down to help her pick them up. When she made eye contact with me, I came face to face with a wall of silent tears streaming down her face and making a God-awful mess of all that mascara she was wearing.

I offered to help her find what she was looking for and we stepped to the side, spread all her papers out in a corner of the hall, and eventually found her birth certificate which had inadvertently become attached to the paper clip on her academic record.

The registrar let her straight back into the queue, but I had to go to the back of the line, my face clearly forgettable as the poor idiot who offered to help.

Carol disappeared into the throng. I forgot all about it. Several weeks later she descended upon me in the canteen, clutching onto a guy with dreadlocks. 'It's her! *This* is the chick I was telling you about. She saved me, I swear, this girl saved my life!' she said really loudly so that people looked at me. I probably wasn't going to finish my spinach pie anyway. This, by the way, is how lifetime burdens are acquired. If you've got a choice between ongoing gratitude or a once-off, always go for the once-off. Carol acts like she has a gratitude servitude over me in perpetuity.

The guy she was dating played the saxophone on weekends at the Swivel. He looked like he had a good story to tell, full of anguish and drama. Turns out he wasn't so much sad and interesting as a heroin addict. He went into rehab just before midyear exams and OD'd three weeks later. Carol asked me to come with her to the cremation. We went out afterwards and I spent a week's worth of grocery money on cocktails. At some point Carol leaned over to me and whispered, 'Would you rather have a one-night stand with Sting, or a long-term relationship with Phil Collins?'

I shrugged. 'Are those the only options?'

'No, you could have either of those with me . . .'

I downed the rest of my cocktail.

'Sorry, I didn't mean to make you uncomfortable,' she said. 'It's just that you have such kissable lips.'

I had always thought my mother saying I had *gorgeous lips* was compensation rather than compliment, the way you struggle to find something nice to say about someone and end up commenting on the shape of their ears or the colour of their eyebrows. There's not much you can do to hide your lips from someone who eyes them like summer peaches. Since then, I've always felt like I'm fending her off, like a beggar who doesn't believe you when you say, 'I don't have anything on me.'

Back then, Carol wore her blouses low-cut (even to funerals) and her charisma made you think of Tequila sunrise. It took me years to work out that the tantalisations she sprinkled like fairy dust on our friendship—*Let's go to South America, why don't we hire a caravan for the summer? I've always wanted to work as a croupier*—was the manic part of her condition.

I glance at Carol.

She smiles, but her eyes are sulking. She's told Corey it's over. Again. She hasn't been suicidal for a while. But the churning in my stomach is a horrible portent that we're not far off another episode. I always see things coming. It gets messy. I am cursed.

Carol suddenly revs my car and clocks 100 kilometres in that last stretch up to SISTAA's front gate.

\* \* \*

*MEMO: To all staff*
*FROM: GENEVIEVE*
*SUBJECT MATTER: IMPLEMENTING 'CARING*
*FOR THE CARERS'*

*SISTAA's primary obligation is to the clients who seek our help. However, our obligation to our clients cannot be discharged unless the carers (yes, that's each of you) themselves are being cared for. If we do not care for ourselves, we suffer burnout. I do not want to lose any staff to burnout this year. In addition to the tips below for avoiding burnout that I have incorporated into our new policy document, we will soon be implementing a compulsory bi-weekly therapy session with two counsellors from the university who are doing research and have offered their services free of charge.*

*Tips on how to avoid staff burnout:*
- *clear job descriptions, responsibilities and accountabilities;*
- *professional boundaries between staff and clients must remain inviolable;*
- *appropriate training at regular intervals;*
- *monitoring of case loads;*
- *staff must take regular breaks and holidays;*
- *regular debriefing and team-building exercises;*
- *whenever you get down, remember you are doing a wonderful job!*

# 12. blood

Nonna says it was the water that did it to her.

She and Nonno Antonio came over from Italy in the 1930s on a boat that took six weeks. Forty-four days 'to be precize'. When they got here, Nonno Antonio, whilst filling in immigration forms, dropped the 'o' from Roberto and added an 's'. So they wouldn't be called Wogs. As if their thick Italian speech wouldn't give it away. Nonna still curses Nonno Antonio for it. But amputation is her sore point, given her pinky. She's the only person I know who can nag the dead. Now it's only her accent that tells a story of where we come from. If I knew how, I'd capture it in a bottle for when she's gone, or else it's just going to get lost like everything else worth keeping.

Ever since the immigration, she feels things 'in her waters'. She began with matchmaking, moved on to healing blisters and fevers, and finally became the oracle in her suburb. Soon her reputation, passed on over fences in quiet whispers, saw neighbours lining up outside her kitchen door, laden with salamis, olives and homemade ricotta tarts to trade in order to hear what her waters had to say.

One of my happiest childhood memories was offering Nonna's home-baked almond and caramelised ginger biscotti on the silver tray Nonno Antonio's parents gave them for their wedding to the crowd patiently gossiping while they waited to hear whether so-and-so's husband was having an affair, or the baby born with a cleft lip would ever marry, or the cancer would go away all by itself.

She once looked me in the eye and told me, 'For you, Faith, love will die, but love will live.'

'Don't things live before they die?' I asked.

'I never wrong,' she said. And mostly, she never has been. The only thing she's been wrong about so far was Nicholas. She never saw that coming. And if she did, love made her keep it to herself.


My mother said it must be period pains and she touched my cheek with that 'my little girl's becoming a woman' kind of tenderness that makes prepubescent girls cringe.

At the age of twelve, I wasn't menstruating yet.

I lay in bed writhing. My mother gave me a hot-water bottle and some aspirin which just made me sweat and feel nauseous. Every hour I got up to go to the toilet to check if there was any blood. But it was as unmuddied as a mountain spring down there. I don't know whether you can call it mystical, or one of those things that is just difficult to explain and hard to name—maybe that's what magic is in the end—but the pain in my belly suddenly lurched out like a phantom projectile hand and snatched at words, 'Nonno Antonio'. The ringing in my ears made my head ache.

'I need to speak to Nonna,' I told my mother.

She rang for me and brought me the cordless phone. She stood at my door and watched me. I winced and waited for her to leave, until I could hear her footsteps down the stairs.

'Nonna?' I whispered.

'*Mia cara?*'

'Where's Nonno Antonio?'

She was silent. 'He's gone to cetch a fish for me, but he be back later.'

'Nonna, Nonno Antonio's tummy,' I said. 'He's sick . . .'

She was silent.

'Sick?'

'Yes. He's very sick.'

'No, he fine . . . he eat a big breakfast, make me cook eggs, sausage, he eat a big breakfast.'

'He's got something in his tummy,' I said, stifling a sob.

Nonna grew silent. I could hear her breathing. Her breathing became ragged.

She cleared her throat.

'You good gal, *mia cara* . . . Ahhh,' she sighed deeply.

'I want to say goodbye to Nonno Antonio.'

'*Sì, sì*, we say *addio* . . .' she said.


A week later, Nonno Antonio was rushed to hospital when blood came out with his poo. *Advanced bowel cancer. Sorry to have to inform you. Nothing we can do. Just make him comfortable.*


On the morning of his funeral Nonna told me to 'put a mattress in'.

'Mattress, Nonna?'

'For the blood, in your penty,' she said, gesturing to my undies.

Nonna never cried at his funeral. She told me, 'You never cry for what cannot die, and love never dies. *Amore eterno.*'

Standing there next to her, holding Nonna's four-fingered hand in mine, the floodgates of my womb opened in a gush in secret synchronicity with the thud of earth on wood.

My mother read a poem she had written for Nonno Antonio. The words 'magic' and 'solid' were both in there, contradictions that blurred into each other making a strange kind of sense.

Libby shrieked when she saw a lizard on a gravestone.

My dad stood there, empty and hushed.

As if losing a father was a simple formality compared to burying a son.

# 13. locket

I am holding my little African violet pot plant which is going to brighten up my office.

As I pass the pink room, I see a young woman sitting on a chair playing with the Zen garden, moving stones. There are bandages around her wrists. Post-rape is high-risk suicide territory. Especially in those who've been saving up their virginity for marriage, like a precious treasure, only to have it snatched away from them by some creep. They should've thought to give it away as a present to their best friend.

Permission. It's such a modest expectation.

It's only another couple of hours until the weekend. But first I've got to deal with another grim tale from the field of horrors. I swear, I should write a book.

As I walk past her desk, Barbara stops me. 'Your Nonna called,' she says handing me a post-it. 'Her appointment is at ten-thirty not eleven-thirty tomorrow.'

I look forward to Nonna's hair days. Every Saturday I pick her up from the Everglades, her retirement village, and drive her to the mall. Clawing the crook of my arm like a baby koala, she insists we stop off first for 'a stiff cappuccino' at Giorgio's. Only Giorgio is allowed to make her coffee. He has the 'Badolato touch'. Nonna was born in a mild Badolato autumn, while her mother was preparing salamis for the winter. It's on my List Of Things To Do. Someday I am going to visit the little walled city in the Italian mountains where Nonna was born, went to school and fell in love with Nonno Antonio.

If Giorgio isn't there, she sends it back with a wave of her hand. Too hot. Too weak. What, no biscotti? *Disastro!* She likes to take a little bag of biscotti back for Mr Abrahams, her neighbour who lost his wife to a brain aneurism when she was just forty-three and who brought up his three girls all by himself, seeing them through puberty, first love and motherhood one by one. 'This,' Nonna sometimes says to me, righteous with emotion, 'is the mark of a real man.'

Last week, she stopped mid-sip of her cappuccino, leaving the perfect shape of her lips imprinted on the rim of the cup in cherry plum, the same lipstick she's been using for fifty years. I was outlining the pros.

'*Operazione?*' she said.

'It's not a proper operation, Nonna, medical technology is very advanced for cataracts these days.'

'No!' She shook her head. 'I see better now,' she said under a huge foam moustache on her upper lip. I leaned over and dabbed it off with a serviette. She's goat-stubborn but she's not to be laughed at.

At Heads Up, Betty always fusses over her. Though Betty's been doing Nonna's hair for more than twenty-five years, Nonna always makes me choose the hair colour afresh, as if this time I might come up with something original. 'No brown,' Nonna reminds me. 'Brown is *molto brutto*. Hugly. Not for *signora con passione*, full of passion,' which comes out more like 'peshen'. 'Choose for your Nonna.'

'The purple rinse is nice. It goes with your lipstick.'

'*Viola* or *porpora*?'

'What's the difference, Nonna, between violet and purple?'

'Look,' she says.

'They look the same to me.'

'You not look properly,' she shrugs.

'Brown is safe,' I suggest.

'*Prudente*? No!'

'I don't want you to look ridiculous. Or for people to make fun of you,' I tell her.

'*Va bene*, hokay, we go for *viola*. What the eye cannot see, cause no pain,' she chuckles.

Blindness is clearly its own form of perfect delusion.


Back in my office I stick the post-it Barbara has just given me on my computer screen. I pull my second drawer out and have a scrabble around at the back. My hand closes around my pair of scissors. I bring it out into the light of day. It looks benign. Useful even.


Despite what horror movies make of it, a 'haunted look', can I just say for the record, isn't just a special effect.

Carol brings a young woman into my office and introduces her to me as Shirley.

'This is Faith Roberts, our legal counsellor. She will be helping you with your statement,' Carol says.

She nods, hiding her bandaged wrists behind her back.

Carol takes a seat next to Shirley. She's here while I take the statement in the event that Shirley breaks down. Shirley is wearing a large man's work shirt like a tent. A boyfriend's, maybe her dad's. Post-trauma, SISTAA's official policy is a recommendation that rape survivors maintain close contact with *supportive loving men*. Around Shirley's neck is a small silver heart-shaped locket.

Shirley is nineteen, a university student studying teaching. She loves kids. Wants to live out in the country and have a little farm some day. Well, she wanted to, we'll have to see now . . . Her punctuation has changed. The paragraphs of her life have shifted. There is a new grammar now, that of the past tense. The present tense has been gouged out of her.

She lives with a flatmate in the city. On Wednesday evening she was alone studying, exams are in three weeks' time. She put out her light after midnight. She was woken sometime later with a knife at her throat. The intruder pulled off her underwear and stuffed them in her mouth. She begged him not to rape her. He called her names.

I stop writing. 'Can you tell me what he called you?'

Shirley looks over at Carol. 'Do I have to?' she asks. 'They're horrible . . .'

Carol puts her hand on Shirley's shoulder.

'We need to know because it may help identify him. It assists us to establish a possible cultural background, ethnic group . . . that sort of thing,' I say. 'Can you tell us the words he used?'

She lowers her head. 'I can't . . . I can't . . .'

I hand her a piece of paper and a pen. 'Can you write them for me?' I ask her.

Her hands shake, like mine do after too much caffeine. She takes the pen in her right hand. At first she cannot still their tremors. She manages. Slowly. *Where there's a will.* Holding her right hand steady with her left hand. She writes three words on the paper and hands it back to me.

*SLUT. BITCH. WHORE.*

A charming little trio of accolades. Just what every woman wants to hear.

'I know that was hard for you,' I say.

'Are you okay to go on?' Carol asks.

She nods.

He turned her around onto her belly and held her legs apart with his knees. He raped her anally. He then turned her around and raped

71

her vaginally. He hit her across the face. He then took his knife and he cut her thigh. I make my notes.

A cry catches in her throat. 'He . . . carved . . . the word *BITCH* on my leg. With a switchblade knife . . .' I look at Carol and she looks at me. Same guy. Shirley is his fourth victim.

Her whole body heaves with the impact of the words she is speaking. Carol and I just sit with her. Carol hands her a tissue. I catch Carol's eye. She has tears in them. In this moment, I decide I will go with her to belly dancing or whatever it is she needs to help her be happy. I'm her friend. That's what friends do.

We wait. Shirley's sobs subside. When it is safe, we ask our questions. She has had a tetanus shot and a medical examination; a vaginal and anal swab have been taken, we are now waiting for the results. She has been given the morning-after pill to prevent a pregnancy. Every orifice of her body is now a piece of evidence. There is a fragile girl in there somewhere who just wants it all back.

'Did they take blood?' I ask her.

She nods. 'What's that for?'

Nonna used to read me that story *A Fish Out of Water* when I was a kid. The boy didn't listen to Mr Carp who said, 'Feed it only so much and no more, never more than a spot, or something may happen, you never know what'. *So much and no more*. That's all Shirley needs to know for now. Blood tells us whether she is welded to her rapist's DNA. The extended family of STDs (syphilis, hepatitis, HIV) is hanging around, waiting to gatecrash the rest of her life. She'll need follow-up blood tests every three months for at least a year as she bleeds her medical aid policy dry until it configures a way of reframing the rape as a 'pre-existing condition'. In her grey tracksuit pants, sitting here in front of me, Shirley is the 'after' picture. There was a Shirley 'before'. They bracket her, like crutches.

'It's just a precaution,' I say.

It's enough. She nods.

'Well done for reporting this,' I say to her. 'You are brave.'

She does not answer me. She looks at me like she needs me to translate 'brave'.

'Will I have to go to court?' she asks me.

'Maybe,' I say. 'If they catch him, if he's charged, if there is enough evidence.'

She starts to shake her head. 'I don't want to go to court . . .'

Carol puts her hand on Shirley's back.

'Let's just take it one step at a time.'

The road she has to travel is long. The next time she has sex it's either going to be with her childhood sweetheart who has stood by her side for ten years while she processes this trauma, or next week in a drunken stupor with a stranger, feeding a wound that just won't heal. Either way, it's no teddy-bear's picnic.

'Can you take her over to HQ to do an identikit?' Carol asks me. 'I've still got two more clients to see today.'

I grab the opportunity for a possible late arrival for dinner with my folks. 'Sure, I say. Let me just finish up with some paperwork.'

Shirley gets up. She walks to my door.

Then before I know what's happened, she gives a little gasp and with her foot she stamps with almighty force on something close to my foot.

'Horrible . . .' she says. 'I hate spiders.'


It is 5 pm on Friday afternoon and Shirley is sitting in the passenger seat of my car.

She is quiet, fingering her silver heart locket. I put on the radio. It fills the space with something other than the mutually acknowledged ghastliness of what has happened to her. Classical music is too noticeably soothing, and therefore patronising. I go for country. We listen to Willie Nelson, and then to Nancy Griffiths singing 'From a Distance'. Though the words are corny, somehow that song always gives me a lump in my throat. I guess it makes me think of Josh.

'Have you just learned to drive?' Shirley asks me.

'No, I just prefer slow,' I say.

As we pull up outside police headquarters, she turns to me and asks, 'Is there any real point in me going through with this?'

'Yes,' I say.

'I don't know what he looks like,' she says. 'I didn't see his face.'

73

'That's okay,' I say to her. 'All the details you can remember help—his clothing, whether he had hair on his face or was smooth-shaven, his accent . . .'

She nods quietly. While you're being raped, you don't tend to memorise the details of your assailant's features. If you're face-down being sodomised it's the rose pattern on the linen, the taste of grass in your teeth or the burn of carpet against your cheek that stays with you. What is asked of rape survivors is unfair and we both know it.

'Shirley, this is going to be very hard,' I tell her. 'But we think the guy that did this to you has done this to other women—this is a serial rapist, and that means he's not done yet. Whatever you can give us can maybe help us prevent it happening to another woman.' Even as I say this, I feel the sting of Priscilla's words, 'I don't care about anyone else . . .' I hold my breath.

But Shirley isn't Priscilla and this clinches it. My tactic of last resort, the preventative argument. Maybe I once believed it. Cynicism isn't the same as experience, but they overlap. Each time a woman gets raped, with a higher social and economic status, the pressure on the police intensifies to make an arrest. In this spate of serial rapes, she is the closest thing to clean and white we could have asked for.

I have so much power in this moment. I could get Shirley to do just about anything I ask. I think to myself that, in the wrong hands, this kind of power could really be dangerous.

'That's a lovely locket,' I say.

She smiles sweetly. 'My sister gave it to me.' She clicks it open to reveal a small image of Jesus on the cross on the one side and a tiny message on the other: *Jesus loves you*.

Josh sang 'Always Look on the Bright Side of Life' from behind his oxygen mask, from that scene where Brian is nailed to the cross. I sometimes have to remind myself that was just two days before he died. There is no reason in the world for me to share this with Shirley. She didn't know Josh, and people who are earnest about Jesus don't appreciate crucifixion jokes as a rule.

'I don't know what I'd do without her . . . She's been amazing to me . . . Do you have a sister?'

'I do.'

She smiles at me. 'I guess we're the lucky ones.'

I cough. The gifts Libby's given me over the years have filled three drawers of my bureau. The expired electrolysis, Reiki and Shiatsu massage vouchers. The bath products and expensive perfumes. The jewellery. Those pearls. All that exhausted generosity.

She twists her fingers over and over in her hand. 'Why do men do this kind of thing?' she asks.

I look out the window. She follows my gaze. 'Shirley, if I knew that, I'd be God.'

'I just thought, since you work with this all the time . . .'

'That, what? I'd have all the answers?' I laugh, perhaps a little hysterically.

I see crimson panic seeping up from her neck. 'You've got blood—is that blood?—on your pants . . .' she says tentatively.

'It's nothing,' I say. 'Just a graze.'

'Are you sure?' she looks at me like she's about to cry. 'It looks like something's bleeding under your trousers.'

'Just a cut,' I say, covering the stain with the open palm of my trembling hand.

I take her up the stairs to the office and there, with Constable Peterson as our guide, Shirley tells us everything she can remember about the night that broke her into pieces. At the end of a long hour we have a black-and-white image of someone who looks like a cross between a bad Japanese cartoon character and the Incredible Hulk. No wonder we never catch any rapists.

> *A rape survivor should make a statement to the police as soon as possible. The law regards a statement made soon after an assault as an indication of a lack of consent on the part of the complainant. The complainant can make this statement at the first reasonable opportunity after the offence. This is known as the 'hue and cry' rule.*

Training Manual, page 167

# 14. sheet

I bled onto his sheet after we had sex.

'Sorry,' I said.

'Don't be,' Josh said. 'It's beautiful. It's you.'

A month after he died, his mother, Mrs Miller, arrived at our house, 'being in the neighbourhood on the way to pick up some pictures at the framers, so no thanks, I won't come in', with a box of things which had my name on it. *For Faith*, Josh had written on it in large blue texta. She looked spick and span; all her corners were tucked in like a hospital bed. I took the box from her with unsteady hands.

'He thought you were very special,' she said to me brightly, in the way a headmistress might bolster a parent's hopes about a wayward child. 'He was . . . lucky . . . to have a friend like you,' she said, and then, as if 'lucky' or 'friend' were words that brought back too much to her senses, she backed away, an ambulatory gesture of spitting out. 'Oh well, you take care,' she said stretching her mouth in a seam of something in the vicinity of a smile.

'Mrs Miller?'

'Yes, dear?'

'What happened to his aquarium? All his fish and hermit crabs . . . ?'

'We donated it to the school,' she says. 'We've got a lovely Biology teacher who's been only too happy to take on the responsibility of looking after all those little creatures that Joshua seemed to love so much.'

I nodded. 'I'm . . . I'm glad . . .' I said, but what I really meant was, 'I wish you'd given them to me.'

'They're in very good hands,' she reassured me, and then she strode, like a woman with an impending appointment, to her car. She waved at me before pulling off. Good. Bye.

Inside the box was our project on water spiders we had done together in sixth grade with our names on the front: *by Joshua Ralph Miller and Faith Ava Roberts*. I told him it wasn't alphabetical, but he would always insist on going first.

> *The fisher spider gallops across the water sprinting up to 75 centimetres per second.*
>
> *They do not propel off the water, but rather row across the water, making small dimples on the surface of the water as they do.*
>
> *Because they are so small, and have a high ratio of surface area to volume, these spiders are responsive to surface forces like surface tension and adhesion. The larger an organism, the more likely they will be responsive to gravity.*

Josh liked them because he thought they were 'magical'. I knew better. When there's a perfectly rational scientific explanation, it's silly to call it magic. Josh said science was magic, and that after Einstein, wasn't that obvious?

Smartarse that he was.

Then there was a picture of us when we were both cards in the school play *Alice in Wonderland* in second grade. He was the ten of hearts. I was the ace of spades. I only noticed now. I was smiling at the camera. Josh was smiling at me.

At the bottom of the box was his sheet all folded up. My blood had turned brown. A stain in a box of treasures. I opened it up and in the middle was a pile of unopened Valentine's Day cards. Eight years' worth from Josh to me. I opened them, one by one, my heart caught like a fish with a hook in its mouth with every word. *Adore. Beautiful. Kind. Wonderful. Perfect. Eyes like the leaves of a Chinese chestnut tree. Best. Love.*

I had always thought Josh was the bravest person I ever knew and that would somehow count towards him getting better. But a box of failed courage showed me something different. He'd quietly been dying alongside me all along.

I folded all those letters back into the sheet and pushed the box to the back of my cupboard and never looked at it again.

I once asked Nonna how she knew Nonno Antonio was the one for her.

'You see this?' she said, holding up her four-fingered hand with the missing pinky that got hacked off 'in the line of domestic duty'. She was only a little girl helping her brother Marcello to chop firewood. Marcello needed glasses but 'we were too poor'. 'Nonno Antonio kissed this hand,' Nonna told me.

'And?'

'All my life I hid this hideous hand in my hapron pocket, away. Children tease. They made me ashame, feel dirty to be "a nine-fingered *mostro*". *Nove dita* they call me. But Nonno Antonio, when he say those words, he pour sunshine in them. He took off the hugly.

78

He say, "Maria, you are *nove dita perfette*." Perfect. As if that is how I was meant. For love, you get one chance. You must concentrate. Sometimes love look funny. Like this,' she said, holding up her hand-less-one-finger.

I suddenly got that feeling when you've not been concentrating and you've put something down and now you need it but you don't know what you've done with it. My loss kicked at me from deep inside, furled in a womb of irritation. At myself. At my carelessness. 'Concentrate, Faith, concentrate,' my mother's said to me all my life. 'Don't be oblivious . . .' And yet here it was again—I had been so busy looking at Tyler's long legs and trying to work out which 'good word' Lisa had put in and where exactly it was she had put it, I had been distracted. That thought doesn't comfort me. But you can only lose what was yours in the first place, and that soothes me, a little. At least I gave Josh my virginity. It wasn't my heart, but I think if he'd had the option of choosing, he would've opted for my virginity anyway.

# 15. envelope

I am the first to arrive at Papuzzi's. So much for my late arrival. I hate being first, having to wait at an empty table with waiters circling you. Piranhas in aprons. *Fuck You*'s all dressed up in *What can I get you?*'s. And in this neighbourhood, you pay double and you get double attitude.

I order a gin and tonic with a double shot of gin. We're going to have to listen to my mother regale us with anecdotes from her latest book tour, how some young woman wept when my mother signed her book, how airline food is 'indigestible and how 9/11 has single-handedly erased the pleasure in international travel, god, no liquids in bottles anymore, what's next?' My mother's heart is big enough to fit the whole world in it. She gives most of the money from her royalties to various charities which in turn wins her all kinds of awards and tributes; the latest is an honorary doctorate at her alma mater, and I *really* did have PMS that night of her acceptance speech which is why I didn't get there. My mother doesn't *value* money because it is an 'energy that you should pass on to others'. My father, on the other hand, believes you should 'put it away for a rainy day'.

Evenings like tonight are at my father's insistence and expense. 'Birthdays are important,' he always says, as if a wish laced with enough desperation could sneak in as a fact. But you can't make something what it isn't. When Josh died, I gave up on birthdays. Waste of time and effort. I realise this is a minority point of view, so I indulge my family and do what is expected of me: I pitch up. My mother always orders the least expensive dish on the menu, and insists that whatever we spend at a meal like this, we donate the equivalent to a charity of someone's choice. I think tonight it's my turn to choose, which is a no-brainer.

Maybe she was always like this. Maybe she got this way after she went away that time. Nonna moved in with us while she was gone and slept with me in my bed. She did the housework, dusting around those framed pictures in the lounge room which could be of a complete stranger for all I know. I don't remember Nicholas. Nonna sucked antacids that smelled of peppermint and always let me have one too. Now *that* I remember.

When I was six, my mother went on to have another child, because she 'always wanted two' and she didn't want me to be an only child. Hence Libby. Liberty Mae Roberts.

If I were to write a manual about how to handle losing a child, based on my mother's experience, I'd go for:

> *Some things you can do when someone you love dies:*
> - *believe they were 'too good for this world';*
> - *pretend they're in a 'better place' right now and that 'we'll be together again some day';*
> - *go on as many courses as you can to understand why you needed your child to drown in the bath in order to become a better person;*

- *replace them;*
- *write a book about their death.*

*No Chance to Say Goodbye* was a 'tour de force of maternal loss, grief and ultimately personal redemption'. My mother's gone on to write fourteen books over the past twenty years, on topics from forgiveness to parenting teenagers, to menopause to the economics of generosity.

Dad just gets on with things quietly. I've watched the silence creep over him like a slow-spreading rash that starts with a patch on your upper arm you hope will go away if you ignore it or dab it with tea-tree oil. Over the years it's overtaken him like that poor kid in the bed next to Josh who scratched himself till he bled, not a square inch of flesh left unclaimed by the psoriasis.

In his study in the bottom drawer of his desk is an old Adidas shoe box he once let me open. It was filled to overflowing with medals: best Under 15 cricketer; best Under 17 rugby player; rugby captain 1958; Long Distance Achievement Award . . . It was a treasure chest of personal victories you would never have known about unless you had spread them out on the study carpet, arranged them in little mounds according to sports, and counted them . . . over one hundred and fifty-eight medals. 'Wow, Dad.' He smiled sheepishly. 'That was a long time ago. They don't mean very much. In the Big Scheme of Things.'

Now all that remains of his sporting talent is his Sunday morning eighteen holes with his old school mate Frankie Sherwood. There's a defeat about him that is depleting, but it's hard to be cross with him. He's gone on no courses, written no books, just kept doing what he always did—working at his job as an insurance salesman. And insisting on going to expensive restaurants for birthdays.

Libby started working in a nail salon last year, which is a place where women go to have false nails put on. Really. All she wants is to get married and have children. That is her life's purpose. Not that there's anything wrong with that.

She was genuinely gutted when she walked in on Charles, her ex-fiancé, with his face between her ex-best friend Kay's legs. It was just three weeks after he'd proposed. Around his ankles were the custom-made boxer shorts she'd given him for Valentine's Day embroidered with *Libby's Treasure* over what I believe is officially referred to as the crotch area while Kay was sucking on my little sister's treasure.

She likes to pretend she's not that smart. But she didn't buy the '69 doesn't mean anything' line. When she called me to tell me she'd broken off the engagement, I told her about the grope.

She didn't talk to me for a month after that.


When Libby first brought Chris home to meet my parents, my mother took Libby aside in the kitchen and congratulated her. 'He's SO good-looking,' she whispered. 'Much handsomer than Charles.'

'I know,' Libby shrugged in a kind of delirious shudder.

My mother had made her special apricot chicken, with a mushroom and asparagus risotto on the side for me.

My mother dished up a huge plate for Chris.

'I don't eat chicken,' Chris beamed his shiny grin.

'Oh.' My mother looked crestfallen. She handed the plate to my father.

'Vegetarian?' I asked hopefully.

'Na,' was all I got back.

'Religious grounds?' I asked.

'Na,' he shrugged. 'I just don't eat it.'

'What sort of religion doesn't allow chicken?' Libby asked me.

'There must be a reason,' I pursued.

'Faith, he doesn't eat chicken and that's that,' Libby said.

'Do you eat meat?' I asked.

'Yeah, love my meat,' Chris said.

'Then I just don't get it,' I shrugged.

'It's not a problem,' my mother smiled. 'We've got mushroom risotto . . . and salad . . .'

'Oops, don't eat mushrooms,' Chris chuckled.

'I can defrost some arabiata sauce . . . with some pasta . . . will that be okay?' my mother asked.

'Does it have chilli in it?' Chris asked.

My mother's expression strained momentarily.

'How about some cheese?'

'Yeah, cheese. Cheese is good. I love cheese,' Chris said.

And Libby cocked her head to the side and giggled like 'cheese' was the punch line to the most hilarious joke anyone had ever told in the history of stand-up comedy.

Last week I was in the middle of a consultation with Christina Bryant when Libby called.

'Chris and I are talking about getting married,' she bubbled.

'I can't speak right now,' I told Libby.

'You're just jealous,' she huffed.

I squirmed in my seat. I'm not saying it's a crime to be a halfwit. Not everyone can have Josh's brain. Chris has walked away with 'Estate Agent of the Month' for four months in a row at Westings Real Estate where they groom celebrity estate agents. Dad says real estate has great 'future' and 'potential', words he casts like hopeful nets, anticipating a bountiful trawl but tempered with the stoicism of fishermen. I'm not the one marrying him. I am not one to judge a person based on a single conversation about where you can get the best leg wax to avoid ingrown hairs. I knew men waxed their legs. The balls took me a little by surprise.

Libby's whole world is cuticle softeners and French manicures, so for her the 'big picture' is matching nail colour to an outfit. 'He reads my emails and SMSs' she told me on the phone.

'Libby, that is wrong,' I ventured. 'It's a violation of your privacy.'

'Faith, someone can say they love you, but that's just words. It's what people do that counts. I wouldn't want to be with someone who didn't love me enough to read my emails.'

'It's jealous, controlling behaviour,' I said.

'I know,' she squealed in delight. 'I swear, no one's ever loved me this much.'

I will walk Libby through her divorce sometime in the next decade after she's survived postnatal depression and Chris's infidelities, and

84

her two maladjusted children now fall into the category of 'kids who come from broken homes'. I won't say I told you so. But I am never wrong about these things.

From the smiles on her and Chris's faces as they walk into the restaurant, I can sense we're in for an Announcement tonight.

I take a huge glug from my G and T. It's gonna be a long night.

I hand my mother my envelope. Nonna doesn't have a 'runny tummy'. I know her bowel habits. She has Special K for breakfast. It's all over by 9.30 am. That's just the old-person fob-off she gave my mother. I know exactly where she is and what she's doing and if I hadn't mislaid it, I'd bet my butterfly pendant it does not involve a toilet. She's curled up on her couch, under a quilt, listening to *Lady Chatterley's Lover* in Italian on tape. 'When you are *veterana*, very old, like your Nonna, you are *invisibile*,' she once told me. 'You can disappear . . . you come and go. No one see.'

'*I* see,' I told her.

I thought she didn't hear because she didn't answer. But then she said, 'You see too much, borrow some of my blindness,' which had this way of making me feel sad but very special.

When I asked Nonna what she thinks of Chris, she sniffed.

'Think?' she said faintly. '*Impossibile!* To think when you can't breathe? A man who needs so much *colonia*, perfume, is hiding *un grande puzzo*—a big stink . . . Nonno Antonio, he always smell like a man, sweat, like the field.'

My mother is looking glamorous and fluffed, her greying hair is silvery. It makes her look wise. I pull out my hair band and try to air my hair. It's not much of a success. I am mildly anxious about being third in line after my father's gift of the latest hand-held word processor 'for long flights', and the seven-hundred-dollar gift voucher Chris and Libby just gave my mother for a day at the most expensive health spa in the city (*which comes with micro-dermabrasion and half an hour of complimentary electrolysis*), to which my mother admonished, 'You're very naughty—I am being very spoilt.' But she didn't do that 'you shouldn't have' thing, which worries me. Maybe she's softened on the whole materialism thing. I have a momentary panic that, once again, I've fucked it all up. My headache has gone only to be replaced with horrible intestinal cramps.

She reads the back of the envelope with interest.

'Oh sweetheart . . . What you have done here?' she says, tearing it open.

She takes the Polaroid of Rania and her son, Jacob or whatever his name is. She has a quizzical look on her face. She reads the back of the picture and, I swear, tears well up in her eyes.

She shakes her head.

'I'm afraid it comes *without* complimentary electrolysis,' I say. 'Or micro-dermabrasion.'

Libby glares at me.

'Don't knock electrolysis,' Chris says tousling Libby's hair. 'It does wonders, doesn't it, doll?'

Libby shines at him.

'How are your allergies?' I ask.

'Under control . . . for now,' he says slowly.

Gwyneth, Libby's cat has, honest to God, one yellow and one green eye. Libby got her when she was a kitten. That's six years before Chris even met Libby. But he's allergic and 'cannot commit' until she gets rid of The Cat. He won't even call her by her name. It's one of those lightning bolt moments, but it hasn't registered on Libby's radar.

Libby tries to take Chris's hand. He moves it away and looks at her like she's the jerk.

I glance at Libby who, despite having just been rebuffed, is eager with devotion, like a kicked puppy who doesn't understand cruelty and reapproaches, enthusiasm afresh just in case there's been a mis-understanding. I suck so hard on my block of ice the membranes of my mouth start to ache.

'This is the *best* present I have ever received,' my mother says.

'Really?' I ask.

Both Libby and Chris look very put out. 'Can we see?' Chris says. He snatches the Polaroid from my mother.

My mother stands up and comes over to me, where she flings her arms around me. I am awkward and embarrassed because people in the restaurant, the waiters in particular, are looking at us. I pat her on the back. She doesn't let go of me. I pat her again.

She takes my face in her hands, and she looks me in the eyes.

'You are such a *good* person, Faith.'

I cough. I feel a little short of breath.

Libby says, 'That was really big of you, Faith.'

'I don't get it,' Chris says. 'Who are these people?'

'Some strays Faith found,' Libby says under her breath. 'Like she needs a few more to add to her collection.'

She and Chris synchronise chuckles.

'So are you one of those "Make Poverty History" types?' Chris asks. 'Like, haven't you ever asked yourself what that actually means?'

My mother coughs. I peer into my glass and count ice cubes.

Dad doesn't even ask to look at the picture. He is engrossed in the menu. 'I think I fancy the marinara pasta . . .' he muses.

My mother goes to sit back in her chair.

'Now I can feel good on the inside as well as on the outside, thanks to my two beautiful daughters . . . and Chris,' she says. 'I am so richly blessed. I give thanks for my children here on earth, and in heaven . . . And now, I am ready to order a wonderful meal,' she says grandly, summoning a waiter.

I smile at my family though my cheek muscles ache.

'Faith, I think it's your turn tonight . . . which charity, my darling? Let me guess . . . sixty-five roses for cystic fibrosis?'

Chris takes Libby's hand. They're working up to something to trump my best-birthday-present-ever gift. A waiter arrives with a large platter of prawns each of which still has his eyes and feelers intact. In the middle is a half lemon in which a single candle has been wedged, already lit. Chris winks at him, 'Good job,' he mouths.

The waiter puts the platter down in front of my mother who seems undaunted by twenty-four pairs of prawn eyes upon her. Granted, they're blind. But still.

'Happy birthday, Mum . . .' Libby says, grinning.

My mother covers her mouth with exaggerated surprise and delight.

'But before you blow out your candle, Mum, we've got an announcement to make . . .' Libby burbles.

I pick up my glass, which is empty but for three ice cubes.

I wonder if there's a name for what I do. Other than psychic or invariably, unrelentingly, miserably right.

### Children from Abusive Families
*Children who have experienced some kind of trauma in the home can suffer from:*
- *stress*
- *guilt*
- *withdrawal*
- *depression*
- *attention and affection problems.*

*Children can also develop physical symptoms through which they exhibit their fears. Such symptoms include headaches, stomach pains and asthma. These are symptoms of deep anxiety.*

Training Manual, page 89

# 16. candles

'Do you want to blow the candles out for Nicholas?' my mother asked Libby.

'Yes, me, only me, not Faith,' she said.

I sat opposite my mother, looking at the chocolate cake she had baked with Nicholas's name scrawled in white icing. There were two finger-biscuit racing-cars with liquorice allsorts for wheels on either side of his name for the two sibling celebrants who could actually eat them.

Libby stood up in her chair and blew out all six candles.

'Now let's cut the cake,' my mother said gaily.

At the dinner table I sat with my hands in my lap.

'I want the first piece!' Libby said. 'For me!'

'You will get a piece,' my mother said, 'you just have to be patient. We're all going to have some birthday cake.'

Libby reached over and tried to grab a racing car and in so doing, ripped up some of the icing.

'Oh that's very naughty, Liberty,' my mother said. 'You've ruined the cake. That's not fair to Nicholas!'

My father, who had been sitting quietly at the head of the table, got up and threw his serviette down.

'Where are you going, Vincent?' my mother said. 'We haven't sung Nicholas "Happy Birthday".'

'Helene,' My father said. '*Per amore di Dio* . . .'

'It's his birthday,' my mother insisted. 'Must we just pretend that it isn't a special day? I went through fifteen hours of labour . . . what, does that mean nothing now?'

My father looked haplessly at me and then at my mother. A thousand unsaid things tumbled out of that look, like a bucket of golf balls inadvertently kicked over.

'Please, Vincent, for Nicholas's sake . . . Just sit down, let's sing him "Happy Birthday".'

My father sat down again. His head hung low. He laced his fingers together and exhaled.

'Happy birthday to you,' my mother began. Libby chimed in, ''Appy birfday to you . . .' she sang.

My father sat in silence.

I mouthed the words but couldn't get my voice to work.

Libby smeared chocolate cake all over the new tablecloth.

And my mother's bright eyes shimmered.

# 17. cat

'Where the bloody hell are you?' I shout into my mobile phone, straining to hear her voice over the noise coming from her side.

'We're at The Leprechaun Did It,' Carol says. She sounds giggly and happy. 'What's taken so long?'

'Big family announcement tonight, Libby and Chris are officially making the biggest mistake of their lives.'

'What???' Carol shouts into the phone.

'Never mind, I'll tell you when I get there,' I say.

I walk into the Leprechaun, which is full of people smoking and drinking. I remember that I actually hate bars and wonder what I am doing here other than digesting the sick look of happiness on my parents' faces when Chris and Libby declared their intention to have a Big Fat Waste of Money. Perhaps I could have timed my comment: 'What about Gwyneth?' 'Not now!' Libby spat back at me. 'God, do you *always* have to spoil everything?'

I feel sick with loneliness. The only one who can see through things, like Superman with X-ray vision, poor friendless bastard. I'm looking for Carol, I remind myself. I see her over at the bar.

As I come up to her I notice that one of the people she is talking to, drinking with and, by the look on his face, flirting with, is none other than Shaun Hamilton. Who was, Carol insisted on telling me 'headhunted by G & C, he never even applied'. I instantly regret having come here. I now wish I had just gone home to the stack of dirty dishes in my kitchen sink.

The first time I met him, he stared me up and down and then he dropped me. You can't complain about staring. People do it, even though it's rude. I'm confident most people know this. But dumping someone like a broken surfboard everyone knows can't be recycled on the footpath because the streamlining's bust, I am pretty convinced, borders on offensive.

SISTAA is an acronym and play on the word SISTER, as in NOT-BROTHER. It is a woman's space. You'd expect a person who ordinarily saunters like he's on a rugby field to maybe take that into account. For someone so smart, so headhunted, there are gaps in the basics.

I'm not an expert. Human behaviour is a science. I'm just making an observation. The thought crosses my mind. What difference does it make to him whether we get rapists convicted or not? He doesn't lie in bed wondering whether that noise was a cat misjudging the dark or the end of your life as you know it. He doesn't avoid deserted beaches, even though they make your heart fly open and your feet itch for the icy water and the gravelly sand between your toes.

'*Odorare,*' Nonna said, fumbling for my face. '*Naso non dire una bugia*—the nose never lie,' she said. She found my face, her fingers squeezed my nose. '*Naso* is same as *fiuto*, hintuition. Like Nonno

Antonio, your nose is *meraviglioso*, gorgeous,' she added for good measure, because she's my *nonna* and she's blind.

Shaun treats our clients with the robustness you reserve for regular people who haven't just experienced sanity-altering traumas. People who answer their doors when they're home alone and don't start sobbing in the condiments aisle. If you survive his questioning you'll make it through cross-examination in court. It's not that I can't do the job. There's just a natural line I cannot cross, because it turns a client into a Them and me into an Us. Shaun doesn't have to pretend to be anything other than a man who has no clue about what it's like to have your face slammed against a doorframe, or to be held down and have some stranger insert his unsolicited erection into you like a kebab stick on a helpless piece of lamb. Though male-on-male sodomised assault is not uncommon these days, men, surprisingly, never anticipate it. This, I have come to believe, is the most notable difference between men and women.

Shaun scuba-dives, skydives and climbs sheer rock faces. Carol thinks it's sexy. Like he'd be good in bed because he bungee-jumps. Personally, I prefer fine motor coordination.

And Carol wants to fuck him. It's at times like this that I wonder whether any of us survives our wounds. Carol's stepfather molested her when she was five years old and that's how she got into this work. I do not judge her. I have no idea what her scars look like and what masochistic contortions soothe them.

'Nice leash,' I say, gesturing to Shaun's fancy silk tie.

'All the better to tie you up with,' he says.

'Oh come on, you two, just be civil, can you?' Carol says.

'It'll kill me,' I say.

'You can do it, I know you can,' she says. 'Faith, this here is Richard, Shaun's colleague. Also at G & C.'

I nod in the direction of a podgy man in a tight-fitting suit. 'Conveyancing,' he says as I nod in his general direction.

'I beg your pardon?' I say.

'I do conveyancing, at G & C.'

'I do rape and battery,' I say. 'At SISTAA. Nice to meet you.'

'Do you want a drink?' Carol asks.

I nod.

Shaun's left hand is bandaged.

'What happened to your hand?' I ask.

'I was teaching some young girls a lesson,' he says, smiling.

'Yeah, well let's hope whoever got the other end of your fist doesn't end up on the other side of my desk,' I say.

'Don't get your ovaries in a tizz,' he says to me. 'Not all men are rapists and abusers, you know. Some of us are just nice ordinary guys.'

The bartender puts my cocktail on the counter, and Richard moves quickly to pay for it, before I can even open my wallet.

'Thanks,' I say, taking a sip.

'The pleasure is all mine,' he smiles.

'What would we do without you, Shaun?' Carol says. 'I think we're lucky to have you. We're lucky,' she says looking at me. 'He does this for free,' she says to me. 'Merissa said she owes him one.'

Merissa Wallace was one of those date-rape cases you pray will never go to trial because who wants to see a sixteen-year-old shredded in cross-examination even if she was a precocious flirt with breasts like the domed crests of billowing jellyfish? You did not want Merissa on the witness stand because she spoke without thinking, which is how she got into trouble in the first place. She told her English teacher that blowjobs were her 'speciality'. When he advanced to test out her theory, she was perfectly agreeable about the blowjob but apparently 'didn't want it to go any further, because what kind of a girl did he think she was?'.

Shaun took one look at her and shook his head. 'Jesus Christ.' When she shrugged her shoulders so that the shoe-string straps on her singlet fell to reveal a lace bra, Shaun approached her and, with a pencil, lifted the strap back up. He then leaned in very close to her face and said, 'Listen here, Lolita, I don't want to see your tits in court, you don't know what a blowjob is, you wash the dishes for your mother after dinner, and you have a childhood sweetheart who's only ever held your hand. Do I make myself clear?' She nodded. Tears pricked her eyes.

'When the defence asks you if you consented, that's when you cry. No histrionics. A few sobs, like your heart's been broken by the captain of the school rugby team. You are everyone's little sister in that court, do you hear me? If one man thinks about your cunt in court, you are fucked. As in, that dickhead gets off to carry on teaching *Hamlet*.'

She nodded again. I barely recognised her in court. She wore a white buttoned-up shirt and a long floral skirt. I think when she cried, she really meant it.

'The thing you do really well,' Carol is saying, 'is that you don't get sidetracked by *emotion*.' She steps over that word like it's a dog turd. She has had far too much to drink already. You wouldn't need a degree in human behaviour to see that she's decided she wants Shaun naked and sweaty underneath her.

Shaun shrugs but he's clearly chuffed. He flicks me a glance to gauge my reaction. Richard is looking at me too. I look around the bar to see if there is anyone else I know here that I can go and talk to.

'When you train for a marathon . . .' he starts.

'You run marathons?' Carol twitters.

'He's an athlete,' Richard croons.

'Kickboxing champion three years in a row and tae kwon do since I was nine. You don't get a body like this by knitting.'

Carol laughs way too much at that. I just sigh and sip my cocktail down to the bottom of the glass. My *nonna* knits. Blind and with only nine fingers. I won't have a bad word said about knitting.

'When you train, you've got to do it in the rain and in the snow. It's called running ugly. Then when you're in the marathon, and it's stinking hot, and your mouth is dry, and your muscles are cramping, and there's still ten kilometres to go, you remember, I've done this before, and I got through it. It's about remembering. When memory kicks in, it gives you a whole new lease on survival. You just keep aiming for what didn't break you before. So with the girls, I always go hard. It's the only way to get them strong enough, they need a bit of mental muscle,' Shaun says.

'Most of our clients are women, not girls,' I say.

'Girls, women . . . there's nothing disrespectful in there, why do you always have to make a point?'

'Accuracy?' I suggest.

Shaun shrugs.

'You just don't understand how difficult it is,' he says. I look at him. Bewildered. I feel disorientated. I blink rapidly. Maybe my radar's gone faulty. Maybe he bleeds and feels like everyone else. Maybe he cries when people he loves get hurt or die. Maybe, just maybe, there's a heart inside there.

Then he winks at Carol, 'Yeah, it's really difficult to control my hard-on when they cry.'

And he laughs.

And Richard laughs.

And my best friend actually laughs a gasp of disbelief, which disintegrates into a proper laugh, and then the three of them are laughing together.

'You are one sick guy,' I say. I feel so steady now.

Richard stops laughing immediately.

'Yeah, Shaun, you're a sick guy,' Carol says.

'Don't you agree with me,' I tell her. 'You laughed at that.'

'I wasn't laughing . . . I was . . . I was . . .'

'You were laughing,' I say.

'Do you find *anything* funny?' Shaun asks me.

'John Cleese,' I say.

'Where's a woman's clitoris?' he asks me.

And before I can tell him that the line is actually, 'Why must you stampede the clitoris, what's wrong with a kiss?' Shaun says, 'Who cares?' He points his finger at me and starts laughing at the look on my face.

'Now that's *not* funny, Shaun,' Carol says, composing herself. Richard decides he's better off not laughing either.

As if that was less funny than the hard-on when women cry.

I swear, if I carry on making excuses for Carol, I'm going to end up hating her too.

* * *

Richard insists on walking me to my car.

'Goodnight,' I say. He stands there, cheerfully.

'You need to fuck off now,' I tell him.

'Yeah, okay,' he says before giving me a small nod and walking back to the bar.

Inside my car, I hit my hand against the steering wheel. I have no idea why. I have a meaningful job. What could be more meaningful than what I do? I'm not stuck in an office churning out advertising copy to convince kids to eat junk food, or exploiting Third World children or destroying the ozone. On a good day, I actually make a difference to someone's life—sometimes women even tell me that I've *saved* their lives. You should see the cards and letters in my bottom drawer. I've got Nonna. I am part of that miraculous statistic of women who has never been sexually or physically abused. My parents have done their very best. I have my health. I think. So far as I know.

I start my engine and swing out into the road. I don't see anything, but I feel a thump as my car hits something. I stop the car and turn off the ignition.

I stand in the road and there in the gutter is a cat. I've hit a cat. It's a tabby. Only male cats are tabbies. It's one of those interesting animal facts I read on interestinganimalfacts.com.

I go over to the cat. It is very still. My heart races.

I take off my jacket and wrap the cat in it. There is no blood. But it's very still. I can't tell whether or not it is breathing.

My head races. The only emergency vet I know is over the bridge. It's going to take me at least twenty minutes if I go flat out. I put the cat on the seat next to me and I drive. 'Please don't die,' I say. I say it over and over again. But there doesn't seem to be any life coming from the bundle inside my jacket. I put on the classical music channel. I figure this is soothing music for a cat that has been hurt. The gentle strains of violins also help calm my nerves.

For a Friday night at 11.25, the roads are quiet. I don't look at the speedometer because I'm afraid to know, but I am sure I am going at ninety kilometres an hour. I race through several lights that are technically red. I arrive outside the Crown Street Emergency Vet at 11.46.

I gently lift the bundle from my seat and I burst through the doors. 'Please help,' I say, unable to stifle a sob.

Behind the counter is a man with a beard.

He comes out and takes the bundle from me, without asking any questions.

Ten minutes later he is sitting beside me on a chair in the waiting room, holding a box of tissues in his hands.

'It happens,' he says.

'I killed a cat,' I say. 'I've never killed anything.'

I am crying embarrassingly but the vet doesn't seem to mind. I'm crying more than I can ever remember having cried. My hair is sticking in bits to my wet face, and it's a mess of mucus and tears and loose hair gummed to me like feathers.

I sit there for what seems like a long time.

The vet just sits with me.

He offers me some water. I accept.

He goes away and comes back with a glass, which he hands me.

I take it from him. He has outdoor hands, with distinct veins. He doesn't bite his nails. There are no nicotine stains.

He watches me drink the whole glass.

He takes the glass from me.

'Are you all right?' he asks.

'My sister is getting married to a man who gels his hair,' I say.

'He must be a real estate agent,' he says.

'And my friend wants me to go belly dancing with her,' I say, stifling a sob.

'It releases a lot of tightness in the lower back and hips,' he offers.

'My best friend died before I could tell him . . .'

I don't finish.

He sits there with me at the edge of silence, like a lake. I feel safe, the lake is there, but it's not brooding, it's just holding. All that life in it and around it. It hums. Alive. The tadpoles, the dragonflies, the frogs, the fish. And I'm in no danger and people don't drown there.

'You can still tell him,' he says. I look up at him. He shrugs. 'Just tell him.'

'What? Now?'

'Yeah.'

'He's dead. He's gone. Lost. He can't hear me.'

'Okay,' he says.

I don't move for a while.

'What was his name?' he asks.

'Joshua Ralph Miller.'

'Ralph?' he asks, grinning.

'Shocking name, I know . . . We laughed about it a lot.'

'Joshua,' the vet says aloud.

'Josh, actually. I called him Josh.'

'Okay. Josh, your friend, who's sitting here with me, wants you to know . . .' and he looks at me with a very clear look from his very unmistakably hazel-brown eyes that have little flecks in them like bits of leaf and beetle wings caught in amber.

'. . . that she loves you.'

We sit quietly. I look at him. He looks at me.

'Now he knows,' he says.

'Yeah . . . now he knows.'

Before I leave, he asks me if I want my jacket back.

'No, I'd like the cat to be buried in my jacket.'

'We don't bury, we incinerate,' he says, almost apologetically.

'In that case, I'd like to take both the jacket and the cat.'

'What are you going to do with the cat?'

'I'm going to give it a decent burial.'

He smiles.

'Where are you going to bury it?'

'I have no idea, but I'll find somewhere nice,' I say. 'Somewhere with a view. Maybe somewhere in Sullivan's Forest. I know a spot.'

'Tell you what,' he says. 'I'm driving out to the Blue Ridge Mountains tomorrow to visit my sister. I'll take the cat with me and I'll bury it somewhere on her farm.'

'Will you?' I ask him. 'Will you really?'

'I will,' he says. 'I know that it's important to honour the things we love.'

'I didn't love that cat,' I say. 'I didn't even know it, until I killed it . . . I don't even know its name.'

'Still,' he says. 'Things without a name still matter.'

He retrieves my jacket for me. It has no blood on it. I was hoping for some blood, so I could at least wash it out. Have a kind of ritual of acknowledgement for what I have done.

He opens the door for me and I walk out into the night.

'I'm sorry your weekend had to start like this,' he says to me.

'Likewise,' I say.

'It's nothing I don't see every day,' he says. 'I just look forward to the animals I can save. I try not to lose sleep over those I can't.'

I nod. I stand there and look at him.

'Why do you do this work?' I ask.

He shrugs. 'I love animals.'

The night is crisp and clear and there is a new moon somewhere high above us.

Those three little words tumble out into the night, stones plopping into water. I gather them up like homeless orphans and I hold them close to me.

'Thanks, you've been . . .' I try to think of a word that doesn't sound corny or pathetic.

He waits. He doesn't move.

'. . . you've been . . .'

He waits.

'. . . here . . . you know, with me . . .' I manage eventually. 'Here with me,' I repeat.

'It's okay. Drive carefully.'

# 18. rat

Josh liked to watch things die.

Not things that weren't already dying. He was a pacifist like me. We'd never kill anything.

But if we came across something that was hurt, he'd want to stay and watch it die.

Flies that were still struggling to escape spiders' webs.

Birds that were still gasping for life after having been mauled by a playful cat.

Half-squashed caterpillars, the wriggling half still sentient and suffering.

He'd get down on his haunches and wait until the fight was over.

I never needed to ask him why. It was just kind of understood.

I suppose he saw himself in all life that was half alive and half not. I think he just wanted to confirm for himself that he wasn't the only one.

Josh knew things. Like the exact movements the black male swan makes with his mate: dancing, dipping his head, calling with his neck outstretched and bill pointed upwards, finally swimming with her in a circle. And that this is called the Triumph Ceremony. Josh made this the sort of thing that was important to know. Through his eyes, I saw more. Small things you would otherwise miss.

We once came across a rat that had been beaten up, by some kids most probably. It looked like it had been used as a cricket ball. It was fighting to breathe; its innards were oozing from its belly. Its little eye fixed on Joshua.

We stayed with that rat for a long time. Eventually I said, 'Maybe we should put it out of its misery.'

Josh shook his head.

'But he's suffering,' I said.

'You don't know what he's feeling,' Josh said. But then he added more gently, 'Faith, some things you just have to let be, you know. No one's asking you to be God.'

'Yeah, well, as if . . .' I said, but I wished I hadn't, because, well, because maybe Josh needed God more than I did.

When you're watching and waiting, things take longer to die. As if life tries harder to hang on if it knows it isn't all alone.

We stayed with the rat until the end came. Its eye still open in a lifeless gaze.

# 19. nail polish

'Where were you this weekend?' Carol says, barging into my office. 'I came past your place three times, saw your car outside, but you weren't there.'

I look up from the Monday-morning headlines in the online news: *GOVERNMENT INVESTS $2 MILLION TO END PROSTATE CANCER.* There is also the identikit image Constable Peterson put together of our serial rapist and an emergency number for *ANY INFORMATION LEADING TO THE ARREST OF THIS PERSON.* A warning that *this man is dangerous.*

'I didn't feel like answering the door.'

Carol narrows her eyes at me. I see the faint shimmer of The Candy Floss fairy's body glitter on her cheeks. I have tried introducing her to the concept of cleansing and toning. But some people don't want to learn.

'Are you saying you didn't want to see me?'

'I wasn't feeling well.'

'If you don't want to see me, why don't you just come out and say it?'

'I . . . I . . . that's not it, Carol . . . I might be coming down with flu or something.' Actually, I feel like I've swallowed a horror story and it's been repeating on me. I fold the note Genevieve left on my desk this morning in two.

'Well, guess what?' she grins.

'Please, spare me the details,' I say.

'Aw c'mon, please be interested in my sex life.'

I sigh.

'So, anyway, after you left the Leprechaun, I went home with him and I fucked him . . .'

I exhale deeply.

'. . . and?'

She holds up her thumb and forefinger. 'Itsy bitsy teeny wiener . . .'

'Bungee jumping has to be an overcompensation for something,' I say.

'But he gives good oral sex. That joke about 'who cares where a woman's clit is' was just crap. Better than Corey ever was. Bastard.'

'Please,' I say to her. 'Too much information.'

'Okay, I'll summarise: he came, I didn't, he left, and . . . I don't want to sleep with him again.'

I look up at her. She's waiting for me to say something.

'Well at least you got that out of your system.'

'Richard had the hots for you. He couldn't stop talking about you after you left. You should have stayed.'

'Conveyancing, seriously Carol.'

'What did you do after you left?'

'I ran over and killed a cat.'

She laughs. I don't. So she stops.

'It happens,' she says.

'Yeah.'

'Maybe it was its time.'

'Yeah and maybe it's in a better place, and maybe it was too good for this world and maybe we'll be reunited again some day.'

'What's the matter with you?'

'Platitude fatigue.'

'Have you found your butterfly pendant?'

'It's lost, Carol,' I hiss.

'Well, forgive me for giving a shit!' She pulls a little packet out of her pocket and throws it down on my desk. 'I bought you something at Fairies R Us, but maybe you've got friendship fatigue,' Carol says as she leaves, slamming the door behind her.

I open the packet.

Inside it is a silver chain with a pendant. The pendant has a silicone butterfly encased in glass.

I put the chain back in the packet and put the packet in my top drawer.

I unfold the note in Genevieve's unmistakable scrawl, with one, two, three, four stingers in *Please come and see me*. Stingers, in case you were wondering, are those little hooks on 'a's, 'c's, and 'd's which, if you know anything about writing analysis, reveal 'anger towards the opposite sex', and someone who likes 'the thrill of the chase'. That is on the 'more information than I need' side of things, and means that whenever I look at Genevieve, I can't help wondering whether she likes Annie to play hard-to-get and whether lesbian hard-to-get is anything as wearying as heterosexual hard-to-get. With the same abstention of interest I apply to my parents', I prefer not to think about Genevieve as having a sex life. To make it worse, the *Please* has been squashed in there, an afterthought.

I try to swallow the wad of cotton wool in my throat. I wonder how she found out about the money I gave to Rania.

I lay my head on my desk. My heart is racing like it's been doing all weekend. Ever since I ran over that cat, replaying memories that should be forgotten.

Like that time we tried to stop the bleeding. When that woman was brought in here by her brother, instead of to the hospital. It was last year, around this time. The weather was turning. I remember. We definitely tried to stop the bleeding. She couldn't speak. Loss of blood, shock. It looked like just another violent rape. It was only later, after the autopsy, that we learned about the bottle that had been inserted inside her vagina before her belly was used as a trampoline. The bottle had shattered inside her, tearing her to shreds.

Things probably wouldn't have turned out any different if her brother had taken her straight to hospital, she'd lost so much blood.

But sometimes, you can't help wondering.

I am standing outside Genevieve's door. Maybe she hasn't seen the headlines yet. Prostate cancer only affects men. We have been trying to get a measly $1.2 million in funding for the past three years for a shelter. Genevieve calls this the 'misogyny of investment preference'. She takes stuff like this personally.

'Come in,' her voice barks. My heart plummets.

I close the door behind me. On her office wall her degree from Harvard is the only framed image, alongside her laminated posters, *A Woman is Raped Every 83 Seconds*, and Sojourner Truth's famous speech, 'Ain't I a Woman?' She is makeup-less. Of course. The Beauty Myth, objectification of women, etc. The only sign of her vanity is a pair of professorial tortoiseshell glasses. Today she is also sporting a massive silver ankh on a leather strap around her neck, but that is certainly in the category of things you would keep to yourself and not share by way of chitchat, as in 'that's a nice chain you're wearing' sort of thing.

I take refuge behind one of the chairs and clutch it with both hands. Her office always puts me on edge. Her bookshelves are lined with titles like *Refusing to be a Man*, *Feminist Politics*, and *Angry Women*. Displayed in the spaces in between is her lover Annie's vessels and ceramic art, which I am always nervous I am going to knock over and break. Ornaments baffle me for this very reason. I do, however, admire the way lesbians refer to their partners as their 'lover'. It keeps love in there, named, unlike wife, husband, boyfriend or, gag, girlfriend. Annie offers pottery as part of our Sistaas-Are-Doing-It-For-Themselves programme here. It's very popular. Vases and salad bowls. Soothing in their own functional way.

Genevieve is in her fifties, and well preserved, as people who have chosen not to have kids generally are, like that thing you put away for the rainy day which never comes. She is about two feet shorter than I am, and stocky. Today her number two haircut is spiked for battle.

Information about Genevieve is all rumour-based, ill-fitting hand-me-down knowledge. Barbara once told me Genevieve's been arrested. Twice. Once for disrupting a beauty pageant, slathered in raw meat, and once for photographing men coming out of sex shops and publishing the pamphlet 'Porn User of the Month'. I believe I would rather donate both my kidneys than get on her bad side.

She wastes no time.

'As you know, we're implementing compulsory debriefing. You're the only person who hasn't signed up for a time that suits you—Barbara has a roster. Once every two weeks.'

I stand and look at her. I don't want free psychological counselling. I *work* here. It is no one's business that I spent most of the weekend in my pyjamas. People cry. Hormonal fluctuations. Flashbacks are just memories. I'm used to feeling things forwards, not backwards. I'm not coming undone.

I even made it to Nonna's, though I considered calling her and cancelling. She took one look at me, which is funny because of the blindness, and put both her hands on my head. It slowed everything down. 'When the garbage is full, you must empty,' she said. You can't ask her what things mean. She gets annoyed at that kind of laziness.

'Yes?' Genevieve asks me.

'Is this . . . strictly speaking . . . necessary . . . for the legal counsellor?'

She rummages for her ankh and swings her Birkenstock-clad feet towards me. I detect the stain and outline of . . . can it be . . . nail polish? I daren't even stare at her toenails in case she catches me thinking, Call yourself a feminist? Nail polish is my sister Liberty's department. The overlap is very disorienting.

'Did you or did you not lose a client last week?'

I nod.

'So you'll go.'

I stand there.

'What is it?'

'I was just wondering . . . about referring some of the DV cases to specialised services . . .'

She says nothing.

'It's just that . . . we're the only organisation that does both rape and domestic violence . . .'

She inhales. 'Faith, when you've worked out the neat line between the two, please be sure to let me know. Our policy is to help every woman who walks through our doors. We know what it takes for a woman to get here. Don't we?'

I blink.

'Refer her on, and there is a seventy-nine per cent fall-out of women who don't ever take up that referral. We can't afford to refer people. And, Faith, Ms Leta, was she a domestic violence case or rape victim? From her file I see she was raped throughout her relationship.'

I sigh.

'Sign up for counselling,' Genevieve says.

I sigh again.

'It's for *your* benefit. And therefore for the benefit of every woman who walks through our doors. Starting this week. Put your name on the roster or otherwise I will.'

I curse on my way out.

'Did you say something?' she asks, looking at me from above the rim of her specs.

I shrug a sort of 'who-me?' gesture. I'm sick of that phrase 'every woman who walks through our doors'. Has anyone ever thought of bolting the fucking doors, maybe with some bright! pink! bicycle! chains!?

'You'll be there. It will do you good.'

I slam the door behind me.

Back in my office, I kick the desk. My stapler falls over. I kick it again. The box of tissues falls off the desk. As I bend down to pick it up I see my African violet and remind myself to water it before I leave today.

> *Unlike other forms of violence, domestic violence is ongoing and repetitive.*
> *Usually violence in the home occurs in a cyclical pattern. This is called the cycle of violence.*

> Training Manual, page 52

## 20. dream

.

Libby painted my toenails for me.

She put little sponges between my toes and blew on my nails so I wouldn't mess them up.

'So, do you think he's going to kiss you?' she asked.

'Shut up,' I told her.

'I bet he'll try to kiss you,' she taunted. 'And it will be all slimy and squishy . . .'

Ron Hadley had washed himself very well, and was in a suit that obviously did not belong to him, not in any sense of the word. He looked uncomfortable and swaddled in finery. He had what he told me was a 'cummerbund' around his waist in a dark maroon colour.

He asked me if I liked it. I shrugged. I guess. He had shaved for the occasion, around the acne, and held a bunch of small, tightly furled roses in his hand. Yellow. For friendship, he said.

We didn't dance. Ron admitted he didn't really know how and I didn't really want to.

So we sat at the table and drank punch.

'Nice nail polish,' he said.

'Yes, it's called Caramel Fudge,' I said. 'My sister Libby painted my nails. She's very accurate.'

'I love fudge,' he said.

'Yes,' I conceded. 'Fudge is very likable.'

At one point, he said, 'I'm sorry I'm not Joshua.'

'That's okay,' I said. 'He's dead. You'd rather not be him.'

At the end of the evening, Ron shook my hand.

'I had a very nice time with you,' he said.

I nodded.

'And . . . I hope you don't mind me saying . . .'

I waited.

'. . . but if you ever just want to . . . hang out . . .'

I shrugged.

He made no move to kiss me.

'. . . well, I'd be happy to . . . hang out with you . . .'

He turned to leave.

'Hey,' I called out.

He turned on his heel.

'Do you want to put your hand on my breast?' I asked him.

'Uh . . . I guess . . .' he smiled.

He came back towards me and gently took my breasts in his hands. I watched his eyes. They glimmered. I can't say if it was happiness. He breathed slowly.

'I guess there's no chance of a . . . kiss?' he asked hopefully.

'Nah,' I said. 'Sorry, just the breasts.'

'That's okay,' he said.

He stood there for a long time, touching my nipples as they hardened under his fingers, which, despite all indications to the contrary, did not fumble or grab, but caressed me with appreciative certainty that this was an aberration of nature, a dream too good to be true.

# 21. teeth

You do things. Not out of choice. Bully is a strong word and Genevieve would object to the insinuation.

I wrote my name on the roster. *FAITH R* squashed in that little box. There wasn't even enough room for my full name. It's a detail, I know. But claustrophobia is claustrophobia. A bit of extra space makes more difference than people give attention to. My pendant gone. The cat I killed. I'm losing things. I don't want to end up in an institution or a hospital. I am certain about this. I am terrified of nurses who reek of garlic.

I watch too much TV. I once saw an *Extreme Makeover* where this bloke had seriously rotten teeth. A combination of smoking and fizzy drinks. 'Today, a great smile is the accepted norm,' he said. As part of the makeover, he got Da Vinci veneers. 'It's a miracle,' he said, at the revelation, crying without inhibition, which made it difficult to doubt his sincerity. Miracle is a big word you want to keep in reserve for things like world peace and a cure for HIV, and not throw about to describe porcelain shells bonded to the front of your teeth, but I could see his point. They even showed him afterwards on a date with a woman. He was kissing her with his mouth of Da Vinci veneers.

Kissing is sometimes more a dental decision than a mental one.

Unless you end up on *Extreme Makeover*, when it comes to poverty, the teeth give it away.

My new client Candy has gold caps on her two front teeth and large glasses that magnify her eyes. She is sitting on my couch next to Phoebe. Like a six-year-old awaiting the tooth fairy, she is missing a single front tooth. On her calf is a tattoo: *Emerson*.

At their feet is a dog. Beyonce. She is a mongrel with a grotesque overbite. She is Candy's 'darling girl'.

Candy reaches out for Phoebe's hand, but Phoebe shifts away.

'They're cool with it here,' Candy chides. 'It's a bloody women's organisation for heavensake,' she clucks. 'They're all lesbians here. A colony of five-legged iguanas,' she whispers.

Phoebe doesn't care. She's not holding hands. Not here. Not in front of me.

Candy and Phoebe live in a small Christian community. Candy's husband is and has always been 'a useless piece of rubbish' (*a poor breadwinner* I write in my notes).

'He couldn't hold down a job, he drank, he swore at me, and gambled every cent he ever earned' (*alcohol abuse, emotional abuse*).

Candy has two grown-up sons but she doesn't know where they are. 'Boys are like that, couldn't give a rat's eyeball about their mothers. Couldn't even give me a daughter, bloody useless sperm on top of it.'

'And Feebs here lived next door. She fell pregnant when she was just seventeen, married Christian and had three children, aged five, three and one.'

'Had?'

'Emerson drowned in their swimming pool last year,' Candy says. Phoebe lowers her eyes.

'I . . . I'm so sorry,' I say.

'It's okay,' Phoebe whispers. 'We've put a fence up now.'

'It's been about—what?—five years since he started hitting her. Specially when he's juiced up. One day, I hear screaming, and Feebs runs into my house, wearing a little nightie with Tweety Bird on it,' Candy winks at Phoebe, 'and she's crying, "Hide me, hide me." After that I hid her every time that bastard came after her.' She pauses. 'I've got a really big pantry in the kitchen.'

They look at each other with yielding eyes. My couch has seldom seen such gentleness between two people.

'I hated that nightie,' Phoebe says.

'But now our problems have started,' Candy continues. 'Our community doesn't tolerate . . . this kind of thing,' she says. 'I've been going to church every Sunday for my entire life—and how old am I now? Forty-six. Forty-six years of Sundays—work it out. I've probably been going to church longer than that Father's been out of nappies. Last Sunday we were just sitting singing hymns in church, minding our own business, when the Father stops the singing. He says, "It's come to my attention that there is sinning in this community. People have turned away from God and His command that a man shall love a woman," and he looks at us like we are some kind of five-legged iguana or something that's never before been seen. And he says, "These sinners are not welcome in our church, they may not sit next to us with their filthy thoughts and pray with us to our God."'

Phoebe nods.

'"They must leave, and not return so long as their minds and bodies are contaminated by the Devil's own corruption." And he stares at us with his crocodile eyes, and then everyone turns and stares at us with their happy eyes, like people do when they're not the ones in the shit. And I look at Feebs and as far as I can see, she got two legs, just like me, not five legs like everyone else in that church—but we're being looked at like God's made a freak of nature. So we gathered up our Bibles and we stood up and left . . . and everyone started cheering . . . like their team had just won the bloody Grand Final.'

'Orthodox religions only sanction heterosexual monogamy,' I say, offering something useful.

Candy's eyes light up. The polysyllabic label elevates her righteous indignation to 'things with a name'. Legitimate.

'That slimy rubbish in a collar tells Feebs she's going to burn in hell,' she continues, gesturing at Phoebe.

I look at Phoebe. She shrugs and shakes her head. 'I just don't think God meant it like this . . . it's not . . . *normal*,' she says mouthing the word with the wistful yearning evoked by foreign destinations . . . *Machu Picchu* . . . *Arc de Triomphe*, *Ponte Vecchio*. 'It's disgusting. *I'm* disgusting.'

'It's more disgusting to hit someone, wouldn't you say, than to love someone?' I offer.

Phoebe's head drops.

'Christian's best mate is a cop out west. He told him a court will put kids in foster care long before they give them to a cunt-licker, excuse my French, even if she's the mother—is that right?'

'The law is unclear in some ways about the rights of lesbian mothers,' I say.

'I'm definitely not a lesbian,' Phoebe says.

'Is he still hitting you?' I ask.

'Only with the flat of his hand,' Phoebe says. 'Nothing serious.'

'Has he forced you to have sexual intercourse?' I asked.

Candy answers, 'He forces her all the time.'

'Does he?' I direct my question at Phoebe.

'Why do you think she had three kids? She didn't want kids,' Candy says.

I direct my question at Phoebe again. 'Does he force you?' I ask.

She nods. I can't tell whether she's been primed by Candy and, like a kid, is only trying to please, or whether she is telling the truth. When someone's been bullied for so long, they can't tell the difference between the bullies that are on their side and those that aren't.

*Custody issues.*

*Temporary shelter needed,* I write.

'Is there anything else I need to know?' I ask.

Phoebe hesitates. Candy nods at her.

'One small thing . . .' Phoebe says.

I look directly at her into her brilliant blue eyes.

'My five-year-old, Sofia . . . has been complaining . . . you know . . . she's itchy . . . down there . . . I just wonder . . .'

Before she even finishes her sentence, I write:

*Possible sexual abuse of children: need urgent investigation.*

I lead them both to the door. Beyonce stands panting at my feet.

Phoebe turns to me and says, 'It's not that I didn't want kids . . . I was only seventeen . . . I told Christian to put that fence up.'

'I understand,' I say to her. 'Why don't you help yourselves to some tea or coffee, and some biscuits, while I make some calls.'

'I kept on telling him, "The kids can't swim."'

'It sounds like you made it very clear,' I say. I feel my chest closing in on me.

'He said, "Stop nagging. You know how I hate nagging." And I know Emerson was his only boy and that made it worse, but you know . . . I told him. I told him.'

'Yes, you did tell him,' I manage to squeeze out of my throat.

Phoebe looks at me like I'm something much more than I know I am. I hope she doesn't have tears in her eyes, but I think she does.

'Thanks,' she whispers.

Candy puts her arm around Phoebe, 'It's gonna be a'right, Feebs,' she says.

'Yes, we do have space,' she repeats.

I'm on the phone to Nicole at one of the shelters we use. It's a secret location, for obvious reasons, and only Genevieve, Barbara and Maryse know where it is. Nicole has two places in the shelter. Just not for Candy and Phoebe.

'So let me understand this,' I say. 'You have two places for women who are trying to get away from abusive situations . . .'

'Yes, but—'

'Hang on a minute,' I say, 'please let me finish ... It just so happens that these two women are in a relationship together.'

'They're lesbians,' Nicole says as if she's explaining my clients' situation to me.

'That's right. If you're looking for a name for it.'

'The other women here won't be happy. They'll feel uncomfortable having women like that around.'

'Nicole,' I say. 'Can you listen to what you're saying. They're not fucking five-legged iguanas. It's not contagious, you know.'

'Look, Faith, I understand it doesn't seem fair to you, but you've got to see it from our perspective. To keep a shelter running, I've got to maintain a very delicate balance. The women here are all very edgy. They don't deal well with unexpected surprises.'

'They're homophobic is what they are,' I say.

'If you're looking for a name for it . . .' she says.

'Hey Nicole,' I say, 'if all the women in your shelter were white, and my clients were black, would you feel the same way if the white women weren't comfortable with a black woman coming in?'

She doesn't answer me directly. 'That's different . . .' She's sensitive about her interracial heritage like I am about cruelty to animals.

I sigh deeply.

'I'm sorry,' she says. 'I just have to consider the shelter as a whole. It's nothing personal.'

'What the hell am I supposed to tell my clients? Sorry, they don't take lesbians, but don't take it personally?'

'Sounds like you're taking this all a bit personally too,' she says. 'Are you doing any debriefing at SISTAA?'

'Fuck you, Nicole,' I say, and I return the phone to its cradle with a great deal more force than is, strictly speaking, necessary.

> *Homophobia: the irrational fear or distrust of gays or lesbians.*
> *Internalised homophobia: a gay person's self-hatred for him*
> *or herself due to the expectation that the only desirable rela-*
> *tionship is between a man and a woman.*

Training Manual, page 147

# 22. sugar

'Suck it,' my mother said through clenched teeth.

It was not the smell of chlorine. Nor the splashing. The sweet taste in my mouth of blueberry. The squawks of toddlers. None of these alone. Together things have a force they lack individually. I was surrounded, everything closing in on me. The hard rock of the lollipop clicked against my teeth. I spat it out.

'Open your mouth and suck it,' my mother begged. I could feel her mounting panic in the grip of her fingers on my upper arm.

I shook my head violently from side to side. Later, when the agony was behind us, she would tell me that people in shock are given sugar to calm them down and all she was trying to do was to help me. The bag with my asthma pump was in the change room. She couldn't just leave me. When you're hyperventilating, it is difficult to hear things. I had been thrashing my head. All the other mothers at the swimming pool were looking at my mother compassionately. She was no stranger to benevolent stares but they still undid her, the way a certain kind of cloying familiarity nonetheless estranges us from ourselves.

Some arbitrary other mother, whose baby was happily drinking from a bottle in his stroller, held Libby for Mum. Libby, who was all of six months old, swaddled in a towel. Not crying. But sucking on her wet hands.

To this day I find the idea of submerging underwater a baby, who can barely sit up by itself, both brutal and unnecessary. I've subsequently read all the theory, but really, a baby that small shouldn't have to know how to swim on its own.

'It's just a precaution,' my mother said.

The moment the swimming instructor dunked Libby's head beneath the water, I started to scream.

'Stop it, Faith, she's fine,' my mother said. Tentatively.

But I couldn't.

I screamed and screamed and continued even after my mother grabbed hold of my arm and said, 'She's okay!' I carried on screaming as my mother scrabbled in her bag and finally offered me the lollipop. My screaming didn't stop until my mother pinched my nose closed between her fingers and forced that lollipop into my mouth.

The lollipop cut the soft interior membranes in my cheek. I remember. How the sweet taste of blueberry sugar overpowers the metallic tang of blood.

## 23. kiss

I knock on Genevieve's door. My heart is gadoofing in my chest.

'Enter,' she says. I walk in with a purposeful stride. Take my position behind a chair. She is on the phone. She carries on talking for a minute, holding her hand up to me. Then she says, 'Just a minute, I've got a staff member in here,' and she puts her hand over the receiver and says, 'Yes?'

'We've got a little problem with the shelter,' I say.

'What sort of problem?'

'We've got a lesbian couple who need some temporary shelter and—'

'Stop right there,' Genevieve says. 'You told the shelter they're lesbians?'

'Yeah, I thought it might be important information,' I say weakly.

She huffs. 'What's the matter with you, Faith? You know that we *never* divulge that kind of information—it's bloody sacred, like HIV status.'

I shuffle my feet.

She lifts her hand off the receiver, 'Listen, I'll call you back, this is going to take a few minutes.' The phone clicks on its cradle. She picks up a red pen and pokes the air in my direction as she talks.

'I don't need to remind you that people who are oppressed are only too keen to find someone else to oppress—battered women would love nothing more than a lesbian couple to beat up on. That's the pecking order. Father kicks wife, wife kicks kid and the kid kicks the dog. Lesbians are right at the end of the food chain.'

It's not like anybody is using my pull-out couch. It would only have been for a week or two. If I'd just taken Sanna back with me. Genevieve would never have had to know.

I shuffle. I rake my fingers through my hair.

'We're not there yet,' she says to me. 'We've got a long way to go.'

I look at her and she looks at me.

'Well, Faith, don't just stand there. You and I are not going to solve the conundrum of gender stereotypes here in my office today.' She waves me away, lifting the receiver of the phone again.

'What am I going to tell them?' I say to her.

'Lie,' Genevieve says. 'Tell them the shelter was full. The shelter was full and we have no fucking money to build any new ones, because our government believes prostate cancer is a worse social evil than gratuitous violence against women and children.'

I nod. I'm not a huge fan of The Lie.

'And by the way, omitting to reveal that two women admitted *independently* are actually in a lesbian relationship together is not strictly speaking against our policy . . . Try the Salvation Army. And the Jewish shelter.'

I nod and turn to leave.

'Faith, if you get them in together, you better get things straight with them—do you get me? No kissing, hand-holding, no heavy petting in the bathrooms. They've got to behave or the shelter will kick them out. There's a hierarchy even if you're a battered woman.'

Within an hour, with Barbara's help, Phoebe has a bed at the Sisters of the Holy Cross shelter and Candy is booked in at the Habayit shelter as long as she observes the Jewish Sabbath, which includes no television, radio or use of phones on Saturdays.

'I know that song "Hava Nagila",' Candy tells me proudly.

'I'm sure that will come in handy,' I tell her.

They greet the news with mixed emotion. To be apart is clearly unbearable for them. Neither shelter takes dogs.

'What am I going to do with you, my darling girl? Saved your life once, but maybe we've come to the end of the road,' Candy says, scratching Beyonce on her chin. Beyonce nuzzles Candy's leg.

I sigh. This is so unprofessional. This is not part of my job. Why do I volunteer for these things?

'I've got a friend, well, not really a friend, I've only met him once, he's . . . a vet . . . maybe he can help. You can leave Beyonce with me, until you can get her.'

Candy nods. 'You okay with that, Beyonce?' She ruffles the dog's head. 'If Beyonce's okay and you're okay, Feebs, it's gonna be okay. It'll be all right, sweetie,' Candy says, a small waver in her voice, a tiny crack in her brave heart.

She hands me the leash. She leans towards me and says in a whisper, 'This dog is a lucky charm.'

I must look sceptical.

'Some kids threw her in a river, tied to a bag of rice. Nice kids. She was real glad to be out of that water, I can tell you.'

Another bloody survivor. I should start a collection.

'And she loves ice cream, strawberry's her favourite.'

I take hold of the leash and make eye contact with Beyonce. She lowers her eyes. It is a sad face. You can't bullshit an animal.

\* \* \*

123

Candy holds Phoebe's hands in hers. She wraps her arms around her lover, and gives her a long, deep kiss on the mouth. Phoebe nods. *Me too.*

It's the last kiss in a long time. But women can survive a long time without kisses. Ask me.


I close the door to my office and exhale. Beyonce stands and looks at me. That overbite is disconcerting. I wonder if vets do Da Vinci veneers for dogs. She looks for somewhere to sit. She shuffles in behind the filing cabinet and settles down with her back towards me.

I look at the telephone on my desk. We're not allowed to make personal calls. Still, it's just a local call. Sometimes abusers hurt a family pet if they know it has special value to their victim. I can squeeze it past Genevieve.

'Barbara, can you put me through to the emergency veterinary clinic on Crown Street, please?' I say to the switchboard.

My heart pounds furiously while I wait to be connected.

'Crown Street Veterinary Clinic,' the voice of a young woman answers the phone.

'Uh . . . hi, hello . . .' I say. 'I . . . uh, brought a cat in on Friday night . . .'

'And you'd like to know how it's doing?' she finishes for me.

'Uh . . . no, actually it died . . . It didn't make it . . . It passed away . . . I ran over it,' I confess.

'Oh, I'm sorry,' she says.

'That's okay,' I say. 'Actually, I was hoping you could tell me the name of the doctor on duty on Friday night. He was very kind, and I just want to send him a thankyou note.'

'Oh sure, that's Dr Caleb Pearson. He sometimes does weekend duty.'

'Thanks,' I say. 'You've been very helpful.'

'No problem,' she says. 'Have a nice day.'

She doesn't know what my day holds, but I appreciate the sentiment nonetheless.

\* \* \*

I write his name on a post-it. *CALEB PEARSON*. It's a lovely name. Caleb. Pearson.

I then ask Barbara to get Ray Osborne on the line for me.

'Can you do me a favour? I need everything you can find on a Caleb (not sure whether it's a "K" or a "C", please try both) Pearson that's P-E-A-R-S-O-N. Is he married? Where does he live? Where does he hang out? Hobbies.' And then just to seal the illusion, I add, 'Previous criminal history and so on.'

'Another wife basher?' he asks me with an eagerness that reminds me that the world is festooned with weirdos who are masquerading as the good guys. Ray Osborne just happens to be one on our side.

'Yeah, we're just doing some preliminary investigations on him.'

'Gotcha,' he says.

I put the phone down. There's the bucket in the corner. I must remember to take it back to the kitchen.

In my belly those words, 'I love animals', now nestle, wrapped up in a scarf of emotions I cannot name.

Fuck, if Genevieve ever found out, I'd be deader than that cat I ran over.

# 24. bucket

Lisa felt sorry for me.

We were at Felicity Baker's party when she came to find me. I was sitting by myself at the pool, watching everyone dance. My mother had bought me a new navy blue halterneck top to go with my jeans. She thought it might 'cheer me up'. I was watching a lizard zigzag between the grouting of the tiles, wondering if there was such a place as heaven and whether Josh was looking down at me. I guess I wasn't expecting how sore it would feel to miss laughing at someone's stupid jokes.

'Come quickly,' she said.

'Where to?'

'Just come.' She was thick with alcohol and some kind of drug. Ecstasy maybe.

She led me up the stairs of Felicity's parents' home to Felicity's bedroom where Tyler was lying passed out on the bed.

'Go fuck him,' she said.

'What?'

She pushed me towards Tyler. 'He'll never know it's you—I've got his glasses,' she said, holding them up. 'Just fuck him. This is your chance.'

And she turned and closed the door behind me. I heard the key turn in the lock.

I stood looking at Tyler for a long time.

He didn't look as beautiful as he did when he was standing tall. Awake. Towering over me.

I sat down on the bed next to him. I touched his face. He hardly moved.

Gently, I put my face next to his. I felt his breath against my cheeks, on my lips. He reeked of cheap wine. I hovered next to his face, which was rough with stubble. That surprised me.

'Lisaaa . . .' he murmured.

I didn't speak.

'D'you love me?' he asked.

'Mmmm . . .' I said.

'Then get me a bucket, I'm going to vomit . . .' he said.

Before I had a chance to react, he hurled all over my new halter-neck top.

It became a joke.

That Tyler had vomited all over me.

No one asked what I was doing alone with him on Felicity Baker's bed.

Lisa never mentioned it again.

## 25. angel

'Are you allergic to dogs?' I ask the couple at the door of my office.

'No, we love dogs, don't we?' she says. He nods.

Beyonce pokes her head out to see who has just come in. Charliena and Frederick each take turns patting Beyonce with that expression you get when you take out the garbage.

'I used to have one like that when I was a little girl,' Charliena says. 'Her name was Kitty. She would always wait for me to get off the school bus and she'd walk me home. Then one day she got caught under the wheels of the school bus right there in front of me. Squashed flat. It was . . . horrible.'

'What sort of person calls a dog Kitty? That's like calling a cat Doggy,' Frederick frowns.

'I didn't name it. My mother did,' Charliena says, fidgeting with her bag on her lap. And then, 'You always have to get the needle in about my mother . . .'

'I've got nothing against your mother,' Frederick says. 'It's wrong. To call a dog Kitty. Am I right?' He looks at me.

I shrug.

'He never liked my mother,' Charliena says.

Melissa, their daughter ('but we call her Melly'), is twenty-five and mentally retarded and has been since birth.

*'I'm so sorry.'*

*'It's okay, we love her, she is very special in her own way. The way God made her.'*

She has been living for the past six years in a state-funded institution for the mentally handicapped, Tranquil Gardens. It came highly recommended. Mrs Talbot's brother is a schizophrenic, 'shame, born like that', she's the neighbour, ('Lives three houses down on the other side of the road,' Frederick corrects). Anyway, he's there. At Tranquil Gardens. They look after them. It's what you'd expect from a state-funded institution, if you can overlook some of the meals they serve. Just a pinch of salt, a herb, a dash of something, to give a bit of taste. It's their brains not their tastebuds that are damaged. But no point in complaining, is there?

Recently, Charliena noticed that the sanitary pads she was buying for Melly were piling up.

The night staff have reported night terrors in the past few weeks. 'Melly's never been one for nightmares except for that time after the fire next door where that little girl died.' She has also started putting on weight.

They have only just discovered that she is in fact twenty-six weeks pregnant.

'Can you believe someone would do this to a mentally retarded girl?' Charliena asks.

People don't realise. A mentally retarded woman is a rapist's ideal victim. A victim with no legal credibility. The mind of a child in a woman's body. Can't testify. Unreliable witness. Rapists lack humanity, not common sense.

'Is it possible . . .' I suggest, 'that the father is one of the other inmates at Tranquil Gardens?'

'That's disgusting,' Frederick says. 'Retarded people don't have sex together. They're like children.'

'Umm, okay,' I say. 'It is going to be difficult to lay a charge. Your daughter is regarded as a minor . . . because of her intellectual disability . . . and I take it there are no other witnesses?'

They look at me weakly. They look at each other. Charliena starts to cry into her embroidered handkerchief.

'We need your help,' Frederick implores.

'I'm not sure what I can do to help,' I say. 'We can't lay a charge against an unknown perpetrator. And Melissa can't testify. The law treats her like a minor.'

'Forget about the law. We don't want to lay charges. We need . . . to make this pregnancy go away,' Frederick says.

I swallow hard. A twenty-six week pregnancy. I shuffle in my chair. 'I . . . don't know,' I say.

Hospital staff hate us 'feminists' with our 'pro-choice' politics. It's hardly a midwife's idea of a good time to have to take a woman through an induced delivery, to stand by, watching unwanted life struggling for breath, when there's equipment and the means to save it, left, right and centre.

The whispers in the corridors, sidelong glances and brisk responses to our questions are restrained accusations against those to whom abortion is a political rather than a visceral issue. Saving life is hard-wired. Especially in nurses who sure as hell don't clock in on time each day for the pay.

'If she has this baby, who will have to bring it up?' Charliena asks me. 'Me and Frederick. Melly can't even look after herself, let alone a child. They won't let her keep a baby in the institution. And we . . . we've been bringing up a child for twenty-five years. We only put her in Tranquil Gardens when she was nineteen. It's been too long . . . too hard . . .'

'What about adoption?' I ask.

Frederick shakes his head. 'I don't want to put Melly through childbirth. It's not fair. She won't understand what's going on. And the pain . . . Why should she have to have that pain?'

'Do you want her to stay at Tranquil Gardens?' I ask.

They look at each other.

'Yes,' Frederick says. 'Once the pregnancy is gone and Melly's sterilised so this cannot happen again, then she can stay.'

'You understand,' I say slowly, 'that sterilising her is not going to prevent her from having sex . . . or being raped again. It will just prevent future pregnancies. Sometimes sterilising mentally disabled women makes them a . . . target,' I say. 'We will have no way of knowing if it's happening again . . . Can you live with that?'

The two of them look at each other. Charliena covers her face with her hands.

'Yes, we'll have to accept that,' Frederick says. 'Because we don't have a choice.'

They both thank me for my kindness.

Maybe there's a word for what I'm doing.

But I know kindness isn't it.

I call Kathleen. I tell her Genevieve told me to phone her.

Kathleen will do anything for Genevieve. There is an enthusiasm there that suggests unfinished business between ex-lovers. It's an over-familiarity that only the subtlest of indicators points to. Kathleen is our Trojan Horse in the medical system. Her lightning bolt moment happened at twenty-one. Date rape, which she once confessed to me was 'so unnecessary . . . If he'd just approached it differently, I'd prob-ably have had sex with him.' She switched from botany to medicine, sharpening her medical degree into a sabre to fight for women who have been hurt. Professor Klueznick hammered it into us: law's objec-tivity. But he never saw Kathleen from his ivory tower. Watching her at work makes me think that *knowing how it feels* fuels a compassion

131

no amount of theoretical distance can match. She does most of our post-rape swabs—women are prepared to wait, unwashed with a rapist's semen inside her for an entire day in order to see Kathleen instead of some man in a white coat and stethoscope.

She is clinical and professional and only wants the details.

'Consider it done,' she says. 'She'll be free of this whole thing by lunchtime on Wednesday.'

At lunch I stop in at Food For Less to buy a dog bowl and some dog food for Beyonce.

At the checkout, I stand behind a woman with a chubby baby in the front seat of a trolley. A toddler wipes his runny nose on his mother's trousers. I flinch.

As she turns, unpacking a Huggies special onto the counter, I recognise her. Time has done her justice. After all. Leigh Flowerday. Her hair's short, a couple of wrinkles have made their home around her eyes. She glances at me, but time has obviously done other things to me. Besides. She's the one who made the impression. Storming out of Prof Klueznick's lecture. Causing his whole face to flush. Now, some fourteen years down the line, she looks encumbered, but not in that saddled way. Locked into her life, a family, a wedding ring, happiness perhaps. It's not the kind of thing you say, but as I stand with my little red shopping basket, Beyonce at my feet, I think of how much courage that took. Leigh Flowerday, in that snot-smeared tracksuit, is a hero in that invisible way that Josh was.

Back at my desk, I call Melissa's parents and tell them the news.

Charliena bursts into tears. I hear her call her husband, 'She's an angel. God has sent us an angel.'

When I put the receiver down, I wonder if maybe I am an angel after all. The Angel of Death.

'Wasser name?' Mr Williams calls out from his shelter of boxes.

'Beyonce,' I say.

'Com'ere Bee On Say,' Mr Williams says, putting out a hand.

Beyonce approaches. She licks his hand.

'There's a good gal,' he says, ruffling her head. And slowly, for the first time since Candy left for Habayit, her little whiskered tail flicks in a wag.

'Watch her for me for a minute, will you?' I say. 'Just need to grab some ice cream.'

I buy a tub of strawberry ice cream and a cheese and bacon pie for Mr Williams. I sit with him on the pavement while Beyonce licks the ice cream from the container and Mr Williams chews his pie. And I swear, her tail becomes a blur of wags.

'Ain't never seen a dog like ice cream before,' he says. 'Guess you can live a long time and not see all there is to see in this mad fucking pig bitch of a world.'

I can't argue with that.

Back in my apartment, Beyonce lies at my front door and watches me with her small sad eyes. I tell her everything is going to be okay. She sighs and turns her head away as if she doesn't believe me.

### Obstacles in a Rape Trial
*The issue of consent of the complainant is one of the greatest obstacles to overcome in a rape trial.*

*If intercourse is proved, the accused will rely on a defence of consent.*

*The issue thus boils down to his word against hers.*

*Credibility of the complainant as a reliable and honest witness is therefore crucial in a rape case.*

Training Manual, page 146

# 26. worm

The official version was that she was having a cyst removed from her ovary and it was 'no big deal, she'd be back for the English test on Thursday'. When Lisa came back from her week in hospital, she looked very pale and she and Tyler weren't going out anymore. I guess that kind of made him 'available', but for me, the romance of Tyler had the lingering smell of bile.

Yet somehow it leaked. My mother took me aside and made sure I understood what happens when you have sex and how it 'leads to unwanted pregnancies'. She told me that I could 'always come to her if I needed anything', and when I nodded, she added, 'like the pill'.

It was coincidence, and just very bad timing. It was the day after Lisa came back to school and we were doing practice impromptu debates in English with Mrs Ellington who clearly hadn't been privy to the leak. I was up against Lauren. Our topic: 'Abortion: for or against?' I had to speak against.

'Life is sacred,' I began. 'Even life that struggles, and needs help to survive, should be preserved at all costs.' I had Josh in mind, since he was back in hospital, it had been a vicious winter of chest infections, but there was a kind of huge sob at the back of the classroom. Elizabeth had her arm around Lisa.

Mrs Ellington told them to 'keep it down and please respect your classmates. We can only expect from others what we are prepared to give ourselves.'

'Fucking cow,' Elizabeth mouthed at me.

Mrs Ellington asked me to proceed.

I looked down at my hands and said, 'The only way we show how much we value life is by how we treat the smallest of creatures. The ant and the worm, the heartbeat in the amniotic sac. If they can be snuffed out at a whim, who's to say when something is big enough to be worthy of our protection? It's not size that counts. It never is.'

Mrs Ellington gave me an A.

Elizabeth and Lisa gave me a death stare.

I slunk out of class, looking for somewhere dark and sheltered to hide.

# 27. memo

In my pigeonhole is the agenda for our staff meeting this morning. Sanna Leta's name is number 2. After *1: Cause for celebration.* Genevieve's 'surprises' remind me that words mean different things to different people. I did my job. I did all I could. Genevieve said so herself.

Behind Barbara's desk is our SISTAA poster: *IN THE EVENT OF RAPE.* Today one line stands out like it's highlighted or something. *REMEMBER THIS IS NOT YOUR FAULT.*

'I'm going to start with the good news,' Genevieve says.

'Yesterday, in the case of State versus Robinson, Judge Hafford's rejected a defence of provocation in a case of domestic assault, *because there is NEVER any form of provocation that a woman can commit that can ever justify a man stubbing out a cigarette on his wife's face or belting her so hard that she requires hospitalisation.'* Genevieve emphasises the word 'never'. It is bolded in the handout Annemarie is passing around.

Around me, people start applauding.

Genevieve is grinning. It appears to be a genuine smile.

'This is what we've been working towards for months, years,' Maryse says. She is hugging Annemarie.

'This is a remarkable precedent,' Genevieve says.

Unlike most judges, who race through their roll to make it home in time for the footy, Judge Hafford actually cares about getting it right. Like every other gay man, he understands fear. It's what makes him one of Us. On a good day, I will actually care that he cares.

Tomorrow, when Melissa is just another file in my closed cases drawer, I will probably want to laminate this memo and put it up in my office next to my African violet.

I reach for my throat. My fingers close around the butterfly pendant Carol gave me.

She notices. And I swear her smile brings sunlight right into that room where victory feels so empty and happiness so sparse.

I smile back at her briefly before letting my gaze fall into my mug to stare at the vortex of my black coffee.


'Turning to the next item on the agenda,' Genevieve says.

'As you all already know, SISTAA lost a client this week. Sanna Leta. A classic case of separation assault and intimate femicide. Faith and Michelle were looking after her.'

Michelle puts her donut down, wipes her mouth with her sleeve and reaches for my hand and holds it. I'm not a hand-holder. Why Michelle doesn't know this is not clear to me.

'Faith, what are the chances of her sister telling the story at a Speak-Out?' Genevieve says. 'You saw her on Friday, didn't you?'

I try to speak. My voice is missing. I clear my throat and try again. 'I . . . I'm not sure this is the right time . . . She's still very much in shock.'

'Fair enough,' Genevieve says. 'Let's give her a bit of time.'

The last time we discussed Survivor Speak-Outs here, things got ugly. There were murmurs amongst the psychologists and social workers about standing up to Genevieve, going on some kind of strike, which of course will never happen—everyone here knows we're like the emergency staff at a hospital. Only our clients suffer if we're not here. It's what you might call a flaw in our leverage position that we care more about our clients than ourselves.

Carol said, 'Speak-Outs mess with my clients' healing. I won't treat my clients like fucking roadkill.' Maryse softened it. She wondered about the ethics of treating people as a means towards an end. She asked, 'Isn't our primary duty to our clients?' There were lots of nods from the others. Genevieve cleared her throat, pursed her lips and clarified matters, 'We will use *all means necessary* to wipe out this scourge in our society. On the day that our phones stop ringing and we sit here twiddling our thumbs because no one is walking through our doors, and there isn't a mother kissing her teenage daughter goodbye who isn't also silently praying for her safety, that's when we stop using stories. Do. I. Make. Myself. Clear? The personal is *political.* Anyone who doesn't understand what that means, either put your hand up now so I can explain it or leave your letter of resignation on my desk.'

No hands went up and no letters of resignation were tendered, though there were a lot of prickly silences in the corridors for days afterwards.

'I'm thinking about a memorial service for her. Here at SISTAA,' Genevieve says.

The others all nod approvingly.

'Michelle, will you discuss it with her sister, what's her name? Priscilla, yes? I'll say a few words about femicide and she can tell her sister's story, the history of abuse, the failure of the system et cetera. Make sure we've got someone from the *Herald* or the *Express*, maybe *Cosmopolitan* will do a feature on femicide . . .'

Michelle nods through her last chews of her donut. Carol's tried to get her to go to the gym over lunch, but Michelle won't allow anyone to see her in a bathing costume or in a tracksuit. She once told me she even closes her eyes when she walks past a mirror.

Some dates are suggested. Barbara will send out a mass email to all our clients and volunteers.

Genevieve continues with the other items on the agenda. Upcoming dates for the diary. Case reports due. Compulsory debriefing.

I wonder whether Christina Bryant, or Rania, or any of our clients caught in their individual crises will come to listen to Priscilla tell the story of how her sister was butchered to death. I wonder whether any of these women will have a chance of something gentler because of Judge Hafford's *NEVER*.

I wonder whether Dr Caleb Pearson buried the cat without a name for me.

I wonder if he just bullshitted me and stuck the cat in the incinerator. As I think it over, I convince myself that no man would bury a cat without a name for a person they had just met, whose name they didn't know.

Then I remember those three precious words. I. Love. Animals. I turn them over and over in my hands, like gems that catch the light. I close the fist of my trust around them, and put them away again just as I involuntarily crumple the memo with Judge Hafford's precedent. Genevieve gives me a quizzical look. I uncrumple it. I smooth it out with both hands.

And I know that he went to the trouble of burying that cat.

And I'm never wrong about these things.

Back at my computer, I delete a poem by a girl with leukaemia, which, if I had forwarded it to thirteen people in fifteen minutes, something good would have happened to me. Apparently *this is not a joke*. But it's hard to know.

Barbara puts a call through to me. I have Charliena on the line. She had told me they would take Melissa out of Tranquil Gardens for a week while she undergoes 'the procedure'. I ask if it would be all right for me to meet Melissa tonight. I am *not* calling her Melly. It sounds like a bad limerick name choice for a line to rhyme with Smelly. They *would be delighted* and invite me over for tea after dinner. I'd like to, out of respect, just ask Melissa myself. You know, if this is what she wants.

I click onto eBay to check up on my green beetle bracelet. I brace myself for disappointment. I never win these bids.

And there it is: Congratulations *missmuffetsucks*. You are the winner of this bid. Please contact *saturnboy* to arrange payment: $25 for the bracelet and $15 for postage. I realise that I've just spent $40 on a bracelet. I don't even wear bracelets.

Victory.

It feels as empty as love.

## 28. snake

After Lisa served Tyler up to me like a dying rat, I switched off. I found the whole idea of sex repulsive and the idea of love grotesque. I took a vow of celibacy.

Boys were carnivorous and I felt like prey. I excused myself from the food chain.

A reputation starts with a story like your friend's boyfriend vomiting all over you. Then it gets distorted and stretched and before you know it people have invented entire scenarios about who you are, what you do in your spare time, and they snigger when you pass them in corridors. If you become the object on which someone who isn't even your boyfriend throws up, you lose rank, as if you've just landed on the longest, deadliest python in a game of snakes and ladders. Down you tumble. Not even to Start. Off the board. I wish I'd known that before I followed Lisa up that staircase.

When that happens, you get lost in the story. You lose the voice to say, 'I didn't know where I was going or what I was being asked to do,' and if you do, people never believe you anyway. You don't have the words to say, 'I was just looking, taking in the fantasy of it all.' No one hears that, much as that truth opens and shuts its mouth, mutely, desperately like a baby bird calling for its mother from hunger. You become invisible.

No, once your friend's boyfriend has chucked up two bottles of cheap red wine all over your new halterneck, some of which is dripping hotly down your forearm and between your nonexistent breasts, you, the one who innocently followed your best friend, you, the one who loved him first, with purity of heart, become the object of ridicule. The slut.

That's how it works.

That's how easily it all gets undone. I wouldn't report being thrown up on.

And we wonder why women don't report being raped.

# 29. apple pie

I knock tentatively on the door.

I am staring at a handmade mosaic plaque on the front door which reads: *THERE'S NO PLACE LIKE HOME.*

The icons of scarcity out in these suburbs are evident here in the low fences, the prefabricated structures and the proximity of the homes to one another, the number of McDonald's and KFCs lining the high street. Still. People here manage to live with dignity, even if Chris would make comments about inbreeding and architectural suicide. There's something honest and unafraid here. People have modest dreams. They put up signs on their doors that declare with pride: we are trying to be happy. You've got to admire the optimism.

Charliena opens the door. 'Come in, come in, Faith ... Ooh, I see you brought your friend with you.'

'It's okay, she can just wait outside.'

'No, no, everyone is welcome here ... Let's see how Melly responds to her.'

She ushers Beyonce and me into a lounge room which is decorated with framed embroidery on the walls. On the sofa sits a heavily retarded young woman who is obviously pregnant. Her belly is huge. I am fluffed with irritation. Why didn't her parents—or the institution—pick this pregnancy up sooner? She didn't just get this size in the past week. There are liability issues here for Tranquil Gardens. Perhaps Charliena and Frederick don't visit all that often. And I am not one to point fingers at the frequency of family visitations.

'Melly, Melly, look, this is Faith, the nice woman who is going to help you ... and her dog ... It's very sweet, tame, why don't you pat him?'

'Actually it's a her,' I say.

'Him, her, what's the difference?' Charliena smiles.

I know this is not the right time or place. But the reproductive organs of male and female canines are worlds apart. Really.

Melissa looks up at me and gives me a goofy smile. Her lower chin glistens with saliva and what looks like biscuit crumbs.

I sit down next to her. Beyonce follows me and sits down at my feet.

'How are you feeling, Melissa?' I ask her.

She smiles at me some more.

'Melly is very happy that you are going to help her, aren't you Melly?' her mother says. 'Faith, would you like something to drink?'

'A whiskey if you've got one,' I say.

Melissa's mother gives out a little laugh. 'Ooh, we ... we don't drink alcohol in this house, I'm sorry.'

'Tea will be fine.'

Charliena nods approvingly and leaves us.

Melissa smiles a huge grin. She takes my hand and puts it on her belly. I flinch. Beneath my fingers I feel the movements of her unborn baby. I get a constricted feeling in my throat. Hot tears prick my eyes.

144

'Bobby,' she says.

'Bobby?' I repeat. 'Is Bobby the person who did this to you?'

'Bobby . . .' she says.

I feel a kick beneath my hand.

I gently remove it from her belly.

Frederick comes in, smiling, so happy to see me. 'Aah, Melly, what do you think of the dog?' he asks. 'DOG,' he says pointing to Beyonce. He takes her hand and places it on Beyonce's head. Melly grabs her ears and pulls them.

'No, don't hurt the nice dog,' Frederick says, removing her hand from Beyonce's ears. Beyonce looks up at Melly and licks her hand.

'Oewuwhaa,' Melly says, but there is delight in her voice.

'She's hard to understand, she babbles a lot,' Frederick says. 'It's nothing to be scared of. She doesn't mean any harm.'

When Charliena returns with a tray of tea and homemade apple pie, I am caught, like a fly in a spider's web, in a tangle of threads of right-eousness and wrongfulness. The apple pie smells delicious but is tasteless and does not dislodge my disquiet. In fact, it gives me excru-ciating heartburn. Beyonce finishes my pie and licks her lips.

Bobby is one vowel away from 'baby'.

Melissa may be mentally retarded, but she's not stupid.

That night I lie in bed with a hot-water bottle across my belly, listening to 10 000 Maniacs while I eat (having just chewed an entire packet of orange-flavoured antacids) eight vegetarian samosas I picked up on my way home. Beyonce lies at my feet, watching me.

Banaz hadn't wanted the baby. I guess it reminded her about how her husband had raped her. But when she lost it, she was sorry. I think just having it there inside her made her love it. Pregnancy is a high-risk time for abused women. Getting thrown down a stairwell is always bad news. Worse when you're twenty-three weeks pregnant. She wrote me a letter. To say 'thank you for all your help'. Her last line hurt: 'It was a little girl.'

She blamed herself. Battered women always do. But by then it's always too late.

My period is two days late.

Stress can do that to you.

I don't ever want to be pregnant.

But I cannot sleep for thinking about the look on Melissa's face. Her body did what any normal woman's would.

I also try not to think too much about whether she really was raped or whether mentally retarded women actually want to have sex, the way we all desperately do.

The truth is, tonight I probably saw the happiest raped woman I've ever seen.

# 30. baby

My mother came to tuck me in and kiss me goodnight.

'I have some wonderful news,' she said, stroking my forehead.

'What is it? What is it?' I asked, sitting up in bed. 'Are we getting a dog?'

She smiled at me. I watched as her eyes filled with tears, and the left eye let go of the tear first, marking a trail down her cheek. I was confused.

'No darling, not a dog. I'm . . . we're going to have . . . another baby,' she said.

'Why?' I asked.

Now her right eye let its tears go, and a tear dripped down onto my sheet.

'Why?' she repeated. 'Don't you want a little brother or sister?'

I fingered my covers.

'We had one,' I said.

'Yes, I know.'

'. . . and we lost him . . .'

'Yes . . .'

'Didn't you always say that if you lose something, then it's bad luck?'

She nodded a little.

'And you can't just get another one?'

'But that's different. Losing something is different from losing someone.'

'Can we get one just like Nicholas?'

'No, we can't. Nicholas has gone forever now. We'll get another one. A different one.'

'Can we get a dog instead?' I asked. 'That way if we lose it, we can get another one from the RSPCA.'

'No, we're having a baby instead.'

'Can we call it Toto?' I asked.

She smiled. 'We will figure out what to call it.'

'Don't you want a baby?' I asked her.

'I do,' she said.

'Then why are you crying?'

She didn't answer. She leaned down to kiss me, wetting me with her tears.

I lay there in the dark for a long time after she left, feeling the cool wet spot on my face dry. 'Nicholas, Nicholas, Nicholas,' I whispered over and over again, trying to seal the gap between my mother's tears and the things we'd lost that had names we didn't speak of anymore.

# 31. notes

*Tell me something about yourself.*

The counsellor smiles at me.

The adolescent specialist my mother made me go and see after Josh died also had this line of questioning. I try to remember what I answered her. The request is so big and so wide that it just locks the gates on the graveyard of my mind.

Two years ago, when I agreed to go on a blind date with Carol's cousin who had just returned from travelling around the US, he also started the evening with, 'Tell me something about yourself.'

James was a smoker. The only thing I could think of to say was, 'I hate smokers,' but, call it intuition, I sensed it wasn't a good way to start an evening. So I just sat there staring at him, until he said, 'Or . . . don't . . .'

So I didn't.

The evening ended sooner than I expected when he got up to get drinks and never came back. I don't suppose working in a woman's abuse centre is much of a drawcard for men. They either assume you're a lesbian or they have a prurient interest in the details of your work. Either way, making conversation can be like passing gallstones.

*Take your time.*

This only aggravates my anxiety.

*Start anywhere . . . What music do you like to listen to?*

I clear my throat.

'I like Zucchero.'

*Who?*

'Zucchero—he's an Italian singer . . . My *nonna* likes him . . . He's quite well known . . . in Italy . . .'

*Okay. Who else?*

'10 000 Maniacs . . . I especially like that song "Trouble Me". It's got a lovely tune . . . And I like the words . . . the sentiment.'

*Go on.*

'Yeah, that's about it.'

*What else can you tell me?*

'I like mangoes, but I'm allergic to them.'

*Really? What happens to you when you eat them?*

'My tongue swells up and I find it hard to breathe.'

*When did you discover that you were allergic to mangoes?*

'When I once ate a mango and my tongue swelled up and I found it hard to breathe.'

*Pause. Right. How long ago was that?*

'About ten years ago.'

*What else can you tell me?*

'Turkish delights are my favourite chocolates.'

*I also like them.*

'But I don't eat them because of the gelatine . . . I'm a vegetarian . . . And you know gelatine comes from animals' hooves.'

*Pause. Right.*

*Long pause.*

'I . . . um . . . I buy really good facial products . . . the kind that hasn't been tested on animals, and I can never understand why when people know you're supposed to cleanse, tone and moisturise, most of them just leave out the toner and go straight from the cleansing to the moisturising . . . Does that happen to you?'

*Blink.*

*Can you say more about this?*

'Not really. That's just a thought I have every now and then . . . It's like we all know what we should do, and then we don't do it. People know they shouldn't eat fatty foods, but they do . . . People know they shouldn't smoke, but they do.'

*Nodding. Earnest nodding.*

*Pause.*

*Long pause.*

'You know how most people are scared of spiders? I'm not.'

*More nodding.*

'And I don't understand why people kill them.'

*Really?*

'They never seem to harm anyone, yet people happily kill ants, cockroaches, flies, bees, spiders . . . It bothers me. That sort of gratuitous violence.'

*Sometimes they become pests, though, don't they?*

'How many people do you know who have ever been bitten by a spider?'

*Shrugging.*

'I can tell you it's very few. The statistics for spider bites are startlingly low. I've Googled it. It's much rarer than people imagine.'

*That's interesting.*

*Pause. The taking of notes.*

*Don't mind me, I'm just making a few notes.*

I know about note-taking. You take notes when there is an alarm bell. A red flag. What did I say that needed a note taken?

I watch her.

*Go on, I'm sorry I interrupted you.*

'No, really, that's it.' I was going to say, just to try out how it feels in my mouth 'Actually, I love spiders . . .' but now I hold back. I want to stall the note-taking which is getting on my nerves. But I say it over to myself. I love spiders. I love spiders. It feels good on my tongue.

*Have you dealt with any cases this week you'd like to talk about?*

I pause.

'Not really.'

*Silence.*

'I just organised the termination of a pregnancy for a client.'

*Silent nodding.*

'Mentally retarded woman. Twenty-six-week-old foetus, if that's the right word. Do you still call a twenty-six-week-old pregnancy a foetus?'

*Nodding.*

'Do you still call something that can breathe on its own a "foetus"?'

*I believe so.*

'It's a bit of a misleading word, don't you think?'

*Shrugging.*

'It's closer to a baby than a foetus.'

*Silence.*

'Yeah, well, I'm off to visit her after this session is over.'

*More silence.*

*I believe the centre lost a client this week.*

'Yes, yes we did. A case of femicide.'

*Tell me more.*

'A client came in last week to get an AVO, we got it for her, and we were working on an exit plan but she went home to get some of her belongings. Without a police escort. He was there, waiting for her. And he killed her.'

*Pause. More note-taking.*

*And how do you feel about it?*

I narrow my eyes. I'm sorry, I just do this instinctively when people ask stupid questions.

'Not so happy about it.'

*Do you feel . . .*

'Responsible? No. Should I? It wasn't my fault.'

*No. How do you feel?*

I pause.

'Relieved.'

The psychologist looks taken aback. I get a momentary thrill of pleasure. She repeats my word: relieved. but it's more of a question like this: *relieved????*

'The cycle of violence is broken. He won't hurt her ever again.'

*She nods. She takes notes for quite a long time.*

*Are you sad?*

'I don't know.'

*What do you mean?*

'I'm more angry than sad.'

*Who are you angry at?*

'At the deceased. I told her not to go back without a police escort. She didn't listen to me. You can't help people if they don't listen.'

*More note-taking. What was her name?*

I pause. 'Sanna,' I say. 'Sanna Najma Leta. She was Somalian.'

*I notice you call her 'your client' and 'the deceased'? Do you think there's some distancing going on there?*

'Well, she was our client and she is deceased.'

*Nodding.*

*Do you think you are suffering from compassion fatigue?*

'I don't know. Am I? Is that your diagnosis?'

*I don't diagnose, we're just having a chat.*

'In that case, can I go now?'

*See you again next time.*

'I'm counting the days.'

## 32. epitaph

'What kind of a person ... ?' my mother's voice was pinched, ensnared in the razor wire of the grief she had strung out and erected over the years, fencing all the horizons. She repeated that phrase over and over. It was just a bit of fun, I don't see what the fuss was all about.

Besides, it wouldn't have happened if she hadn't been nosing around in my room. She had, in her self-absorbed generosity, bought me a bunch of huge yellow sunflowers with faces so enormous they were monstrously human, to 'brighten up my room', because it was 'time to see the light again' . . . because after six months, one needed to move forward and place the pain in its rightful place . . . because she knew how I felt. She was arranging them in a vase on my desk when she came across it.

It had been Josh's idea. It was just to occupy us and divert attention away from all those pipes and that oxygen mask. 'Let's write epitaphs,' he suggested.

Josh thought it would be fun to pick out the handful of words by which we'd each be remembered.

He begged me to get his parents to drop the 'Ralph'.

'I'll do what I can, but let's face it, they chose it and they're going to want to include it in the finale.'

'Isn't there some children's rights charter that says kids have the right to veto their parents' stupidity?' he asked.

I promised I'd check it out when the time came.

He wrote mine and I wrote his.

I don't know why my mother got herself all knotted up about it. She shouldn't have been looking through my things in the first place. It's not like I was hiding any secrets from her. After Nicholas died, she appropriated all spaces, as if she had a right to be everywhere, checking up on us, making sure everything was fine and that 'the channels of communication' were open.

It wasn't a death wish. I wasn't suicidal. I wasn't even thinking about dying. Don't all kids play these games?

I had written: *Joshua (Ralph—to be omitted if family agrees) Miller, who got stuck with faulty lungs, and a huge heart, missed (especially for his snot and very crap jokes), who always wanted to go first. Why? I didn't say it was okay. Rest in peace.*

He liked it. It made him laugh.

*Faith Ava Roberts*, Joshua had written, *arachnophile par excellence and perfect friend. Who died of a broken heart. Aged 17. Sorely missed by a family who never understood her anyway. She sure was SOME GIRL.*

My mother sent me to an adolescent specialist for six months after that. Where I sat in silence, and counted all the ways in which it was possible to be misunderstood even though all the things you were saying had names that were supposed to be there for understanding, the way Nonna had explained. So that when you asked for a spider, you didn't get a bunch of fucking sunflowers.

# 33. rolling pin

*Abortion is lawful if a doctor holds an honest and reasonable belief that a woman's physical or mental health would be in serious danger if she continued the pregnancy.*

Training Manual, page 187

People go there to commit suicide. That stretch of road along the cliff. It happens to be on the way to the hospital, even though it is the long way round, which arguably makes it 'out of the way'.

There's a sign there: *Beware of the Edge*. It's not an invitation, though some people take it that way. Last year two teenage girls jumped off holding hands. Their bodies were washed up several days later, spotted by some poor guy going for his early morning run. MySpace was filled with poems and tributes about the sea, loneliness and oblivion for weeks afterwards. I never think about dying when I get there. But it's a perfect view if you're going to make it your last.

Today there are Goliath-like autumn swells, and the sea is dotted with the little ant-like bodies of surfers.

Some days the water is choppy, and the wind stirs it up into little white cuffs. Then there are days when the sea has a temper, and you're head over heels in love with land for being so sturdy.

You can expect no mercy from the ocean. It doesn't know its own strength and shrugs you off with the same indifference as a human will crush a spider underfoot.

I have the floor and ward number on a post-it in my hand. I left Beyonce with Barbara. Hospitals have hygiene issues with animals, which is fair enough, they sniff each other's butts and all. But you do wonder about the logic. Humans are garbage bins. Microcosms of destructive microbes. Far worse than any flea-bitten canine.

The ward is full of women—some are here because of miscarriages, some have come for D and Cs, some hysterectomies.

I stand at the door of the ward. I see Melissa's parents sitting on chairs at her bedside. Frederick is reading the *Herald* and Charliena is crocheting. They wave enthusiastically when they see me.

I walk over gingerly to the bed where Melissa lies. She looks quite drugged. Her belly is still swollen, but not taut, puckered like a balloon that's a few days old.

'She's just come out of recovery,' Charliena says to me. She has an obscenely genuine smile on her face.

I go over to stand at the side of the bed.

Melissa opens her hazy eyes and focuses on me momentarily. She gives me a goofy smile.

'Hello Melissa,' I say softly. 'Are you feeling okay?' I have a tremble in my voice, but I clear my throat. 'I bought you some chocolate,' I say, putting a huge slab of dairy milk chocolate in her hand. When you don't know a person's preference, plain milk is best, I always think, though I wish I knew, and I wish there were a way of knowing whether Melissa loves hazelnuts, raisins, mint or caramel. Somewhere inside there is a person who actually knows what she wants.

The nurses who circle give me the evil eye. You can't help what you feel. It's what I most want to know. Whether the baby they delivered and allowed to die was a boy or a girl. Here, with Melissa lying on her hospital bed, hands on her belly, bleary from anaesthetic, I know it was a perfectly healthy little girl. That's prescience. I feel her everywhere. I want to say I'm sorry.

I try again, 'Are you feeling all right?'

And Melissa drops the chocolate, which slides off the bed and falls to the floor as she takes my hand and puts it on her vacant belly, where her Bobby no longer keeps her company in the monastery of her self.

And she smiles and she smiles and she smiles.

There is no weather in hospitals. It's a perpetual season of artificial warmth and ambient fluorescence. Squeaky trolleys and nurses in sensible shoes mark the passing of time. I know this for sure: if heaven is grassed and canopied with sky, hell is an endless hospital ward with garish cartoons along the walls trying too hard to make you forget.

I am relieved to be back in my office, depressing as it probably is from a feng shui point of view. Beyonce looked up at me and even thumped her tail under Barbara's desk when I came in, but she did not move. She's used to shuffling her allegiances, like children of divorcees who take their affection where they can. I don't take it personally. Though it hurts a bit more when it's an animal doing the shrug-off.

There are three emails in my inbox. One is from the Organ Donation Register. This month, if you can inspire a friend to sign up, you get a special discount on your next purchase of medication from Grayston's Chemists. I save it under 'correspondence'. I might find someone. Not Carol, who will only quip, 'Donated your virginity, next your spleen, your pancreas . . .'

The other two are from Ray Osborne. The first email reads:

MESSIAH DEMAS
Husband of Rania
Born 14 December 1961 one of six children
No HSC certificate
No traceable marriage certificate
Has worked: packer at Textile Industries (1987–1989)
Labourer at Western Propshafts 1990 (fired for drinking on the job)
Labourer at Wicker Manufacturing 1991
No other traceable jobs—must have done casual labour since then
One other maintenance claim pending—from one **Mary Shetland**.

He's got kids with another woman.

I think of little Jacob, or whatever his name is. I think of those lollipops I handed him in the face of such a rotten deal. Daddy's not coming home.

Maybe I should find another job. One where I get to say things like:

'Mrs Oefenpoof, your poodle is all washed and manicured and is ready to be picked up,' or 'Mr Delacort, the chocolate brown drapes definitely! set off the leather chaise lounge more eloquently than the fawn!'

A job where the only thing I've got to save are invoices for tax purposes.

I click onto the next email:

CALEB PEARSON
Born 30 June 1969 one of a twin (brother Noah)
Qualified as veterinary surgeon in 1999
Hobbies: surfing (member of Surf Life Saving Club); active member of Greenpeace and volunteer at RSPCA
Drives green VW numberplate JKV 987C
Works at Crown Street Veterinary Clinic
One sister, co-owner of small holding in the Blue Ridge Mountains

Unmarried. No children

Admitted to hospital after car accident in June 1989 with fractured ribs, broken leg

Unfortunately no traceable criminal record history.

And then, a comment in brackets: '(atypical abuser profile)'.

I press print. And dash out of my office to Barbara's desk to be there when it comes out. When I am back in my office, I fold it and stuff it deep into the belly of my handbag.

I wonder if Tranquil Gardens has a spot for me.

I could do with the break.

I bring Barbara a cup of coffee.

'Thank you,' she says. 'Your dog has been so good, haven't you girl?' she says scratching Beyonce's head. Beyonce looks at her adoringly, panting from that crooked jaw of hers. I laugh out loud. 'She's not my dog,' I say.

Barbara raises her eyes at me. 'You reckon?'

'Yeah, her owner is coming back for her.'

Barbara laughs. 'We'll see. There's no shortage of people in my family who'll love her if you get stuck with her. I'll bet Tyler'd adore you . . .' she says to Beyonce. 'He's got a thing for ugly dogs.'

'Don't you already have a dog?' I ask.

'Honey, I got a house full of mutts, a pair of love-birds Dave gave me for our anniversary and an honest-to-God python Jai is feeding live mice to . . .'

I shudder at the thought of a live mouse going down a python's gullet. 'Can I get some sticky tape and a stapler?' I ask. 'Oh, and a red pen?'

She unclips the key from the chain around her neck.

I gulp. This has to be a first.

She just smiles with those white teeth.

\* \* \*

At the stationery cupboard, I fumble with the lock. My hands are shaking. I read somewhere this is how Michael J Fox realised he had Parkinson's. I am too young and nowhere close to ready to contract a debilitating disease, but then again, look at Josh.

The cupboard finally yields to my fumbling. It is full of unused stationery. Boxes and boxes of pens and pencils and reams of paper. A hoard, like people prepare in anticipation of war. The abundance is almost thrilling, and then I realise that it is an abundance of things I do not need. Like all those gifts Libby gives me. I hope she knows it doesn't matter. *It's the thought that counts.* I believe that. Social dyslexia may not be officially recognised as a condition. I have problems. Working out the significance of Luis Vuitton handbags and Issey Miyaki fragrances is one of them. I do try.

I wonder if loneliness is a destiny, whether perhaps that statement 'there's someone for everyone', which my mother uses when referring to Frankie Sherwood and his highly strung wife Angie, is just a cliché. The thing you say to the spinster so she doesn't ever quite give up. I am, I guess, almost one myself. A spinster. Names pinch. Well here is my predicament. My soul mate decided to pack it all in at the age of seventeen. Fuck you Josh.

I remove exactly one red pen, one box of staples and one ream of sticky tape. Then I quickly close the cupboard. I hold up the red pen, staples and the sticky tape to show Barbara as I drop the key back on her desk.

It makes me very nervous when people trust me.

I knock on Carol's door. There is no answer. I open it and walk inside. Her office is a mess.

I open her top drawer to put her stationery in. I wasn't looking. Not scrounging, no. It was semi-impossible to miss. *Barely Legal Bondage.* A very young woman—a girl, to be exact—is tied up with ropes, and a gag. She is also displaying her clean-shaved vulva to me from the front cover of a magazine.

I flick the magazine open . . . *I slid my steel-hard cock into the wettest pussy . . . groaned for more . . . give it to me hard . . . Rock Hard, 21* writes on the letters page.

Carol once told me all these letters are written by the editors, that no one actually sits down and writes to a porn magazine to share how much semen he spurted all over the face of a young Spanish retail assistant he met while trying on clothes in a store. That put to rest one of the many unanswered questions I have about life.

On page 48 'Wet Willow' has a cascade of glorious red hair. Honestly the kind you'd like yourself if appearances were a matter of choice. I understand things. I appreciate that the reason she has handcuffs on and a rolling pin up her vagina is that she needs the money. People do things they'd probably prefer not to, all things being equal. You can go longer without dignity and self-esteem than three meals a day and somewhere to live. I wonder if it makes me sexually repressed. That I really don't want my vulva publicly splayed like a piece of human origami. But rather dived for, by patient marine biologists, hoping for a glimpse of a bashful sea anemone.

She could walk other people's pets. Or become a hair model. I shouldn't care one way or the other. Handcuffs and a rolling pin. I want to believe that no girl grows up with this in mind.

'You're so fucking judgemental,' Libby chided me.

'No fighting,' my mother begged. 'It's your father's birthday.'

Libby was debating whether she was hungry enough for the special: lobster fois gras. 'Don't look at the prices,' my father said. 'Have whatever you want.' So Libby selected a live lobster which arrived half an hour later on her plate, served with duck liver pate. Despite its French name, there is no euphemism for what goes on there. Slicing off a duck's beak and force-feeding it to 'marble its liver' is plain and simple animal torture. I am sure I am not mistaken about this.

I am not Willow. And she is not me. She has enormous breasts. And very little pubic hair. Actually none. I quiver to think about the practicalities involved. Carol once asked me to have one with her, but I prefer to keep Brazilian something I associate with coffee.

That time Josh and I were buying drinks at the café and those boys came in, I tried to look away, to pretend I didn't see. They were laughing, buying cigarettes, swearing and joking over a porn magazine. One had a swastika on his T-shirt. From where I stood, I could see Josh's lowered eyes. I saw him shiver, despite the heat.

Sadness is sometimes like that. It's not yours. It's someone else's. Like Gillian Brown. Leigh Flowerday. When you see it, it sticks to you, the sadness, like a smell. But not everyone sees the same.

Maybe Libby's right.

The way I see it, Wet Willow comes home, plops her bag in the hallway, hangs her keys on the key rack and thinks, I hate my job. And not because she's never going to get promoted to broom handles. But for all I know, she wakes up in the morning and muses over her Weetbix and coffee, I love Thursdays. It's the rolling pin up the fanny day.

If Genevieve saw this magazine in her drawer, on SISTAA's premises, Carol would be in the kind of deep shit nobody needs in their lives on top of an STD and a married man who won't leave his wife. Genevieve uses words like 'holocaust' and 'crimes against humanity' to describe the sex trade industry. She did her MA on pornography as a hate crime. Genevieve would not be so quick to condemn all those human rights violations that trickle out from detention centres if those being tortured were pornographers. The beauty of a double standard is its loyalty to the things we hold dear.

I flick through the magazine. There's a jokes page.

*What is black and blue and hates sex?*

Answer: *A rape victim.*

I swear, if I smoked, right now I'd need a cigarette.

'Barbara, where is Carol?'

'She called in sick today.'

I return to my office as the cold feeling in my belly slithers its way up my oesophagus like a tapeworm heading in the wrong direction.

My stomach feels like someone's crocheted a tea-cosy out of my intestines.

I wonder if you can get cancer from lack of sex. Cancer of the clitoris. Of the G-spot. Of the heart. Where cells just turn on each other. Like people do, pursuing a nameless swirling longing they cannot pin down but end up chasing, like a cycle they're caught in that has no beginning. No end.

*Porn is the theory.*
*Rape is the practice.*

**SISTAA poster**

# 34. monkey

'It's from the new baby . . . just for you,' my father said, handing me the bar of chocolate. It was a special kind of Italian chocolate, *cioccolatino* the kind Nonna used to give him when he was little. It had a picture of the Dolomite mountains with the village of Nova Case in its lap.

'How can the baby buy me a chocolate? It can't even drive yet,' I said, inspecting the bar of chocolate. It's not that I didn't want it. The mountain tops were covered with snow.

'The baby asked me to buy you this special chocolate,' my father tried again. 'It comes all the way from Italy, like Nonna and Nonno.'

I sat on his lap in the lounge room, holding the bar of chocolate in my hands. I had seen the new baby earlier that day, wrapped up in a cocoon of blankets. It looked very squishy and a lot like a monkey. It also cried a lot and made my mother cry too.

'It can't talk yet,' I said. 'That baby can only cry.'

My father sighed.

'*Va bene*, Faith, I bought you that chocolate because I don't want you to be jealous of the new baby.'

I squinted at him. He was telling the truth.

'Why will I be jealous of the baby?' I asked.

'Your mama is going to be very busy with her for the next while, you know small babies need a lot of attention, they cry a lot and they need to be fed and changed and . . . bathed . . .'

I fiddled with the chocolate wrapping.

'She can't have any of my books,' I said.

'That's okay, she won't be able to read for a long time,' my father assured me.

'And she can't use my asthma pump,' I said.

'Hopefully she won't have asthma,' my father said. 'Not everyone gets it.'

I opened the top of the chocolate, careful not to rip the picture of the mountains with snow on them like icing sugar. I bit off a piece. It was smooth in my mouth, and coated my teeth.

'I wanted a brother,' I said to my father.

My father blinked at me.

'We don't decide these things.'

'Who does?'

'God, I think.'

'Nonna says it doesn't matter. As long as the baby is healthy.'

'You must listen to your Nonna,' my father said. 'She is wise.'

'We lost Nicholas. So we should have got a boy.'

'God thinks differently,' my father sighed. I broke off a piece of chocolate and handed it to my father. He took it from me.

'God god bo bod, banana fanana fo fod, me my mo mod . . . Go-od,' I sang with a mouth full of chocolate.

'What's all that babbling?' my father smiled. Laughing, almost.

# 35. pills

I have the phone on speaker.

Carol's voice is bunched up into little sobs followed by long stretches of monologue.

'I'm never going to find anyone to love me . . . for who I am . . .' she grieves. 'I think this time I'm really going to do it, Faith, I really am . . . Corey . . . shit . . . I've wasted so much time . . .'

'Don't do it,' I say. I am not being absentminded here. I have trodden through this valley of self-pity before. I could walk its tracks in my sleep.

'I've got the sleeping tablets,' she says.

'How many have you got?'

'About fifty.'

'How did you get them?'

'Kathleen prescribed them for me. I told her I was having trouble sleeping.'

'You've got lots to live for,' I say.

'Like what? My fucking herpes has come back. Corey's never going to leave his wife . . . what was I thinking?'

I stop reading.

I look around my office.

'Weren't we going to travel next year to India?' I say.

'I've got no money saved up,' she says miserably. 'I've spent it all.'

'On what?' I ask her. 'You were supposed to be saving.'

'I know . . .' she says. 'I'm fucking hopeless. I can't do anything I set my mind to doing . . . I just say I'm going to do stuff and then I don't . . . I can't . . . I'm useless and pathetic . . .'

I inhale and roll my eyes. I can't believe I actually have to say this, but I do anyway. 'No you're not.'

'No one wants to fuck me . . .'

'What do you mean?' I say. 'Shaun Hamilton wanted to fuck you . . . Do you want to know how long it's been since I've had sex?'

'How long?'

'Ages.'

'How long?' she pushes.

'Months and months . . . Actually it's probably years and years now.'

'Who was the last person you fucked?' she asks.

'Hugh Mungous,' I say.

There is silence.

'You fucked Hugh Mungous?' she asks.

'We had sex. A couple of times.'

She starts to laugh. I am feeling very annoyed. But this is what you do for a friend who is suicidal. You parade your history of miserable sexual encounters with little men so she can laugh at how much more pathetic you are than she is.

'Hugh Mungous, that poor excuse for a stand-up comedian at the . . .'

'He had one or two good jokes,' I say.

'He was fat.'

'He carried a bit of extra weight.'

'He's about three feet shorter than you.'

'Don't exaggerate.'

'Faith, he was practically a dwarf.'

'I don't believe that is factually correct,' I say.

'That was four years ago . . .' she says.

'Is it that long?'

'You haven't had sex for four years, Faith?'

'It appears to be that way . . .'

And now she is laughing a full-bellied laugh. She is giggling and pissing herself.

'Jesus, that explains a lot.'

'Like what exactly?' I ask.

'Like how fucking uptight you are . . .'

I inhale. I exhale.

'If you're not feeling so suicidal anymore, I have work to do . . .' I say.

'You need a good shag,' she tells me.

'I'm putting the phone down now, Carol. Try not to take an overdose will you?'

'Okay, I'll try,' she says. 'Faith . . . ?'

'Yes, Carol?'

'Will you come with me to belly dancing?'

I drop my head onto my desk. 'Of course I will,' I sigh.

'You're the best, you know that? You are, really.'

'Carol, are you there?'

'Yes, Faith.'

'Can you come in to work tomorrow? We've got Hazera coming in, Shaun's preparing her for trial.'

'Fucking Shaun Hamilton,' she says. 'He hasn't called me since he fucked me.'

'I thought you didn't want to fuck him again,' I say.

'I don't,' she says. 'But he could at least have phoned.'

\* \* \*

169

In my hand I am holding the post-it with the Crown Street Veterinary Clinic's phone number on it. Eight digits. I pick up the receiver and . . . my fingers just won't go there. I put the phone down. He won't even remember me. There's nothing more embarrassing than having to remind someone who you are. 'Remember me? Yes, the one with snot all over my face . . . crying, yes . . . in the waiting room . . . you promised you would . . .'

Nothing more pathetic in the world. With Carol's gibes, I've had enough humiliation for today.

I distract myself with the million things on my to-do list. I phone to leave a message for Rania at the telephone number she has left for me.

'Hi Rania. Faith Roberts here from SISTAA. How are you going? Umm . . . hope all is well. Please come and see me as soon as possible,' I say into the answering machine. 'I have some . . .' I scrounge for a word that does not induce panic but that prepares a person for news they were hoping not to hear, '. . . unexpected information about your husband.'

I look at my African violet. It looks like it's just heard bad news. Wilted and neglected. I have no water in my office, but I get up and empty my half-drunk black coffee into it. What doesn't kill you makes you stronger.

I wonder if perhaps that's meant ironically.

Barbara puts her head around my door and Beyonce squeezes through her legs and comes to me. I pat her. 'There girl,' I say.

'Everyone's gone, Faith. It's past your home time. Go home.'

'Just finishing up some details for tomorrow's clients,' I say to her.

'You work too hard,' she says. 'Why don't you take up a hobby?'

'Carol wants me to go belly dancing . . .'

'That'll do you good.'

'I'm not doing it for me.'

'You need some love in your life,' she says. 'You need a man.'

'Like a fish needs a bicycle,' I say.

'There are some good ones out there,' she reprimands.

'Maybe you got the last one,' I say to her. 'Did you ever consider that?'

She chuckles a deep throaty laugh. 'Twenty-five years is a loooong time to love one man. And not long enough. And besides, I've got three sons I'm working on making into three good men. I couldn't do this work if I didn't love men,' she says. 'You never loved a man?'

I pause. 'No . . . yes, maybe a boy . . . when I was fifteen . . .'

'Fifteen? What do you know about love when you're fifteen?'

I shrug.

'That is way too careless for my liking,' she says. 'Love doesn't plop into your lap like some bluebird of happiness. You gotta hunt it, Faith. It doesn't come to you. You go to it.'

I smile.

'Stop thinking,' she says.

I nod.

'Gently gently,' she says to me.

'What does that mean?'

'Far as I know, that word's only got one meaning.'

I sit in the catacomb of my office, in the quiet empty SISTAA house. It's just me and Beyonce. Darkness is spilling in through the windows. Leering, a voyeur. The windows in my office do not have curtains. I cannot shut out the night and all the hiding places it offers to men with switchblades who can't just be satisfied with a defrosted TV meal and a particularly medically improbable episode of *House*. I wonder what safety feels like. And whether once you've been raped, you never feel safe again, or you feel safer than you've ever felt, knowing you've survived every woman's worst nightmare.

I pick up the phone.

I dial the number of the Crown Street Veterinary Clinic.

'Hello,' a young female voice answers. 'Crown Street Veterinary Clinic, how can I help you?'

My throat feels tight. Gently gently. I speak, 'Can I please talk to Dr Caleb Pearson . . .'

'I'll get him on,' she says.

I get put on hold. I listen to a verse of Dolly Parton and Kenny Rogers singing about being islands in the stream with no one in between.

The next voice that comes on is . . . the same female voice.

'He's just busy with a client,' she says. 'Can I take a message and he'll get back to you.'

I wasn't prepared to leave a message. In my head I was ready to say, 'Hi, this is Faith. I don't know if you remember me. I killed a cat last week, actually I ran over it by accident, and you said . . . you mentioned . . . you would bury it for me on your sister's farm in the Blue Ridge Mountains . . . would you like to be the first man I've slept with in four years since Hugh Mungous?' So I don't say anything for a minute.

'Are you still there?' she asks.

'Uh, yes, I am . . .' I say, composing a shorthand version of the above. 'Can you just tell him . . . tell him . . . can you please ask him . . . to call Faith.' And I leave my number.

'And it's concerning which animal?' she asks.

'The cat without a name,' I say.

# 36. ghost

After Josh died, I watched the sea. I told my mother I was doing after-school chess.

Instead of coming straight home from school, I'd take the bus south and get off at the end of the bus route. I'd make my way down the rickety steps to Starling Bay and find a rock hidden from view.

I wasn't looking for trouble and I didn't think about strangers and what opportunities they saw in others' loneliness.

One day I got down to the bay and there was someone else on the beach. He looked about nineteen, he was wearing a denim jacket and he was smoking a cigarette he clutched as if it was something small he was keeping alive between his fingers.

I walked over to my rock and sat down. He wandered over, greeted me in broken English. Jose, from Brazil, still struggles with English, misses home, his family there.

He used the word 'lonely' fifteen times. He smoked seven cigarettes. We thought we spotted dolphins. No, maybe it was just the reflection of the light on the water. Maybe a porpoise. Isn't a porpoise a dolphin? No, just like an alligator is not a crocodile and a toad is not a frog. It's not? He seemed genuinely surprised. I told him every dolphin has a signature whistle. Just like every human has a unique fingerprint. We looked at each other's hands. He thought I knew a lot about marine life. I shrugged. Not as much as some people.

The moon in the afternoon sky collapsed day and night into something hovering towards twilight.

He talked. Reeling my thoughts.

'. . . hard to find people to talk to . . .'

'. . . wonder if I'm crazy . . .'

When the sun started to drop and the shadows stretched above us like canopies, I got up to leave.

'I've got to get home,' I said. 'My parents will start to worry.'

He stood up too.

As I turned to leave, he grabbed hold of my arm.

'Please . . .' He said.

I turned to face him.

'Please . . . kiss me . . . I haven't kissed a girl in so long . . .'

He had hazel eyes with the craziest long lashes. They made him beautiful. Things had happened to him that had made him sad, on the edge of being lost. I knew I would never see him again. I leaned in to this stranger's face. And watched myself in the brown reflections of his eyes. It was a perfect kiss filled with all the frustrated longing for everything I had been denied and lost. For a moment I felt as if I was floating in a magical place of tongues and hearts and breathlessness.

When I came up for air, his cheeks were flushed. 'What's your name?' he asked.

'Faith.'

'Faith . . .' he implored.

174

I fled.

I know he was not a ghost. But where he ended and I began was hard to tell, a shimmering divide, just as uncertain as whether that day folded into night, or the approaching dark swallowed up daylight's remains.

# 37. bells

Because I said I would. That is the only reason.

I am standing next to Carol with my shirt rolled up and tucked around my bra so that my bare stomach is visible. Me and eleven other women. Gina, the belly-dance instructor has a tanned, bejewelled, belly-ringed body. There are bells attached to her wrists and ankles. She sounds like a carnival when she moves. The warm-up exercise involves us rotating our hips like we're stirring porridge with a rolling pin up our fannies. I am missing a *60 Minutes* special on 9/11 to be here. While terrorism is changing the world we live in, I am rotating my hips in a group environment. There is something needless about this.

I look over at the door where Beyonce is sitting with cocked ears, titillated by the tinkling of chimes. Gina allowed me to bring her in, which was very nice of her, not everyone thinks about animals the way I do. Her smile was more of an enquiry as to how anyone could attach oneself to anything as unlovable and unsightly as a dog in need of maxillofacial intervention.

'This movement, which is called *undulation*, releases your lower chakras to allow more sexual energy to flow through your body,' Gina says. 'Just breathe into your yoni . . .'

There is giggling. Everyone around me is undulating. To undulate, you need a certain distance from your own sense of dignity.

I most sincerely do not want to breathe into my yoni. I do not want to be doing undulating exercises with my pelvis as a group activity, I don't want to open any chakras. My friendship with Carol is causing me to do things I am beginning to associate with mild insanity.

'Look, Carol, this isn't working for me,' I say.

'Keep undulating,' Gina smiles at me. That smile brooks no resistance.

I stop undulating altogether.

'It just takes a bit of practice,' Gina encourages.

'She needs to stay,' Carol tells Gina. 'She's very repressed.'

'Please Carol, no diagnoses,' I say to her.

'We don't force anyone,' Gina says. 'I know it may be uncomfortable, but as soon as we start drumming, you'll relax.'

'Excuse me,' I say and walk over to Beyonce, who stands up and wags her tail as I approach. I reach for my bag, remove my asthma pump and take two huge puffs from it.

Gina steps lightly to the corner of the room and switches on a CD player. A light drumming sound begins.

'Now what I want you to do is to close your eyes . . .' Gina says soothingly.

I shuffle back to my position in the circle and shut my eyes tightly.

'And then I want you to allow the music to enter you—just let it find its way in . . . There isn't a special opening, each of us is different . . . For some of us, the music enters through our feet, for others of us, it's through our fingers, for others, it's through the yoni, and for others, it could be through the heart . . . Just open yourself, and let the music in.'

I keep my eyes closed, the drumming feels quite soothing the way a pounding headache can eventually start to have its own rhythm.

'Let the music in . . .' she repeats. I open my eyes and take a look around me. All the women are swaying, some with beatific smiles on their faces. I feel exposed and ridiculous. I close my eyes again. My body starts involuntarily to sway from side to side.

I try not to think about how I look.

I try to imagine what it feels like to be unwatched, unjudged, unlabelled. I close my eyes. The scars on my leg begin to throb. Gently at first, then with more intensity.

I wonder if Shirley's scars have healed and whether the B might fade. One could learn to live with ITCH.

I wonder whether the guy that did this to her is in the pub playing pool or walking the streets, his switchblade twitching in his pocket.

I wonder whether the police have arrested Sanna's boyfriend.

I wonder where my butterfly pendant is.

*You may be in shock and not even know that you have injuries.*
*Do not wash, eat, drink or brush your teeth. Do not tidy anything including yourself as this may destroy evidence.*
*There is no right or wrong way to react. Whatever you are feeling is normal.*
*You may feel vulnerable, powerless, humiliated and depressed.*
*It is very normal to feel afraid.*

I wonder why I am mentally reciting the *WHAT TO DO IN THE EVENT OF RAPE* poster.

My scars are throbbing.

I am in the bath. There are bubbles and I am splashing. I am reaching for something. Someone. I am laughing.

\* \* \*

When I open my eyes again, and look at my watch, I am aware that twenty minutes I cannot account for have gone by.

Gina asks us each in turn how we feel.

People giggle.

'Wonderful!'

'Relaxed!'

'Renewed!'

'Mildly nauseous.' Gina is not discouraged by my answer. Instead she smiles.

'Now, I am going to show you how to shake your belly.'

Carol grins at me. 'I love you,' she mouths silently.

In the car, Carol turns to me.

'Will you read a poem I wrote?'

'Sure, Carol.'

She hands me a folded piece of paper.

'I think there's a market for a battered woman's magazine,' she says. I nod slowly.

'I just need something more . . .' she sighs. 'Don't you reckon there's got to be more than . . . this?'

I nod briefly and get out of the car before she sees an excuse to hug me. When her car drives off I open the piece of paper.

'*I'll callous up my vulva . . .*'

I stop at the first line. I glance briefly at the last line, '*As I dance into the sunset.*'

I fold the paper in half and then in half again. Is this just sad? Is it sick? Is it literature?

That night, I lock Beyonce out of my bedroom.

Alone in my bed, I close my eyes and I imagine what it would be like to kiss Dr Caleb Pearson. I picture the wiry mesh of his beard on my mouth. I visualise his strong kind hands on my little breasts . . . and then his strong outdoors fingers finding their way into the part of me that I don't share with anyone anymore.

179

In my sleep, I have an orgasm that has been four years in the coming. I wake to a new day with an ache inside me that stretches endlessly. Like the ocean, I'm holding a world beneath a moody surface of briny hunger.

# 38. rain

The first time I had an orgasm, I got a fright.

I was still in my funeral clothes, my mother had bought me a black skirt and blouse especially for the occasion, because until then it was her philosophy that 'young girls shouldn't wear black—it's the colour of mourning'.

Mrs and Mr Miller stood at the gravesite holding hands. Josh's little sister Naomi stood alongside them, blowing her nose.

He would have hated his own funeral. Josh hated crowds. Even Lisa turned up, dressed in a miniskirt. She embraced me with the garrulous enthusiasm of one who does not want to be excluded from grief as though it was a sleepover party or something. As if bereavement were the latest must-have accessory along with legwarmers and headbands. I think she just wanted to get the morning off school and skip the Maths test.

My mother said I didn't have to go back to school that day, and that I could spend the day 'quietly reflecting'.

So I went into my bedroom and closed the door and put a big sign up on the outside, *In Mourning, Do Not Disturb*. That word held currency in our family. It bought you space. Excused bad behaviour. One of my mother's more successful books was called *The Mourning After*, which you can find in the self-help sections, and is about 'living with loss'.

I lay down on my bed and thought about Josh's body in the coffin, his blond hair, his little hands, his lopsided smile, his brown eyes, his . . . penis. It had been only a few months back. I found myself thinking about how it felt going inside me.

I put my hands inside my undies and felt around. It was so soft and warm inside there.

Then I started thinking about Tyler and what it would be like for him to touch me with his long fingers, and before I knew it, the tiny patch of precipitation broke into a glorious storm that sent rumblings of thunder and darts of lightning all through my body. No wonder the earth loves the rain.

It was such a surprise, in a nice kind of way, like a ticklish spot you never knew you had but you want to keep on touching to make sure it's still there. It made me wonder what else my body could do that I hadn't known about—what other tricks it had up its sleeve.

I wondered if Josh was watching me, and suddenly I felt self-conscious.

I wondered where my G-spot was and how to go about finding it. Whether it came to you, like love, or you had to pursue it like a hunter. It was there, inside of me, sheltered and shy. If I rushed at it, would it swim away like a frightened seahorse, or approach, like one recognising a friendly hand?

## 39. anaconda

I don't usually look at myself too closely. I've seen the wretchedness discoveries of individual blackheads have provoked in my sister Liberty. I can't help thinking there is something deeply masochistic about an overly familiar relationship with a mirror, especially the magnifying sort.

This morning, however, I got stuck in front of the bathroom mirror while brushing my teeth. I wondered if you could stab someone to death with a toothbrush. The one end is quite pointy. With enough force. You could certainly blind someone.

Maybe she didn't understand 'police escort'. I could probably have explained that better.

I never knew, perhaps because I've never looked, how noticeably tears mark a face. They actually leave tracks.

Libby goes shopping. Carol goes to bars and gets laid. My mother goes for massages. Dad hangs out in Giorgio's reading the Italian newspaper. Beauty is not my department. There is nothing rational about it. But this morning I am up early enough and I make my way to Heads Up with Beyonce at my heels. Before I have a chance to work out what I am doing there, a hairdresser 'but call me Shepard' has me under a black cape and has 'layered' my hair, which I guess is hairdresser-ese for 'cut it'. Beyonce sits patiently at my feet.

'Fabulous!' he gloats.

I try to tie it back in a ponytail, but all these bits fall out, here there and everywhere.

'I can't seem to get it all in a ponytail,' I say, to which Shepard winks and says, 'Exactly, darling.' As I am paying, he leans in close to me and whispers conspiratorially, 'You need a colour.' A 'colour' is pretty low down on the List of Things I Need, certainly in the Big Scheme of Things, but standing there in a salon full of bottles and people taking their hair seriously, I actually succumb to this novel idea. *I need a colour.* It feels purposeful. I would even say a bit hopeful. Shepard books me in for four-thirty later this afternoon. He is still 'going to give it some thought', but right off the top of his head, he's feeling 'burgundy'. Burgundy. Not quite an adventure, but a brave world apart from brown.

'So who's the lucky man?' Barbara asks me.

I shrug. 'Man?'

'Don't try to fool me,' Barbara chuckles.

'I needed a haircut, for crying in a bucket.' I give her a look. 'And I also need a colour.'

'Talking of buckets,' Barbara says, 'what's the mop bucket doing hanging out in your office?'

'I was going to use it to escort a spider who lost his way outside again.'

'And?'

'And one of my clients stood on it and killed it before I got to him,' I say miserably.

'The story of your life,' Barbara says, with a chuckle.

I look at her, this big generous woman with the braids and the mole on her cheek. I stop and really look at her.

'What you staring at?' she asks cheekily.

'You're way too smart to be a receptionist in an organisation like this,' I say to her. 'You should be studying psychology or Fine Art . . .'

She laughs. 'I am. I'm studying at night to become a counsellor, to work with kids at risk . . . that way I get to play all day . . . Didn't you know that? Everybody's gotta have a dream. Sistas are doing it for themselves, Faith.'

I shake my head.

See? I am completely psychic.

Beyonce settles down at my feet. I compose myself. I straighten my desk. My butterfly pendant has not magically appeared in my top drawer. I send out an email to everyone in SISTAA entitled, '*Reward. I am offering a green beetle bracelet as a reward for anyone who finds my butterfly pendant.*'

Carol will hopefully be back at work. She better be. After what I put myself through last night in the line of duty. Shaun Hamilton will be in today. Cross-examination prep is never a tango in the park. Not that I can tango, but it is an expression. At least I look good. Well, better than I did last week. Just in case he calls back. Which of course he won't. But just in case.

Carol and Shaun come into my office together. It's choppy between them, fraught with little white horses tossed up by too many cocktails, indiscriminate libidos and that plummeting postcoital abyss from which not even a whimper of intimacy can be resuscitated. You can feel these things. My mother calls it 'energetic baggage'. Right now I can feel how right she is about certain stuff. Watching makes you seasick.

I raise my eyebrows at Carol.

'I'm fine,' she clips.

I nod.

'Nice haircut,' she says. 'What's the occasion?'

Shaun looks me up and down, doesn't say anything. He returns to his examination of Hazera's statement in her file.

I give an insouciant shrug. I'm not like Carol. I like the personal to stay just that.

'I'll just go and see if Hazera is here,' she says.

She leaves us in the office.

Shaun looks up at me. 'Do me a favour,' he says, 'just don't interrupt me the way you usually do.'

I clear my throat.

'I'll do what I think I need to do to protect my client.'

'You don't need to protect your client from me. I'm on her side, remember?'

'Yes, well I'll use my discretion,' I say.

'What bloke hurt you so badly to turn you into such a manhater?' he asks.

I lock eyes with him. I look at him so he knows I know he slept with my friend Carol. And I say, 'Could we leave the personal comments out of this? Could we just focus on the job at hand?'

'Are you jealous because I fucked your friend?'

'Now why would you think that?'

'I know you've got a thing for Carol,' he smirks.

I shake my head.

'So you do swing both ways or you only like girls?'

I sigh.

'Because I'd pay good money to watch,' he laughs, adjusting his trousers.


'Where were his hands when he was sitting on your chest?' Shaun asks.

Hazera is huddled on the couch, with Carol by her side.

'One of them was gripping both my hands which he'd tied with the nylon, and the other . . .' her voice comes in exerted spurts.

'I'm sorry, which hand was holding the nylon?'

'I think it was his left hand.'

'You think or you know? It makes a difference—they trap you on the detail.'

'I'm pretty sure it was his left hand . . .'

'Are you certain? If not, think and get sure.'

Hazera pauses, dropping her head and squeezing the bridge of her nose between her thumb and forefinger to locate the ugly memory in all its crucial inconsequence, and then says, 'I'm sure.'

'Go on.'

Hazera's face is mottled with emotion, her voice subdued by the calamity of a girlhood derailed. 'He forced his . . . his . . . penis into my . . . my . . . mouth.'

I look down at my hands so as not to give her the feeling I am looking at a person who had a rapist's penis in her mouth and am grateful it was not me.

'Did he have an erection?'

'What do you mean?'

'An erection? Was his penis hard like this?' Shaun straightens his forefinger. 'Or limp, like this?' He lets it droop.

She squirms in her seat. 'I . . . it was . . . no, I don't think it . . .'

'What was it? Erect or not?'

'. . . not . . .'

'You think or you know?'

Hazera closes her eyes and says as if it does not matter, 'I know.'

'And at that point you stopped struggling?'

A murmur, 'He was angry . . . I was scared . . .'

'Just answer the question. Why did you stop struggling?'

Shaun holds her with the pincers of his gaze. Hazera does not answer.

'You've told us that you hit him with your fists when he first grabbed you, you scratched his face with your nails, but then you stopped fighting precisely at the moment when YOU were in control. Why was that?'

Suddenly there is a crackle of unusual silence, different from other silences. Hazera finally opens her eyes and slowly, as if words were rehabilitated steps she was taking after an accident, she says, 'What. Do you mean. *I was in control?*'

Calmly. So staggeringly calmly, Shaun says, 'If someone was holding me down and forced their penis in my mouth, I'd have just bitten him. If you'd done that, you wouldn't have been raped. Why didn't you bite his penis when you had the chance? By then, had you changed your mind? Did you decide that you were enjoying it? A nice Muslim girl like you doesn't get much chance to enjoy some premarital sexual experimentation . . .'

I look at Hazera. Hazera looks at Carol. Carol looks at Shaun. Shaun looks at Hazera. And in this ricochet of glances, Hazera's face breaks, a shattering wall of glass. Shaun doesn't flinch. He asks it again.

'Why didn't you bite him?'

In my belly, a beast turns, like an anaconda rising.

'Surely they won't ask that?' I say.

Without turning to address me, Shaun says, 'Shut up or get out.'

Hazera starts to cry. Almost inhuman noises come from her throat. She rocks back and forth, her arms clutching tightly around her skinny bones, like an autistic child. Carol puts her arms around Hazera's shoulders. I catch Shaun's glance. His eyes tell me I have messed things up. Again.

Carol escorts Hazera out to the comfort room at the back.

Shaun snaps the file shut and says under his breath, 'I don't know what your problem is. Why can't you just let me do my job? They may not ask that, but if she can answer me, keep it together here, she'll waltz through cross-examination in court. What part of that don't you get?'


I drive to the city. I park in a loading zone.

I walk into the Red Cross and wait while the nurse looks for my donor card. She pricks my finger with a pin and tests my blood.

Around me several people are hooked up to drips where half a litre of their burgundy blood fills bags.

'Sorry love, not today . . .' the nurse says.

I look at her quizzically.

'You're anaemic. Get some iron tablets,' she says. 'Come back in a month.'

She must see the look on my face. She leans forward and puts a sticker on my shirt. *I donated blood today.*

'It's the thought that counts,' she smiles.

I'm back at my desk drinking a Coke I am using to swallow iron tablets when Barbara puts a call through.

I answer absentmindedly.

'Hello, it's Caleb Pearson here. Is that you, Faith?'

### The questioning of a complainant in a rape trial

*The complainant will be questioned about:*
- *her relationship to the accused;*
- *the circumstances leading up to the rape;*
- *the details of the incident itself;*
- *the effects of the incident on the complainant.*

*Since the prosecutor must prove all the elements of the crime, it must be proved:*
1. *that the accused had sex with the complainant (that penetration took place);*
2. *that this took place without the complainant's consent;*
3. *that the accused acted unlawfully and intentionally.*

*The more details the complainant can remember, the better the chances are that the judge will find her a credible witness.*

Training Manual, page 79

# 40. balls

'The trick to giving a good blowjob is to watch your teeth,' Lisa taught me. 'You gotta cover your teeth, or you can do some serious damage . . . Trust me. It's a real art.'

I smiled casually into my cheese sandwich.

'And rhythm,' she added. 'Once you got the teeth sorted out, you gotta get a rhythm going. Hand-eye coordination. And then it's over quick. Pull away before they come or you get a mouthful. And it's like—gross. Keep tissues handy.'

'Sounds like a lot of work,' I suggested.

'Why do you think it's called blow*job*?'

She was an expert in areas I had only ever read about in puberty myth-busting books. Along with wet dreams, menstruation and breast development. She wielded her knowledge like a magical power. As if only she knew the secrets to boys' hearts.

That was before Tyler. And the cyst on her ovary. And my anti-abortion speech. But I'd stored the information, a quiet apprentice, assuming some day it might come in handy.


'Why do dogs lick their balls?'

I looked at Josh with a bored expression. He loved this sort of joke.

'I can't wait to find out,' I said.

'Because they can!' he cackled, buckling over.

'Yeah, as if. You wouldn't lick your balls, would you?'

'You don't think I haven't tried?'

'You are totally sick,' I said. And then more tentatively, 'Does one . . . strictly speaking . . . have to . . . actually . . . lick the balls . . . in a blowjob?'

'Faith, anything involving a mouth and male genitals is a blow-job,' Josh said. Officious-like, and I was too unacquainted with the mechanics of sex to correct him, curiosity being a loyal sidekick but an unreliable substitute for knowledge. 'The proper name for it is fellatio.'

'Wasn't that a character in a Shakespeare play?' I asked.

'That's Horatio, you nutter,' Josh laughed.


Josh kept his shirt on, because he didn't want me to see his chest. I knew the feeling, so in solidarity I kept mine on too. But I let him unsnap my bra for access.

After he had touched and kissed my breasts I rolled him over and moved my face towards his boxer shorts.

But he tried to pull me back up again.

'Come on, let me,' I urged.

He laughed nervously, 'I . . . I don't want you to . . .'

I could see the lie firm in his shorts.

'I just want to let you know that, all evidence to the contrary, I am not a Bigus Dickus,' he smiled.

'Thanks, that makes it much easier for me.'

'Stop if it's horrible.'

'Okay, I will,' I gulped. 'And Josh?'

'Mmmm?'

'I'm not going to lick your balls.'

'Fair enough,' he said. 'I wouldn't lick them either.'

I barely had a chance to cover his penis with my mouth before he lifted my head.

'Premature ejaculation alert,' he said. 'If you carry on doing that, we're never going to get to the sex.'

# 41. steps

He knows my name. He knows my name. He knows my name.

And then I remember I left a message for him with my name. Idiot.

'Yes?' I say, my heart hurtling.

'How are you doing?' he asks.

'Me?' I say as if there's someone else he might be asking about.

'Yes, you,' he says, a smile in his voice.

'I'm . . . I'm okay,' I lie. 'Actually I've just had a pretty terrible session at work.'

'I'm sorry to hear that,' he says. 'What work do you do?'

I pause. Okay, here goes 'well it was nice chatting to you excuse me while I run a million miles'. 'I work with raped and battered women.'

There is a long pause on his side of the phone. I'm expecting to hear the click of a receiver.

And then . . . he laughs. Maybe he thinks I'm joking.

'Shit, and I thought I had a heavy job,' he says. 'I'm sorry, I didn't mean to laugh.'

'That's okay,' I say. 'I don't get to hear many people laugh in a day's work here.'

'Yeah, I'll bet,' he says.

I try to sound relaxed. He sounds relaxed. He's probably got a girl-friend. Ray Osborne didn't find that out. A nice guy like this would certainly have a girlfriend. Without needing to go online or anything like that. You don't need to advertise when you're relaxed like this. People go for relaxed. It's very relaxing. Maybe he's even married and doesn't wear the ring at work because of animal bodily fluids. He's probably gay. Decent guys are gay these days, as if the species is changing its mind and is retreating to the harmonies of likeness.

'So . . .' he says, 'you left a message for me to call you back.'

'Yes,' I say. 'I was just wondering about that cat . . .'

'Yes, the cat without a name.'

'Yes, that one.'

'It has a beautiful resting spot out at my sister's place. There isn't a clear view of the mountain because of all the trees, but just a few hundred metres beyond you can see Athena's Peak. There's also a little creek that runs through there.'

'Really?' I ask.

'Really,' he says.

I have a huge lump in my throat. It's not unrelaxing, just hard to swallow. He really did it. He buried that cat. Because. He. Loves. Animals.

'Thank you,' I say, but my voice comes out all squashed and squeaky.

'That's okay,' he says. 'I could tell that it was important to you.'

I don't speak. Tears are pouring down my cheeks. I am afraid to sniff in case he'll know that I am crying—again. And he'll think I'm a nutcase for sure which maybe I am.

194

'I can tell an animal lover from a mile away,' he says.

I still don't speak, because it's hard to make chitchat when you have mucus pouring out of your nose, onto your lip and down your chin.

'Hey Faith, are you there?'

'Mm,' I manage.

'Would you like to take a drive out to the mountains sometime this weekend? If you're free. You can check where I buried your cat.'

'It wasn't mine,' I say.

'When you bury something, it becomes yours . . . in a way,' he says.

I smile into the phone.

'So . . . ?'

'I'd like that,' I say. 'Really, I would like that very much.'


'Aren't you going to eat that?' Carol asks, pointing at my salad. In my lap is a dish with the half-moons of avocado pear, crumbles of feta cheese, the slender bodies of green beans, and the orbs of baby tomatoes. We are sitting on the steps outside the kitchen at the back. The noon sun is friendly on our skins in that tempered autumn touch. I feel like stretching out and rolling on the grass. Like a cat. Not that there is any grass out here. It's all concrete and brick. But grass, like lazy picnics, is always a nice thought.

'Yeah, I'm getting to it,' I say, spearing a baby tomato and biting into it so my mouth fills with the sweet explosion of that sap, those little seeds.

'Listen, it wasn't your fault,' she says.

'I didn't watch where I was going, it was most definitely my fault,' I say.

She looks at me oddly. 'Hazera?'

'Oh, sorry, no, I meant the cat . . . You know, the cat I killed last week.'

'Why are you thinking about that cat now?' she asks me.

'No reason,' I say. 'It's just that when you said it wasn't my fault . . . and by the way, I don't think what happened in there was my fault. Shaun was out of line. He goes too far.'

195

'It's *my* job to protect my clients,' Carol says.

And before I can stop myself and remember that Carol is my friend and that she has a condition, and is kind and generous and is just looking for someone to love her with all her wounds, and that I would rather stick pins in my eyes than hurt her, I say, 'Then do it . . .'

She cowers. 'Are you saying I'm not doing my job?' She shifts and turns to look at me head-on.

I scramble for the rewind button to erase what I was just about to say to her, which would have been something like, 'You are a suicidal masochist who has wasted seven years of your life on a married man and are now overcompensating by sleeping with every thing that breathes, and I'm worried about your ability to do anything for anyone else . . .' But all that comes out of my mouth is a feeble, 'No, I'm not saying that.'

'Then what are you saying?' She has, as she says this, tears in her eyes.

'I'm saying . . . Carol, that you are not an invitation to the best party of someone's life . . . you are not a party, Carol, you are a person. How long does a party last? A few hours? Maybe a night? You are not a party . . .'

'Okay, so I'm not a party . . . It's just a phrase.'

'It's factually incorrect.'

'So what? It's just an advertisement. At least I'm trying to find someone to love me.'

'If we don't look after ourselves first and foremost, we can't . . .'

A huge tear rolls down her cheek. It is very distracting to try to think clearly when someone you love is so observably hurt by every word that comes out of your mouth, no matter how cautiously you have selected them.

'. . . we can't . . . I mean . . . we don't do our clients . . . or ourselves . . . any favours.'

'I haven't let any of my clients down,' she says to me. 'And,' she says, blowing her nose on a serviette, 'you're a right one to talk . . .'

I clear my throat. I was, just a few minutes ago, feeling so elated at the prospect of this coming weekend, and taking a drive with

Dr Caleb Pearson to the Blue Ridge Mountains even if it is just to look at a mound of dirt. But just when you can see above the treetops, with the clouds beckoning, your best friend heaps the boulders of the self-hatred, which she's been storing up since she was five years old and some paedophile of a stepfather decided to stick his dirty dick in her mouth, into the hot air balloon of your day. Why? Because you happen to be sitting next to her on a step, in the sunshine, eating your lunch.

'Look at you,' she says. 'You're the one who doesn't want to go into therapy. You're the one who feels guilty about your baby brother's death and has never admitted it or dealt with it. You're the one who hates men and never has sex. You're the one who doesn't even cry when a client of yours is killed. You can't even say, "You wrote a beautiful poem, Carol," you can't even bring yourself to say it . . .'

Her diatribe contorts into a laugh that is more a gasp. 'And you're calling me fucked-up. Sister, take a good look at yourself before you come with your advice on how to fix me up.'

She gets to her feet and storms back into the house.

I exhale. She leaves me with a basket full of accusations I will need weeks to unpack, figuring out what to own and what to discard. For now, I decide to just shove the whole lot in the freezer of my mind.

I stab my fork into a piece of yielding avocado pear flesh and put it in my mouth.

I am usually a fan of avocado pear. It is wholesome and rarely disappoints. But today it is unable to soften the unbearable dictatorship of concrete, and the hopeless absence of grass.

# 42. jonquils

They were on our doorstep when I arrived home from school.

A bunch of jonquils with a large green envelope. My name was written in capital letters. *FAITH ROBERTS.*

I had not had much experience with Valentine's Day cards, having only ever received one from Ron Hadley. It was Libby who always received half-a-dozen.

I picked up the flowers. They were adorable, with little yellow centres surrounded by white petticoats. Jonquils fling their smell in your face. They are not easily ignored.

I opened the card with trembling fingers. I tried very hard not to hope it might be from Tyler Holden.

*When the sun comes up . . . I want to be there.*
*When the moon appears . . . I want to be there.*
*When your smile comes out . . . I want to be there.*
*When your tears freely flow . . . I want to be there.*
*Be My Valentine so I can be there for you.*
*Love from your Secret Admirer.*

My mother gave me a vase for my jonquils.

Later that day, I went into Libby's room. She was painting her toenails.

'I got a Valentine's Day card,' I told her.

'You?' she laughed. 'Who from?'

'A secret admirer,' I said.

'Can I see?' she asked.

'Close your nail polish,' I said. 'I don't want you getting it on my card.'

She obliged.

I handed her the envelope.

She opened it and read it. I waited. She wasn't the only one with secret admirers.

She read the card again, then she sniffed it. She sniffed it again.

Then she began laughing.

'This is from Mum,' she laughed at me. 'I can smell *Emerald Dream* on the card!'

I snatched the card away from her. The heady aroma of tangerine and honeysuckle clung to that card like desperation, the way smells do.

Behind the closed door of my room, I tore the card into tiny bits. And pulled the heads off every single one of those cheerful jonquils until they were a confetti of crushed petals.

Their smell lingered for days, though.

# 43. burgundy

Shepard assures me it will look 'stunning'. I assume he's using it as an ill-fitting synonym for 'better than it usually looks'. Beyonce is seated at my feet, unruffled by the nests of hair she's lying on.

I try to resist the impulse to scratch my itchy head, which will stain my fingers and get them full of gunk. Vanity-remorse kicks in. Why did I think that this might be a good idea?

'So, gorgeous, is there some special occasion?' he asks me.

I assume he is being ironic. I look at him. He is not. 'You mean other than just another dreary day in my life?' I ask.

He giggles. This is how he keeps his customers satisfied. Inane chitchat is not my forte, which is really an understatement. But I recognise it has its place.

'Don't tell me you don't have a hunky boyfriend?' he asks me in a sort of singsong voice. 'I love hunky boys,' he says conspiratorially, dropping his voice an octave.

I shake my head. 'No hunky boyfriend.'

'Do you like them hunky?'

'How do you mean?'

'You know, tanned, big muscles, clean-shaven . . . tight arse . . .' he whispers.

I try to imagine a tanned big-muscled clean-shaven tight-arsed man being interested in me. It's like scrounging in the dark for a dropped contact lens.

'Actually, I'm not that fussy about the tan or the muscles . . . or even the clean-shaven part.'

'You like your boys scrawny and effeminate,' he says. 'I know the type you like—the artists, the musicians . . . the Johnny Depps, the Rupert Everetts, am I right? Tell me I'm right.'

I sigh. He is just doing his job. This is the stuff normal people talk about. What I do must be the crazy stuff. People preening in front of the mirrors for hours and hours, fussing over split ends, flaky scalp, products and sheen, is perhaps about something less vacuous than vanity. Maybe it is about hope. That if we have a swish enough haircut, a burgundy enough colour, something in our lives will change. There will be vividness. I can only assume that, deep down, this is the reason I am in this chair with this foul-smelling concoction in my hair.

'Yeah . . . maybe,' I say vaguely.

I look around the salon. It is a busy place, filled with people, young and old, having their heads wrapped in plastic and tinfoil, their hair heated and curled, snipped and shaved. On the chair right next to me is a man in his fifties in an expensive-looking business suit I have overheard is having 'strawberry-blonde highlights', which I don't know for sure but can't imagine are what they sound like— pink. I try to imagine what might possess a man in a business suit to highlight his hair when it seems that the natural aging process has got all of that under control. A midlife crisis? An affair?

In the mirror I can see a girl who cannot be older than fourteen, in a private-school uniform, on the other side of the salon. 'Hair extensions,' Shepard tells me. Again, I am a little at a loss, there are gaps in my education, but I would have thought that if you just leave your hair, it extends all by itself. She is sipping on a very large smoothie and paging restlessly through *Vogue* magazine where anorexia beckons alluringly. She is long-suffering, and inspects and comments on each extension with listless impatience. I hope she is not planning on hitching a ride home, not at this time of day. It's going to be dark soon. Not in a school uniform. There is a serial rapist out there.

'My worst is men with beards,' Shepard says from behind me. He rolls his eyes with exaggeration. 'I mean, there is nothing more off-putting than a boy with too much facial hair—it's just so sloppy.'

I nod again. 'I don't really . . . mind . . . beards.'

'Have you ever been kissed by someone with a beard?' he asks.

I shake my head.

'It's revolting,' he says. 'Disgusting. Don't do it.'

'Okay.'

'Smooth is where it's at,' he says.

'Smooth,' I repeat.

An hour later, Shepard holds a mirror up to 'show me the back'. My hair glistens with a deep crimson glow when the light catches it. Burgundy. Even I have to admit, *you can't go wrong with burgundy.*

I dish out the $99 for my colour. The thought of how much time that would have bought Rania and her offspring gives me mild indigestion or a feeling practically indistinguishable from it.

I cross the salon floor, Beyonce at my heel, to where the fourteen-year-old is having her extensions finalised.

'Hi,' I say to her.

She looks up at me with the straw in her mouth. 'Hi,' she says, revealing a jaw of metal attachments. She probably won't need Da Vinci veneers. That is almost assured. She flicks her gaze to Beyonce. I am grateful Beyonce is immune to unvoiced teenage judgements.

'I was just wondering . . . are you getting picked up . . . or would you like a ride home?'

She twists her mouth into a kind of scorn overlaid with a frown. 'My dad is picking me up in half an hour,' she says. 'And anyway, what's it to you?'

I shrug. 'Sorry.' I start to retreat.

As I do so, I hear her say, 'Dyke. Pervert.'

I am grateful for the evening air outside which drinks me in, burgundied to the roots, tussling my layered hair in the wind that is coming from somewhere across the ocean. Beyonce runs ahead and barks at birds which I don't have the heart to inform her are actually bats.

I wonder if it is too late to drop in on Nonna.

I usually call first. So she's expecting me. But I'm trying something different. It's not exactly 'dancing into the sunset', as Carol's poem puts it, but it's spontaneous. Which, all things considered, is a kind of personal renaissance.

I sign in at security. Old people are vulnerable. At her retirement village the systems they have in place are 'designed to give you peace of mind' and certainly cover them for any mishaps so they can say 'we did our job'. I have to leave my driver's licence at the security entrance, an ostensible deterrent to those intent on getting up to no good with one of the geriatric residents and crashing their way through the boom gate in a hasty escape. Which could still happen, but one would be a fugitive without one's driver's licence.

I park in the visitor's parking. Beyonce hops out of the car and squats down on the grass where it says, *Please do not walk on the grass*, though I've never understood the point of grass if it may not be walked on. She squats and doesn't lift her leg to pee. When she's done, she rolls onto her back. It looks like the canine equivalent of fantastic.

We walk down the well-lit pathway towards Nonna's ground-floor apartment. Beyonce stops ahead of me, growling. I feel a tremble in my lower belly. Rapists go for old folk for the same reason they go for mentally retarded women. Not much of a fight. Easily subdued. The

203

aged sometimes die from shock, relieving one of the headaches eye witnesses can become when one is insisting on one's innocence. My panic swirls, then recedes. It's a false alarm.

Beyonce can't tell the difference between a rapist and a moth. She wolfs it down. It didn't stand a chance. She's different from Bernard Baker in the school playground. Hunting is nature. Torture is nurture. I think one's sanity depends on believing this to be true.

Through the closed curtains I see that Nonna's lights are on. That's odd. One of the perks of blindness is that one's electricity dependency drops right off. Nonna's ecological footprint is the gentlest of all house-dependant creatures. I'm usually the one who puts her lights on, and switches them off when I leave.

I ring her doorbell.

I wait.

Time ticks by. I ring again.

'Nonna?' I call out.

'*Sì, sì,*' I hear from inside.

I hear voices. Fumbling at the door. What's going on in there?

Eventually, the door opens. It is not Nonna. It is Mr Abrahams. In his dressing-gown.

Something isn't right with his face. It looks blotchy. Is it blood? A nasty rash?

'Faith . . .' he smiles. He looks flustered.

'Is Nonna here?' I ask, leaning to the side to look past him. Inside I see Nonna straightening her blouse.

'She's here . . . We're here . . . we're both here . . .' he smiles.

'*Mia cara,*' I hear Nonna say as she walks towards me.

I look again at Mr Abrahams' face.

Dear Lord. It couldn't be, could it? It is. Those blotches are Nonna's cherry plum lipstick. All over his face.

I can't think of a single thing to say. So all I say is, 'Burgundy, Nonna. Next time, I'm choosing burgundy for you.'

*Secondary traumatisation (or vicarious traumatisation) is the experience of trauma-related stress caused by repeated exposure to trauma and an overdose of exposure to victim suffering.*

*Symptoms:*
- *feeling numb, apathetic and blocking off of senses*
- *sadness, depression, withdrawal from others and communal activities*
- *cynicism, loss of compassion, loss of faith/trust in humanity*
- *loss of faith in beliefs that previously gave meaning to life*
- *Over-identification with clients*
- *Hypervigilance: seeing danger where there is none.*

Training Manual, page 217

# 44. cape

Rachel Abbey. It was a name I heard a lot over our dinner table for a couple of months while my father was working on the insurance payout. It made for sensational headlines. It sparked passionate debates on *Newsline at 6, bringing you the latest when it breaks*. The feminists siding with the unions against the big law firms. Has feminism gone too far? Rachel Abbey became a name used in the same sentence as Lorena Bobbit.

She was a hairdresser. Nothing fancy. Just cuts and blowdries. The kind you get for $15 as long as you weren't after anything spectacular or stunning.

She was locking up when Ahmed Arafat, respectable in a suit and glasses, knocked and asked if she would squeeze him in. He had a job interview the next day. Would she mind, he knew it was late. He was happy to pay a bit extra.

She said she'd do him a favour. What the hell. She didn't have anywhere else to be. She covered him with the hairdresser's cape and went into the back to retrieve her scissors and combs which were soaking in disinfectant for the next day.

When she returned, she saw Mr Arafat making vigorous arm movements beneath his cape in the 'vicinity of his groin'.

Rachel Abbey panicked. She was a woman alone in a hairdressing salon with a man. She returned to the back, picked up a set of hair straightening tongs, returned to the unsuspecting Mr Arafat and hit him over the head with them, rendering him unconscious.

Rachel Abbey called the police. She explained that a man had been masturbating in her salon and was about to rape her.

When the police arrived, Ahmed Arafat was still unconscious. When they removed the cape, Mr Arafat's trousers were fully zipped. The glasses he had been cleaning beneath his cape, however, had fallen to the floor and the glass in the left lens had smashed.

'It was a perfectly acceptable mistake. In the circumstances,' the unions argued. 'A woman's perception of harm is qualitatively different from a man's,' the feminists proposed.

'Jumping to conclusions . . . not all men are rapists . . . when was the last time Rachel Abbey had sex? She was a forty-five-year-old spinster with a history of failed relationships, she wanted to have sex with him, it was all her own projections . . .' his lawyers argued.

Rachel Abbey lost the case. Apparently no man would have thought he was in danger had the situations been reversed.

Once a man stopped Libby and I as we were walking to school. 'Remember me?' he asked. I didn't. 'Go away, leave us alone,' I shouted. I grabbed Libby's hand and made her run all the way home with me.

My mother made me write an apology note. Apparently, Mr Rodriguez, my father's colleague whom we'd met once at a Golden Insurance Christmas barbecue, had been most upset at the insinuation.

Desperate measures don't translate well in retelling. Sometimes you just had to be there. Danger is always attenuated by the security of recall. And sometimes people make mistakes. It Happens.

# 45. drawer

There are nine messages on my answering machine when I get home. Eight of them are from Carol in various states: consoling, blaming, self-deprecating, apologetic, hysterical. I can't even work out if suicidal is mixed in somewhere there. I wonder if I actually don't care anymore.

The only other message is from Libby. She and Chris are planning an engagement party. At a vineyard in the Valley in three months' time. She wants me to be 'involved' with the preparations. Can we go shopping together for a dress? She's thinking ambers, saffrons, autumn colours. She wants her only sister to be her 'maid of honour' at her wedding. *And!* Chris is giving her an early engagement present. Breast implants. Size D. It'll be done before the wedding! *Really a dream come true!* Her voice, I recognise, is truly that of a happy person, and not one who is in touch with the fact that she is marrying a scumbag.

I suddenly feel very warm. I pull off my blouse and sit on the carpet next to the phone. Beyonce cocks her head and looks at me.

'Little boobs,' I say by way of explanation, like in case she was curious. I wonder if Mr Abrahams had his hands on Nonna's boobs. I notice I am not hoping he did not. It is nice to have your breasts touched by someone you like. I think about how I let Ron Hadley touch mine and how much he smiled. I think about how lovely it would be if Caleb Pearson put his strong outdoor hands on mine.

I cup my breasts in my hands. They feel tender. PMS. Bloody PMS. I scrounge around in the wastepaper basket of my emotions to find the 'be happy for your sister' feeling that must have inadvertently fallen in there while I wasn't looking. But I rifle in vain. That was Nonna's lipstick all over his face. I think maybe this is funny. I wish I had someone like Josh to call and tell. It's lonely not having someone to tell stupid things to. Laughing, unlike undulating, is more gratifying as a group activity.

Maybe I should buy my little sister a locket that says *Jesus Loves You*. But I know she just wouldn't take it the right way. I have no idea if Jesus loves Libby. I think Jesus would think she has perfectly lovely breasts just the way they are.

The right thing to do is not always the thing we can do. It complicates matters, the ill fit between them. I know it would make Libby happy if I called her and told her that I'd LOVE to be her maid of honour, and what a great guy that Chris is, paying for breast implants—we should all be so lucky. That's all she wants, really. Her big sister's blessing, as if it would make any difference in the BST.

Everything inside me is balled in a tight frond. Even the Red Cross rejected me today. My butterfly pendant is gone. My sense of style is not something that ought to keep Libby awake at night. I can dress myself. I don't want a chaperone to come shopping with me for a dress. I can shop. Black and brown are perfectly respectable colours for a wardrobe—I think they were quite 'in' last winter. My ire peaks and suddenly ebbs. I am not her and she is not me.

I consider phoning her to tell her I just had a haircut and a hair colour. Burgundy. Maybe I'll tell her that I have a 'date' with someone. Not really a date. Does visiting a gravesite constitute a 'date'? I guess if you're me, it could.

It is possible that I am about to have one of the Biggest Disappointments of my Life.

This would happen if:

1. Caleb Pearson is married and has only invited me to see the gravesite of the cat I killed because he feels sorry for me. Pity is not a good foundation for an ongoing relationship. See Me and Carol as an eg.
2. Caleb Pearson is gay. Again, not a good basis for a relationship unless we're talking friendship, and right now, friendship is not on the List of Things I Need in the BST. Carol is more than enough.
3. Caleb Pearson is a smoker. My asthma and all.
4. Caleb Pearson is a psychopath serial rapist masquerading as a nice, decent vet to lure ordinary women like myself into his car where he will drive me out to a deserted place on a farm where he will proceed to . . .

I reach for my asthma pump. Just as the phone rings again.

It is Carol. And she's hysterical. All I manage to get out of her is 'Shaun . . .'

I tell her to stay where she is and I'll be right over.

I buzz her apartment number. The street is quiet for a Thursday evening.

'Who is it?' she asks.

'It's Faith,' I say. 'And Beyonce.' Beyonce wags her tail at the mention of her name.

Carol buzzes me in. I don't wait for the lift, I take the stairs to the fourth floor, two stairs at a time. Beyonce's claws *clip-clap* on the tiles.

When I knock on her door, Carol opens the peephole first to check that it is in fact me. She has, I suspect, officially gone off the rails. I may have to get her certified before the night is up.

She opens the door and before I can even step inside, she flings her arms around me. She has black rings under her eyes.

She pulls me inside and shuts the door behind me. She then bolts it with two security locks.

'Faith, you were right about him,' she says to me, her eyes wide, pupils dilated. I recognise this as someone very much in the throes of a freak-out.

'About who? Shaun?'

She nods frantically.

'What was I right about?'

'He's sick . . .'

I just nod. 'Yeah.'

She takes both my hands in hers and looks at me with desperation. I hope she hasn't swallowed any of those pills yet. Stomach pumping is not on my list of things to do tonight. I am all hospitalled out. She flicks her gaze to Beyonce.

'That dog better not crap or piss in my apartment,' she says.

'Don't worry, she's done her stuff outside for tonight,' I say, trying to retrieve my hands. She doesn't let go.

'Faith, I've just been on the phone with Hazera for the past hour,' Carol says. 'And you won't believe this . . . but Shaun . . . called her . . . this afternoon.'

'Called her?' I ask. 'How did he get her number?'

'Exactly!' Carol is squeezing my hands very hard.

'And why is he phoning her? He's not supposed to have contact with clients outside of SISTAA's hours.'

'Exactly!' she repeats. 'But it's bad . . . it's worse than bad . . .'

'Why, what happened?' I manage to manoeuvre one hand free. The other Carol clutches like a blanky she's trying to keep from the washing machine.

She sobs. She stops. She inhales. 'He said he thinks he knows what kind of guys she likes . . . and that he wants to take her out . . . on a date.'

'What!?' I say. Carol drops my hand. She covers her face with both of hers.

'Can you believe it? He asked her out on a date. And she said, "I don't think it's appropriate . . . given all the stuff . . . that you know about me . . ." and he said, "Well, I know you're different from other girls . . . and that you won't mind trying a few tricks . . ."'

Carol drops her hands from her face, looks at me unswervingly and finishes, '". . . with some *nylon* thread . . ."'

Lightning bolt.

Suddenly my head is spinning in crazy orbits and everything I've loathed in jagged bits about Shaun and couldn't put together slots into place. As the image sharpens, the blade of clarity nicks me with a coo-ee under the chin.

'Fuuuuuuck . . .'

'He's sick. There's something badly wrong with him. He obviously gets off on all this . . .'

I exhale. 'Are you sure it was Shaun?'

'Jesus, Faith, would I make something like this up? Would Hazera? After what she's been through? Believe me, I wish it wasn't him.'

I look at my friend. She is gaunt and depleted. Sadness and exhaustion have tagged along for the ride.

I drop my head.

This is bad. Very bad. Possibly as bad as it could get.

'I don't know how we're going to figure this one out,' I say, 'but we will.'

She nods. As she does, two tears roll down her cheeks.

'Nice hair colour,' she says to me.

I take my sleeve and I wipe her tears.

'Thanks,' I say. 'It's burgundy, you know.'

I lean against the wall in her entrance hall and sink down onto my butt. I wasn't paying attention—again. I wasn't concentrating. I am furious. Why didn't I trust my intuition and nail him with that hard-on comment? Maybe I just figured that anyone that depraved inside wouldn't let it show.

'And Faith . . . There's something else I didn't tell you . . .' Carol sinks down next to me.

'What?'

'You know that night . . . that night I fucked him?'

I nod, my heart tapping with adrenaline.

'We did it at his place . . . He got up to go to the toilet after we had sex . . . and, I know I shouldn't have done this, but . . . I opened the drawer next to his bed . . .'

I try to still my spinning cranium. 'Drugs?' I ask weakly.

Carol shakes her head. 'It was full of pornography.'

'What kind?'

'The worst kind . . .' she says faintly.

'Kids?'

'No, not kids . . . but S & M . . . really rough stuff . . . you know, where girls look like they've been raped and battered.'

I inhale. *Barely Legal Bondage*.

'I stuffed one of the magazines into my bag . . . I took it to work . . . I don't know why I did it, it was completely impulsive . . . maybe I knew I'd need it as . . . evidence.'

'So what do you reckon? What does it mean?'

'I don't know.'

I can barely breathe through the knot in my chest.

'Most men use pornography,' she offers.

'S & M?' I ask.

She shrugs. 'Women too . . .'

I feel myself squeezing my thigh. I need my asthma pump.

'And there's something else . . .'

I look at her with wide eyes.

'I saw his birth certificate.'

'You were *rummaging* in his drawer?'

She shrugs. 'I was curious.'

'And what?'

'The name on his birth certificate isn't Shaun Hamilton. It's Shaun James Brimble.'

'He's going under a false name.'

Carol nods.

'Do you think . . . he could be . . . I don't know . . .'

'The serial rapist?' she finishes.

'Right now, I think he could be anything.'

I shudder.

'Please don't go,' she says to me, grabbing onto my hand again.

'I won't,' I say.

We lock the windows and lie half-awake and half-asleep in her double bed, attuned to every sound and squeak that comes from the streets below. Carol eventually falls asleep with her arm across my belly. I can't believe how far away I am from where I want to be right now.

I swear, when you do this work for long enough, you start to go mad eventually. Or the madness in the world finds you. One way or the other.

*Pornography generates images of women enjoying sexual violence, desensitising men to the realities of violence and contributing to a climate which normalises the physical and sexual assault of women.*

Training Manual, page 208

# 46. magazine

It was the summer we were both turning fifteen, and Josh dreaded it because the heat made him sweat even more than usual, his body working overtime. After school we'd hang out in the game arcades where it was airconditioned and he didn't have to feel like such a freak. Sometimes we'd make it to the public swimming pool, but he didn't like me to see him half-naked, not with his half-konked-in chest and his skeletal limbs.

'I'm a scrawny prawn,' he'd say. 'Don't look at me.'

'I'll look if I want. You're my friend, don't be shy.' But he was. So I made my gaze neutral. Devoid of judgement or yearning. So we could swim and splash like kids to whom bodies are not verdicts.

\* \* \*

It was a Friday. Summer was having a tantrum. We were all being punished. Teachers made us go for water breaks halfway through lessons. The streets burned our feet through our shoes. School came out at 2.30 and we caught the 2.45 Central bus which took us all the way to the Junction where Josh wanted to buy some sea lice for his aquarium.

In the pet shop Josh looked longingly at the seahorses.

'Why don't you get one?' I asked. 'They're so beautiful.'

'They don't thrive in captivity,' he said. 'They get stressed in an aquarium. It lowers their immune system and makes them susceptible to diseases.'

He put his finger near the glass of the tank. The seahorse jiggled closer. Joshua was a seahorse whisperer. But he left just with the sea lice.


I was at the back of the café, scanning the fridges for ginger beer. Root beer. Lemonade. Orange fizz. Fanta grape. All lukewarm. Times like this, I felt the world just didn't accommodate my needs. I settled for an icy cold Coke. I pressed it to my temple.

Up front Josh was ferreting in the freezer looking for a Mint Crisp.

Suddenly four brawny teenage boys sauntered into the café, taking up all the space with their shouts and whoops. They threw a rugby ball to each other with belting thuds.

'Wachout! Fucken dickhead!'

'Belt up, pimp.'

'Grab some fags.'

The tall one had a swastika on his T-shirt. Later I wondered if that was even legal, given history and all that. But in that moment, I just stopped breathing.

The one with the shaved head walked up to the magazines and flicked one open.

'Sweet cunt,' he grunted.

The others crowded around him and joined in a chorus of yelps.

Gripping the Coke in my one hand, I inhaled, and began the long walk up the aisle, holding my school skirt down with my other hand.

I made it past the cans of tinned sardines and baked beans on special, two for $2.50.

'Give it to her up the arse,' said one.

I stopped. From where I was I could see Josh up ahead. His hands in the freezer. He didn't move either. And he didn't turn to look for me.

I stood for a while, holding my Coke. Small electric shocks of adrenaline surged through my body. I needed someone next to me. Josh was frozen. He wasn't budging. I wished my dad who is six foot three would step out from behind the washing powder and walk me to the till.

As I came out of the aisle, one of the boys looked up at me.

'Look, there's one,' he said, sniggering.

The others looked up at me. All four of them started making pelvic-thrusting gestures towards me, laughing, the *Hustler* magazine floppy in their hands. The one with the Nazi T-shirt approached me, rubbing his groin, his tongue flicking back and forth in his mouth. 'You want a bit of tongue action, baby?' he growled. I backed up into a stand of postcards.

'That's enough,' the old man behind the counter said to the boys. 'You leave this nice girl alone.'

I paid for my Coke and left the shop, not waiting for Josh.

I ran all the way home in the scalding furnace of the afternoon.

Ten minutes later Josh rang my doorbell. When I opened it for him, he was drenched in sweat. He looked like he'd been crying. In his hand was the can of Coke I had dropped somewhere between the café and home. It was dented. The Coke puttering in a slow fizz from the damaged tab.

'I'm sorry I'm not Tyler,' he said.

'Fuck you, Joshua, I don't want you to be Tyler.'

'I'm such a wimp.'

'You're not a wimp, you just . . .' the tip of my blade hovered at his flesh.

He waited for the blow.

'. . . can't protect me,' I said, leaning in, thrusting all the force of my body behind it.

I watched as every part of his face fell.

'You don't know what it's like to be a girl,' I said, with pitiless assertion.

The packet of sea lice slipped from his hands. It plopped at our feet in a wet thud. It's not like gravity means to be cruel.

But Josh *did* know. And I knew he did. It is one kind of pain to be the target. But his invisibility hurt as much and in as many ways. He was not oblivious to the fact. He had wanted to save me. He knew I was drowning. But he was drowning too.

How can two people who are drowning save each other?

# 47. circus

The morning lies on top of me, like a lover who doesn't respect dream space. Garish and needy, it hovers, waiting for my reaction. My first thought is, Jesus Christ, even Nonna's having sex!

Neither Carol nor I got much sleep. We tossed all night, human dinghies in a storm. I kept on getting up, standing at the windows and looking out at the streets. Things look sinister by night. That's darkness for you. Unreliable, unnerving. Figures in the shadows could just as well be lovers drunk on romance. Harmless homeless people.

Everything around me looks evil. Is it everything? Is it me?

\* \* \*

This morning when I look in the mirror in Carol's bathroom my burgundy swish haircut I got yesterday looks like it's just stumbled in after a big night of *and-I-can't-remember-what-happened-after-that*. I wonder if Shepard does refunds.

'We have to speak to Hazera today, just to check her story,' I say to Carol. 'Before we do anything further . . .'

'She was so distressed when I spoke to her yesterday, I don't know if she'll even want to talk about it again.'

Carol's hair must have grown an inch overnight, revealing her brown roots. I can't believe I actually notice this. One burgundy colour and my brain has changed lanes. Overnight I've become a hairdresser's salary.

My mind is twisting and turning, scuffling for order, a way to make this okay. The thought of having to face Genevieve and all those ceramic ornaments makes me blister with sweat. I just know I'm going to break something today.

Beyonce jumps up so her front paws are on my lap and I scratch her behind the ears. Carol lets me open a tin of tuna for her. Beyonce dances around the kitchen like an orphan on Christmas Day when the Salvo's van pulls up. Carol soothes me by making me French toast with apricot jam and a huge mug of coffee.

'S'funny,' she says, while watching me eat. 'I fucked him. I was up that close to him.'

'What's funny about that?' I ask.

'You know, that you can be that close . . . to something so perverted . . . And,' she pauses, 'and not know it.'

'Maybe you did know it . . . in some way,' I say.

She looks at me from the startled orbs of her black-ringed eyes. 'No, Faith, I'm telling you. I didn't.'

I am at my desk when the phone rings. I nearly jump out of my skin.

It's Libby.

'So I take it you're not interested in being part of the engagement party at all,' she says. 'You can be *such* a bitch, Faith.'

I don't know where to start with my little sister. With the cat I

221

killed? With Carol? With Hazera? Shaun? A drawer full of S & M pornography? My life is a circus of miseries. She would think I was lying if I tried to tell her the truth.

'Sorry, Libby, I didn't go home last night,' I lie. 'Did you leave a message for me?'

She pauses, assessing whether to believe me or not.

'Yes . . . did you not get my message?'

'No, sorry. I spent the night at Carol's. She's having another one of her "episodes",' I say.

'God, Faith, when are you just going to dump her and get a normal friend? A normal life? Do you want to be miserable your whole life?'

I pause. It is possible that I am, for all intents and purposes, a weirdo, the way my sister sees me. I can hear in Libby's voice pity and embarrassment not entirely without kindness. There is so much I want to say to her, but I know that whatever comes out of my mouth, like 'you deserve more than Chris', will be contorted into the antonym of my intentions. My love will be broken and arrive in her hands as an insult.

'I am. Trying. To be normal . . .' I say.

'Are you? How?' she gibes.

'I had a haircut yesterday. And I got my hair coloured.'

I can hear her smiling. 'Did you?'

'Burgundy.' I say it like it's a sweet nothing.

'I can't wait to see it. Don't you feel better for it? I mean, don't you just feel like a different person?'

Perhaps there is a way. To tell her that as soon as I have outed the pervert lawyer who gets off on hearing our clients tell their rape stories I will feel much better about myself, not to mention my burgundy hair. Perhaps. But I can't see it right now. Is this how cripples feel? The longing to walk, to dance, to run, stripped of the ability? It is so strong in me, it roars. I am sure she would also welcome the information that a potentially normal man is driving me out to his sister's farm on the weekend. But that would be too much. She will think I'm bullshitting.

I reach for my throat where Carol's butterfly necklace sits. I look up. My African violet lives. It seems to even have a new purple flower in its midst. I cannot believe how this lifts my spirits.

'Hey Libby,' I say. 'It's great about you and Chris. The breast implants—truly terrific. In time for the engagement party, and all . . .'

There is a long long silence.

'I thought you didn't get my message last night,' she says, her voice clipped.

I don't move a muscle. I am fucked.

'You know, it is SO hard to have a relationship with you,' she says. 'I really try, but you know what, I think you just don't like people. I think you just prefer your screwed-up clients to ordinary normal people who just want to love you.'

The buzz of the receiver hums in my head for a long time as I sit and hold the phone to my ear.

Yesterday, Hazera huddled rabbit-startled on my couch. In twenty-four hours claws have grown. Today the waters of her distress shimmer with the meniscus of anger. Her mother sits alongside her, a silent co-sufferer, with a blue chador on her head, holding Hazera's hand between her two like something small you're trying to keep warm. She looks as if someone's kicked her legs out from under her. *You should see the look on her face.* Her eyes are grey with righteous resignation.

I hate the fact that we have to make Hazera tell us her story again.

Her mother coos to her intermittently, a lullaby of consoling murmurs. I cannot tell by the tone in her voice if Hazera is blaming me or Carol or both of us. Her mother is not blaming. She is just holding up the sky for today.

Hazera repeats the conversation she had with Shaun while I scribble notes wildly. I ask for details—time of call, exact words used, her response.

She answers us with staccato impatience.

I ask her if she has any questions.

She puffs up, spine erect. She pauses, bites her lip. She looks at Carol and me directly.

Why does SISTAA allow men to work here? Aren't there policies against this sort of thing? Don't we know that raped woman don't want to have to deal with men?? She agreed to court preparation by Shaun Hamilton because *she trusted us*. All she knows for sure now is that she does not want to go to trial. She's a good Muslim girl. How would she know that biting would stop a man from raping you? And don't we screen people first? To make sure they're not psychopaths?

I hang my head low. Sometimes silence is your only refuge.

Carol and I each swallow a tranquilliser from Carol's cosmetic bag. There's a stash there to still a sanatorium or pull off a triumphant suicide. Migraines aside, I don't, as a rule, resort to pharmaceutical interventions but this, I recognise, is a bona fide emergency. We are about to enter Genevieve's office. There is no other way. I guess that's why lambs cross the threshold into the abattoir, despite their best instincts.

We breathe in deeply and knock on Genevieve's door.

Before I know it we're outlining the 'situation'. Summary of Hazera's story. I refer to the notes I took, to avoid eye contact with Genevieve and to take my mind off the battalion of ceramics with which we are surrounded.

In all the time we talk, Genevieve remains quiet, her mouth a tight seal of displeasure.

When we have run out of facts, she asks, 'Is that everything?'

We look at each other and nod.

'Emergency meeting in the staffroom. Right now. I want all the staff there. Everyone.'

There is the warrior about her, always prepared for battle. Nothing surprises her about men. Nothing. I heard her say that a few months ago when some research came back that made Barbara so furious. From some Harvard postgrad who interviewed over a thousand ordinary men between the ages of eighteen and thirty. Two thirds answered 'Yes' to the question, 'If you knew you could get away with it, would you rape?'

I found Barbara in the toilet, shaking her head, dabbing her eyes.

'I don't believe it,' she said.

I handed her a tissue.

'It's bullshit,' she said. 'I've got four good men in my life, five counting my late dad, may his soul rest in peace. I've got a brother who's a man of God. That means four of my good men would rape if they could get away with it . . . Bullshit . . .'

I sat with her while she splashed her face with cold water, not knowing what to say, or what to believe. Barbara's anger shone, like mother-of-pearl.

'Hey Barbara, want to know why dogs lick their balls?' I asked.

And I swear she laughed so much at the punch line, she had to brace her enormous bosom with both hands as if she might lose her balance.


Barbara explains to the waiting room that 'there is an emergency that needs to be dealt with. No one will be able to be seen for the next two hours.' No one budges. Where have they got to go? In a lifetime of hell, another one hundred and twenty minutes between these bleak walls adorned with a few bright posters and information pamphlets declaring *You have the right to safety in your own home; rape is a violation of human rights; remember this is not your fault* is a curious kind of luxury.

# 48. raisins

It happens on an ordinary day. That's the first surprise. That you wake up, just the same as on any other day, you check your clock, you can lie in for five more minutes. You change your mind, because it's a bonus to get to the bathroom first before everyone else begins their ablutions. You do your wee, you splash water on your face. You cleanse, tone and moisturise while Libby does her wee. In the normal course, sisters are perfectly amenable to a toilet audience.

Back in your room you check for a clean school shirt. Find one. Dress. Check your pencil case. That your asthma pump is there. Your 'Aspects of Fate and Love in a *Midsummer Night's Dream*' essay is in a folder ready to be handed in. Without an extension, despite Josh being readmitted last week.

You make it to the fridge, pour your orange juice, put two slices of raisin bread in the toaster because there isn't any plain. Get the peanut butter out.

Still, at this point you have no idea of how close you are to the edge. You pick out the raisins one by one. You lay them in a little heap on the side of your plate. You spread your peanut butter on the toast. Even when the phone rings, you do not fall as if you've just had a baseball bat pounded into the belly of your soul. Phones ring in the morning. Nonna needs a ride to the market. Dad's work. Mum's publisher. Anything is possible at this time of day.

You hear your mother's voice. 'I see . . . and I'm so sorry . . .'

You chew a little more slowly, because something is inching closer, and by now you're fully awake and your prescience is kicking in. But it's gradual, a slow climb up a hill, not a freewheel down.

When she is standing in front of you clutching her dressing-gown tightly at her throat, as if trying to hold back what she needs to say, you see it.

'Faith . . .' your mother says.

You do not swallow what is in your mouth.

'It's Joshua,' she says.

You look at her because perhaps she is not meaning what you know she is saying. Perhaps what she is saying is, 'He's taken a turn for the worse,' you've seen him take many turns. But her eyes are not letting your friend have a turn for the worse or you an ordinary day today or another ordinary day for a very long time to come. Perhaps she doesn't understand.

'I'm sorry,' she says, 'he . . . passed away in the night.'

You swallow now, because you have nowhere else to put this peanut butter toast but down your gullet where it will be absorbed by your stomach and converted into energy which will help you make it through this very unordinary day. You knock your plate, perhaps by accident; it falls to the floor, where it does not break, but the raisins fall haphazardly at your feet. You will need to clean that up.

'No, no, no, no, no,' you say. Involuntarily, it patters off your tongue, a morse code of denial.

And she shakes her head. Slowly. Sadly.

You never liked raisins before.

But from that day, their desiccated sweetness and shrivelled little bodies will mark the beginning of a time you will come to know as 'after'.

## 49. hatchet

Carol and I take turns filling everyone in.

We are all convened in the staffroom. There is a crackle of exhilaration. Crisis situations perk people up. Like that fizzy vitamin C drink they advertise. Everyone is abuzz with the effervescence of the macabre. Disgust. Fury. Outrage. Like fireworks compared to the mundane executions of our daily in-trays. Maybe we all secretly crave it. A touch of gruesome corruption. The kind of stuff that makes for good stories. Looking around me, there is vitality in this room that could fuel a rebellion.

There is a hushed silence. Some are shaking their heads in disbelief.

'Finally, I would just like to say,' I add, 'that it is my feeling that we should have a policy of *never* allowing men to work here. Not face to face with clients anyway.'

There are several nods in support.

'There are conflicting positions on that issue,' Annemarie says. 'A lot of new research is showing that post-rape, supervised intermittent contact with nonthreatening male figures actually counteracts some of the impact of Rape Trauma Syndrome . . .'

*I'm all about integrity.* Those were his words. My fists curl tightly.

'Wasn't he screened?' Michelle asks from the lattice of her apple Danish.

Eyes turn to me. 'Yes, Ray Osborne checked him out. He's got no *official* criminal record . . .'

'What do you mean by that?' Genevieve asks.

I shrug. 'Who knows what he's gotten away with?'

'Can we afford to turn help away, when it's being offered free of charge?' Maud asks. 'He seemed genuine . . . we've had some good results in court since he's started here, haven't we?'

'Men offering to help out here should be treated with automatic suspicion,' Michelle says, wiping her mouth. 'If men want to work in this field, they should do preventative work, with men.'

I nod.

Others offer their opinions.

Finally, Genevieve has heard enough. 'Okay, I've listened to all of you. We are in a situation where we have severely compromised one of our clients, both her safety and her healing, and we need to take responsibility for that.' She pauses. 'I also think we have to take a principled stand once and for all about men's involvement. We can't screen volunteers for perversion and sexual distortions. I recommend, based on what I have heard, that Shaun Hamilton's involvement with SISTAA be forthwith terminated. Do I have a seconder?'

Me, Michelle, Maud and Annemarie all put up our hands.

'Right, that's settled then,' Genevieve says.

Carol doesn't say a word. She just looks at her hands which are folded in her lap.

Within the hour, we have a formal, documented resolution. The only question remaining is how to go about terminating Shaun's involvement. He can't be fired. He's a volunteer.

Maud suggests a formal letter from SISTAA, outlining that due to client feedback, Shaun's services are no longer required, and suggesting that he seek help from a professional to deal with whatever his own issues are. 'We can even suggest names of some psychologists, I know several who specialise in sexual deviance.'

Michelle froths at this suggestion. 'Are you for real? We should go straight to the senior partner at his law firm and expose him. The guy is a goddamn lawyer—he should be publicly humiliated and struck off the roll . . . Is there such a thing for lawyers?' she asks.

'He could get disbarred,' I say. 'It's the same thing.'

There is some discussion that this is too extreme, too public and will do SISTAA's reputation as much, if not more, damage as Shaun's. 'We look utterly incompetent,' Genevieve says dismally. 'It is a serious breach of our professionalism.'

'Do you think we should maybe give him a chance to defend himself?' Maud asks. 'Just like, for the sake of hearing someone out?'

There is silence in the room. I hold my breath as if to try to stall the shifting winds of compassion. It only takes one—like that single juror in *Twelve Angry Men*. Things can turn around real quickly.

'Defend what?' I ask. Internally, the quills of my ire tremble. At times, women's organisations can really overdo this feely-feely feminine justice bullshit. 'Own worst enemy' is a phrase doing somersaults on the trampoline of my mind. I can feel Shaun Hamilton slipping out from between my fingers. Right now I want the brisk hatchet of guerilla justice. The drawn-out even-handedness of civilized adjudication seems limp. Handcuffs and rolling pins. If only they knew.

Genevieve nods. 'I suppose we do need to hear what he has to say. It's a hell of an accusation, and we should give him a chance to defend himself.'

'Yeah, maybe Hazera misunderstood . . . maybe it was a cultural thing . . .' Annemarie says.

'Misunderstood what? Why would she lie?' I ask. 'And what about "you can show me some tricks with nylon" don't Muslim women get?'

Annemarie ignores me.

'Nobody thinks she's lying, but maybe she interpreted it in the worst possible light. Maybe there was a context . . . Let's just hear him out,' Maud says.

Others nod in agreement. Carol too.

'Give him a chance to bullshit some more,' I mutter.

Genevieve is firm. 'It's over for him no matter which way you look at it. Let's at least give him the dignity of defending himself, that way we've covered all our bases and can't be accused of a witch-hunt. We have to practise what we preach. I guess this is a hard one, but we're setting an example.'

'I know stuff about Shaun that makes this look even worse,' I say before I can stop it.

Carol swivels around to face me and raises her eyebrows in an arc of disbelief.

'Well . . .?' Genevieve asks.

'Personal stuff . . .' I murmur.

'Like what?' Genevieve asks. 'Don't be obscure, Faith.'

'I think he has . . . identity issues . . .' I say lamely.

'Don't we all?' Genevieve asks.

Carol glares at me.

I feel my lie—my omission to speak up—heavy in my stomach. Carol looks down. What friends will do to protect each other, it's ridiculous.

'Maybe we should call him to a meeting here and confront him publicly,' Maryse suggests.

'No,' that's Carol's voice. It's the first time she's voiced her opinion. 'That would be like a firing squad. I think since Faith and I are the two that know him best and have worked with him the most, we should confront him privately and report back to all of you.'

Everyone seems to think this is a Sensible Suggestion. Everyone that is, except me.

'Time to get back to work,' Genevieve says. 'We've got a waiting room full of people out there . . .'

As Carol and I leave the staffroom, Genevieve calls us back in.

We stand before her.

'So, you two—what do you have to say about all this?'

I look at Carol. She does not look at me.

'What do you think?' Genevieve asks me.

'I think it is time Shaun Hamilton was brought to his knees.'

'And you?' Genevieve asks Carol. 'You've been pretty silent through all this. What do you have to say?'

'I think Faith was right not to trust him,' Carol says.

Genevieve swings her gaze at me like a cleaver. 'You haven't trusted him?'

'I never have,' I say.

She takes two steps towards me so that she is claustrophobic-ally close. And she says, very precisely, in a tone that is hard to take in any other way than how it is intended: 'Faith Roberts, if you ever keep silent in the face of your distrust again, I will not have you working another day in this organisation. Do you hear me? Your first and foremost allegiance is to your own inner voice. You have jeopardised the safety of one of our clients by ignoring it.'

'Yes, Genevieve,' I mutter.

'And as for you,' she says turning to Carol, 'when you fuck people you work with, you lose the ability to be objective. SISTAA is not a pick-up joint.'

'Yes, Genevieve,' Carol mumbles.

She waves us away with her hand.

We both leave, scorched and lame as if we've walked on coals. I suddenly have a mutinous headache behind my eyes. I take four aspirin with a Coke I find in the fridge. It relieves my headache but gives me a burning sensation in my stomach.

By lunchtime, I am doubled over in pain. I hobble to Barbara's desk and tell her I am taking myself home for the afternoon.

'Go home and rest, girlfriend. Lord knows, you need it,' she says. 'You look like hell.'

As I'm about to leave, the phone rings. It's Candy.

'Hey Faith,' she says, her voice a tumble of exclamations. 'How's my darling girl?'

I look over at Beyonce who is lying with her head on her paws next to the filing cabinet. 'She's good, Candy. She's fine.'

'I've got the best news . . .'

I wait.

'They said I could bring her here if she stays outside in the day and in the laundry at night and I clean up her poops in the yard . . .'

My headache immediately refers a small pinch to my chest.

'But . . . but isn't it against the shelter's policy . . . to have animals?'

'It is! But they're making an exception . . . for me . . . they think it will *facilitate my healing*,' she laughs.

'So . . . umm . . . when can you get her? On Monday?'

'Jennifer, she's the shelter sister, has to do some grocery shopping and she said she'd swing by SISTAA this afternoon!'

'Right . . .' I say, swallowing. 'That's . . . great news.' I rearrange my stapler on my desk. I wonder if you could kill someone with a stapler. Staples are very sharp in their own right. If you got the right spot. Like the jugular for instance.

'So can you get her back for me from your vet friend?'

'Actually, she's right here. With me.'

'Fantastic!' she whoops.

'Yeah . . . any news of Phoebe?' I ask.

'They let me call her every day . . . She's, what they call it here? *coping*,' she chuckles, chuffed with her new shelter vocabulary.

'That's good.'

'Hey Faith?'

'Yeah?'

'You know how it is when you're holding your breath under water? And you feel like you're not going to be able to hold it in

234

anymore? When I'm away from my Feebs, I feel like I'm holding my breath.'

'I see,' I say.

'But then you know how you suddenly see the light coming through the water and you know the air is there?'

'I know,' I say.

'That's how I know I can hold it in just a little bit longer.'

I look over at Beyonce and that desperate overbite of hers.

'You're going to be okay, Candy,' I say into the phone. 'You, Phoebe and Beyonce.'

'Yeah,' she says. 'All thanks to you.'

I deposit Beyonce in Barbara's care.

One last pat on her mangy head, and I leave quickly.

For the first time ever, I leave SISTAA's offices without saying goodbye to Carol.

# 50. apple

Nonna taught herself how to read.

Her parents couldn't see the point of sending her to school when all girls were supposed to do was to find a good husband and make a good lasagne. Her brother Marcello went to school. Nonna had to help out around the house.

'I get cross. I make hugly face. I tell my mother, "Is not fair, I want also to be clever. Write a book." She tell me, "You be clever, marry a good man."'

Then when Marcello chopped off her pinky by accident, her mother felt so guilty she enticed Mr Sardi, who was an ex-teacher, and lived across the square, to teach Nonna a few lessons by way of compensation in exchange for some pork salamis.

'Three thing. A girl must know. How to read. How to say No. How to say Yes.

'I sit with this man Mr Sardi. He is fat and with lots of eyebrows. He look at me with pig eyes. I read his eyes. He put a book on my lap. He put his finger in my penty. I say, "No Mr Sardi. We must learn from this book." He say he want to put his finger in my penty. I tell him this is not a good way to teach. He tell me I must not tell anyone about his finger in my penty. I say "Yes, I will not tell anyone." But I lie. I tell Marcello. Marcello tell Mama he will take salami to Mr Sardi. And Marcello take the skin of salami and fill it with sawdust. And he take to Mr Sardi. And all his friend collect the horse manure and put it outside Mr Sardi's door. Every day for a month that man step in horse shit every time he leave the house.'

Nonna threw her head back and laughed at the memory as if it were a story about love in all its sweetness.

'That's a horrible story, Nonna,' I told her.

She looked at me oddly. 'Horrible? Is wonderful story.'

'How is it wonderful?'

'Boys are good,' she said.

'What about Mr Sardi and his fingers in your panties?'

Nonna laughed. 'He was bad. But he is one. All the other boys is good. Sometimes, one apple is rotten. But you cannot throw out all the apple. *Mia cara*, if you throw out all the apple, you will be very hungry.'

# 51. book

Carol once made me do a water aerobics class with her over lunch. You can try your hardest, but water has its own idea. It slows things down. Right now I feel like I am moving in water's slow motion.

Maybe I overdid the aspirin.

I seem to be walking funny, like I've got a slow bleed in the stomach.

I consider that it has been a rather full-on week. I say the words aloud to myself, 'It's been a rather full-on week.'

I am sitting on my couch in my apartment with a hot-water bottle on my belly. My place is a mess. I should tidy it up. I especially want to get rid of the dog bowl in the kitchen. When things just stand there, empty, it's hard to forget. Like Sanna's shoes. One can begin to have feelings for something. Just because it's there. Affection grows from presence. I wonder why I never knew that before. Maybe Barbara's right. You have to have something to love before you can feel love.

I reach over to my desk and I grab a pen and paper, on which I write:

*My full-on week:*
1. *Sanna*
2. *The engagement*
3. *The cat without a name*
4. *Dr Caleb Pearson*
5. *Enforced counselling*
6. *Carol's suicidal episode followed by diatribe*
7. *Shaun Hamilton*
8. *Beyonce—coming*
9. *Beyonce—going*

I sigh and close my eyes. My neck and shoulders are in spasm. I need a massage. If I look through my drawer, there will, I am certain, be a voucher from Libby, perhaps one that hasn't already expired. It feels quite nice to need something for a change.

I scan my apartment. There is my basket of dirty laundry waiting to be washed. There are papers on my desk that need filing. There is a dirty coffee cup I left there sometime last week. There is my bookshelf full of books haphazardly arranged. Unlike my mother's which are alphabetised 'and need to please be put back in the right place'. I am not looking for it specifically. But it's that cover she chose that stands out. Bright pink. Luminous, if one is to speak frankly of colours. Anna Kay Li hot pink. She wanted a cover that would 'jump out at people', though why you'd want a book about losing a child to 'jump out at people' strikes me as emotionally sadistic, not that my mother is. Wouldn't you want it nestling with subtlety among the pastels of *Six Ways to Forgive Yourself* or the gentle greens of *Life is a Garden*? She wanted her pain to be in everyone's face. She even says in the book, *I wanted to etch on my forehead, 'I lost a child.'* The covers of subsequent books have been more understated, which she would say has to do with her *healing* and nothing to do with advice from her publicist.

I stand up and make it to the bookshelf.

I reach out and put my fingers around its spine. I pull it out.

The book comes to me, like a lover.

A picture of Nicholas's smiling face is faded in the background, overlaid by what looks like entries to a journal, *Nicholas smiles 6 weeks 4 days; Nicholas rolls onto his stomach 15 weeks, 2 days* and so on. Though babies are all much of a muchness in my opinion, there are certain telltale features whispering that he belonged to our family (though my mother would fret at the use of past tense)—he has Dad's dark Italian eyes, the way they are deep-set like that, Nonna's chin, my mother's neat nose.

I wonder if I was happy when he was born, whether it was exciting to have a baby brother or whether I resented him. I wonder if my mother ever let me hold him. Nonna once told me that I used to sing to Nicholas when he cried. I can't remember.

I flick the book open. *Dedicated to my children—on earth and in heaven. Because a mother's love never dies.*

I haven't exactly read the book. I've done a cursory skim, out of respect to my mother. It's not easy to read without taking some of the stuff personally. As an example, my mother writes that she *always wanted to be a writer.* She wrote poetry throughout her childhood and teenage years. But after she had me, *it was too difficult to follow my dream of being a writer and being a mother at the same time, so I chose to focus on my children.* The way she puts it is that *motherhood got in the way.* Like it was a lorry stalled in the middle of the highway she couldn't manoeuvre round. Even though she's the one who parked the truck in the first place.

I think now of Hazera's mother's face, and how she masked her anguish, the way mothers do. How she didn't chide us for what her daughter had to go through. I think of how she thanked me—thanked me!—when she and Hazera left SISTAA this morning. That kind of love terrifies me. It's like you're volunteering to have the crap beaten out of your heart.

Look at what happened to Nicholas. He drowned when he was only nine months old.

Terrible accident.

In the bath.

Apparently I was with him at the time.

I have no memory—of him, or of that bath.

But in *No Chance to Say Goodbye*, my mother writes on page 54:

*Faith was having a bubble bath with him. Nicholas loved bubbles. He was, I thought, secure in a bath ring, happily splashing. I left the bathroom for a few moments. I couldn't have been gone for more than two minutes. When I returned, Nicholas was submerged under the water. The bath ring had come loose. Faith was happily splashing next to him, oblivious to the fact that her baby brother had just drowned.*

*Oblivious to the fact*—that phrase might as well have been carved into my flesh with a switchblade. I was playing with a rubber duck in the bubbles and he just drowned next to me. If I'd known he was drowning, I could have just reached out and pulled his arms and he would be thirty-one years old today, maybe an engineer, or a musician, even an architect. I could have saved him. It would have been so easy. That's the difference between knowing and not knowing.

But when you're *oblivious to the fact*, drowning looks just the same as splashing.

I sometimes wonder how my life would have turned out had my mother not stepped out of the bathroom on that day.

Would I be a thirty-four-year-old legal counsellor for raped and battered women with a suicidal social worker as a best friend, having to confront a psycho solicitor for getting hard-ons when he cross-examines raped women?

Would I be a hairdresser flouncing alongside Shepard, layering hair and gossiping about men with tight arses?

Or would I, like Libby, be planning a wedding to someone I loved?

Somehow this thought pierces right through me, gouging open a flap. Something terrible seeps into me, filling all my empty spaces. The fullness feels suffocating.

In the bathroom, I strip off my jeans. Standing naked in the bath, I open the packet containing my new Gillete blade. I cut a very neat incision on my right thigh, right next to last week's one which is almost healing. Sanna's. I don't know what to call this one, but it aches and aches, and I bleed and bleed.

And I feel so much better.


'Hello . . . Dad?' I say into the phone.

'Faith?' he says.

'It's me, Dad.'

'Why are you phoning in the middle of the afternoon?' he asks. 'I thought you don't make or take personal calls during the day . . .'

'Yeah, I don't generally, but I'm not feeling so good today . . . so I took the afternoon off.'

He pauses.

'Is everything all right?'

I swallow. 'Everything is just great, Dad,' I say. 'How about you?'

He sighs. 'Things are fine. Work is work. Nothing to write home about, but it gets me through to five o'clock and a glass of sangria,' he chuckles.

I chuckle in reply.

'So . . . Everything okay?' he repeats.

'Yeah,' I say. 'Actually, Libby is really cross with me.'

'Oh,' he says. 'I'm sure the two of you can sort it out. You're both adults.'

'Yes, we are,' I say. 'And Dad?'

'Yes, Faith?'

I clear my throat, 'Isn't it just *great* news about Libby and Chris?'

'It is,' he says. 'It's good . . . We'll have a party . . . it will make your mother happy . . .' he chortles into the phone.

I am holding a wad of tissues over my latest incision. The wad is turning redder and wetter, but I can feel the platelets gathering to make a scab. That's the thing about wounds. Barring the misfortunes of haemophilia, they're so reliable.

My father's voice is soft and gentle in my ear.

'Do you want me to get married?' I ask.

He pauses. He pauses for much too long.

Then he says, with what is too much love in his voice, 'No, my girl. I just want you to be happy.'

'Aren't I happy, Dad?' I ask.

He pauses again.

'No, *mia cara*. No, you're not.'

# 52. elephant

The day my mother came home from hospital with Libby she insisted I hold the baby.

'But I don't want to, Mum,' I said.

'You must,' she insisted.

'Helene . . .' my father ventured tentatively.

'It's okay, Vincent,' my mother said. 'I need her to overcome her anxiety.'

My father looked on helplessly. 'Just give her time . . .' he murmured with the tortured uncertainty of the parental understudy.

My mother propped me up against the couch, with a huge cushion in my arms. She placed Libby, swaddled in a baby wrap, on my knees. Then she let go and stood back. 'Watch her head,' my mother said.

'I can't . . .' I said, gulping for breath.

'Calm down, Faith,' she insisted. 'Nothing's going to happen to the baby . . . I'm here . . . I'm here,' she said patting her body as if slaps on flesh could still the nerves.

'Now just hold that,' she said, as she took a photograph of *Liberty Mae Roberts, one week old, on her big sister's lap.*

Everyone who ever saw that picture in the album always asked the same question: 'Liberty looks so peaceful. Why is Faith crying?'

My mother entrusted Libby to my care more and more often with the strategic vision she had once applied to her games of chess.

'Making friends with responsibility' was the name she gave to my supervising Libby in the backyard, or pushing her on the swings in the park. 'It's not your fault if something happens to her,' my mother always said, which had the same effect as, 'Whatever you do, do NOT think about a pink elephant.'

When Libby started school, I was the one who had to wait for her and walk her home.

On days when I didn't have too much homework, we'd take a short cut through the park so Libby could screech down the slippery dip and have a go on the swings.

'Just keep an eye on her.'

'As long as you know where she is.'

'You're in charge.'

One day, I didn't feel like going to the park and pushing Libby on the swings. Josh was in hospital again and I was anxious to get home to call him and find out how the pneumonia was going and if he needed me to clean out his aquarium. But Libby insisted. 'I'll tell Mum you didn't keep an eye on me,' she said spitefully.

Despite my pulsing guts, which I thought had to do with Josh, I took her to the park.

She ran ahead. I saw the bull-terrier. It was supposed to be on a leash. The sign at the park clearly had a dog with a big red line through it. I knew what was going to happen. I shouted out, 'Libby! Watch out!'

But she ignored me.

\* \* \*

According to his owner, 'Winston had never hurt a flea in his life.' He offered to give us a ride home, but I said 'No thanks, we don't accept rides from strangers'. Libby was inconsolable. I carried her all the way home on my back. She bled onto my school uniform. She needed four stitches in her calf and an anti-tetanus injection.

'Don't worry, it wasn't your fault,' my mother said. About ninety-five times in twenty-four hours.

I had pink elephants dancing around in my head for weeks after that.

# 53. shopping

People are puzzles. Like human sudoku grids with missing numbers. There's no magic to figuring them out. It's logic.

The trick to getting people to believe that cards can magically stick to the palm of your hand is wearing a ring with a toothpick through it, and sliding the card under the toothpick. While your audience is concentrating on 'abracadabra' or 'simsala bim', you're sliding cards between a hidden toothpick and your finger. It doesn't make you a genius or a magician. It just makes you one step ahead of everyone else.

If you know what matters to people, you can get them to do pretty much anything.

Right now, I have Libby on the phone. And this is what I am saying to her—but there is no need to be cynical about it, I genuinely need her help.

'Hi Libby.'

'What do you want?' she quips.

'I need your help.' I am hoping I sound humble.

'What for? You've managed to make yourself miserable all on your own.'

'I've got . . . a . . . I'm going on . . . I'm seeing someone on the weekend.'

There is a long pause.

'Like a man?'

'Yep, a man. I've surprised even myself.'

'Who is he?'

'Someone I met . . . um . . . He's a vet . . .'

'Vets are lovely,' she says. 'They love animals.'

I feel extremely annoyed by this remark. Is it that obvious? Maybe I've really made too much of Caleb's words. Maybe florists love flowers. Teachers love children. I feel deflated. A 'Made in China' sticker is stuck to the bottom of my profound discovery.

'Anyway,' I say. 'I need help with an outfit for tomorrow.'

I close my eyes. I cannot believe I am stooping this low.

'My help?' she asks eagerly.

I manage a small, 'Yes,' with what I am sure is enough enthusiasm in the circumstances.

'Do you want to go shopping?' she asks brightly.

'Uummm, maybe we don't need to go that far,' I say. 'Maybe you could lend me something from your . . . terrific wardrobe.'

'Something of mine?'

'Yes, if . . . if you don't mind.'

'Why, because you'll never wear what I pick out again? Are you not planning on seeing this guy more than once?'

I stop.

'No, I might like to see him again,' I say. 'It's just a first date and I'd like to see how it goes before I commit to a wardrobe.'

248

'That's just your problem, Faith,' she says. 'You have no faith. Why don't you buy something that you will wear again? Why don't you go on the date with the thought that you will see him again?'

For an irritating little sister who's about to make the biggest mistake of her life, she's not a moron.

I concede.

We will go shopping together tomorrow morning after Nonna's hair appointment.

'Can we go for a coffee first?'

'Sure,' I say. 'We can even have a slice of cake.'

'I don't eat cake, you know that!' she giggles. 'I'm getting married.'

'Sorry,' I say. 'How about some celery juice?'

'That sounds divine,' she says.

As I said, once you know your customer, the rest is plain sailing. There's no magic in it.

It's mathematical.

### *Types of abusers*

#### *Type A*
- *never been to jail, law-abiding in most respects*
- *known to the outside world as a 'gentleman'*
- *a bully who won't fight back if confronted*
- *batters when sober*

*Appropriate Action: letter or telephone call to warn him if it happens again, legal action will be taken. Perhaps secure AVO.*

#### *Type B*
- *has had brushes with the law, not afraid of cops*
- *batters when drunk, becomes unpredictable and volatile*
- *could lose temper if confronted*

*Appropriate Action: secure AVO so that if he hits her again, he will be arrested.*

*Type C*
- *has served periods of imprisonment for domestic violence*
- *previous AVOs have been ignored or have resulted in violent outbursts*
- *violence escalates each time*
- *has omnipotent fantasies, fearlessness, coupled with threats to kill her, take children away or kill himself*

*Appropriate Action: work on exit plan from relationship. Secure emergency shelter space. Only then secure AVO, lay criminal charges if necessary.*

Training Manual, page 189

# 54. cake

My mother did not bake for pleasure. This nearly disqualified her in Nonna's eyes as a suitable match for her only son who had been brought up at her apron, mixing flour with his bare hands and peeling tomatoes with a knife most parents wouldn't allow their children to pass to them even with the blade down. To my mother, baking made too much unnecessary mess when life was messy enough and there were lunchboxes to be made each day, meals to be put on tables, laundry to fold. If Nonna hadn't allowed me to mix the mascarpone with the sugar and taste the coffee and whiskey first before drenching the finger biscuits, I'd never have known the laboured delight of homemade tiramisu. It's the patience in handmade things. The way pearls are made, eventually.

My mother refused to indulge me. It was the single evidence of her miserliness.

The only time my mother ever baked was for her Meetings. The house would suddenly be cleaned, vacuumed, cushions plumped on the sofas, and fresh flowers bought for the dining room table. Lilies, mostly, with sprigs of jasmine in spring. And then the house would fill with the smell of something sweet. Rhubarb tart. Plum cake. Date and walnut loaf.

I always asked if I could help her, but she made it clear, 'This isn't a fun activity, Faith. I'm baking for my Meeting.'

Teacups would be laid out on the fresh tablecloth. My mother would even scatter rose petals on the table if there were aging roses in the flowerbeds, which she'd send me out to collect. On the coffee table in the lounge room my mother always made sure there was a box of tissues with a single white tissued mast sticking through the plastic flap.

It started off with just three women. But after several years, the meeting had grown to at least twelve. I can't recall any of the individual women, they seemed to pass through the rooms of our home in a faceless mass, but Sonia I remember well. She smiled a lot, but it was a smile that made you unsure. Sometimes you couldn't be certain whether it was in fact a smile or that thing people do with their mouths before they are about to start crying.

I was always sent out to the back to play. I was never allowed to sit with the grown-ups. Sometimes I'd position myself outside the window to the lounge room. If the window was open, I'd catch snippets of conversation.

'. . . never wanted to live . . .'

'. . . just to know why this happened?'

'. . . ways to go on . . .'

There was always a lot of crying. Serious crying. With quiet pauses, cooing. And then there would be a gathering as all the women got up and huddled around the crier, holding her in a big group hug.

At the end of the meeting, I was allowed to come in and say goodbye to all the ladies. I would take it all in. The red eyes. The smudged eyeliner. The scrunched-up tissues in their hands. The precious half-eaten cake my mother had made, left on the plate. Somewhere in all that I understood that Something Important always happened in these meetings. I knew these women had something in common, I just didn't know what.

Until one day when I was ten and I was in the kitchen peeling an apple for Libby with the potato peeler, trying my best not to let it break. Libby liked the snake that came off the apple as long as it was in one piece.

Sonia waddled past the kitchen on her way back from the downstairs loo. She stopped short when she saw me standing there at the sink, a long twirled ribbon of apple dangling from my peeler.

She gasped. I got a fright. I didn't know what she saw.

And she began to cry.

'I'm sorry, I'm sorry,' she kept on saying over and over again.

'That's okay,' I said. I was used to crying in our house.

'I'm so sorry,' she said, wiping her eyes.

'What are you sorry for?' I asked. I was peeved because her crying had made me lose my concentration and the apple peel plopped to the floor and I was only halfway through peeling the apple.

'You just look SO much like my Mary, standing there . . . so grown-up.'

'Is Mary your daughter?' I asked.

She nodded. Very vigorously. Too vigorously. 'She . . . she was abducted from a shopping centre when she was your age. We found her body in the bushes behind the parking lot out at Cliffdale. They raped her. They suffocated her with her own pink T-shirt . . .' she heaved. 'She was just a little girl . . .'

I stood there looking at Sonia. I knew all about suffocate. Josh and I were practically experts on how it felt not to be able to breathe. But 'rape' I hadn't heard of before.

'Why are *you* sorry?' I asked. 'It wasn't your fault.'

At this, Sonia began to sob so heavily that I felt afraid. Libby began to cry too. It wasn't something easy for a child to look at.

I picked Libby up in my arms and ran towards the door, just as my mother burst into the kitchen.

'What is going on in here?' she asked. She took Libby from me and held her.

'I'm sorry, I'm so sorry . . .' Sonia kept on saying over and over again.

'Let it out, Sonia, just let it out,' my mother soothed. 'It's okay . . . It's really okay . . .'

I stood there, unheld. Ignorance pounding in my veins, the smell of my mother's plum tart rasping in my throat. I suddenly understood—our house was full of mourning mothers. Mothers who had buried their children. My mother invited them into our house and baked for them every month. Ours was a house of tears for lost children. Children that lived in the heart but who did not need lunchboxes made or nag their mothers to bake with them.

Cherry pies and carrot cake should have been for celebrating. Instead they were fertiliser to feed the soil of my mother's grief. In our house flourished a society my mother had created around herself. She borrowed from the sorrow of others to dilute her own loss so that the cathedral of her mourning would always be frequented by a thriving congregation.

# 55. bra

I do not have a wilful disregard for the rules of fashion, as my sister claims. I am certain I don't make an obstinate point of wearing colourless, creepy, shapeless outfits. Libby thinks I dress as I do 'to make a point' or to 'say something about myself'.

I've tried to break it to her that I don't give clothes any thought at all. If my clothes say anything about me, they're doing so behind my back. If I make a 'statement' by wearing jeans and T-shirts, it's one I haven't signed. My sister reads things into clothes the way detectives scrutinise crime scenes. One stray grey sweater and she's made a whole case against me.

For the sake of world peace today, I have decided to put her in charge. I am going to take all the abuse, the innuendos about my sexuality, my repression and my weirdness, in my stride. I have, with calculated effort, refrained from even commenting on the T-shirt she is wearing, which she tells me Chris gave her 'as a joke'. Across her C-soon-to-be-D cupped bust is the rhetorical question, *Who needs a brain when you have these?* I have, as a consequence, excruciating indigestion.

I am standing in a cubicle in a large department store while she passes clothes to me through the two little curtains.

She has insisted that she see *everything* I try on.

I told her I want 'low-key' and 'casual'.

'Leave it to me,' she has said.

I don't see any jeans in the clothes she is passing to me. There are items here with more buttons than is sensible and fiddly bits that I have no idea what to do with—do they hang, do they tie, what kind of management will be required and do I have the training?

This afternoon. The thought of it makes my stomach break out into a clumsy cartwheel.

He left a message on my answering machine this morning saying he'd be at the Crown Street Veterinary Clinic at 1 pm and did I want to meet him there?

I contemplated for about an hour whether that message required a return call to say yes, or whether one is expected to call back in the case of regrets only. I called Nonna, who evidently understands how to get a date. She said, 'Make nice. Say *grazie mille*, see you later.' So I dialled the clinic, and when the receptionist answered, I said briskly and matter-of-factly, 'I'd like to leave a message for Dr Pearson: Faith Roberts will meet him at 1 pm at the clinic, thanks, goodbye.'

So now I've covered my bases.

I've just got to get through this shopping expedition with Libby.

Libby, bright-eyed, is wearing a very hefty diamond on the forth finger of her left hand. '*Jan Logan*,' she whispers. I know that means something, I'm just not sure what. I smile. 'Wow,' I say. It is a word that comes in handy and covers a lot of ground, especially when you're uncertain. Libby's hand gestures have become exaggerated as if her shiny dazzling ring is like a bottle of Moët champagne and cannot be enjoyed in solitude. I am doubled over with gratitude to the middle-aged woman who hands out numbers in the change room when she notices, actually comments on the ring. 'That's a mighty fine stone you got there, honey,' she says. 'Only six items at a time . . .'

Libby billows with bridal expectancy. 'Yes, it is lovely, isn't it? Three carats. Jan Logan.'

'Ya got yerself a good fella?' she asks, handing over the plastic tag.

'Tall, rich and handsome,' Libby smiles.

'No guarantee of good,' the woman mumbles, but Libby has moved on.

Libby passes me clothing in a range of colours I have seen grown people who call themselves The Wiggles and Teletubbies wear. Something she calls cadmium lemon which looks like bright yellow to me. Thistle. Slate. Firebrick. Burnt umber. Deep ochre. Chartreuse. Mint. Cornflower. Viridian. Sea green. I stop. I like sea green. I've never looked at it before as a colour you could wear. It comes in a chiffony-type top. And there is a halterneck in . . . is it . . . cerulean?

'Can you wear this with a bra?' I ask from inside the cubicle.

I take her snort as a no. I don't know whether one ought to go on a first date with a man one potentially likes without the dignity a bra affords. I doubt Caleb will have the opportunity to think in any sort of serious way about my breasts. Besides, they'll only disappoint.

I emerge from the cubicle wearing a pair of chocolate-brown slacks and the sea green chiffon top. It is pretty see-through.

Libby looks at me.

'You know, Faith, you're actually quite . . .'

I wait for it. Ridiculous? A fashion disaster? A walking commercial for bad style?

'. . . attractive,' she says. 'When you're all dressed up.'

'Yeah, I'm pretty revolting when I've got nothing on,' I say.

'No, I don't mean that . . . it's just that you hide all your prettiness . . .'

I roll my eyes at her.

'Prettiness?' I say to her. 'That's got to be a first.'

'What do you mean? You know you're pretty. You're the tall one, with the figure like a bloody ramp model . . . You're the one everyone thinks looks like Carol Sippel.'

I look at her. I can take a joke. But she's not joking. Ramp model? Carol Sippel? 'Who . . . um . . . is Carol Sippel?' I actually ask.

She gasps. 'Carol Sippel . . . the Brazilian supermodel. The one who models for Women Paris?'

I shrug.

'Supreme NY? Women Milan? Select London?'

It is sobering. The realisation that you and your only sister actually speak different languages.

I give her an exasperated smile.

'Anyway, Chris thinks you're very . . . attractive,' she says.

I shuffle.

'That's . . .' I flounder, I flounder some more, '. . . sweet of him,' I manage to squeeze out.

'Attractive in a sister-in-law kind of way,' Libby adds.

'Yeah, yeah,' I say, trying to move right along. 'Look, Libby, umm, I just want to feel comfortable today. I need to feel relaxed if I'm not going to make a complete fool out of myself.'

'Faith, he already knows what work you do, so we're doing damage control right now. We have to counteract his expectations by showing him a bit of sex appeal.'

'I don't feel very sexy,' I say, 'in an outfit that is showing off my bra. I mean, it's *under*wear for a reason, isn't it?'

'That's because your bra reached its use-by date ten years ago,' she says. 'You need new underwear.'

'My boobs haven't grown in the past two decades . . . why do I need new underwear?'

'If I didn't know your IQ,' she says as she disappears into the lingerie section. I'm going to feel like a corsetted poodle today. I know it.

I wonder if Dr Caleb Pearson is out this morning with his twin brother choosing new underwear and shirts for our date this afternoon.

I realise that I *am* ridiculous. Right now he's probably doing mouth-to-mouth resuscitation on a dachshund, or has his hand up a labrador's fanny delivering a litter of puppies. He's just being kind. He's making space for me, the way I should have done for Sanna. Just to get through a rocky patch. This 'date' is just part of his job. He's got to appease people when their animals die. Then I remember that cat wasn't mine. And it's this thought which gives me a flicker of hope that maybe this afternoon has nothing to do with that dead cat and has everything to do with me.

Hopefulness is indulgent. Disappointment, if anticipated, offers the familiar comfort of things that don't pounce on you out of nowhere.

I think about sitting next to Caleb Pearson, the vet with the strong outdoor hands, for an hour in the confined space of a car. It will be nice to drive out into the country, up towards the mountains. I can't remember when I last did. I will try not to think about the vet who loves animals sitting beside me and all the questions I want to ask him, like what kind of animals he likes the best and whether it's true what they say about twins, that they can feel each other's pain.

Libby appears, a smile from ear to ear, carrying what looks like— a lace bikini.

'Bras!' she declares like she's just discovered a cure for AIDS.

In her world, getting me to wear a lace bra is a laudable lifetime achievement. And because there are no crowds or honorary degrees to applaud her effort, I manage to wring out a meek smile.

While she's handing them to me one by one and I am examining myself in the mirror, I ask, 'Have you decided what you're going to do with Gwyneth?'

'Put her down,' she says.

I pull back the curtains to my cubicle. She's got to be kidding. Libby shrugs.

'Kill her?'

'Don't be so dramatic, Faith. She's just a cat, she's six years old, which is six years more than she would have had if I'd left her at the RSPCA. Chris is my soul mate—cat, Chris . . . it's a no-brainer.'

She said it, not me.

## 56. saccharine

'What happened to Sonia's little girl?' I asked my mother. She was standing at the sink washing the dishes, wearing purple rubber gloves.

She stopped scrubbing the frying pan and turned to look at me.

'She . . . died . . .' my mother said. 'You know, like Nicholas.'

'Yeah, I know that. But how did she die?' I asked.

My mother inhaled deeply. 'It was not a very peaceful death . . . It was a difficult death.'

'Difficult like how?' I asked.

'She was hurt,' my mother said.

'Hit?' I asked.

'Yeah, kind of.'

'With what?'

'I don't know, Faith,' she said. 'But a man hurt her really badly.'

'Why?' I asked.

My mother's head wilted on her shoulders. 'It's not a question I can answer,' she said. 'That little girl did nothing wrong, that man who hurt her was a bad man. He had no right to do what he did to her.'

'He raped her,' I said.

My mother looked as if someone had just punched her in the jaw.

'Who told you that?' she snapped.

'Sonia,' I said.

My mother shook her head.

'What is that, Mum?' I asked. 'Rape?'

She did not look up at me.

'What is it?'

She did not answer me. My mother's head was heavy on her neck. When she looked up at me, she said, 'I never want you to know anything about rape,' she said in a kind of whisper. 'If I can ask of God one thing in this life, after all I have lost, I pray that you and Libby will never know what rape is. Some things you just don't need to know.'

She stopped. She wasn't saying any more.

'What happened to the man who hurt Sonia's daughter?' I asked.

'Unfortunately, they never caught him.'

'Where is he now?'

'Far away from us, he can't hurt you . . .'

'How do you know?' I asked.

She smiled at me. 'Some things, a mother just knows . . .' she said sweetly, but that smile made me think of those little white pills she put in her coffee to make it sugary which I once tasted and spat out.

She must have seen the look on my face because then she said, 'He will pay for what he has done, my darling . . . In life, whatever we do, we have to pay the price, if not now, then later. Whenever you do something bad in life, you get caught. Eventually.'

'By the police?' I said.

'Or by God,' she said gently.

I accepted these offerings from my mother gingerly, nervous about where I was going to store them. Lies? Truth? Fairytales?

I went straight to the dictionary and looked up 'rape'.

> *Rape: (n) a type of European plant grown as food for sheep*
> *and pigs and for the oil produced from its seeds.*
> *(v) to have sex with, against the woman's will.*

I still didn't understand.

Sonia's daughter was a ten-year-old girl. Not a sheep, not a pig, not a woman.

# 57. itch

I am so close I could put my hand out and lay it on his knee.

He is wearing khaki pants with pockets, low-slung, and he has an earring in his left ear. I didn't notice that before. My stomach does a perfect tumble turn, like Libby used to be able to do in the water. Men in jewellery. Do I really hate it? I am fixated on the way his hands hold the steering wheel. He has sturdy hands. Hands that hold animals writhing in pain and, just by touch, instil calm. There is a big scar in the space between his left thumb and forefinger, running down to his wrist. Probably a terrier who mistook the firm grip of kindness for viciousness while the doctor was trying to save its life. I want to ask him about it. But we're not on to our wounds yet. We're still in the shallows of 'How's your week been?'

I am sitting in the passenger seat of his truck and we have a cocker spaniel by the name of Nancy sitting between us. I am grateful for her panting presence even though her breath is hot and fuggy and she likes to lick my hand every now and then. Three always takes the pressure off and right now she is distracting me from how I am feeling about wearing a new lace bra that feels like a colony of ants is break-dancing on my back. This morning, while Libby was whizzing through the shoe department for me, I quickly pulled what looked like a blue T-shirt off the shelves with *Dolphins are our only hope* on it. But when I got home and tried it on, it was a little tight. So tight you could make out the outline of my new lace bra. A simple chill or stray thought about strong hands on my breasts would turn my nipples state witness against me. At the last minute, I decided to go with the new bra and the sea green chiffon top. I then threw an old greyish sweater on over the chiffon blouse. I know Libby would be disappointed if she knew. 'What was the whole point of going shopping?' she'd huff. And she'd round it off with a 'You don't really care what I think, do you?' and then the whole retail exercise, sisterly bonding and all, would have been a waste of a Saturday morning when I could have been wrestling a few dating tips out of Nonna.

Libby did take my hands in hers, eye my bitten-down nails and sigh, 'There's no time or point in even trying to fix these—you may as well wear gloves.'

I looked at my hands and had to concede that my fingers don't look very . . . inviting. In fact 'gross' is the word that springs to mind if we eliminate self-esteem as a factor in the choice of adjectives we use to describe ourselves.

'Like what kind of gloves?' I asked her.

'I'm JOKING, Faith, you can't wear gloves on a date.'

'Oh,' I'd said. Now I am incredibly self-conscious about my hands, though Nancy doesn't seem to mind my chewed-down nails.

I stuffed the new T-shirt into my bag. Just in case. I am wearing jeans, and I'm glad for them. Nancy has drooled on my knee a few times. Jeans can accommodate a bit of saliva. Even the odd bit of blood.

'Sorry,' Caleb says every time she does that, scratching her behind her ears. 'Nancy, leave Faith alone,' he chides lovingly.

Caleb has had Nancy for sixteen years. I didn't ask for a history, but he told me anyway. Nancy has some kind of cancer but he doesn't think she's 'ready to die'.

'And when will she be, d'you think?' I asked him.

'She'll let me know. For now, she's still got quality of life. I mean, just look at those eyes, that face . . .' He says this with such tenderness I have to look away.

We pull out of the city onto the highway and soon we are on the open road. It feels as if the sky is calling and the road leads straight to its heart.

'So, Faith,' Caleb says, 'did you go belly dancing with your friend?'

'I did,' I concede.

'And?'

'It does release a lot of tightness in your lower back and hips, like you said.'

'It does.'

'I showed my *nonna* how to . . . undulate.' I think now of Mr Abrahams' beaming smile, covered in cherry plum lipstick. Because Nonna couldn't see, I had to put my hands on her waist and tell her to 'make circles'. I can see now how I may have been overcompensating. It was very disorienting to think of things to say with Nonna's lip prints all over Mr Abrahams' face.

Caleb laughs. I think it is one of the nicest things I've ever heard. I could listen to it and not get annoyed for a very long time.

'Can she undulate?'

'Perfectly . . . and those are eighty-four-year-old hips . . .'

He gives a gentle chuckle.

I am not minding at all that we are in traffic and 'it might take us longer than just over an hour to get there'.

'You'd had a hectic day the other day when I spoke to you,' he says.

'Every day is hectic where I work,' I say.

265

'I'll bet.'

There is silence for a bit.

'What do you get out of your work?' he says.

'Other than recurring stomach cramps and a couple of coffins a year?'

'You're funny, you know.'

'Is that a euphemism for weird?'

'No, you are funny. You make me laugh.'

I look down at my hands. It's hard to look at someone when they say nice things about you. It makes you feel looked at.

'How do you manage the stress of your work?' he asks.

I shrug. I look down at my chewed up nails. 'Not as well as I could.'

'Did you know,' he says, 'that humans, seals and otters are the only animals that cry due to stress.'

'Seals and otters cry?'

'Real tears,' he says.

Seals and otters have always been two of my favourite animals. My affection for them seems enlarged by this revelation.

'What's your favourite animal?' I ask.

'Hedgehogs.'

'Of all the animals in the world . . . ?'

'Yup.'

'Why?'

He turns to smile at me. 'Well apart from the fact that they are almost impossibly tricky to get up close to, they are also innocent of their greatness.'

He loves hedgehogs. I have to look out my window in case he recognises that I find his confession ridiculously irresistible.

'Do you enjoy your work with women?' he asks me.

I don't answer him. I don't want to talk about work today. He senses my hesitation.

'We don't have to talk about it if you don't want to,' he says.

'It's okay,' I say. I inhale. We are out of the traffic now and the passing landscape is so restful on the eyes. It feels lovely to be driven. 'Do you like puzzles?' I ask him.

'I'm all right at crosswords. Not so good at riddles. I get a kick out of figuring out what's wrong with a sick animal that can't tell you where it hurts, is that what you mean?'

'My work is a bit like that.'

He doesn't interrupt. He waits. There is patience in his waiting. Not like 'Tell me something about yourself'. Very different from that.

It is easy to carry on. 'When women come to see me, they're caught in a riddle of love and violence. They can't work out which is which and they can't find their way out.'

He nods.

'People don't want to believe that someone who loves them wants to hurt them. It's a kind of blindness. When someone's just been beaten up, she sees the violence. Right about then we work out an exit plan from the relationship. But then he sends flowers and chocolates, he says, 'I'm sorry, I'll never do it again,' and she can't see the violence anymore, only the love. It's like an optical illusion that changes shape before your eyes. When you remind her about the violence, she gets cross, like you're forcing her to see something that isn't there. It's more complex than that. It's often about money, having nowhere else to go. And sometimes it's just about hope. That the person you love is actually not a monster.'

I exhale. Caleb doesn't speak.

'I don't love my work. I don't even like it.'

Caleb nods. 'It's more complicated than I imagined.'

I sigh. 'Domestic violence makes the Poincaré conjecture look simple—you know, that unsolvable maths puzzle that only geniuses can work out? Rape is straightforward. If she doesn't want to go to trial, it's only because she doesn't want her sexual history paraded, as if any of us would. A raped woman never feels sorry for the creep who did it to her. I don't mind dealing with rape so much. The justice part is easy to figure out.'

Caleb sits quietly while I talk.

'But with battered women . . . we're in the territory of the heart . . . it has no rules. It doesn't listen. It changes its mind. You can't keep the love and kill the violence. You sometimes just have to let it all go. And some people would rather hold onto something rotten, for that one taste of something sweet. People are that desperate for love.'

'Do these women actually love the men who hit them?'

'Depends what you mean by love. People call a bad habit love. You have to be careful of the names you give to things. Because that's what they become.'

'So what happens?'

'Sometimes our clients turn on us. Become hostile witnesses. After we've lined everything up. They tell the judge, "I love him, he didn't mean it, and I was forced to make my earlier statement." We sometimes end up fighting against a woman just to protect her. It gets messy.'

Caleb exhales '. . . so you get no thanks . . .'

I laugh. 'Sometimes you get accused of breaking marriages when you're only trying to help. If you put an abuser in jail, you often end up making a woman destitute, if he was her only source of income. The whole system doesn't really work. We haven't figured out yet how to manage this properly.'

I can feel him taking in my every word, even with his eyes on the road ahead.

'And people don't listen. They can't hear the thing they most need to hear. You tell them, "Don't go back to the house without a police escort." You say it. They nod. You say, "It's dangerous." And then they do something stupid. And you're left wondering, was I clear? Did I do my job? Did I make a mistake?'

I look out the window. Sanna did not look me in the eyes when I spoke. I should have insisted on eye contact.

'What's the best part of your job, then?' he asks.

I sit with his question for a little while. It snuggles in the curve of my lap. He doesn't press me for an answer.

'What I hate most is when I'm right. I see things before they happen, and then when they happen, and I haven't been able to prevent them from happening . . .' I find my sentence has run out before I've finished my thought.

268

'So . . . logically, the best part of your job is when you're wrong?' he asks.

'Yeah . . . when someone inverts my expectations, or I make a mistake because I've thought the worst of someone . . . that is very possibly the best part . . . It's pretty sad, really.'

He nods softly.

'In a way, that's what Nancy's about. I know she's going to die. But I just want to be wrong for a bit—I want to see how far she can get on love alone.'

'Yeah, I get it,' I say.

He turns to look at me, momentarily.

'You're easy to talk to,' he says.

'It's my job,' I say. 'I get paid to listen.'

'You're not working now. Just take the compliment. Suck it up,' he laughs.

I squirm.

'All right,' I say.

'Have you got fleas or something?' he asks.

'Why?'

'Because you're scratching your back against the car seat like a dog with fleas.'

I am not going to tell him that my little sister took me shopping this morning for a new lace bra and a chiffon blouse, which are now driving me nuts. I don't want him to think I went shopping *because of him*. Because then he'll assume I'm going to have sex with him. Which I'm not. I'm not even thinking about sex.

'Nah, I've just got a rash on my back,' I say. I am aware that there are half-truths creeping into our banter, which invariably set us up for a crash later when those chickens of truth come home to roost, as they always do, in the barnyard of our own bullshit.

'What sort of a rash?' he asks.

'I don't know. An itchy rash.'

'You should let me look at it. I'm a doctor, remember.'

'An animal doctor,' I remind him.

'Do you have allergies?' he asks.

'I don't know,' I say.

'To any kind of food?'

'Mangoes.'

'What a bummer.'

'It's okay,' I say. 'But I don't eat meat.'

'You're a vegetarian,' he says, like this is some kind of endearing quality.

'Aren't you?' I ask.

'Nah,' he says. 'There's nothing like a good steak or hamburger.'

'How can you eat meat when you're a vet?'

'I don't eat the animals I treat,' he says.

'That's hypocrisy. I'll bet it makes your patients nervous.'

'Faith,' he says, 'I'm full of horrible contradictions. You might as well get used to them.'

'Do you smoke?' I ask.

'Only when someone sets me alight,' he laughs.

'That is very weak,' I say to him.

'Yeah but I'm trying to make a good impression,' he says.

I put my hand on Nancy's head.

'You're doing okay,' I say.

He takes his eyes off the road again to look at me. And he smiles with all of his face, most especially his eyes.

I try to pretend that that smile hasn't just made my stomach gurgle.

An hour and twenty minutes go by very quickly, as we drive along the mountain road which meanders through hilly undulations and little towns nestled in crevices. Mountains beckon, like whales. Asking for, needing, nothing.

We don't listen to music. We speak. Where we've travelled. Books that changed us. Delivering a breach baby goat. Joshua and his cystic fibrosis.

'We're almost here,' he announces.

He turns off the road and heads down a sand road. It is lush out here, compared to the city which doesn't seem to know what to do with the kindness of rain. We churn up a trail of dust behind us which infiltrates the car. Nancy blinks her eyes and is panting for some water. We pull up outside a beautiful old Georgian house with gables and a huge verandah snuggling around the building. There is a stone chimney on the western side, and lanterns and all sorts of hanging chimes and coloured glass sun-catchers dangle from the rafters.

To the left of the house is an old willow tree with a child's rope swing attached to one of its branches. Beyond, out on a small hillock is a windmill. I feel oddly like I'm dreaming. Children's bright pink bicycles, balls, prams and spades are strewn in confetti-like abandon, evidence of long days of outdoor play.

Nancy takes a single considered leap from the car and trots to the bottom of the stairs where she laps at a bowl of water that has clearly been left there for her and other thirsty animals. Two collie dogs bound up and smell her butt while she is drinking. They then turn their attention to Caleb. He is already down on his haunches to hug them; they are grinning from ear to ear with doggy smiles.

When he stands up, he has dog prints on his shoulder, but he doesn't notice or doesn't mind.

'Nathalie is married to Bill, and they've got two kids,' Caleb says. 'Tanya is three and the baby Kim is six months old—they're both cutie-pies.'

*Cutie-pies.* Who uses a word like that? A man who likes children, that's who, I think. A man who is about to introduce me to his two nieces. Am I going to have to hold the baby???? I suddenly feel besieged. First there was Nancy, then there was a sister, now there's a sister's husband and two children. Children. That was never part of the deal for today. And I'm all decked out in a lace bra and a chiffon blouse. I should always always always follow my instincts. Overalls and gumboots. That's what I should have worn today. I silently curse Libby and her 'fashion advice'.

Caleb must see the look of trepidation on my face.

He comes over to me and slings his arm around my shoulders like we're best mates.

'It'll be fine,' he says.

'I'm not so good with . . . family . . . and children,' I say.

'Nathalie's not scary,' he says. 'She's my big sister, you'll like her.'

As he says this, a woman in her early forties with hair down to her elbows, streaked with grey, appears at the door, a baby attached to her exposed breast. She is wearing a hand-woven garment from a country where people celebrate in Turquoise! Green! Pink! And Purple!

'Hey bro,' she smiles.

Caleb propels me towards the bosom of her presence. And I was worried about an erect nipple through a T-shirt.

# 58. socks

Sometimes when I was alone in my room, I would put a pair of socks into my bra and walk around imagining what it would feel like to have breasts. Real ones. Ones that made an announcement about my gender.

*Great Expectations*. That's what I had for my mammary glands. Lisa had delicious breasts she sported like two corsages. They were radiant. They pushed up against her blouse and made you think of things you'd like to squish in your palm like silly putty.

But instead, the story of my breasts was more like *Waiting for Godot*. It was like they forgot they had an appointment. My biological intelligence needed a bit of extra tuition. I was failing puberty.

At fourteen, when my breasts were just buds, I thought maybe I was being punished.

'Nonna, when are my titties coming?' I once asked her.

'Tette?' she shrugged. 'We wait,' she said.

'How long?' I asked.

'How long is spaghetti?' she asked. 'We wait, we wait . . .'

So I waited. And watched.

And Josh watched too.

He eyed my school shirt with two tiny little bumps like I was Loni Anderson from *WKRP in Cincinnati*.

When finally I lay beneath him and he put his hands under my shirt to feel my breasts, I felt an apology coming on.

'Sorry,' I said. 'They're not very impressive.'

'More than a mouthful is a waste,' Josh smiled, sliding my shirt up so he could see them in all their unimpressive glory.

But from the look on his face, and the way my soft nipples hardened into little plum arrows under his fingers, I saw that size was a vanity and that their beauty lay in the eyes of my beholder.

# 59. stones

I am sitting on a huge sofa made up of different cushions. They are covered in sari material, Persian weaves and Mexican textiles which Nathalie picked up on her voyages around the world when she was a 'hippie'. It makes for a very relaxing sitting experience. Perhaps relaxing runs in their family as a genetic trait. The living area and kitchen form one enormous room which is cluttered—and I mean cluttered in that there is not a single bare surface—with crystals. Large chunks of pink, blue, transparent, green and purple crystals line the windowsills, sit clustered on the coffee table, side tables, and mantelpiece. How this makes me feel is that a lot of the outside has been brought inside. It's bewildering in a soothing way.

In the centre of the room is a huge wooden kitchen table with long benches so that, squashing up, there will always be space for a few more. In the centre of the table is a ceramic bowl toppling with lemons and apples. It's an Aladdin's cave of a trillion bright and wonderful things.

I am holding a mug of homemade gluhwein in my hands. The smell of lemons, orange, cinnamon and cloves kisses my nose. The sweet warmth thaws me. Nancy is sitting beside me. She is sleeping now. In this moment, I can see that she is, despite her best attempts at exuding a playful demeanour, a sick animal. I pat her head. It is so easy to love things that are dying, I reflect. It's the living we have trouble loving.

Caleb has taken Kim from Nathalie and is winding her on his shoulder and talking to her as if she can understand 'There's a lovely girl, what big blue eyes . . .' She obliges and gives a massive burp.

The next thing she has vomited up a whole glob of breastmilk on his shoulder.

'Jesus, sorry,' Nathalie says, wiping it off with a cotton nappy.

'It's no big deal,' he smiles, making big-mouthed gestures at Kim. She gurgles and laughs.

I don't think I knew that babies laugh.

Caleb walks over to me, carrying the baby.

Before he can even ask it, I say, 'I don't hold babies.'

'Don't worry, I wasn't going to ask you to hold her,' he teases. 'See—you were wrong.'

'Yeah,' I say, taking a huge sip out of my mug. Caleb sits down next to me and seats Kim on his lap. She leans forward to try to grab my cup, which I move just an inch out of her reach. She looks up at me with long-lashed eyes. Quizzical.

Nathalie is still walking around with her breast out of her blouse. It is very distracting. Caleb doesn't seem to have noticed. There is a huge drop of breastmilk on her nipple, which is dripping down onto her skirt. I feel a latent sense of panic.

'Don't mind me,' she says, 'I'm just getting dinner ready,' and she potters around in the open-plan kitchen with the original stone fireplace. Fat copper pots and pans hang from large hooks from the wooden rafters.

Caleb sees me looking around.

'This place belonged to our folks,' he says. 'We grew up here.' Kim now has each of her tiny fists wrapped around two of Caleb's fingers. What big fingers you have, I think. My nipples seem to be eavesdropping on my internal conversation. I can feel them straining.

I nod. 'That must have been fun.'

'It was.' Kim lets go of one of his fingers and grabs onto the sleeve of his shirt which she puts in her mouth and begins to suck on.

'Bill's just taken Tanya to the herb garden to get some basil and tomatoes for dinner,' Nathalie says.

I nod. I sip my gluhwein. I snuggle next to Nancy. 'So, have your parents passed away?' I ask.

'Yeah, they died within a year of each other. Dad died of lung cancer three years ago and Mum followed a year later with breast cancer,' Caleb says.

'I'm so sorry,' I say.

Caleb shrugs. 'It's not so sad when people die after they've lived a full life, had kids . . .'

'I guess,' I say.

'We have our own family graveyard, up beyond the orchards.'

'Really?'

'Yeah, my dad's parents are buried there and their parents, and now both my folks.'

'That's very unusual,' I say.

'Yeah, it is.'

'Is that where . . .'

'I didn't bury the cat there,' he says. 'But I buried it just outside the enclosure. In fact, Nat, I might take Faith for a walk up there now, before dinner, if that's okay.'

Nathalie comes back over to us. I can see both her naked size-D breasts pendulously swinging inside her shirt. If this is what Caleb is used to . . .

She takes Kim from his strong hands.

'I hope you eat chicken,' Nathalie says to me.

'Not this one,' Caleb laughs, squeezing me on the shoulder. 'She's a vegetarian.'

'Never mind,' Nathalie says.

'I'm sorry, I don't want you to go to any trouble . . .' I say.

Nathalie stands and looks at me with a baby on her one hip and her hand on the other.

'Now why would you say that?' she asks. 'Around here, we call "going to trouble" making our guests feel welcome. So you go and see where he buried that cat, and leave the trouble up to me. Okay?'

I feel chided as if I were being reprimanded by a headmistress. One who really secretly adores kids.

Out here, the rest of the world feels so far away. Carol. Shaun Hamilton. Hazera. Melissa. Candy and Phoebe. Faint stirrings of time with my father suggest themselves to me as I follow Caleb through the wonderland of the outside. As far as the eye can see, there is just openness. Trees and bush. In the far distance, the containing presence of mountains which are here for the long haul. Towering and sturdy.

On the path through the trees, following Caleb, I encounter lanterns hanging from branches, bird-feeders filled with old fruit and seeds, hanging chimes. We walk over a bright yellow bridge that has ceramic fairies on either end. Everything here—unlike everything about me, according to Carol—invites participation. I feel my chest expanding. I suddenly realise I've left my asthma pump in my bag in the house.

Caleb tried to get Nancy to come with us, but she wanted to rest on the sofa. I could see how this clenched at his heart.

Now he chatters away about how his father's dream was to grow grapes and make his own wine. But that it didn't work out and now they have just a small orchard of orange, lemon and apple trees and a herb garden. There are also some cows and hens so there's always fresh milk and eggs. Oh and the three collies, Abraham, Isaac and Jacob and four . . . maybe five now, cats.

My mind boggles that anyone would voluntarily care for that many creatures. I mean, this is a choice, right?

278

I follow his large stride. He is tall and lean. He hides a lot under his loose-fitting jeans and oversized T-shirt. I suddenly wonder about the tightness of his arse. I curse Shepard. At one point Caleb stops ahead of me. I nearly crash into him. I watch as he lifts the strand of a spider's web with his finger and beckons for me to duck down. I do, and he does too. He then reattaches the web to a protruding twig. I walk ahead now, grateful he cannot see my face. We walk in silence for about fifteen minutes, by which time I am panting. I remove my sweater to reveal my new chiffon shirt.

'Wow, that's a lovely colour on you,' he says, almost involuntarily.

I blush brazenly, still huffing from the exertion of the walk. 'It's sea green.'

'Sea green . . .' he repeats.

I lower my gaze.

'We need to run you,' he says.

'Excuse me?' I say.

'Animals love to run,' he says. 'They do it naturally. They crave the feeling of running.'

'If I ran, I'd pass out,' I say. 'I am very unfit.'

'Don't you like the outdoors?'

'No, I love the outdoors but . . .' and I stop. I've just said 'I love the outdoors.' Can that be true? When did I last do anything in the outdoors? I spend my life indoors. But as I hold this thought, I recognise that I am always happy when I'm outside. I used to go birdwatching with my father. In the Royal National Park. We'd spend hours and hours sitting with binoculars. I didn't want to be anywhere else and I wanted it to go on forever. That was over twenty years ago. Now, my work fences me in a razor-wire of phrases: *Asking for trouble. Dark and deserted places. What was she doing there in the first place?* I've been trying to bring the outside inside. That's what the African violet is all about. I hope that caffeine revived it. I didn't mean to kill it.

'. . . but you never get there?' Caleb finishes for me.

I nod.

'It's not going anywhere,' he says. 'The outdoors is always there.'

'I don't go out very much,' I say.

279

'You're like a mushroom. You like cool dark places.'

'No, I hate cool dark places,' I say. 'I like bright warm places.'

He nods at me. 'And you think I'm full of contradictions,' and he gives me a playful cuff on the arm.

'We're almost there,' he says.

'Thank God for small mercies,' I huff.


To the right of the hand-built stone wall no higher than my waist encircling the family graveyard is a patch of freshly turned earth. A small pile of stones has been put down to mark the spot. And—this is what gets me—a handmade wooden plaque has been nailed to a wooden stake, with these words:

*The cat without a name. For Faith.*

I drop to my haunches. With my index finger I trace the contours of each word. They have been chiselled into the wood. And then blackened with charcoal. I look at my finger. It is black from touching. As I do so, I feel my bottom lip shaking out of control. I blink many times. But it is no good. I cannot stop the tears from pooling in the cups of my eyes, and soon I even see the earth darken in plops where my tears fall.

Caleb Pearson doesn't say anything at all. He is leaning on the stone enclosure watching the horizon, where the sun is heading. And then he is looking at me.

I swear this is the nicest thing anyone has ever done for me.

And I know as he is sitting there looking at me, he knows this.

And I don't know whether I am crying from happiness or sadness, or whether, in fact, it even matters.


When I stand up, he points to a clearing up ahead. There is a path laid out in stones.

'A labyrinth,' Caleb tells me.

'A labyrinth . . . I've never seen one before.'

'Do you want to walk it?'

'I don't know . . . What will happen to me?'

'It's believed to have mystical powers.'

'I don't believe in magic,' I say.

He shrugs. 'It works whether you believe in it or not.'

'Oh yeah?'

'Let's give it a go,' he says, taking my hand.

I like him, so I follow him.


Don't ask me about walking a labyrinth.

You just follow a path.

It goes this way and then it goes that way.

It goes that way and then it goes this way.

No lightning bolts.

Your breasts stay exactly the same size.

The dead are not resurrected.

The mistakes you've made are still there.

Nothing changes.


'So, how do you feel?' he asks me. We are standing at the exact point at which we entered the labyrinth.

'No different,' I say.

He smiles. It's a very knowing smile.

'Come,' he says. 'Got one more thing to show you.'


I'm actually not a morbid sort of a person.

Graveyards don't do anything for me. Since Josh's funeral, I try to avoid them.

But in this case, it was like he wanted me to see. I follow him back up the hill to the family graveyard. He opens the little wooden gate to the stone enclosure. He leads me in. I follow.

There are one-two-three-four-five-six-seven gravestones. I walk from one tombstone to the next, reading to myself, the names, the dates the handful of words chiselled into each tombstone, the little token of words for people who have gone, *a man who loved the world and its beauty; for a woman who cared for all creatures, great and small; lovingly remembered; missed by his wife and his children.*

I usually see this sort of thing coming. But this time I didn't. There is a tombstone of a severed tree-trunk, like Josh's. It usually means only one thing.

*Noah Jonathan Pearson:*
*30 June 1969–14 December 1988*

*Taken from us too soon.*
*Forever in our hearts.*

Thirtieth of June 1969? Ray Osborne's fax: that's Caleb's birthday. That's his twin brother buried there.

I whip my glace to look at Caleb.

He shrugs.

'Yeah . . .' is all he says. Then: 'My twin, Noah, car accident . . . I was lucky to make it . . .'

I don't think. I just move towards him, gently, gently, and put my arms around him and hold him. I feel his arms around my back. He is holding me too. He doesn't cry. I'm the one who's crying. I think I'm whispering, 'I'm so sorry . . .'

When we arrive back at the homestead half an hour later, he is holding my hand. I think he's been holding my hand all this time. But I can't be sure. I don't believe in magic.

But things got a little weird out there.

# 60. binoculars

There are certain words my father never uttered. The notion that 'fuck', 'shit' or 'cunt' could come out of his mouth always struck me as mildly ludicrous much as they dangle like ripe verbal apples for the plucking especially when someone cuts you off in the traffic. It was more than refinement or good manners. It was almost a deficiency, a question of reach.

Some Sunday mornings, to 'give my mother some space', Nonna would take the baby and my dad would pack a flask of hot sweet milky tea and a whole packet of shortbread, and we'd drive, 'to find birds'. Then, we'd sit crouched together for hours in the bush, looking through the special binoculars my mother had bought him for their tenth wedding anniversary, with *The Little Black Bird Book* open on my knee. Every so often I'd look up to find my father staring at me with a look that cupped my face in the palms of its silent touch. 'You're a good girl,' he'd say. That was an almost unbearable surfeit of words for my father. He used them sparingly, as if language was currency and he was saving up for something.

My mother told us she loved us at least three times a day, as if it were a habit of cleanliness or nutritional necessity. 'I love you, my darling,' she'd say when she woke me up in the mornings. 'I love you, Faith,' she'd say, kissing me goodbye for school. 'Don't forget that I love you,' she'd say before kissing me goodnight. She used those words like daily moisturiser, as though vigilant application could hold back time and prevent the perishing of the things you want to hold onto.

If you don't ever hear a word spoken, you start to wonder if it exists at all, if in fact, it is not just an optical illusion.

And if you say a word over and over and over again, it becomes meaningless. A jumble of letters unmoored from its connotation.

Between my father's parsimony of speech and my mother's munificence there was some kind of perfect equilibrium.


In the slow-motion of birdwatching, I would sometimes get a glimpse of who my father had been in a time before fatherhood became a word that ached.

I never saw him lose his temper, perhaps he had none to lose. He was bleached of anger, and at times I feared it had been replaced with something untouchable, unnameable. I knew he wasn't perfect. But his faults seemed so distant, so far-flung, I never wanted the binoculars of my affection to enlarge them. As he aged, as if needing some tiny quirk or human flaw, he grew his one patch of grey hair long enough to comb over his bald head. When the wind ruffled it and blew it back, a tussle of undone vanity, I would look away, never wanting him to seem ridiculous.

Every so often, in those soft patient moments, hoping for birds, I'd catch his eye, and my heart would flutter wildly. I saw something loose, a flap, and I'd be tempted to open it, like the corners of those paper chatterboxes we made at school that told you whether the boy you liked would marry you.

Even though words like 'It will be all right, Dad,' would press themselves up against the inside of my mouth, I knew that whatever was in his eyes couldn't fit into the box of 'all right' and that I couldn't make things mean more than they do. I always hid back inside the binoculars, hoping that when I looked up again from spying on a red-tailed finch, it would be gone so I wouldn't have to be the one to reach out and pull him back to safety.

# 61. neck

A small girl is playing with my hair. She wants to be a hairdresser when she grows up.

She is brushing my newly styled and coloured hair and is sticking all sorts of hairclips and baubles into it. It is remotely uncomfortable and remotely soothing.

Every now and then she comes round to face me and looks at me and laughs. 'You look pretty,' she says to me.

I nod. I think I even smile. Children see things adults can't.

'Just let me know if she's bothering you,' Nathalie says. Thankfully, both her breasts are back in her clothes and, for now, the baby is sleeping.

Tanya tells me that she knows why the old lady swallowed a fly.

I ask her why.

'It was an accident, see?' she says. 'I once swallowed a fly, and it was an accident . . . and it tasted very yucky.' She scrunches her face up.

'Did you swallow a spider to catch the fly?' I ask her.

'No!' she giggles. 'I don't like spiders.'

'Why not?' I ask.

'They're scary.'

'Do you know,' I say, dreamily, 'they are very very clever little insects . . . and they look scary, but they're just ugly . . . and ugly things don't hurt us just because they're ugly.'

'Uncle Caleb is ugly,' she says to me quietly.

'Is he?' I say conspiratorially.

'His tummy is very ugly,' she says, shuddering. 'But he's not scary.'

I feel almost as if I am falling asleep. I have the taste of tomato and basil soup in my mouth. I ate two huge bowls of it, with about four slices of grainy bread slathered in butter as if I hadn't seen food in a month. I didn't eat the chicken, but there were roast potatoes with rosemary and garlic, a salad of wild grasses and nuts, and a home-made pear cake with vanilla ice cream. In addition, Bill, Nathalie's huge husband of the bluest eyes and a lot of chest-hair sprouting out of his checked shirt, poured me a glass of 'the best red in the cellar'. I have overeaten. I have drunk too much. There is a fullness in me that could just burst.

I look over at Caleb, who has Nancy's head on his lap. He is sipping on a cup of chamomile tea, the kind of thing that could be effeminate on someone else. He is murmuring to Nancy, little words, grunts of affection. I understand now what it means to die happy. This dog looks like peace itself.

I can feel it. Here in this room. Right now with a three-year-old's fingers in my hair. I want to call my dad. I want to stand up and declare, 'I am happy.'

But I don't know if this is my happiness to keep, or whether I am just borrowing it from this family.

Even with all their losses—planted in severed tree-stump tomb-stones—there is still a joy here. I tasted it in the fresh tomatoes. My

287

hair follicles are twitching with it. A seeping, inescapable warmth unbattered by things that should never have happened.

I don't want to leave, but I fear I may want this more than I can bear.

'I'm ready when you are,' I say to Caleb.

He looks up at me. 'So soon?' he says. 'Since it's so late, don't you think we should just sleep over and leave first thing in the morning?'

Panic surfaces in me.

'I haven't brought any pyjamas.' I realise as I say this how foolish I sound.

He looks at me and shakes his head with a grin.

'It's up to you—it's a long way back. We can leave first thing.'

Nathalie smiles.

Caleb smiles.

Something billows in me, a wave of fear gathering every instinct I have come to call my own. But then, something solid dives clear through and I hear my voice from far away, as if it were someone else saying, 'Yeah, okay.'

Everyone has gone to bed. Everyone except Caleb and me. He is sitting on the huge sofa. I am reclined in a huge easy chair, in my socks.

Now that the wine is starting to wear off, I have—no, not butter-flies, but a swarm of wasps in my stomach.

Nathalie left us some blankets and cushions which she plopped on the couch before saying, 'Goodnight, sweet dreams,' kissing Caleb on the top of his head and trundling off to bed. I've always scorned contentment as unfortunate and unoriginal, something settled for, not claimed. But here, it feels oddly miraculous. Not like Da Vinci veneers. But the way that word can bring you to the verge of unex-plained tears.

Suddenly silence shifts its way between us. Now that it's *that* time of night. I so don't want awkwardness to take over from the ease and the softness of the past few hours, but I can feel myself getting odd.

Caleb looks up at me. 'Don't stress,' he says gently.

'How do you know I'm stressing?' I ask.

'I'm a vet, remember. I work with nonverbal cues. And besides, anyone with fingernails bitten down like that is stressing way too much.'

I tuck my hands under my bottom. Libby was right. I should have worn gloves.

'Why do you bite your nails?' he asks me.

I shrug. But I don't shrug his question off. I pull my hands out from under my bottom and look at them. They look as abused and unloved as the women that stream towards me day in and day out. Some of my fingers actually ache from where I've gnawed them.

'To get to the pain before anyone else does,' I say.

Caleb gives me a look I find hard to interpret. He nods.

We sit quietly for a while.

'I'm not having sex with you,' I say before I have a chance to think.

'Okay,' he says. He looks relieved. Maybe that was just the stupidest thing I could ever have said.

'I just mean . . . not tonight . . .'

'That's okay,' he smiles. 'Anyway, when you get to know me, you might decide you don't want to have sex with me at all.'

'Really?' I ask him. 'Why?'

'Aw . . .' he trails off. 'I'm not as together as I'd like to be . . .'

'Well, that's a relief,' I say. 'Because neither am I.'

'Two fucked-up people . . . what chance do we have?' he smiles.

'I object to that description of me. I am only partly fucked up. I think the most fucked-up people are masquerading as normal.'

'Now that is true,' he says.

'My sister Libby is getting breast implants as an engagement present from her fiancé. Is it just me or is that seriously fucked up?'

'That is seriously fucked up,' Caleb says.

'If I told her that, she would say, "Faith you are so WEIRD." And that's the word she uses when she's feeling affectionate towards me.'

Caleb cocks his head to the side and grins beneath his beard.

'If someone asked you to put her cat down because her fiancé was allergic to cats, would you?'

Caleb grimaces. 'Not me . . . but there are vets who will do it.'

'Really? Isn't that like . . . illegal?'

He laughs. 'No, animals never come first . . .'

'Would you ever have highlights put in your hair?'

'What?'

'Highlights, you know, bits of colour they put on your hair at the hairdresser. With tinfoil.'

'You're joking, right?' he says.

I hope he can't tell how much I like him in this moment.

'You try so hard to be unlovable, don't you?' he says. 'Like a hedgehog.'

'No, I'm unlovable without even trying,' I say.

'What do you mean?'

'Just that I can understand that you don't want to have sex with me.'

'I didn't say that . . . *you* did,' he reminds me.

'You didn't have to . . . I can feel it,' I say.

'What can you feel?' he asks.

'That you're not attracted to me. And it's really okay. I don't expect you to be. You did a really nice thing for me, burying that cat and bringing me out here, it's really been very kind of you.'

'You're wrong,' he says.

'About what?' I ask.

'There's a lot about me you don't know, that you can't see.'

'Like what?' I ask.

He sighs. He turns his eyes to the window. 'I have a horrible scar under this beard,' he says.

'Do you think someone like me would be scared of scars?' I laugh out loud.

He looks at me. Suddenly serious. I stop laughing. Moments pass. I think I am holding my breath.

And then, without any warning, he lifts his T-shirt to reveal a series of scars down his torso, including a huge surgical scar from his bellybutton up to his chest. 'I lost a kidney, needed bowel and bladder reconstruction and my windpipe was punctured . . . the car accident . . .' he says.

I look at his ravaged body. If ugly things hurt my eyes, I wouldn't be able to look at it.

'You *are* lucky,' I whisper.

I stand up and cross the floor to the couch. I crouch down and look at his scars. His body tells a story. Metal. Glass. Scalpels. Stitches. All that history is etched there.

'Can I touch?' I ask.

He shrugs.

Gently, I reach out and put one of my unsightly fingers on his scar. He shivers. And then, as if I were tracing a line on a window-pane after the rain, I run my index finger all the way up and all the way down. Beneath my jeans my row of scars throbs, each one in its own special way. What I love about scars is how the skin that grows back is numb. You have to sacrifice feeling for healing. I then put my hand flat against his chest. I feel his heart beating under my fingers. He puts his hand over mine.

He pulls his T-shirt down again and gives me a hand up to sit next to him.

Now I shiver.

'Was it that bad?' he asks me.

'It's pretty graphic,' I say to him.

He nods. 'Hard to feel sexy when you've been stitched together.'

'It's harder to feel sexy when you're dead,' I say to him. 'You're lucky.'

He nods again. I don't know why but I shiver again.

'Are you cold?' he asks me.

'No, I think I'm nervous,' I say.

'Are you sure that's not disgust?'

'I see hundreds of scars every week,' I say.

'Not on people you've decided you're *not* going to have sex with,' he says.

'True . . .' I say.

'Don't be nervous,' he says.

'Okay, I'll try not to be.'

'Can I put my arms around you?' he asks.

'I'm not sure,' I say.

'Okay, I'll wait,' he says with his hands folded in his lap.

'Okay, you can,' I say.

He puts his arm around my shoulders. This just makes me shiver more.

And he leans into me and asks, 'Can I just smell your neck?'

'Is this vet humour?' I ask him. 'You've been hanging around with dogs for too long,' I say. 'Besides, aren't you supposed to ask if you can smell my butt?'

He laughs. 'Yeah, I'm warming up to that, but I figured I'd start with your neck.'

And like that, he folds his face into the space between my ear and my neck and he gently breathes me in.

'You have the most beautiful green eyes,' he whispers into my hair. 'Like nature was showing off.'

I stop shivering.


Tyler Holden aside, I have never actually wished someone would kiss me.

But now, with Caleb's lips this near, I know what it feels like to really want someone to kiss you. It starts shy, and gains courage in the quiet space between breaths, a mounting wish for a gap to seal, and heal, like a new skin.

To wish for something so small feels so big.

# 62. scalpel

'Do you want to listen?' the doctor smiled at me.

I shook my head.

'Go ahead, listen to the baby's heartbeat,' he encouraged.

My mother beamed at me from her position on the examination table. 'Go on, Faith, listen . . . what can you hear?'

I allowed the doctor to put the stethoscope pieces into my ears. He placed the stethoscope on my mother's swollen stomach.

My own heart was beating so loudly, I could barely hear the galloping pulse in my ears.

'What does it sound like?' my mother asked.

'Like horses,' I said. 'Lots of horses, galloping on the sand.'

My mother put her hand on my head. 'My precious girl,' she said.

I took the stethoscope out of my ears. 'It's very noisy,' I told my mother. 'It sounds like more than one baby.'

My mother laughed nervously.

'No, it's only one,' the doctor smiled reassuringly.

'Phew,' my mother chuckled. 'I don't think I could handle twins.'

'So what do you want? A baby brother or a baby sister?' the doctor asked me.

'I want a dog,' I told the doctor.

'A dog?' the doctor smiled.

'Yes, I want a dog called Toto.'

'Well then, you're going to be disappointed,' the doctor said, feeling along my mother's belly. 'You're nicely engaged, it shouldn't be too long now.'

'What's that?' I asked, pointing to a scar under my mother's belly.

'It's a scar, where the baby comes out,' the doctor said.

I looked at my mother for confirmation. She nodded.

'You didn't want to come out the way other babies come out, so the doctor had to cut my tummy open.'

I looked horrified. 'With a knife?'

'A special knife called a scalpel,' the doctor said.

'Did you bleed?' I asked my mother.

'A little bit . . . but the doctor stitched me up.'

'Did it hurt?' I asked.

'Not much, because the doctor gave me medicine to take the pain away.'

I touched the scar. It felt smooth.

'That's *your* special scar,' my mother said. She said it proudly. But I didn't hear that. I wondered how you could love something that had made you bleed and need stitches.

Something that had left its mark on you, seared you for life.

294

# 63. brother

I have a bunch of humble jonquils in my hand. They don't take up much space but their scent is redolent with the outdoors. I haven't called to say I'm coming over. I'm doing a 'pop-in'. Given the results of my last pop-in, I am prepared for any manner of surprise.

'Sweetheart,' my mother exclaims as she opens the door. 'This is a treat! Are those for me? Oh you darling girl, I *love* jonquils,' and she buries her face in them. Babies and flowers always make people happy. It's a fact. I notice these things. She takes them from me and gives me a peck on my cheek.

'I like your new blouse,' she says, winking.

'Libby chose it for me.'

'Yes, she told me you went shopping together yesterday. That is wonderful. You have no idea how much joy it gives me when my girls play nicely together.'

She ushers me into the living room. Dad is reading the Sunday papers.

'Hello,' he says dropping the paper down long enough to give me a quick brisk smile. 'Feeling all right, are you?'

'I'm . . . great, Dad,' I say.

'That's good,' he says. 'Work stressing you out too much still?'

'Work? No. I haven't really thought about work this weekend.' As I hear myself say this, I feel a lightness. Like you get when you sip freshly squeezed juice and your body sucks it up.

'And how's Carol?' my mother asks, arranging the jonquils in a little cut-glass crystal vase.

'Mad,' I say. 'Sad, too.'

'I don't know where you find them,' my mother says.

'Actually, they're everywhere,' I say.

'Who?' my mother asks.

'Fucked-up people,' I say.

'I suppose you're right, my love, it's just that some of us conceal it better than others.'

I nod. 'I believe Libby is getting breast implants from Chris as an engagement present.'

My mother holds up both her hands and sighs. 'I know, I know . . . she's just going to have to figure it out for herself. There's no point in getting worked up over it. It's her journey, her body and she has to find her peace.'

'Do you mean you also think it's fucked up?'

'I'm trying to avoid using judgemental language,' my mother says.

'But it is fucked up?' I ask.

My father clears his throat. He doesn't like foul language. It's 'unbecoming' which is one of those remarkable words that does not mean what it sounds like: to disappear.

'It's her choice,' my mother says. 'I think she's got beautiful breasts, but she has to love herself enough to own her own body.'

'I'm . . . the wedding . . . the outfit . . .'

'We have to support her, my love. We have to. Don't be jealous.'

I know she means this in the nicest way.

'I'm not.'

'It's perfectly normal to feel jealous,' she smiles.

I shrug.

'Your time will come. As a mother, I just know that is true. So . . . to what do we owe the pleasure of your company this morning?' my mother asks, draping her suspicion with magnanimity.

'I just felt like coming over,' I say.

'Are you . . . all right?' my mother asks, a small tone of alarm creeping into her voice.

'I'm fine,' I say.

'You're not pregnant or on drugs?' she asks.

I shake my head.

'Because you know we're here for you . . . no matter what.'

'I know,' I say.

'So will you stay for a bite of lunch?' my mother asks. 'I've made a gorgeous waldorf salad with the crispiest green apples and these heavenly organic walnuts.'

'I will,' I say.

And I do.


After lunch we are sitting on the lounges in the sunroom. I am thinking about this morning when Caleb dropped me off at the Crown Street Veterinary Clinic.

'Thank you,' I said. 'I had fun.' 'Fun' sounded foreign in my mouth, not to mention ridiculous given that we spent a lot of time standing at gravesites.

'You're welcome,' he said. 'Me too, by the way.'

I wanted him to gather me up in his arms and maybe even kiss me, even though I hadn't brushed my teeth because I hadn't packed a toothbrush. I gargled with toothpaste this morning while little Tanya stood and watched me in her Care Bears nightie. She smelled of milkshake. Mornings are awkward. Is it the light? Is it something

297

about a new day? Maybe it's the smell of eggs frying that scrambles the brain and makes you think: Did I dream touching his body? Were there scars or did I just make that up? Were those his lips on my cheeks, was it really him who said, 'God, but you're beautiful . . .'? Dawn is a thief, robbing us of the inches we cross in the weary moments before sleep. It's as if that holding never happened. But I know it did. I know it did.

As I fumbled for my bag in the car, I noted that in just under twenty-four hours I had no need to use my asthma pump. That is a first in about four years.

But he didn't. Kiss me. For one thing, Nancy was in the way.

I patted Nancy on the head. She licked my hand.

'Okay then . . .' I said.

I opened the door.

He didn't grab my arm and beg me to stay with him.

He let me go. Just like that.

So I stepped out of his truck and walked over to my car.

He waited for me to get into my car. To start the ignition. He waited for me to pull off. Only then did he hoot and drive off in the other direction.

As I lie there on my mother's lounge I think to myself that

1. if he really liked me
2. if he wanted to see me again
3. if it is true that I have the most kissable lips and I am a Carol Sippel (whoever she is) lookalike

he would have kissed me. Wouldn't he?

I wonder if I will hear from Dr Caleb Pearson again. Probably not. I think of his breath on my neck. Maybe I will hear from him. I don't feel so sure about things this morning.

As I think this I notice my mother has a notebook and pen with her, as she always does, and she is furiously scribbling away.

'What are you writing?' I ask her.

'This and that,' she says vaguely. 'Notes for my next book.'

'What's it about?' I ask.

'Mothers and daughters,' she says to me.

'Really?' I ask, sitting up. I don't like the sound of that at all. 'What about mothers and daughters?'

'I don't know yet—that's what I'm figuring out,' she says, smiling.

I lie back. She continues to scribble away.

I sit up again.

'What is it that you're trying to figure out?'

She sighs and looks up at me from above the rim of her glasses. 'The dynamics . . .' she says vaguely. 'The expectations, the unspoken agendas, the hidden truths . . .'

I lie back again. Caleb's breath on my neck. The warmest of stillnesses. A pulsing softness.

'What expectations?' I ask.

She sighs again. 'Faith, it's really difficult to concentrate with all your questions. I'm brainstorming a few ideas, it's nothing to panic about.'

I think at some point he pressed his lips to the spot in my throat where Josh's pendant used to sit. I have checked my car. No one at SISTAA has responded to my email. It's lost.

'I don't want you to write about me in a book,' I say to her, sitting upright now.

My mother removes her spectacles. She coughs gently. 'My love, that is not up to you, is it?' she says. 'And I'm not writing specifically about you or Libby or anyone. I'm writing generally.'

Too much of my own history I've read about in the books my mother writes. Is it normal? What's wrong with a conversation?

'I would prefer it if you didn't write about me—even generally,' I say.

My mother purses her lips.

'Is everything all right, Faith? Work? Carol? You seem a little . . . on edge?'

'I'm good,' I say. 'Actually better than I've been in a long time.'

'You know if you're depressed, we can talk about it.'

'I'm . . . not.'

'And if it gets really bad, I can chat to Dr Steinberg. A short dose of antidepressants can just get the chemical balance right . . . No need to suffer in silence . . .'

'I'm really not. I would just prefer not to have a book written about me.'

'Sweetheart . . .' my mother starts.

'I really would,' I say. 'I'd rather you . . . talked to me . . . if you have things you want to say.'

My mother smiles. 'I always say what I need to say . . . it's not that. I write books for a living, you understand that, darling? I know you do. You wouldn't deny me that, you're not the selfish kind . . . Not a selfish bone in your body, isn't that true, Vincent?'

My father harrumphs from behind his newspaper.

'You are kindness personified . . . that's your problem, you take on everyone else's pain. You need to protect yourself.'

'I'd rather find out what you think . . . if you just say it,' I say to her.

My mother drops her head. 'I don't think you're hearing me, my love. I've said everything I need to say.'

My father ruffles the sports pages to let us know that he is not liking the way the conversation is going.

'Maybe you think you have, but—'

My mother lets out a small laugh. 'Of course I have. I never keep what I'm feeling from you.'

I look at my mother. At the little lines around her eyes. The textured colours of her irises that ebb and surge as the light of her emotions dance. My mother has spent her life spreading her love like an endless astroturf of vocalised affection, so that no matter where Libby and I fall, we've always landed on its cushioned safety. What does it feel like underneath and who is she protecting? I wonder. In that moment, when she knew, really knew, understood in that impossibly unalterable way that her little boy had died and there was nothing she could do to change that brutal fact, did her face change, like Hazera's, crumpled, broken, as if the bones forgot where they belonged? Could she ever feel love without the violence of loss mottled into it, a battered woman caught in a cycle with no way out? She changed. She must have. But she pretended otherwise.

'Why did you stop playing chess?'

My mother looks at me quizzically. She straightens her back, cocks her head.

'I . . . I . . . lost the desire . . .' she says. 'I just stopped wanting to.'

'Did it seem . . . frivolous?'

'I guess I never thought about it like that . . . Yes, maybe it did.'

When my baby brother died, the mother I knew died too.

I fiddle with a piece of my hair that is glorious with burgundy. Something is swirling in me, gathering a momentum. I am paddling in the ocean of nameless things. I grasp at something.

'You never asked me for your black queen back. Remember, you gave it to me . . . before you went away?'

'Did I?' she smiles awkwardly. 'I don't remember that.'

She must see my face fall.

'I . . . there was so much going on . . . Faith, I just can't remember.'

I swallow. I've been waiting for so long for something that was never going to happen. She's forgotten.

'Do you remember that bird I found outside when Libby was a baby? It had fallen from its nest . . .'

She shrugs. 'I'm sorry, my love.'

'I wanted you to take me to the vet. But you said that once a human hand had touched it, the mother would kill it.'

'That's what happens in nature,' my mother says.

'You helped me bury it. In the garden.'

'Did I?'

I nod.

'I'm sorry,' she says. 'I was . . . distracted.'

I press down on my thigh. My muscles ache with gladness from the exertion of yesterday's walk with Caleb. The *outdoors is always there*. It's not going anywhere. Nothing can keep me from it.

'Did I keep you from your writing?' I ask.

'No! Why would you say that?'

I shrug. 'I read it in your book.'

My mother sighs. 'You shouldn't take that the wrong way . . . I always knew I wanted to write . . . It was difficult to juggle being a mother, a wife, and trying to fit writing in . . . There were priorities, you, you were my priority, at the time. You'll see, when you're a mother, it's just hard to fit everything in.'

'And then, when Nicholas died, writing became your priority?'

'No, no, no, darling. I just had to write. It was my way of surviving.'

'Did it make you feel better?' I ask.

'It helped,' she says softly. 'I was able to move on.'

She puts her notebook and pen down in her lap and takes off her glasses.

'Losing a child was a life-defining experience for me,' she says. 'But, having children too . . . having you, Libby . . . that has meant everything to me.'

I look at my hands in my lap. Hands that pass a box of tissues across my desk each day. Libby's right. I should wear gloves. Miraculously, Caleb didn't seem to mind my hands.

'I don't remember Nicholas,' I say quietly.

'You were so little, my love, how could you?'

I look up at the photos on my mother's wall. Three portraits of her children. Here on earth, and in heaven.

'I was only three . . . I'm sorry, I didn't realise . . . in the bath . . . if I had . . .'

My mother inhales, 'No, no, Faith . . . I have never blamed *you* . . . God, no, not you!'

'But I was . . . oblivious . . . oblivious to the fact . . . that he was drowning . . .'

'How could you know? You just thought he was splashing . . . I didn't blame you,' she whispers.

Suddenly I find that I am shivering. My body is jiggling from the inside. I am cold and hot and there are tears streaming down my face. 'You didn't have to, Mum,' I say, softly. 'I did that all by myself.'

'It wasn't your fault,' she says. 'It wasn't.'

She stands up and comes over to where I am sitting. She sits down next to me. 'Shh,' she says. 'It wasn't your fault.'

'But if I had just . . . reached out for him . . .'

'You didn't know. It wasn't fair for me to leave you alone in the bathroom.'

302

She sits beside me and puts one arm around my shoulders. The other she puts on my hand. I have never noticed before, but we have the same hands. Long fingers, a thick vein beneath the ring finger. My mother turns my hand over and clasps mine in hers. Her breathing shudders. I look up at her.

'I should never have left you alone in that bath,' she says softly. 'I'm so sorry.'

I nod.

My mother inhales.

'I have had to work so hard to forgive myself for stepping out of that bathroom for two minutes . . . That's all it took, you know . . . two minutes.'

We sit quietly. I am underwater with my eyes open. Everything is blurry and I am holding my breath.

My mother lifts my hand and looks at my nails. She kisses each finger. One at a time.

'Don't you dare blame yourself,' she whispers.

My hands feel good held in her hands. She has strong hands, my mother. They warm mine. Mine are warming hers too. The light is coming through the water, I can make it. I break the surface. 'Did I like him, Mum? Was he a . . . cutie-pie?'

She smiles. There are tears swelling in her eyes.

'Oh yes . . . You're the one who nagged and nagged for me to have a baby. You so wanted a little baby brother or sister.'

I wish I could remember that.

'You used to hold him and sing to him, "Somewhere over the Rainbow". You loved rainbows. He always stopped crying when you did that. He liked your singing. And you'd help me bath him. Sticky Nicky. That was your name for him, because he was teething and used to dribble all over you. You loved him.'

I loved him. I loved my little brother. I hold on to those words, I tug at them, they fall loose and I gather them up.

'And then after he died, you used to ask me, "Where's Sticky Nicky gone?" and I'd tell you he had gone to a better place. And you used to say if you were good, could you also go to a better place with him?'

I smile. *I loved my baby brother.*

'And I said that if you went too, I'd have no reason to live anymore . . . that I needed you more than Nicky did, that he would wait for you . . . but without you, I'd be lost . . .'

I reach for my mother's face with my eyes.

*She needed me. Without me she'd be lost.*

'Then when I had Libby, I thought you would transfer all the love you had for Nicholas to her.' She sighs and rakes her fingers through her hair. 'But that's unfortunately not how it worked out.'

'I didn't like her?'

'You told me to send her back and get a dog instead. When I tried to breastfeed her, you would hit her on the head.' My mother gives a dark little chuckle. 'Who could blame you?'

'But we're getting on better now,' I say to her.

'Yeah, it's only taken twenty-eight years,' she smiles. She sits back and looks at me. 'That colour really suits you,' she says. 'You look gorgeous.'

She *needed* me.

'I've met a vet,' I say.

'Really?' my mother smiles.

'He's . . . kind of fucked up too.'

She reaches out to touch my face. 'Everyone has pain,' she says. I watch a tear roll all the way down her cheek and hang on for a moment at her chin before it plops onto her trousers, leaving a little mark. 'But the human heart can endure a great deal . . . more than we can ever imagine . . .'

I squeeze her hand. I feel the bones beneath her skin. Her Estée Laudered palms. The weathered sadness in her fingertips.

'How do you . . . know . . . if . . . someone is not going to hurt you?' I ask her.

She shrugs. 'You don't . . . you never know, really. Loving someone is a choice you make. Then you have to live by your choice, and work hard every single day to make sure your choice was the right one.' She turns to look at my father, still hidden behind his newspaper. 'I wanted your dad to be the right one, but it was only when you were born and I held you in my arms for the first time, that I knew he was. That's why I called you Faith. You gave me faith in love.'

I feel my body heaving. A little sob comes out of my throat. That's the nicest thing I've ever heard about me. Maybe even nicer than Josh's 'perfect'.

*Baby Nicholas. Taken from us too soon. Forever in our hearts.*

'And Mum . . . ?'

'Yes, Faith?'

'What was so important that you left us alone in the bathroom?'

My mother bites her lower lip. My father puts his newspaper down and looks at us.

I don't see it coming. But a gasp breaks out from my mother's mouth and she stifles it with her hand. She is breathing very hard, in ragged breaths, and for a minute I think maybe she is having some kind of seizure.

It is my father who speaks.

'She went outside to have a smoke,' he says.

# 64. bubblegum

'It wasn't me.'

My mother shook her head at me. She stood with her hands on her hips, in a stance like a roadblock.

'I'm sorry, Faith, but you have to own up. Those were your father's special binoculars. They cost me a fortune.'

'I didn't take them, Mum,' I said. 'I'm always very careful . . .'

I had taken them on previous occasions, but I'd always asked. The way Dad said I should.

'Tell me, who else in this house ever uses them? Just tell me—did you drop them and put them back? Did you think no one would notice?'

I shrugged. She was right. I was the only one who ever used them. Rainbow lorikeets sometimes came to the plum tree in our back garden to feast, and through my father's binoculars I could see exactly where a feather of midnight blue on its belly gave way to a bright orange and then to an emerald green.

'Telling the truth is very liberating,' my mother said. 'I will be very disappointed in you . . . It says a lot about a person, if they can take responsibility for what they have done, people respect them more, not less.'

I looked at her helplessly. They had cost her a fortune.

'Are you ready to tell the truth?' she asked.

I sighed.

'I want you to go away and think about it, and when you've decided to tell the truth, you come out and apologise and we will talk about it then. You can start saving your pocket money to replace them.'

My mother turned and walked away down the passage.

From the doorway of my room I could see Libby watching, she was climbing the doorframe of her room, legs and hands on either side like a spider, blowing enormous bubbles. She was the president of the Bubblegum Club at school, and officially the very best bubble blower. Twenty-seven kids in her year had signed up to be part of the club, an honour that could only be bought with a pack of Bubblicious donated to the president. As soon as my mother passed her room, she fell back down to the floor on her haunches and darted back into her room. From behind her closed door, I could hear the snap of bubbles.

Back in my bedroom, I flopped on my bed.

Downstairs I could hear my parents bickering.

'. . . make a fuss . . .' my father was saying.

'. . . trying to teach her responsibility . . .'

'. . . not a big deal . . .'

'. . . let her get away with things . . .'

I put the pillow over my ears.

An hour later I came downstairs.

I looked at my father. He lowered his eyes.

'I'm sorry, it was me,' I said.

My mother smiled. 'See, don't you feel better now that you've owned up?'

I shrugged. 'I guess.'

'Now what did you do with them?' she asked.

'I . . . I must have . . . dropped them.'

My mother's smile was victorious.

'Well, since you have owned up and accepted responsibility for what you've done, you only have to pay half to replace them . . . Does that sound like a fair deal to you?'

'Sure.'

My mother came up to me and put her arms around me. She gave me a hug. Over her shoulder I caught my father's eye. He looked defeated. He did not look like someone happy to see the guilty confess. But like me, he didn't have a way of proclaiming what he knew. Innocence is mute that way.

## 65. fence

They are extravagant. The kind you get when someone dies. I don't have a prejudice against flowers per se. They're lovely out in nature, wild and copious. The bunch of flowers on my desk is large enough for me to hide behind should I need to for any reason. It is Monday morning and I am at work in my tight *Dolphins are our only hope* T-shirt. I am also wearing my new lace bra, the outline of which you could make out through my T-shirt if you were paying that sort of attention.

Barbara has put them on my desk because 'there sure as hell ain't room for them anywhere else'. I battle to squeeze past the azaleas and carnations and lilies and other spiky bits sticking every which way. They belong in hospitals and funeral parlours. I scrounge around for a note.

*For Faith, Our Angel*
*Thank you for your help.*
*We will never forget you.*
*May God bless you and keep you.*
*May he cause his light to shine upon you.*
*Frederick and Charliena Bergeron*

I put the note in my drawer with all the other letters.

Carol comes into my office without knocking.

She peers at me from behind the flowers.

'What the hell are these for?'

'Compensation for murder,' I say.

'Who did you murder this time?' she asks.

'Some twenty-six-week-old foetus that just happened to end up in the wrong womb at the wrong time . . . possibly the spawn of a rape.'

'Jesus, you've done it a favour,' Carol says. 'Don't beat yourself up about it. They're very pretty, must have cost a fortune.'

'You can have them for the comfort room.'

'Are you serious?'

'Yeah, I can't do my work with them here—they're taking up the whole office.'

'Well, I won't say no.' She leans in over the desk and looks at me. 'He's gone away on business.'

'Who?' I ask.

'Who?' she repeats. 'Shaun.'

'Really?' I say.

'Yeah, business.'

'We can't read anything into that.'

'Really? When was the last time he couldn't come and help us out because he'd gone away on business?'

I ponder this. Never, actually.

'It's guilty behaviour. He's buying time, he must know that we know. He must know that Hazera would have told us,' Carol whispers.

'You think?'

310

'Yeah, I do.'

'So when will he be back?'

'The secretary couldn't say. She says he's gone away for a trial.'

'That's good, it gives us some time to figure out what to do.'

'What if he's just taken off, never to be seen or heard of again?'

'Then that solves all our problems,' I say.

Carol strokes the stem of an azalea. 'The sick fuck.'

'I've already asked Ray Osborne to do some investigations for us. I want to find out everything about Shaun Hamilton, his full history, where he went to school, where he grew up, who he's dated, the whole picture.'

'What do you think you're going to find?'

'There's got to be something there we've missed . . . Some of it just doesn't make sense.'

Carol takes hold of the pot of flowers and lifts it off the desk.

'And I've been meaning to say . . .'

'Yes?'

'I didn't mean all those things I said the other day . . . you know . . . out at the back . . .'

'I know,' I say. 'And I didn't mean—'

'I know,' she says.

'You wrote a . . . lovely poem . . . it's a great idea, the *Battered Women's Weekly* . . . There's definitely a gap in the market.'

She smiles. She concedes too easily to kindness.

'You okay?' I ask.

'So so,' she says. 'You?'

I pause.

'I've been better . . .'

'Really?' she says, replacing the flowers on the desk and coming over to stand next to me. 'I've never heard you say that before.'

'It's no big deal,' I say. 'Just remembering stuff . . . things I thought were lost, forgotten . . .'

I try to smile.

'Don't make light of it. This is what we call a "therapeutic breakthrough".'

'It sounds horrible,' I say.

'I'm proud of you,' she says. 'Now stand up and give me a hug.'

'Please don't,' I say.

'Just get over it, Faith. You're getting a hug and that's final,' she says, tugging at my sleeve.

I stand up awkwardly. She wraps her arms around me and buries her head into my neck where Caleb Pearson found a place to burrow. I wonder if it was always his spot, just waiting for him to find it, or whether finding it made it his. It takes me a while—I mean a good few seconds—to realise that Carol is crying. I am trapped. Tears, why now? I pat her on the back.

'I'm not letting go until you hug me back,' she mumbles into my shoulder.

I sigh. I wrap my arms around her.

I hope no one walks in on us. Carol presses her body into me, pushing her breasts against my chest. I try to relax. I count very slowly to ten. With 'crocodile' in between each count. That is surely a reasonable time limit on a platonic hug.

I gently gently disentangle myself from her.

She looks at me with red wet eyes. 'You are so bad at intimacy, Faith. I just wanted a fucking hug. I wasn't trying to seduce you.'

She turns to leave, remembers the flowers, changes her mind about them and throws this at me as she walks out the door, 'You can stick your flowers where they fit best.'

'I have an appointment with a paediatrician and child psychologist,' I tell Phoebe on the phone. 'We just need to arrange access for them to assess your daughter.'

'I don't know . . . her father's going to be angry . . .' she says.

I fidget with a carnation.

'Look, Phoebe, I understand that. He doesn't need to know. We can do it during school hours.'

'I . . . I don't know . . .'

'Are you or are you not worried that Sofia is being sexually abused?' I ask.

312

She is silent on the other end of the phone.

'Do you know what happens to girls who are sexually abused?' I ask her.

She doesn't answer.

'They grow up unable to trust, to form relationships with other adults. They feel violated. And when they're old enough to understand what happened, they blame themselves—for not saying no, for allowing it to happen. They overcompensate. They grow up to be women who dress up as fairies for children's parties. They blame their mothers for having allowed it to happen to them. They can't decide if they love or hate men. Phoebe, you owe it to Sofia to find out what is happening. She won't ever be able to have a normal relationship if you don't intervene.'

There is still silence on the other end of the phone.

'Phoebe, did you hear me?' I ask.

'I heard,' she says.

'I don't think you begin to understand the impact of sexual abuse on small children,' I say.

'I understand,' she says.

'Do you?' I don't mean to shout.

'How do you think I got to be so fucked up?' she says.

Now I am the one who is silent. The carnation withers in my hand, bruised by my insistence.

'I'm sorry,' I say.

'It's okay. It was a long time ago.'

'Who was it?'

'My brothers,' she says. 'All three of them.'

'Did your mother know?' I ask her.

'I don't know. Maybe. She wasn't exactly . . . the . . . how would you say it? . . . give-a-shit-about-your-daughter type of mother.'

'Well,' I fumble, 'don't you think Sofia deserves not to have the same start in life . . . don't you want something better for her?'

There is more silence. I wait. I think I hate carnations.

'Look, Faith, there you sit in your fancy job, with your fancy title, and a fancy office, and you don't understand what it's like . . . My

313

mother was fiddled with by her grandfather, and I was by my brothers, and now my daughter is by her father . . . It's normal . . . for us. I don't want to make a fuss. I just want a happy life. I just want . . . I want what you've got.'

I crush the carnation between my fingers.

'And what do you think is so happy about my life?' I ask her.

'Well, you seem happy to me,' she says.

'Well, I'll tell you what,' I say to her, 'I'm not happy. My father told me on the phone that I am unhappy . . .'

She sniffs. 'You? Why are you unhappy?'

'I don't know . . . things happen and I can't change them . . . or make them better . . . and there are things I want that I can't have.'

'Like what?'

I sigh. 'I want your daughter not to be abused by her father. I want men to stop raping women, and husbands to stop bashing their wives . . . okay?'

She gives a little chortle. 'And so then you'll be out of work,' she laughs.

'I would love nothing more than to be out of work,' I say to her.

'Well, I think you are the best person I have ever met,' she says. 'And I know I am a nobody compared to you, but someday, you'll see, I'm going to find a way to say thanks . . . for what you've done for me.'

'What have I done for you?' I ask.

'You made me into a person. Just a normal person.' Her voice is small. 'You know, I used to think I was the one who should've drowned. God made a mistake with Emerson. It should have been me, not him. Shame, he was just a little boy . . .'

I don't say anything.

'You never chased me away like a disgusting thing that should've drowned instead of her own baby boy. You helped me and Candy . . . You don't have to feel responsible for us, but you do . . . You know, it's like you put the fence up around the pool, without me even having to ask you.'

'Listen, Phoebe, this is my job,' I say to her. 'I don't feel responsible. I get paid to take responsibility.'

She laughs. 'You're such a liar. I know you care . . . even if you say a hundred times you don't.'

'Phoebe,' I say to her, 'if you don't organise for your daughter to be assessed by the doctor and psychologist I've organised, I am going to approach child services to have you declared an unfit mother.'

She is quiet.

'See?' she says. 'You care more than anyone I've ever met.'

# 66. nuts

'My sister Faith talks to gravestones,' I once heard Libby tell Patrick Sheridan. He was captain of the school rugby team and had been kept back to repeat a year. His Maths wasn't as good as his forward passes. But he had outstanding pectorals and a cleft in his chin.

I was the 'good girl', Libby the 'pretty girl'. Like the Christmas present of sixteen different lip glosses bestowed by relatives ignorant of your likes and dislikes, I always accepted the designated labels with good grace and manners, even though privately I envied Libby, wondering why, in fact, there couldn't have been a modest over-lap. A shared yard. A common driveway. Even I recognised that 'prettiness' would have come in handy on the odd occasion. Tyler Holden being one example.

Unlike me, boys clustered around Libby, like she had hidden diamonds or an autographed football in her underwear. It also helped that she didn't tower over anyone other than Nonna. Around her, boys always felt big and brave.

On that day, with Patrick Sheridan in our kitchen, I was in the pantry eating salted cashew nuts from the jar, but Libby didn't know this. Every now and then my vegetarianism would catch up with me and I'd get a protein craving and have to eat a jar of peanut butter or an entire block of cheese. I had also become distracted watching a cockroach.

'Is she weird or what?' Libby said.

In the pantry I stopped chewing. The cockroach, as if shadowing me, stopped crawling. We each waited for the other to make the next move.

Until then I'd never thought about what a perfect foil I was for Libby—next to me, she was deliciously sane and glorious, not to mention petite.

'Yeah, that's seriously odd,' the crackly voice of teenage testosterone came back.

'She sits at her friend Joshua's tombstone and she tells it things . . . like what they're studying at school, and who's fixed up with who.'

Libby giggled. Patrick snorted. 'Kinda crazy,' he said in a voice that really meant, 'Can I feel your tits?'

'Can I tell you a funny story?' Libby said.

'Uhhuh.'

'Once, when we were little, I broke my dad's binoculars. It was an accident. I was spying on a boy across the road I had a crush on, but I'm over that. They were like my dad's most prized possession. And my parents blamed my sister. And you know what she did?'

'What did she do?'

Libby started to giggle. 'She owned up!'

Patrick laughed.

'She said, "I'm sorry, it was me!"' Libby said. 'My parents made her save up to replace them. And like, she did . . .'

317

Patrick stopped laughing. 'That's fucken loopy.'

In the pantry, the cockroach twitched. His feelers trembled, assessing danger. I wasn't going to hurt him but he didn't know that.

When you first walk into the butcher's or the fish market, you retch from the smells of blood and death. But after a while, the body slowly concedes a gradual homeostasis, making disgusting normal.

Josh always said when I asked him how it felt to always be sick, 'You get used to anything, Faith, you can get used to drinking turpentine if you have to. For me, this is normal.'

I could see how, looking in from the outside, I seemed like a weirdo to my sister. I never wore nail polish or said '*Ciao*' instead of goodbye. Inside, a freak feels as normal as the next person.

'I feel so sorry for her,' Libby ventured. 'She's never going to get a date.'

'Maybe she'll meet someone in the cemetery talking to another tombstone.'

'Yeah . . .' they laughed.

I shrank down against the pantry door. My knees propped there for a while. I ate the entire jar of cashews until my bum was numb and cold and my tongue was bruised with salt.

The cockroach stayed with me, though.

# 67. prince

'Look, Faith, he's probably just not that into you,' Carol says, pulling on the longer bits of her hair.

I am irritated by this remark. Annoyed at myself for having told Carol anything at all about my 'date' on Saturday, even if the complete rendition went like this: 'We drove out to his sister's farm, he showed me where he buried the cat, I met his sister, it was late, we slept on the couch.'

It is Wednesday already and Dr Caleb Pearson hasn't called me.

Then again, I haven't called him either.

Maybe Carol's right. He's *just not that into me*. A handful of words like sawdust, depleted of the plump succulence of those hours in the mountains. I feel a misery as big as the ocean inside of me about to flood my beaches. I must NOT give in to this sense of loss. What have I lost? I never had anything to start with.

I focus on little victories—like the fact that my African violet made it through the weekend on caffeine. I then focus on my list of things to do today. I've already spoken to Phoebe's daughter's kindergarten teacher who has set aside three hours tomorrow when Sofia can be both examined by the paediatrician and assessed by the child psychologist. I am driving Phoebe down south so she can be with her daughter during the examination. So that is something to look forward to. I try not to think about Tanya's hands in my hair, and the look on her face when she said, 'You look pretty.' I try not to think about someone forcing sexual contact on a person that small. I try.

Carol comes into my office hyperventilating.

'Oh my God, he's back.'

'Shaun?'

'He's back,' she repeats breathlessly.

'Did you speak to him?'

'No, I left a message for him to call me back here later.'

'Well, let's see if he does.'

'Creep.'

'Psychotic pervert.'

'I fucked him,' Carol sniffs.

'You weren't to know,' I say.

'I should think before I fuck,' she says.

'Always a good rule of thumb,' I offer.

'But I wasn't to know,' she says, wounded.

'Well . . . there were signs,' I suggest.

'Yeah,' she sighs. She looks at me quizzically. 'So what was it like? With Joshua with cystic fibrosis?'

It was such a long time ago. I blink. 'It was . . . awkward . . . and funny . . . and embarrassing . . . I kept my eyes shut through most of it.'

Carol smiles. It is a sweet smile. It makes her lovely.

320

'He was the luckiest little bastard on the face of this earth,' she says.

I look down at my hands.

I think of Nancy and her last few days on earth. I think of Caleb Pearson's words, 'I was lucky to make it.' I think of Nathalie's milky breasts and Tanya's tiny fingers in my hair. Happiness is not an abstraction. It attaches to small things and hides in the crevices. So easily mistaken for nothing.

Carol comes into my office again.

'We're meeting him tomorrow evening,' she says.

'Shaun? Did he call you back?'

'He did,' she says.

'How did he sound?'

'Like there was nothing in the world the matter,' she says.

'What did you say to him?'

'Just that you and I wanted to discuss some work-related issue with him . . . and that it was quite urgent.'

'And what did he say?'

'Do you really want to know?'

'Yes, I do.'

'He said, "Do you have to drag your dyke-friend around with you wherever you go?"'

'Is that so?'

'Yeah, those were his exact words. You're not upset are you?'

'Carol, I've got a potential five-year-old sexual abuse case on my hands, my sister is getting married to a man who gels his hair, and I've just found that my mother went outside for a cigarette whilst my baby brother drowned . . . do you think my world would be rocked by the fact that Shaun Hamilton—who gets hard-ons when raped women cry—thinks I'm a lesbian? Is that a real question, Carol?'

She looks aghast.

'Your mother left you alone in the bath for a smoke break?'

'Yes she did.'

'Fuuuuuuckkkkk!' she says.

'I'll say.'

'Well, that lets you off the hook then.'

'I'm so pleased that you've managed to see the up side,' I say.

After a week in a women's shelter something has changed in the way Phoebe carries herself. The starch of anxiety has been washed away, replaced with the suppleness that comes from not being told to shut up every time you speak. She carries her posture, with guiltless poise as if it really is hers. Not something she borrowed by mistake with a hundred apologies for taking up so much space.

In the passenger seat of my car she natters away with the delirious incontinence of a newly acquired freedom of speech. She's made *friends*. She's never had friends before. Not really. Except for Candy of course, but that's love. With another woman in the shelter. She's never known a real live Hindu. Sapna. The Hindus don't eat meat. She knows a lot of tricks with vegetables. And! She's learning how to sew.

'Me!' she laughs. 'I'm so bloody useless at everything, like I got ten thumbs, but you should see how Sapna has taught me—cross-stitch, and tacking, I'm making a dress for Candy . . . We found some old curtains down in the basement the shelter staff said I could use. We got most of the stains out with NapiSan . . .'

I let her jabber away in her luminous innocence, captivated by the optical illusion of safety in shelter life. But just for now, in this small moment, with her sitting beside me—excited to be seeing her daughter—she is happy. She tells me as much. Even if it's not real and it can't last.

On mother-daughter reunions let me say this.

They're never easy and they always make me cry. Now that I know. Mothers need their daughters. They are lost without them.

A little girl with brown streaky hair, and features strikingly similar to Phoebe, bounds up to her and wraps her arms around Phoebe's legs. Phoebe picks her up and twirls her around and around.

'Mama!!' the little girl laughs. She buries her face in her mother's hair and sniffs it.

'You smell like the sea,' she says.

'And you smell like grass,' Phoebe says. 'Have you been playing with the elves again?'

'Yes, I have!' Sofia says. 'And they said you are very naughty for running away.'

Phoebe's face falls. 'I didn't run away,' she says, shutting down. She stops twirling.

'Yes you did!' the little girl berates. 'And Daddy says they going to send you to a place for naughty mummies and I'm not going to see you again.'

'That fucking bastard,' Phoebe says. 'You tell your father he's a fucking bastard from me.'

'Okay, I will, Mummy,' Sofia says. 'He's a fucking baa-stud.'

'You're a good girl,' Phoebe says, kissing her daughter on the forehead before putting her down.


There is a waiting room full of people to see Dr Baninger. Sofia sits quietly on the chair beside her mother chewing gum. When we stopped at a petrol station so Sophia could use the toilet, Phoebe bought Sophia a whole roll of Bubblicious with what looked like her only five dollars.

'Will your read me a book, Mummy?'

'No, now be a good girl.'

Sofia swings her legs.

'Please read me a book, Mummy,' Sofia says, looking over to where a mother is reading to her child from *The Lion King*.

'No, now shut up and stop asking,' Phoebe says, flicking through her magazine.

I cannot believe I am about to do this. This is not part of my job description. I don't even like children.

'I'll read to you,' I say.

Sofia looks at me.

'What's your name again?' she asks.

'Faith,' I say.

'Are you my mummy's friend?' she asks.

'Sort of,' I say.

'She's my lawyer,' Phoebe says. 'Tell your daddy I've got a lawyer.'

'What's your husband's name?' Sofia asks me.

I clear my throat. 'I don't . . . uumm . . . I don't have a husband.'

'Why?' she asks.

'Stop asking stupid questions,' Phoebe says to Sofia.

Sofia looks up at her mother. 'I'm not stupid,' she says, beginning to cry.

'No, it's not a stupid question,' I say. 'I haven't . . . found the right person.'

'Oh,' she says, her tears stalled.

She hops off her chair and goes to rummage in the box with toys and books.

She stands opposite me holding a well-thumbed version of *Snow White* in her hands. 'Don't be sad,' she says to me.

I nod.

'Some day your prince will come,' she says, handing me the book. I manage to get to the part where Snow White is lying dead in the coffin and the prince falls in love with her when we hear Sofia's name being called by the receptionist.

Some objects, no matter how you look at them, don't get easier on the eye. Diminutives have a reputation for cuteness that is unwarranted. Fancy dresses, handbags, high-heeled shoes all designed for a four-year-old induce a cooing that frankly bewilders me. By its very design a pair of stirrups in a gynaecologist's examination rooms isn't friendly, telling you in no uncertain terms which parts go where and that penetration is non-negotiable. But when they are child-size, they just shatter the heart. No child should have to. Though I've referred countless cases, I have never before actually seen such small stirrups designed only to determine whether a child has been molested or raped. I haven't had anything more than a black coffee and a slice of peanut butter toast today, but I feel a dry retch coming on. I recite the history to Dr Baninger and ask to be excused. I explain that the mother will stay with the child while she is being examined.

* * *

Back in the waiting room, I finish reading *Snow White* trying not to think about Sofia's little legs in those stirrups. I hear her crying through the closed door. I read *Snow White*. I get to the end.

I read the words over and over again. I don't call this praying. I don't believe in God anyway. I don't have a name for this.

> *And they all lived happily ever after.*
> *And they all lived happily ever after.*
> *And they all lived happily ever after.*

She eats her cheeseburger and all the fries, dipping each one into a squirt of tomato sauce which is 'play-play blood'. She plays with the Happy Meal toy, a plastic alien with a crossbow that actually shoots the arrow, but not far due to the fact that it is attached to the toy with a string. An insurance against disappointment. You've got to hand it to Ronald McDonald. He seems to have thought of everything to make a child who has just had a doctor's hands examine her most private of privates content. I drink a coffee. Phoebe is also tucking into a double cheeseburger and fries. I am glad to pay for this food despite my arsenal of objections to how it was produced. I guess this is what is meant by a happy meal.

I will have to wait until tomorrow to speak to Dr Baninger for his report. I wonder whether a child who is being sexually abused would be enjoying a McDonald's meal as much as Sofia is doing now. I have arranged for the psychologist to come to her kindergarten tomorrow morning to do the assessment. Just as I think this, my mobile phone rings. It's Carol.

'Don't forget about tonight,' she says.

'Tonight?' I ask.

'You're hopeless Faith—we're meeting Shaun at the Leprechaun at 8 pm.'

I sigh. The silence in my ears is ringing so loudly I can barely hear Carol's voice at all.

\* \* \*

Back inside my apartment, I drop my handbag to the floor before collapsing on my bed. As I do so, I feel the squish of something soft and warm between my legs. Finally! I sigh. In the bathroom, I spit out the chewing gum I've been chewing for the past three hours—Sofia's parting gift to me when we dropped her back at her kindergarten.

'Be good,' Phoebe had said to her, kissing her goodbye.

'Be safe,' I said to her.

'Don't go, Mummy,' Sofia said, getting tearful.

'I've got to,' Phoebe said.

'When will you come back?' she asked, grasping her mother's hand.

'I don't know . . .' Phoebe said.

And that's when Sofia started to wail as if her mother was a plaster being ripped from her flesh. It seemed to make Phoebe cross. The kindergarten staff had to intervene.

I don't know why Phoebe didn't just lie and say, 'Soon.'

Children can survive for so long on lies. They just need mothers who can tell them.


I strip bare. I need a long shower. I've still got Shaun Hamilton to get through tonight.

As I walk naked from my bedroom to the bathroom, I notice there is a message on my answering machine.

I press the button.

'. . . Yeah, hi, it's me. Caleb . . . Just want to find out how you . . . how you are . . . and . . . yeah, just to let you know that Nancy's not doing so well . . . I think I might need to take her for her . . . last walk sometime soonish . . . ummm, yeah . . . give us a call if you're around. Cheers.'


In the shower I feel the pellets of water against my skin. And I bleed and I bleed and I bleed from all my wounded places.

I watch as the pink water swirls at my feet, and then gets washed away.

## 68. suitcase

'It's only for a few weeks,' my mother said to me. She was standing next to a large brown suitcase on wheels. Nonna was holding my hand, tightly, as though I was a kite the wind might rip from her grasp at any moment.

'But that's a long time,' I said. 'Seven days in a week, times by a few is about fourteen or fifteen or even more . . .'

'You're my clever girl,' my mother said, kissing the top of my head. 'I just need to go and have a bit of time to myself . . . to . . . feel better . . .'

'Are you feeling sick?' I asked her.

'A little. I've got a sore place in my heart, and I have to go and get it better, so I can be a good mother to you and Liberty.'

'But you *are* a good mother,' I said.

My mother's eyes filled with tears. 'Darling girl,' she said in a whisper.

'Please don't go, Mummy,' I said. I felt Nonna's grip on my hand tightening.

'I have to.'

'I promise I'll be good if you stay . . . What if you don't come back?' I asked her.

'I will be back, and when I do, I will be much stronger, and a mummy has to be strong, for her children . . . and besides, Dad, Nonna and Nonno Antonio will be here too, so you will have lots of people to look after you.'

'*Sì*,' Nonna said.

I reached out to my mother, pulling my hand from Nonna's, and clung to her. I buried my face in her skirt which smelled of the heartbreak of tangerine and honeysuckle.

Gently, she untangled me. Holding my hand, she led me to the cupboard in the lounge room where she opened the chess set she had got as a little girl. She removed the black queen and held it out to me.

'I have a very important job for you—will you look after my black queen while I'm gone? Mummy needs her black queen, it's her lucky charm, it always helps her win. Will you keep her safe and give her back to me when I come back?'

I took the black queen from her and closed my fist around it. It felt hard and cold in my palm. I clutched it for dear life.

# 69. sweat

Shaun is twenty minutes late. Carol and I have already each had two double shots of tequila and lime to relax us. I've been doing coin tricks for her. She is either truly impressed or exaggerating out of nerves.

'So how should we start again?' she asks me for the hundredth time, though that is an exaggeration. It is in fact only the seventh time.

'Not we, YOU. You're the one he likes, and if I start he'll just get suspicious and defensive. I'm just here for moral support,' I say.

'Okay, how about this: "So, Shaun, made any threatening phone calls lately?"'

'No, I've got a better one: Shaun, it's come to our attention that your hard-ons are interfering with your professional judgement . . .'

Carol explodes into a fit of jumpy giggles.

'That *is* a joke, Carol,' I say. 'You shouldn't really say that.'

'You think?' she says.

'Do you still find him sexy?' I can't help asking.

'Does it matter?' she asks.

'Maybe not,' I say.

'I am so fucked up in so many ways,' she sniffs. 'Let's just have another drink,' she says, downing her third tequila.

I join her. My head is now officially buzzing. I realise this may impede my professional judgement.

'Do you think he fantasised about raping me while he fucked me?' she asks miserably.

'Did you tell him about what happened to you?'

'Yeah,' she sniffs. 'God knows why. Really, it's time to move on from that. Just meet some nice, normal—unmarried—bloke who doesn't mind the herpes, prepared to work around it, have a few kids . . . You know, just try to be normal.'

'I think you'd be . . . a kind mother,' I say, hoping my words have been chosen vigilantly enough so as not to carelessly make something worse.

She looks at me with yielding eyes in which sorrow has burrowed so steadfastly and so long. 'What would I do without you?' and she leans forward to move an imaginary tendril of my hair from my face.

'I don't want to alarm you, but he's just walked in,' I say under my breath, and look up to face the face I now know why I hate.

Shaun saunters in, looks around and, seeing the two of us, smirks and walks over. Carol smiles back and asks him how he's doing. He hardly looks at me, and I like it better that way. Maybe he's always known I've been on to him. I watch him from behind my glass.

'Scotch on the rocks,' he gestures to the waitress, winking at her.

He removes his jacket, loosens his tie and sits back in the chair. He complains about how hard he's working, the trial he's been away for, very complicated business fraud, talking lightly about this and that, amiable, pleasant, charming. Fucking psychopath.

'So, ladies, what was so urgent that you needed to speak to me?' He looks from Carol to me and back at her again. Carol looks at me.

'Shaun, this is not pleasant,' and I am talking before I know what has taken over and now I've got to run with it.

'Yeah?'

'Hazera. You know Hazera?'

'Sure,' he nods. 'The cross-examination prep we did the other day?'

'Yes, that's the one. We received a call from Hazera later that day. She told us that you called her. Would you like to tell us your version of that conversation?'

'Nope,' he says.

'Why not?'

'Because I didn't call her,' he says.

'You haven't phoned Hazera at all?' I repeat just to make sure.

'No. Why would I call her?'

'Well, she claims you phoned her.'

I look at him. He shrugs. 'I didn't.'

I wasn't prepared for this outright denial.

'Really? She also says that you offered to come over to her place . . .'

Shaun squints at me, puzzled.

'. . . and that you'd bring some *nylon* with you,' I emphasise.

I look him straight in the eye and for the first time I feel mightier than him. His eyes narrow. Blood is rushing to his face. He looks as guilty as if I'd caught him with the phone in one hand and the other in his trousers.

'What?' he spits.

'You heard me,' I say.

Suddenly he looks confused and frightened and I am staring evil in the eye.

Shaun looks at Carol but she is looking at me.

'Is this some kind of sick joke?' he asks.

I shake my head. Carol shakes her head.

'She's lying,' he says.

'Who? Hazera?' I ask.

'She's lying. I don't know what she's trying to do, but she's lying,' and all of a sudden he looks crazed, raking fingers through his hair, cornered, back against the wall. There are half-moons of sweat swelling under his armpits.

I have never wanted justice more than I want it now.

'Why would she lie?' I ask him.

'How the fuck would I know?' he says. 'Jesus Christ, these fucking Muslims . . . you turn around and they stab you in the back . . .'

Don't stop now baby, let it all hang out. Let it show.

'I'm telling you now,' and his tone is pleading, 'it wasn't me. I'm not a lunatic. And I'll prove it. Give me the date, and the exact time of that phone call.'

I write 8.15 pm on a serviette and the edges bleed into the softness of the tissue. As I hand it to him, I see it. A deer caught in the headlights, its innocence fatally startled.


The phone rings shrilly. It is past 2 am. I am lying wide awake in my wide empty bed, listening to the night outside beyond my curtains which are tightly drawn. I have kept a night-light on.

'It's me.' It's Carol.

'Are you also still awake?'

'I can't sleep.'

'Me neither.'

'Faith, Shaun's phoned me three times already tonight. I've just gotten off the phone with him again—he sounds irrational. Seriously, he's scaring me.'

'What did he say?' I ask, shivering.

'He says someone's trying to frame him. Maybe someone at the office who doesn't like him or is jealous of him professionally. Or . . . maybe someone else . . .'

'Who? Like me?'

'That's what he thinks.'

I laugh. Carol doesn't.

332

'Faith, he asked me whether I believed it was him. And I told him no, because I was really scared. He says he knows he can trust me, but that he doesn't trust you.'

'Carol, I've had a weird feeling about him all along. There's darkness there. Serious damage. Right now he'll say anything to get out of this. Watch, he'll turn this whole thing around. He'll find someone else to blame.'

'His back's against the wall,' she says softly. 'People do weird things when they're cornered . . .'

I am quiet, laying out all the bits of what I know, like provisions for a dangerous expedition.

'Everything fits, Carol. Everything. His interest in this work. The fact that he doesn't want payment. The pornography. The cut on his hand. The hard-on comment . . . The only thing that doesn't . . . is that he's smart. Someone that smart must have known he'd get caught.'

'You know what frightens me about him, Faith? If he was drowning, he would pull us down with him.'

'I'm not going down with him, and neither are you,' I say.

She laughs gently. 'You were brave tonight.'

And right now I know what Carol's problem is. She can't tell the difference between courage and vengeance.

# 70. queen

She lied. She never asked for it when she came back.

After six weeks, my mother returned from her 'rest'. She told us that she was very happy to see Libby, me and Dad and that we were 'the most precious things in the world, the light after darkness, the meaning within the meaninglessness'. She had learned how to meditate. From then on, every morning and every evening, she would have 'an appreciation ritual', and light some incense and sit on a cushion and close her eyes and smile like she could see something beautiful no one else could. I sometimes came and sat with her and closed my eyes but all I ever saw was blackness.

My mother had learned to 'manage her grief' with new 'techniques' for handling stress, which involved a lot of very slow breathing as if you were learning how to do it from scratch and closing of her eyes and tinkly music that made the house feel eerie. I liked the incense. From then on our house always smelled of something your nose was interested in. Like damp forests. A bonfire of cedarwood. Or the secrets in flowers.

She didn't shout or cry so much anymore.

But something larger and unseen had changed in my mother during her time away.

On her return, my mother stopped playing chess. As if that part of her had been deleted while she was gone.

I didn't even like chess. Chess was my mother's game. She only ever played black.

'Everyone thinks the game is over when you checkmate the king,' my mother would say in the days when I'd watch her beat everyone who ever challenged her, 'but it's the queen you need to keep your eye on. Once she's gone, the king loses heart. So you have to protect the queen as if she's the one that needs to be saved.'

She promised she'd take it back from me when she got home.

But she forgot.

And I kept it, hoping someday she would remember again.

# 71. hole

*Is there anything you'd like to share with me?*

'My little sister got engaged.'

*That's wonderful news. Congratulations.*

I nod.

'I've been asked to be the maid of honour.'

*That's exciting.*

I really don't mean to laugh. Not in that derisive way.

*Is something funny?*

'People should feel free to make their own mistakes. I just wonder about inviting a whole crowd of people to collude with you.'

The counsellor smiles at me. I think she means to encourage me to go on.

'My sister's getting breast implants . . . as an engagement present from her fiancé. She has, I should say, very decent breasts, just from my perspective. She's putting Gwyneth down because he's allergic. To cats. Gwyneth's got these two different coloured eyes. She's an artwork. You don't see that often. Nature gives you surprises like that. And there are distinct expectations about an outfit with frilly bits. In autumn colours. Which I have to wear. In front of all these people.'

*Long pause.*

'She's going to get divorced anyway. In about six years' time.'

*Not all marriages end in divorce. I've been happily married for the past fifteen years.*

'There are always exceptions.'

*Don't you want to get married?*

A small inescapable snort emerges from my mouth.

*I'll take that as a no. Are you in a relationship with someone at the moment?*

I shake my head.

*Do you want to be?*

I shrug. 'Maybe. If there was someone out there worth being in a relationship with . . .'

*Do you feel like you are open to a relationship?*

'I don't know. That depends on what you mean by "open".'

*Do you like yourself?*

I inhale.

'I'm okay.'

*What don't you like about yourself?*

'My sister could give you a comprehensive list.'

*I'm asking you. I'm not interested in what your sister would say.*

I look out the window. Autumn is winding down. Making way for the early darknesses of winter, the biting mornings, so unfriendly on the extremities.

The counsellor is looking at me. Very intensely. I really don't like it.

'I don't have the best fashion sense.' I look at my hands. 'I wouldn't mind stopping biting my nails . . .'

I think. I am sure there is more.

*And what do you like about yourself?*

I shift in my chair. 'I think I'm good at what I do . . . here, you know, at SISTAA.'

*And how does that make you feel?*

'How's it supposed to make me feel?'

*Do you think what you do makes a difference?*

'On a good day. Maybe . . . to some . . .'

*And how many good days have you had since I last saw you?*

I think about the past week.

'There have been a few moments . . .'

*But generally, it's pretty depressing work?*

'Aren't you supposed to be cheering me up?'

*No. That is not the aim of these sessions.*

'What's your point then?'

*What I'm getting at is that if you don't feel like you make a difference on a daily basis, what motivates you to do this work?*

I want to say, I love women. Or something like that. But I can't. The words just won't come out. What can I say? What's the right answer?

*You don't have to answer now. You can think about it. Maybe tell me how you got involved in this work in the first place.*

I am trying to be open-minded about these sessions. But like remarks by far-flung relatives who say, 'So how did you get to be so big?' these questions stunt the imagination. It just happens, doesn't it? It's not like I grew up saying, 'I want to be a legal counsellor for raped and battered women.' It's not childhood-dream material.

I close my eyes. Just say something. Anything.

'Professor Klueznick.'

*Tell me about Professor Klueznick.*

'He was my criminal law lecturer at law school.'

*Go on.*

'He wore those funny little woollen waistcoats, the kind your Nonna knits for you. And if you got up too close to him, he smelled like peppermint. I think he sucked breath-fresheners or something. He had thick glasses and a bald patch.

338

'My mother always said, "You should be a lawyer, Faith, you've always got an answer for everything." And Dad thought it would be a good profession "to fall back on". So between my big mouth and insurance in the event of an accident, I studied law. This was despite the fact that my favourite subject at school was biology. I really loved studying animals and insects. They have such purpose and dignity. There's no bullshit with them. But nature is nature, and it's there, it's not going anywhere, my father always said—which, by the way, he's wrong about because the giant panda, the great white shark, the Malayan sun bear and harpy eagle are becoming extinct at an alarming rate, along with several other species of innocent wildlife.'

*She smiles. Nods.*

'The first day in criminal law Prof Klueznick handed out these course outlines which covered all the topics for the year. Possession of stolen goods, robbery, theft, murder . . . A female student put her hand up and asked him "What about rape?" "Don't worry about it," he said, "it's not important." And this student said, "How can you say it's not important?" And the Prof said, "I can practically guarantee you will never have to defend a rape case in practice. Most rape cases never get to court, so we don't need to cover it here."'

*Go on.*

'She got very worked up, this student. She had a goofy name— Leigh Flowerday. Like a character from *Anne of Green Gables*. She was large, you know, the kind of person my sister's fiancé calls "fat", and had long blonde hair in these two plaits down her back. She got very upset, and because of it, and the fact that she wasn't thinking clearly about how she was standing in a crowd of unsympathetic listeners, she announced that she had been raped, and the guy had never been caught and that's why she was in law school and here Professor Klueznick was taking away from her the one thing she wanted to study.'

*Nodding. Earnest nodding.*

'Prof Klueznick got very flustered and he said, "There's nothing to stop you from studying the cases and reading up on it at home—but it doesn't form part of the curriculum. You won't be examined on it."'

*Go on.*

'Anyway, one of the boys in the row in front of me said under his breath, "Who'd want to fuck her anyway? She was raped in her dreams," and all around him boys chuckled. Leigh didn't hear the quip but she heard boys laughing and she had this terrible look on her face, a mixture of tears and rage and helplessness. The Prof asked her to sit down. But she grabbed her books and her bag, got up and walked out of the lecture hall, you know, like as a protest. Prof Klueznick had this red colouring seeping up his neck and his glasses kept on slipping down his nose. He gave us seventeen cases to read for the next day.'

*And where were you in all this?*

'I was sitting in the back row where I always sat.'

*I mean, how did you feel about it?*

'Like I was drowning.'

*That's an interesting phrase. What do you mean?*

Drowning. Do I need to say more? I look at her. Clearly I do have to say more.

'You can't breathe. You're trapped. You're suffocated in silence.'

*You felt like you were drowning in silence?*

I nod.

'There was this glaring hole in the justice system. And we all just sat there. Not a single person in that lecture hall—and there were about two hundred of us—came to Leigh's defence just to give her a bit of courage, so that she wasn't so alone. We all saw Leigh Flowerday fall into this gaping silence and we all turned a blind eye. I never saw her in lectures again.'

*Do you know what happened to her?*

'I saw her the other day at a checkout at Food For Less. She's married with kids.'

I wait for her to say something. She does not.

'I mean, once you realise someone is drowning you have a responsibility to save them, that's how I see it. Whether you feel like saving them or not. You can't say you were oblivious to the fact. Once you know, you know. Whether you like it or not, you have to do something.'

340

*And Leigh Flowerday was drowning and you didn't save her?*

I shrug.

'We all watched her drown. And when you do that, you become part of the silence too. You collude. You're an accomplice.'

*So you felt responsible in some way?*

'Prof Klueznick said, "You'll *never* have to confront rape in practice." How could anyone be so certain?'

Shrugging.

I ask her directly, 'How could anyone be so certain?'

More shrugging. *Maybe just his experience?*

'No, there was his proof in his classroom. Women don't speak up. We all sat by and watched someone drown rather than risk being pulled down with her. That's how come he was so certain.'

*Do you feel like you've been able to fill the silence?*

I look at the counsellor. Her name is something like Jeanette or Janelle, she's told me before, but I've forgotten. She looks middle-aged. She has wrinkles around her eyes and dyed hair. I wonder what Shepard would call it—auburn, maybe. There are fancy names for ordinary things like hair colour.

'Silence isn't a hole. It can't be filled.'

*What is it then?*

'It's a thing that happens to you. Like rape. You don't ask for it, you don't see it coming. But once it's got you, you're never the same. And you always feel like it was partly your fault. Like you should have done something to avoid it.'

The counsellor looks at me. She looks taken aback.

*That's a very powerful statement you've made.*

She writes something down.

*Why do you continue with this work?*

I look at my hands. I feel sorry for them. I think about the scars on my legs. I think about how ironic it is that I think Libby and Carol are both fucked up.

'You've either got to be stupid or hate yourself.'

*And which are you?*

I know she doesn't mean to be idiotic.

341

'Well, I'm not stupid.'

*One last thing for today, Faith.*

I look at her.

*When did you become an asthmatic?*

'I had my first attack when I was about three.'

*And did it coincide with any traumatic experiences? Did anything traumatic happen to you when you were three?*

'No,' I say.

'No,' I repeat.

'Maybe . . .'

She nods, waiting for me to say more.

It's amazing that you can sit and look at a person for a very very very long time without moving. Or speaking.

After ten minutes of silence, she says: *I think we're done for today.*

And I agree.

I think we're done.

# 72. silk

My mother hated spiders.

She sprayed them with Spi-die and squashed them beneath the soles of her shoes, despite me begging her not to.

When she was pregnant with Libby and her belly bulged like a full moon beneath her blouse, I asked her, 'Where do spiders get their silk?'

'I don't know,' she admitted. 'It's just in them.'

'Like the baby is in you?'

'Yes, I suppose . . .'

'But how come they've got so much?' I asked.

'I guess they just keep on making more and more,' she said. 'Because their webs keep on getting destroyed, so they have to start all over again.'

'What do you call that thing?' I asked.

'What thing?'

'That thing that makes you carry on making something when you know it's going to get broken again?'

I watched my mother swallow. The skin under her chin puckered and fell. She opened her mouth and found that what she wanted to say had escaped. She closed it, swallowed, as if lowering the net to find her words.

When she opened her mouth again, she said, 'It's called Faith. Like you.'

My mother writes in *The Mourning After*:

> *Love is like a spider's silk. It is within us, and infinite. From the spinnerets of hope, we can weave love again, even after the web of our heart has been shattered. If you've ever watched a spider parachuting through the air on a silken rope, you will know the magic of bold courage and what is possible when you take a leap of faith. In the end, it is only love that saves us.*

# 73. soup

I want to phone Caleb back to tell him how much I want him to smell my neck again.

As I dial the Crown Street Veterinary Clinic I make a decision: I am going to stop biting my nails. From now. Caleb has no choice about how his stomach looks. It's what's happened to him. My nails give me a new chance to start afresh just about every day. I wonder why I have never recognised this replenishment as a form of generosity.

I am put on hold.

'Caleb Pearson,' his voice sends a current of tickles through my body.

'It's Faith,' I say, my mouth feeling quite dry.

'Faith . . .' he sighs. But then he doesn't say any more.

'How's Nancy doing?'

'Not great . . . I think this may be her last few days. I'm going to have to put her down this weekend.'

'I'm truly sorry.'

'Yeah . . .' he says.

I don't know what else to say. I just enter the silence, trying not to overanalyse whether it is tight or relaxing. It just fits. If I stop thinking, it feels very calming to have him breathing on the other end of a phone line, a beating-hearted human presence. I hope he cannot read my thoughts.

'She's lucky,' I say eventually.

'Lucky?'

'If I had a week left to live, I'd want to spend it with you. And if I had to die, I'd also want it to be you putting me down . . . If I was an animal,' I add.

He is quiet. I wonder if the word 'lucky' is one of those painful jabs for him, reminding him of his brother's death.

I panic. 'If I was an animal . . .' I repeat.

'Thanks,' he says.

'Well, if you need me for anything . . .' I say.

'Yeah?'

'Just call me.'

'I did,' he says.

'Oh, right. What do you need me for?'

'I want you to be with me when I put Nancy down.'

I gulp. 'Sure . . .' I say. 'When?'

'What're you doing this weekend?'


While I am doing my grocery shopping I see her from behind. It's the shoes I notice. Olive-green Hush Puppies.

She has aged in all these years of lying in bed at night wondering what he would have looked like, who he would have become. Her boy.

She is holding two cans of soup in her hands, examining the two by way of comparison.

346

I come up to her and say, 'Mrs Miller?'

She squints at me from behind her glasses.

'Yes?' she says cautiously.

'It's me, it's Faith Roberts.'

'Faith!' she exclaims. 'It's been a long time . . . My dear, can you tell me how much fat content is in this can,' she says, handing it to me. 'My eyes are a little fuzzy.'

I search the tiny print of the Special Minestrone for her. 'It's fourteen per cent,' I say, handing it back.

'Fourteen!' she says with genuine consternation. 'What on earth do they put into these soups?'

I shrug. 'Animal fat,' I say lamely.

'Yes, yes, they do put a lot of animal fat into these packaged goods, don't they? I ought to just make my own soups . . . but you know how it is, it's just so much easier . . .'

'It is,' I concede.

'. . . when you're in a hurry, and you don't have time to sit and stir and watch the soup . . .'

I nod.

She puts the soup with the fourteen per cent fat into her trolley.

'Well, Mrs Miller, it's been nice chatting,' I say.

'Yes, my dear, it's lovely to see you . . . Are you married?' she asks hopefully. 'Kids?'

I shake my head.

'Oh well,' she says with genuine regret. 'It's not too late . . .'

'No,' I say.

She looks at me as if she wants to say something more. 'Naomi had a little girl last year . . . I became a granny,' she says proudly.

'That's . . . wonderful,' I manage.

'She's got the same smile as Joshua.'

'I'm really happy to hear that,' I say.

'Well, my dear, take care of yourself,' she says.

'I . . . I'm trying to . . .'

I stand in the tinned soup aisle for a long time after her trolley disappears. Josh is an uncle. That is kind of cool.

'You're an uncle,' I say aloud, surprising a young woman who passes me with an odd stare, clutching a hand basket filled with Lean Cuisine stir-fry and Diet Coke.

I am holding *No Chance to Say Goodbye* in my hands for the second time this week.

I open it. The inscription my mother has written in the front reads:

> *'Spiders don't complain when you break their webs*
> *But in memories we are never alone,*
> *Everyone knows that trees make the best umbrellas*
> *Covering the abyss with joy and light.'*
>
> *To my Faith, thank you for always writing poems with me.*
> *And for reminding me that sadness is not all there is.*
> *I love you,*
> *Mum*

Memory—it's as unreliable as a battered woman. I'm always getting cross with my clients for forgetting. But here it is: I too have forgotten. My mother and I used to write poems together. I haven't thought about that in years. But those first four lines in the inscription come from a poem she and I wrote together. I must have been about ten. We were sitting outside on the double swing. She had a broad-beamed orange hat on. She was sipping on a drink that had a wedge of lemon in it. She let me have the lemon to suck on. It was icy bitter. I remember because I had to ask her what 'abyss' meant.

'. . . it's the space between steep cliffs . . . an endless fall.'

Once my mother told me that when she was pregnant with me there was no space between us. She could hold me close without having to reach for me. Once I was born, she says, the distance began. She says that inch by inch, we lose our hold of the things we love, and before you know it, what you once held nearest to your heart stands apart, that intimacy just a memory, folded into the body, beyond reach.

But the truth lives in the memory.

Now, holding her book in my hands, the inscription so clear in her neat handwriting, I see something for the first time. I hold the book close to my face. I rest my cheek on the words.

My mother and I. Held together by the gossamer fibres of one small word.

She. Love. Me.

# 74. abyss

It was her idea.

'You start,' she said. That was her way of bringing me close. I scanned the surroundings, like you do when you're playing *I spy with my little eye*. It's hard to come up with the first line of a poem. You feel like so much depends on it. 'It doesn't have to be about a thing,' my mother said. 'It can be a feeling, or a colour, or a thought . . .'

As I wrote I covered my line with my other hand, even though my mother was looking away. I didn't want any cheating.

> *I wish I had a dog*
> *A moth sat on my windowsill for four days*
> *I didn't ask for a baby sister*

My mother did the folding. The rules were that you weren't allowed to see the line the other person had written. But you got a prompt word for the next line so you could continue.

And so it went, back and forth, back and forth, until the page was folded into a long thin wad.

The best part was always unfolding the page and reading the poem you had written together. My mother always let me do it. Sometimes our poems were so funny we'd laugh and splutter at how a tree 'asked the hardest question' or a spider 'danced across the ballroom of my mind'. My mother never seemed to mind that our poems never made sense. She said that was the point. But I always felt they showed how far away from each other two people could be. I wanted to write about insects and dogs and trees. But her lines were always about things that were lost that were never coming back and the ache in your heart, like an infinite abyss, that you had to make believe wasn't there.

## 75. syringe

'That's a beautiful bracelet,' Caleb says.

'Thanks. I won it on eBay.'

He nods.

'I paid a ridiculous amount for it.'

'Because you wanted it,' he says.

'Because I wanted to see if I could get it,' I say. I am huffing and puffing. That's what happens when you're carrying twelve kilos of dog between two people. Nancy is in a sling-type contraption Caleb has devised. She is lying quietly with her eyes open as we trudge as carefully as we can from Nathalie's house up towards the cemetery.

I wonder if, like an animal going to an abattoir, she can smell death. Maybe what we are doing is not kind. Maybe this is cruelty.

Maybe we should have put her down first and then brought her out to here to bury her. Caleb is adamant, he wants her last breaths to be outdoors.

'It suits you,' he says.

On his back is a small backpack carrying my asthma pump, some water and the syringe with the medication in it that will finally put Nancy out of her suffering. Around my waist is the jacket I was wearing the night I killed the cat without a name. Caleb says we can bury Nancy in it.

We gently put Nancy down under the tree.

Caleb takes off his backpack, takes out a water bottle, gives me a sip, takes a sip himself and then squeezes a few drops into Nancy's mouth. She licks it gently. He then removes a little pouch. He and I sit on either side of Nancy. I put my hand on her head and gently stroke it.

Caleb removes a bottle and a syringe. He fills the syringe with the clear fluid. I see he has a stethoscope in his bag too. He puts it in his lap.

Gently, he lowers his head to touch Nancy's.

He does not speak.

He kisses the top of her head.

'Travel safely,' he says.

He squeezes her fur between his fingers and gently inserts the needle of the syringe.

Looking at me he says, 'It's over very quickly.'

'What do you mean?'

'I just don't want you to get a shock. It happens within seconds.'

'Oh . . . Okay . . .' I don't know what I expected but suddenly I feel afraid that it will be too quick.

'Goodbye, Nancy,' I whisper. 'Say hello to my baby brother, Nicholas.'

Caleb stops. He looks up at me. He is supposed to be injecting Nancy.

'I lost a brother too,' I say. I have stinging eyes.

It looks like Caleb has stinging eyes. He looks at me for a long time.

'Nancy was Noah's dog. Just a pup when he died, weren't you, girl?' He nuzzles her neck. 'Go find him . . .'

Then he pushes the plunger of the syringe.

He's right.

It happens very quickly.

You wouldn't think so. That something could be alive. And then not. But that's how it happens. Her eyes were still open, her body still warm. He checked her heart with his stethoscope. And he nodded. And that's how Nancy died. There, between us. With the afternoon light at a slant, falling through the trees like patchwork. With both of our hands on her, interlaced.

Digging holes is not for sissies. It looks easy, but it's hard work. We dig a hole for her until we are both sweating. We spread my jacket out on the ground.

'Can you give me hand?' he asks.

Together we lift Nancy's body onto the jacket. Caleb makes sure her eyes are closed. So that the dirt won't get in them.

Then we wrap her in my jacket and we bury her.

At the last minute, I take off my bracelet and I put it between her paws.

With stones, we write on the upturned earth, *NANCY*.

And then, Caleb says: 'Let's run.'

'Run?' I ask.

'We have to run,' he says.

He doesn't even wait for me to explain to him that I am asthmatic and that running isn't good for me.

He just grabs me by the hand and starts running. I don't know how long we run for, or how much it hurts my lungs, because I don't remember the last time I ran, but when we finally stop, I fall onto the ground gasping for air.

When I eventually get my breath back, Caleb smiles at me.

'Why did we do that?' I ask.

'Because we can,' he says.

'We can?'

'Yes. We're alive. And we can run.'

I quite like the way he put it.

So we run back to the homestead.

## 76. popcorn

I liked to go to movies alone.

I'd sit in the back at the Norton Street Cinemas during the foreign film festivals where no one could find me. Not that anyone was looking.

He arrived a little after the start of *Il Postino*. I was already sitting in the back row. He sat two seats away from me. I kept on stealing sideways glances at him. His froggy lips seemed much more kissable now that he had stubble on his face and wore a beanie, even in summer. In fact, his full lips had a veteran eroticism about them.

By then Ron Hadley had grown into what my father referred to as 'a very respectable young man'. He was studying engineering and lived in a commune in the inner city. He was still on the chunky side, which on a teenager made one think of gluttony but somehow on a man of twenty seemed less of a transgression and more a statement about the kinds of issues that were important in the BST, like good taste in music and knowing who directed *Casablanca* or *The Graduate*.

I had seen him before on the odd occasion, sitting alone in the middle of the back row, eating a huge tub of popcorn and laughing softly. He had the comfort of someone who has long since ceased to care what other people think.

At the end of the movie I looked up and saw two streams of tears down the side of his face.

I made eye contact with him. 'Remember me?' I asked.

'Sure,' he said, without wiping his tears away. 'Faith Roberts . . . don't you cry in movies?'

'Nah,' I shrugged.

We went to see *Cinema Paradiso* together. In the final scene Salvatore sits in the cinema watching the reel he inherits from the projectionist Alfredo, of kiss after kiss, spliced and cut from all the movies over the years. Round about then, I leaned over and asked Ron if he wanted to be part of my experiment.

He shrugged. 'What sort of experiment?'

'To have as many orgasms as possible through oral sex.'

'Sh . . . sure . . . I guess . . .' he stammered, spilling the entire tub of popcorn into his lap.

Enthusiasm is entirely underrated as a quality in a sexual partner.

Ron was undemanding. He let me steer lest he disturb the balance of what he once described as 'the best arrangement a bloke could wish for'. I asked him not to spend any money on me and I told him I didn't like flowers, especially jonquils. He was gentle and intrigued, the lucky stowaway on the ocean liner who, due to mistaken identity, ends up with the penthouse. Mostly, he was quietly grateful.

For four years, Ron and I had sex once a week on a Thursday afternoon.

I learned over the years that watching the face of someone as they climax is the closest you can come to knowing another person. Done softly, looking becomes its own kind of tenderness. I remembered Josh, and his open eyes, like fleece on my skin.

I wondered, watching Ron, what it would be like to orgasm outwards like that, like a big show of fireworks, instead of inside, the way I did, which was private and quiet, like the water table beneath the surface of the earth, rising to surprise a barren wadi.

I thought long and often about Josh and how he would watch things die, not shying away from what was exquisitely vulnerable.

Looking back, I was sorry I had kept my eyes closed in those final moments with Josh. I hadn't wanted to embarrass him.

I'd always thought those unposted Valentine's Day cards meant Josh wasn't brave.

But really it was me who was the coward.

# 77. alibi

I am at work in my *Dolphins are our only hope* T-shirt. That's because I spent the whole weekend with Caleb at Nathalie's house. I think I am good company when you're burying something you loved. He definitely liked kissing my breasts and he did say, 'God, how I love your breasts,' in the way that makes your stomach lurch, and all sorts of bodily sensations open your . . . yoni. I watched him, with my eyes wide open.

We lay together well into our dreams.

Barbara puts a call through for me. 'Got Dr Baninger on the line.'

I take a deep breath. It's always a good thing to take a deep breath in the event of bad news.

'No evidence of sexual abuse.' Those are his words.

I ask him if he is sure. He doesn't like the way I ask that. He reminds me he is a professional and has been doing this work for thirteen years. I apologise and say, 'It's just that I am very relieved.'

'Yes, it's always a good result . . .' he says.

The joy makes me giddy. I feel as if someone has just cut me loose and I am unravelling a taut spiral that has gripped me by the guts.

When Carol comes into my office she finds me with my head in my hands.

She panics. But no need.

'I'm just crying,' I say.

She stands there with her mouth open.

'Bad news?' she asks.

'No, good news, actually.'

She shakes her head. 'Your wires are all crossed. You're supposed to cry when you're sad and *smile* when you're happy . . . What is it?'

'No evidence of sexual abuse in the little girl—you know, the lesbian couple.'

Carol twitches her mouth. 'That fucks your case, though,' she says.

I look at her.

'You know what I mean? At least if you had sexual abuse on your side, you'd have a much stronger custody argument for the mother.'

Something inside me snaps. Finally.

It has been the longest morning in the history of time. I am trying hard to listen to Hazera but her words are not welcome and I do not want to blame.

'Well . . . maybe it wasn't him.'

'Try to think, Hazera. Think about the exact words the caller used.' I am tired.

'Well, if he's got such a strong alibi, it couldn't have been him, could it?'

'It seems unlikely.' Someone who doesn't care at all is speaking through my mouth.

There is a silence while she thinks. 'Now that I think back, the caller didn't actually say he was Shaun. It sounded just like him . . . what must have happened is, yes, now I remember. The caller said "Guess who's speaking?" That's right. I found it quite strange, because I'd seen him earlier in the day, and given how the session ended . . . I guess I thought he was phoning maybe to apologise . . . but he said "Guess who's speaking" and I must have said "Is it Shaun?" and the caller said "Yes".'

I am wishing that somehow I had known this in an age before tequilas at the Leprechaun and sleepless nights. Guess who's speaking? is the standard opening line of an obscene phone caller. It is either a shocking coincidence and therefore very bad luck, or someone who knew what had happened to Hazera and was acting on a 'dare'. You'll be amazed at what some people classify as 'humorous'. What is worse is that I know this stuff. I wrote the training manual. It's there on page 148. A caller lures the woman into naming someone and then plays a role, feeding off the information she offers him.

'And how did the caller know about the rape?' It's all just a matter of going through the motions now. Finding out what really happened because this piece of paper bright and white and official in my hand is unravelling her memories.

'I think I must have asked him something like, "Do you always make rape victims cry?" . . . something like that . . . I must have mentioned it first. I know I said, "Are you phoning to apologise?" and he said, "Of course I am . . ."'

'The nylon?'

'I said, "Do you think they'll ask me about having my hands tied with the nylon?"'

It's all flowing now.

'And he said, "They'll definitely ask you about that . . ."'

I sigh deeply. 'So basically, you gave him all the information . . . is that right?'

She doesn't speak for a while. 'I feel really bad now, you know, for accusing him,' she says.

'Don't feel too bad,' I tell her. 'It was a perfectly acceptable mistake, in the circumstances. It happens.'

I am holding the signed declaration of the senior partner at Gallagher and Cullinan Solicitors. *This is to confirm that Mr Shaun Hamilton was ... at all times relevant to this inquiry ... in my personal presence ... consultations with the following clients ...*

It is what you might call a watertight alibi.

'It wasn't Shaun.' Her voice is clipped, accusing. 'You were mistaken.' Carol is standing in front of me. Her arms folded across her chest.

'I was mistaken? I'm not the one who accused him. It was Hazera. She seemed so certain.' I am feeling something hard against my back.

'Yes, but you wanted it to be him.'

I am silent. What did I not see here?

'Carol, hang on, hang on now—we agreed on this thing together remember?'

'You seemed so convinced. I just said I'd help you confront him, but he said you made him feel guilty. You can't deny that you thought all along it was him. You believed it was him, didn't you?'

'Yes ... yes I did. And I was wrong, but the circumstantial evidence was compelling—he made that comment about getting hard-ons—and that's what did it for me. And what about the pornography you found?'

'So maybe he's an insensitive asshole who likes to wank over S & M, but he's not a psychopath obscene phone caller, and that's what you accused him of.'

'Don't do this to me, Carol. Don't make me into the villain here.'

'Shaun is spewing. He told me he never wants to see any of us again, and that he's going to the newspapers. He said we're a bunch of man-hating bitches out to prove that all men are bastards. He said we can't even tell when someone decent is just trying to help.'

'I don't see what choice we had.'

'Maybe you should have just told him Hazera's story and let him defend himself. Maybe you should just have given him the benefit of the doubt.'

There are too many 'you's in what she's saying and suddenly I'm receding like the tide and the waves are crashing all around me . . . Her voice sounds vague and faded, like a memory I'm recalling, and the space between us is filled with 'you's and not 'we's and I know she's rewriting history so she won't be sinking with me.

'Yeah, well, as I've said, I don't think . . .'

'That hard-on comment was just a joke,' she interrupts me.

Alone in my office, something happens. A sensation so new it sweeps me sideways, like an unexpected rip. I don't fight against it.

I reach for the phone.

And I dial my mother's number.

# 78. bubble

My earliest memory is of being in a bath.

I liked baths. I liked the bubbles the tap could churn up in them. I liked the splashing you could do in them. The fact that you could have company in them. Baths are not lonely places.

But that's as far as memory takes me. There are blanks and voices and ghosts it won't show me. I guess it wants to keep its tricks to itself.

Memory is the slipperiest of senses. Just when you feel yourself closing in on what it is you're reaching for, it pops, stinging your eyes with great big bubble lies.

I have come to think that things that have happened which we can't remember are optical illusions.

I don't remember being in the bath with Nicholas, but I read it somewhere in my mother's book. Language has grouted the gaps for me. Bath. Bubbles. Nicholas.

Nonna once told me that things must have a name for understanding. That without names, things become lost, forgotten.

In the end, perhaps the meanings of things are secreted inside them, like unborn or lost children. And the very thing we cannot find is the thing we must give.

Names don't give us meaning. We give meaning to the things we name.

# 79. windscreen

*FUCKING FEMINIST BITCH CUNT* is spray-painted over the windscreen of my car. It made my stomach recoil. Violence need only be a whisper. It startles. I started to laugh from the shock.

There were no eyewitnesses. We laid a charge of vandalism. It's been filed. Police came to take fingerprints. *They did all they could.*

'Is there anyone who may have something against you?' the police officer asked me.

I didn't know where to start. I told him not to worry. It was probably just some drunken kids having fun.

The truth is that there are hundreds of men out there who hate my guts and think I'm a *fucking feminist bitch cunt.* When you spend your life helping wives and girlfriends secure AVOs or having people's salaries attached to maintenance orders, or sending letters telling them that despite their fancy jobs, fancy titles and fancy offices, you know who they are and what they do in private, this is what is called the fallout and it's no use complaining. '*Ondignified*', as Nonna would say.

Anyhow. I have my suspicions.

Barbara made me a strong cup of coffee with two sugars.

'Don't you let it upset you, honey,' she smiled at me. 'Let me catch the bastard who did that to your car . . . and I'll wash his mouth out with soap and tell him his mother brought him up wrong.'

Carol didn't say anything. She went into her office and closed the door.

There is one man who doesn't think I'm a *fucking feminist bitch cunt*.

I phone him. I tell him I made a terrible mistake of judgement. I accused someone and I was wrong.

'So you're having a good day?' he asks.

'Actually, I'm having a crap day,' I say.

'I thought you told me that the best part of your job is when you're wrong.'

'Yeah, well I was wrong about that too,' I say.

There is silence.

'I think . . . maybe . . . I've been wrong about a lot of things . . .' I say. I look around my office. At my desk in this small room on the south side of SISTAA's premises which does not, never has, inspired or consoled. It is not because it is second-hand, covered with large coffee stains, ballpoint pen scribblings and a few incomprehensible carvings. It is functional and useful. Those are underrated qualities. It's not the desk. I look at the box of tissues on its left-hand corner, a tissue groping out of the plastic slit, waiting for someone to reach for it, dab her eyes, as I hold the broken world of her heart. I notice the squishy stress ball on the right-hand corner. For kneading between desperate fingers. I take in these walls that have buttressed my unhappiness. My unhappiness? What do I have to be unhappy about?

As I think this, I feel a shaking gasp break from my throat.

'I'm here, Faith,' Caleb says. 'I'm here . . .'

And with him, there for me, on the other end of the telephone line, I let out a wail, a curdling, demented cry, that breaks free in ever-widening circles, loosening me from its grip.

I have my box of tissues on my lap. I have blown my nose and dried my eyes. But the tears still come.

'We all make mistakes,' he says.

'No platitudes,' I say.

He pauses. His pause stretches into a silence I can feel is heralding something big that gathers up the moss of that first moment he took a lifeless bundle from my arms, and all that has passed between us since. I realise in this instant, I have been waiting for this moment. Waiting, it turns out, is just a presence. Like Beyonce. Except of the self.

'I also made a mistake,' he says so quietly I wonder whether I have conjured it.

'It was just another ordinary night out with our friends . . . We were hanging out at this bar called Friskies because we'd heard there was a team of Spanish netballers who were coming there after training. Noah was into Spanish girls. He was even taking classes. Just hearing Spanish made him horny. When you're eighteen, you don't think about anything except what's under that little netball skirt. Like how many you've actually had, who's driving . . . if you can't see it, it doesn't exist . . .'

I am holding my breath.

'I didn't see that Merc coming,' he says. 'I swear to God . . . I didn't even see it.'

I let out a sigh. I sniff.

'I didn't see it . . .'

'You didn't,' I say.

'Trouble with mistakes is that they're like things underwater. You can't tell if they're big or small or near or far, until you stick your hand in, and what seemed far away is actually near . . . little things . . . like forgetting to indicate.' He exhales a little puff of what could have been a laugh in a different story. 'Most of the time, you'll get hooted at for that. Worst case—you get called an asshole . . . I got to bury my brother . . . the one person I loved and would have died for . . . I guess that's what they call irony . . . except it's my life.'

I take this information in, a tainted bequest, and clasp it close like a struggling creature. It beats against the walls of my ribs. It hurts.

'We all make mistakes, Faith . . .'

I have nothing I can give him back that words can hold so I just sit in the silence. But I reach into it, and press my unlovely fingers on the source of his bleed, and I hold them there. He is quiet. For the first time since I was a little girl sitting birdwatching with my father, silence becomes a holding place, like water where things shift in suspension and not something that happens to you, forcing itself on you so that you are never the same again.

I hear him exhale. And then he says to me, 'Maybe it's time for you to think about doing something that isn't so stressful.'

'You just don't like my chewed-up nails,' I say.

'I'll match your chewed up nails and raise you an abdominal scar.'

I chuckle.

'I'll come and help you to scrub it off later,' he says.

So now we're having a date to remove misogynist graffiti from my car windscreen.

In my world, this is what is called making progress.

# 80. myth

I wrote the manual. So I know what's there.

**Myth:** It only happens to certain kinds of people. It cannot happen to me.
**Fact:** It can strike anyone at any time. Age, race, gender, ethnic group, social status has no bearing.

**Myth:** You can prevent it if you really want to.
**Fact:** Nothing you do can prevent it.

**Myth:** If people avoid strangers and going out at night, it won't happen to them.

**Fact:** It happens between friends, co-workers, colleagues, acquaintances and often in the home. It occurs any time, any place.

**Myth:** If it happens to you, you were probably asking for it.
**Fact:** No one asks for it. It is not something you have any control over.

**Myth:** It only happens to young beautiful women.
**Fact:** It happens to women irrespective of their age, physical appearance or how they are dressed.

**Myth:** It is rare and affects very few people.
**Fact:** It happens all the time; most likely it has happened to someone close to you.

I wrote it for the chapter named RAPE.
But it could just as well be for a chapter named LOVE.

# 81. beach

I am early. The travel agent didn't keep me waiting. I just wanted some information. Badolato is 447 kilometres from Naples, and on the little country roads it could take forever. Right now that sounds like some version of heaven.

Caleb and I have arranged to meet at a beach that is off the beaten track. I am sitting in my car looking out at the beach. 'Off the beaten track' is a euphemism for 'dangerous' and 'where women get raped'. But really, when used accurately, it means the beach is rugged and wild with beauty. I consider how long I have lived surveying the outdoors from the bolted cubicle of a locked car. I wonder what it would feel like to walk barefoot on that beach without the fear that some opportunistic sadist might pounce from behind a rock and rape and murder me and bury me in a sand dune never to be discovered so that my mother would lament not being able to bury me.

It would be tricky—I would venture impossible—for me to be raped and murdered in a quarter of an hour. It would have to be someone working very quickly. There would definitely be no time to bury my body parts.

I unlock my door. I swing my feet onto the ground. I unlace my shoes and take off my socks. These shoes are really ready for the bin. I hold them in my hands and I close the car door.

It's been three months since I left SISTAA. Barbara cried. Dave baked his 'if-I-die-now-I-can-die-happy' cheesecake for my farewell party, though I can confirm this is an exaggeration. There are still some things on my list before I'll concede that. Genevieve thanked me for my contribution and wished me all the best in my future endeavours. Since then, I've been walking other people's pets. Caleb put me on to his clients who need a dog-walker. So now I spend a lot of time outdoors picking up dog poo with a special contraption. You know, there are worse things in life than picking up dog poo for a living.

Spring is so close I can taste the hope of jasmine in the air.

I look around. There seems to be no one about. I take a few steps on the gravel. The hard cold stones bite into my feet. I don't remember when last I was barefoot outside. As I walk past a bin I throw my shoes in. They clatter on the aluminium on their way down. If Libby were here she'd be applauding. There is a pathway between the shrubbery leading down to the beach. I head for the water.

Just before I reach the sand, I see a spider scuttling for cover. 'Hey . . .' I say, dropping to my haunches. But he's gone, disappeared into the shelter of bushes. I can't blame him. Sometimes we are mistaken about the things we think are going to hurt us.

The sand is like velvet under my feet compared to the stones. As I walk across the beach I see something pink. I bend down. It is a vial of pink lip gloss. I open it and smell it. It smells of honey melon, ripe as summer. I look around. No one is watching. I squelch some onto my lips. My lips smell delicious. The taste, however, is an undeniable disappointment. I put the lip gloss in the pocket of my jeans.

It will be autumn in Italy soon.

'Ray Osborne on line 2 for you,' Barbara said. That was the day I left SISTAA. About ten minutes before I resigned, to be precise.

'Ray?' I said.

'Got some interesting news for you on that Shaun Hamilton you asked me to investigate.'

My heart beat violently.

'Tell me,' I said.

'So the reason I seem to have missed all this is that he was in fact born Shaun James Brimble. He was brought up by his grandmother, one Edith Brimble. Turns out his mother, Susan Brimble, was killed by his father in a domestic violence incident when he was five years old. Quite grisly by all accounts—he beat her to a pulp with a chisel. A case of . . .'

'Femicide,' I said.

'Yes, I believe that is the correct term . . . Anyway, the grand-mother got custody and changed the boy's name from Brimble to Hamilton. Father served a fifteen-year sentence and was killed in a pub brawl less than eight months after his release. He's done it hard—grandmother died when the boy was seventeen, went into foster care until he was eighteen, and won a scholarship to study law.'

In that moment, I could feel the shell cracking all around me.

'He's a bit of a martial arts expert, runs workshops for teenage girls at risk, self-defence stuff . . .'

Pennies were dropping all around me. *Clink clink* fucking *clink*.

'He seems like a really nice guy . . .'

I make it to the edge of the water.

Last week there was a message on my answering machine. It was Genevieve. 'Just thought I'd let you know the good news. The police have made an arrest on our serial rapist. Big celebration today on the front lawn, if you're interested in coming. It would be good to see you. Bail hearing's tomorrow, and we're all gathering with placards at 10 am if you want to join us . . . and . . . there's a parcel that's been left here for you . . . looks like a pair of man's boots. One of your ex-clients who came in for the Sistaas-Are-Doing-It-For-Themselves programme left it here for you. She said you'd know what to do with them.'

I erased the message.

I'm not oblivious to the facts anymore. It's just that sometimes the facts get in the way of other things. When catching a serial rapist becomes the thing to which you attach the term 'good news', you can't use that phrase anymore in a sentence like this: my 'good news' is that Gwyneth and I adopted a kitten. Caleb saved its life after it had been doused with petrol and set alight. She's battered and scarred, like the rest of us, but she's . . . a cutie-pie. I called her Nancy. She sleeps in my bed with me and licks my toes in the morning when she wants to be fed. With Gwyneth, Nancy and my African violet, it's like we're almost a happy family.

I brought Caleb home to meet my parents last week.

My mother made an entirely vegetarian meal. There was even macaroni cheese for Chris.

Chris cornered me in the kitchen while I was refilling the wine glasses.

'It tastes weird,' he said.

'What?'

'Chicken.'

'Chicken?'

'Yeah, when it's raw it's all slimy and when it's cooked you can see the wings, the legs . . . We kept chickens when I was a kid . . . I don't like to be reminded.'

I looked at him. He *is* handsome and since that is on Libby's list of what matters, I'm glad he is.

'Fair enough,' I said to him.

He blinked at me. 'It's really decent of you,' he managed, 'to take Gwyneth off Libby's hands.'

'Sure,' I said. 'Allergies can be hell. You don't want to see me eat a mango.'

A wave comes and tickles my toes. I cry out, something like, 'Hoi . . . yeeks, whew . . .'

I think I giggle.

Another wave comes, and this time I misjudge it and it splashes me and wets my pants up to the knee on the left-hand side. I cry out something like, 'Hey, ooh, hhhaaaaa, hhaaaaa . . .'

Now I am wet.

I consider how uncomfortable it feels to be wet. And how glorious it feels to be uncomfortable.

I did go back for Sanna's memorial service. I wanted to see Priscilla. I wanted to find out how to say, 'I am sorry for your loss' in Somalian, but the website didn't give that as an option. Instead, I learned how to say, 'I am happy to see you.' *Waan ku faraxsanahay gagtidaada.* I figured it would suffice.

I came up to her from behind. She was very neatly dressed. She was holding the hand of a little girl. Sanna's I would guess.

As she turned to face me I noticed two things. Her eyes had softened. Anger had melted and grief had come in. There was a fullness.

And I saw my butterfly pendant around her neck.

I forgot how to say 'I'm happy to see you' in Somalian, despite how many times I had practised it.

She saw me looking at her throat.

'It was my sister's,' she said. 'They found it in her possessions the night she was killed. It's beautiful, isn't it?'

'It is,' was all I managed to say.

The last time I saw Carol she was eating pizza with some guy in a denim jacket who I assume is her new lover. I hope that means she's given Corey the flick. He messed her around for longer than is right. She deserves a better kind of tenderness. She pretended not to see me. Or maybe she wasn't looking.

I think of her. Every time Caleb and I visit Nathalie's place and I see Tanya prancing around in fairy wings, I think of Carol.

But I have lots of new friends. Most of them walk on four legs and require me to pick up their excrement. But none of them are suicidal.

'He's got a horrible scar on his stomach,' I told Nonna.

'Good, good. Love looks funny,' she said.

'And he loves animals,' I said proudly.

'Aah . . .' she smiled and clasped my hands in both of hers, kissing them with her beautiful wrinkled lips.

'Is enough,' she said.

'What, Nonna?'

'No more,' she said, making a gesture with her hand like a knife. She then rested her hand with the amputated pinky on my thigh.

I swallowed.

'Yes, Nonna. It's enough.'


I feel now, standing in the sun, with the wind in my face and the sand in my toes and the salty water on my feet, the cruelty of denying an African violet the sun. I think fondly of my little plant. I brought it home with me the day I left SISTAA. It hasn't given up on me. Despite who I am and my obvious flaws in the nurturing department. I feel a flicker of something beneath my sternum, which I might once have mistaken for heartburn but right now is closer to that part which unjustifiably thrills when a plant opens a new bud. As if it has anything to do with you.

'Hey, Josh,' I yell into the sky. 'I'm here!' and I raise both my arms up to the sun and lift my face.

The next thing I feel a hand on my shoulder. I tense momentarily.

'It's only me,' Caleb says. He is barefoot too.

Only Him. As if there's anything Only about Him.

We stand at the water's edge looking out at the ocean.

And then he is quiet, so I step into his quiet with him and stand there for a long time. The stillness becomes a place and we are there together in it.

'Everything you wish for is in that sky,' he says to me.

I raise my eyes to the sky and feel it towering over me. Holding me to this earth. I close my eyes, and . . . make a wish.

When I open them, we are still standing on the beach.

'I'm scared of loving something, and then having it taken from me,' he says softly, putting his hand on my shoulder and gently squeezing it, like . . . like a breast, I suppose.

I nod.

'All I know for sure, right now, is that when I'm not with you, it's like I'm just waiting. Until I can be with you.'

'Internal conflict is so . . . conflicting . . .' I say and my skinny little heart hops about inside me like a grasshopper.

Caleb's hand on my shoulder moves to my neck. He snuggles his hand under my hair. Little shivers remind me of the way he traced my scars with his fingers and then kissed them one by one last night.

'Caleb?'

'Yes, Faith?'

'It's autumn in Italy,' I say.

'I love autumn,' he says.

I turn to face him. I smile him into me.

There is a name for this, what I'm feeling. I don't want to forget it, I don't want to lose it. I want to hold it to me, gently, gently and deliver it into Caleb's strong hands, which I'd trust to pull a baby out of my womb if my womb ever changes its mind. I've never believed in love or happiness or happily ever afters. But I'm not so sure about things anymore. I just know there is a name for this.

On the beach sandpipers gossip. Something stirs out at sea. Dolphins, maybe. We gaze out, watching for other surprises which can take your breath away, without you needing your asthma pump. You never know what you'll see if you're prepared to wait.

But somewhere in that waiting, Caleb pulls me close. And that's when he swoops, his lips to my face, and begins to kiss it all the way from my forehead to the closed lids of my Chinese chestnut tree eyes, to my freckled nose, my cheeks, my chin and then very much to my mouth.

Every part of me throbs as the fist of my heart uncurls and the air rushes into me, for the first time, like a baby taking its first breath.

Shepard was wrong. About men with beards.

*Nonna taught me how to see.*

*'You have to close your eyes,' she said. So I did.*

*'What you see?' she asked.*

*'Nothing, Nonna, it's just black.'*

*'Look more,' she said.*

*So I looked.*

*'Actually, it's not really black, it's kind of . . . red . . .'*

*'Rosso?' she asked.*

*'Sort of . . .'*

*'What you want to see?' she asked.*

*I felt a small pulsing from my thigh where seven scars sighed, silver memories etched in flesh of things lost but not forgotten.*

*'Will I be . . . happy?' I said. I opened my eyes. Nonna was smiling through the milky cataracts of her ancient eyes.*

*'For you, Faith, love will die, and love will live.'*

*'What does that mean, Nonna?'*

*She shrugged. 'I not make the world. I just read the story.' And she chuckled.*

*'Close your eyes. What you see?' she asked me.*

*I closed my eyes. I saw Caleb. Standing on the beach. The wind sweeping his wide forehead. He was holding onto someone.*

*I couldn't speak for a while. 'SOME MAN,' I said finally.*

*'Amore,' she sighed, patting my arm with her four-fingered hand.*

*I kept my eyes shut for a while longer.*

*Watching my love living. Saving myself from drowning.*

# acknowledgements

With gratitude:

To all the women who shared their stories with me during my years as a legal counsellor at POWA (People Opposing Women Abuse), wherever you may be in your lives.

To all the women and men who work to end violence against women, for your stamina, your vision and your commitment to a better future.

To Jane Ogilvie and Karen Lazar for reading early drafts and offering insightful feedback.

To Alan and Eva Gold for their gift of four days in their secluded haven in the Blue Mountains.

To Jo Paul and Catherine Milne for the love and care they devoted to this book (twenty-three pages of comments was a hell of a LOT of editorial love).

To Catherine Taylor and Julia Stiles for precious input in shaping the final story.

To Alexandra Nahlous for her fine eye for detail and for loving Caleb.

To Marco Gianni for assistance with Italian translations (*grazie mille*—is that right?)

To Sophie Hamley, who supported me in keeping what mattered to me by simply asking, 'What would Alice Walker do?'

And to Ellie Exarchos for a cover that brought tears to my eyes.

To my family, without whom none of this would matter—to Jesse and Aidan for always understanding and bringing me home.

And to my love, Zed. Who has never lost faith. How'd I get so lucky?

Joanne Fedler is the author of *When Hungry, Eat*, *Secret Mothers' Business* and *The Dreamcloth*. Her books have sold over 350,000 copies worldwide. Of her many awards and scholarships, she is proudest of *Asshole of the Month* from *Hustler* magazine in 1995 in response to her work on gender equality.

Joanne studied law at Yale on a Fulbright scholarship, and was a law lecturer and a volunteer legal counsellor at People Opposing Women Abuse (POWA) in Johannesburg, South Africa, before setting up and running a legal advocacy centre to end violence against women. She was appointed by the Minister of Justice to sit on a project committee of the Law Commission to design new domestic violence legislation.

Some day Joanne hopes to set up a writer's colony, grow her own vegetables and live in a place where she will never be stuck in traffic. She currently lives in Sydney with her husband and two kids.

www.joannefedler.com

# appendix: what's in a name?

When writing a book, an author has the freedom to choose any names for her characters. I have elected to use the names of people who have lost their lives to domestic violence or in the course of sexual assault. I came across these people's stories in the press from various countries (including Australia, South Africa, India, Jamaica, Canada and the USA). Below are a few lines that describe the trauma and loss of each life, which nevertheless can never convey the dimensions and horrors of their suffering. I have, with respect to all those who have died, borrowed their names to tell this story.

**Faith Battaglia** (nine) and her sister **Liberty Battaglia** (six) were shot by their father John David Battaglia in Texas in 2001, who was about to be arrested for violating probation on a domestic violence charge. He was sentenced to death in 2002.

**Priscilla Mohlabakoe** was a 29-year-old mother of two who worked as a clerk at the Supreme Court of South Africa. She was killed by her boyfriend on New Year's Day 1996.

**Sanna Nani Moeketsi** was fourteen when she was gang-raped and murdered in South Africa in 2005.

**Carol Stuart** was pregnant when her husband falsely claimed she was shot by a robber in 1989 in Boston, USA. She was in fact killed by her husband.

**Ann-Marie Edward, Ann-Marie Lemay, Maud Haviernick, Michelle Richard, Maryse Leclair** and **Maryse Laganiere** were six of the fourteen women who were killed by Marc Lepine on 6 December 1989 in Montreal, Canada. He shouted, 'You're all feminists and I hate feminists' before firing and killing the women. The names of the other women who died were **Annie St-Arnealut, Annie Turcotte, Nathalie Crouteau, Sonia Pelletier, Barbara Daigneault, Barbara Marie Klueznick, Genevieve Bergeron** and **Helene Colgan**.

**Jai, Tyler** and **Bailey Farquharson**, aged ten, seven and two, drowned when they were driven into a dam by their father Robert in Melbourne, Australia, on Father's Day in September 2005.

**Rania Arafat:** after falling in love with a man of whom her family did not approve she fled from her home in Jordan and lived in hiding for a while. When she returned on the promise that she was forgiven, she was shot by one of her own brothers.

**Gillian Escobar** was murdered in March 2004 in the USA. She was twenty-six years old. Her killer was caught stuffing her body inside the trunk of his car.

**Banaz Mahmod** was a twenty-year-old Muslim woman who was murdered by her father and uncle in 2006. Her family accused her of shaming them by ending an abusive arranged marriage. She was strangled after being tortured and sexually abused, in a so-called 'honour killing' in Britain.

**Candice Williams** and **Phoebe Myrie** were involved in a lesbian relationship when their bodies were discovered in Jamaica in June 2006. The motivation for their dual murder is suspected to be homophobia.

**Shirley Ledford** was a teenager who was raped and murdered in Los Angeles by two men who audiotaped the torture-femicide.

**Charliena Steinmetz**, fifty-six, was shot by her husband in front of one of their dinner guests in their home in Cape Town, South Africa, on 21 December 2002.

**Sofia Rodriguez-Urrutia Shu** was eight years old when she was abducted, raped and murdered in a disabled toilet in a busy suburban shopping centre in Perth, Australia, in June 2006.

**Melissa Demas** was nine years old when her naked, battered and raped body was found in a motor spares shop in South Africa.

**Gillian Hadley** ran naked, screaming from her home, holding her baby whom she handed to a neighbour, before her estranged husband dragged her back inside and shot her in June 2000 in Ontario, Canada.

**Rahima Brohi** was axed to death by her husband and father-in-law in September 2003 in Pakistan.

**Diane Brimble** died in the cabin of four male passengers after being given an overdose of a date rape drug on the P & O cruise liner, *Pacific Sky*, in September 2002.

**Susan Hamilton-Sithole** was killed by her husband on 25 November 1995 in South Africa.

**Lisa Steinberg** was six years old when she died of child abuse, torture and neglect at the hands of her adoptive parents, Joel Steinberg and Hedda Nussbaum, in 1987 in the USA.

**Sapna Akhter**, aged twenty-eight, was killed by her husband who poured kerosene on her body and set fire to her in Pakistan in July 2004.

**Naomi Rose Ebersol** (seven), **Marian Fisher** (thirteen), **Mary Liz Miller** (eight), **Lena Miller** (seven) and **Anna Mae Stoltzfus** were killed by Charles Roberts in a tiny Amish school in Pennsylvania, USA in October 2006, after he had let the boys go.

**Merissa Naidoo**, a ten-year-old girl, was kidnapped in South Africa in 2005. Her body was later found in a suitcase.

**Leigh Matthews** was twenty-one when she was killed by her kidnapper in South Africa, despite the fact that her parents had paid the ransom.

**Tanya Flowerday** was raped, strangled and dumped on a grassy verge in South Africa on 14 June 2004. She was eighteen years old.

**Hazera Khatun**, aged eighteen, was killed by her husband at a hotel in Bangladesh in February 2006.

**Rachel Susan Miller** was pregnant with her husband's baby when she was raped and brutally murdered by her ex-husband on 26 April 2000 in the USA. Her heartbroken son **Tyler Edmond Miller**, twelve years old, subsequently took his own life on 11 June 2001.

**Vincent Sardi** was stabbed by his wife while he was driving a car. He died three days after the attack, in the USA. He was thirty years old.

**Kim Abrahams** was six when she was found strangled, in August 2005 in Cape Town, South Africa.

**Nicole Brown Simpson** was killed on 12 June 1994. She was the ex-wife of US football player OJ Simpson. She was found murdered at her home in Los Angeles, USA, along with her friend **Ron Goldman**.

**Gina Marie Lupson-Holden-Young** and her two sons **Shaun Edward** (four years old) and **Joshua Lee** (seven months old) perished when her husband doused their home with gasoline and set it alight on 9 June 1993 in the USA.

**Helen Betty Osborne**, or Betty Osborne, was a Cree Aboriginal woman who was kidnapped and murdered in November 1971.

**Cameron Noah** and **Christian Caleb Ellington** were two-year-old twins who, alongside their mother, **Berna Ellington,** were beaten to death by their father Clayton Ellington. The three died on 17 May 2006 in Georgia, USA.

**Matthew Shepard** was twenty-one years old when he was attacked and killed by two men in Colorado, USA, on 7 October 1998. He died some days later surrounded by his family. Matthew was targeted because he was a gay man.

**Emerson Ray Batchelor Jnr** died on 8 October 2004 in North Carolina, USA, when he was stabbed by his stepfather. He was twenty-eight years old. His mother **Sandra Kay Pearson** died on the same day when she was stabbed in the back by her estranged husband.

**Richard Whitcomb Jnr** was murdered by his ex-girlfriend after he ended their relationship. He died on 19 January 1996 in the USA. He was twenty-four years old.

**Antonio Robles** was thirteen years old when he was killed in March 1992 in the USA by his sister's ex-boyfriend who broke into the house believing his girlfriend was there. When he couldn't find her, he shot Antonio, his mother **Elva** (forty-three) and two cousins **Naomi** (ten) and **Jose** (six). Jose was the only survivor.

**Tammy Lea Pugh-Schaefer-Jones-Bryant** was shot by her husband while she slept in February 1996 in the USA. She was thirty years old.

**Sheila Abbey** was forty-seven years old when she was beaten to death by her husband in the USA on 31 December 1995.

**William Corey Dave** was twenty-seven years old when he was stabbed and murdered by his girlfriend on 20 October 1996 in the USA.

**Kathleen Peterson** was forty-eight years old when she was beaten to death by her husband, author Michael Peterson, on 9 December 2001 in Durham County, USA.

**Lauren Elizabeth Hafford** was twenty-two years old when she was shot in the back of her head by her husband on 13 April 1999 in the USA.